PREDICTION

TONY BATTON

TWENTY-FIRST CENTURY THRILLERS

PREDICTION

- A stolen top-secret nuclear reactor
- A young lawyer falsely accused of murder
- A government project to build a quantum supercomputer
- A secretive consultancy that can fix any problem

All connected by invisible strings.
But who are the puppets and who is the puppeteer?

Prediction - First Edition v1.1

First published in August 2019 by
Twenty-First Century Thrillers

Cover photographs © Shutterstock
Cover Design by Books Covered

Find out more about the author,
and get a free short story at:
www.tonybatton.com

ALSO BY TONY BATTON

Interface

Resurface

Unstolen

Artificial Inheritance (a short story)

PRAISE FOR 'INTERFACE'

"Batton seems to be a natural in writing a good thriller as Interface has more twists and turns than the Pacific Coast Highway. Just as you think you have figured out the plot, Batton throws yet another curve ball. Even though the premise of Interface is emerging technology, Batton doesn't use a lot of techno-speak. This should please those of you that like to read thrillers, but shy away from techno-thrillers because of the overly complicated lingo, yet at the same time, Interface keeps those of us that do like the techno in techno-thrillers intrigued. For those of you that like a good thriller, Interface will be sure to please." - A Thrill A Week

"A terrifyingly real feeling Technothriller. The scariest kind of fiction is that which feels like it's either already true or could become true any moment. Batton takes one of those scary 'what if' scenarios and turns it into a woah' kind of story. I honestly felt like I couldn't put it down. The pages and minutes just absolutely flew by. [Batton] could be the next **Crichton** *or* **Douglas E Richards.** *- Brian's Book Blog*

"The short chapters and the quick dialogue give Interface a movie like quality that adds to the breathtaking pace. Interface is a well written book with a great plot premise and Batton has the ability to infuse his writing with authenticity which makes Interface highly readable and an enjoyable thrill ride." - Spectrum Books

"An intelligent, fast moving and exciting techno-thriller that is a storming debut novel" - Goodreads reviewer

"...the pages pretty much turned themselves" - Amazon reviewer

"Shades of John Grisham meets Jo Nesbo meets Michael Crichton! New kid on the block Tony Batton's debut novel is a stunner" - Amazon reviewer

"Absolutely gripping from start to finish" - Amazon reviewer

"4am and I couldn't put it down. Thrilling scifi'esque, with twists and turns all the way." - Amazon reviewer

"If you read only one book this year read the Martian by Andy Weir, but if you read two then you should pick up Interface. Make sure you pick it up before Hollywood" - Amazon reviewer

"A hugely impressive debut work" - Amazon reviewer

"a fast moving technothriller that successfully captures the reader from the first page" - Amazon reviewer

"...the best book I have ever read! ...the first book that has knocked Daphne du Maurier's Jamaica Inn from top spot on my book list... I really don't want to give too much away. I suspect you get the best read if you open it reluctantly to give it a go. So sorry for spoiling that! ...one of those books you feel genuinely sad to finish" - 4 Kids And A Chicken

For Sarah, Alex & Nathan

ONE

It was a perfect day for sailing: placid seas, a steady south-easterly – certainly not the type of conditions in which you would expect something to go wrong. Yet in the middle of the Indian Ocean a fishing ship listed as registered in Dubai, was sinking.

At least that was how it was meant to look.

A woman in blue overalls stood on the deck next to three other crew members, watching their rescuers approach. Her plastic-rimmed glasses sparkled as the 10,000-ton container vessel pulled alongside, crew ready with ropes to tie the craft together. The ship's captain, a blunt-mannered Englishman, had barely hidden his irritation at receiving the distress call. Yet he had responded: there was no other craft within a hundred-mile radius, and he could not afford to draw unnecessary attention to his ship by ignoring such a call.

As the two ships slowly drew together, the captain peered over the railing at the woman who was holding a stiff, grey plastic folder.

"What's your situation?" he asked.

"Still taking on water," she called back as a gangplank slid into place, connecting the two ships. "Our pumps are losing the battle."

"My engineer will inspect the breach. And we'll get our own pumps connected up. Who's in charge?"

"Skipper's below decks." The woman strode across the plank, holding out the grey folder. "I was asked to give you this."

The captain took it, an expression of confusion on his face. "You don't look or sound much like a fisherman." He sniffed the air. "Don't smell like one either."

She reached into the pocket of her grubby blue overalls and pulled out a handgun, aiming it at his chest. "Don't do anything stupid."

The five men standing behind the captain froze, though the captain did not look so panicked. "Is this your idea of a joke?"

She took a step forward, gesturing with the weapon. "I'm not known for making them."

He cleared his throat. "You might have taken on more than you expected." Behind him more than a dozen figures clad in black combat gear swarmed onto the deck, automatic rifles held with precision. They spread out, targeting the woman and the three crew on the deck of the fishing ship. "Now," he said, "shall we start again?"

The woman straightened. "Sixteen guards?"

The captain shook his head. "Not your lucky day. I'll take that gun." She shrugged, turned it around and held out the grip. He took it from her, hefting it in his hand, then looked puzzled. With a practised motion he ejected the clip and examined it. "Empty?"

She smiled. "It was just a distraction. The system needs a little time to prep."

The captain glanced quickly around. A pattern of red dots had appeared on the man nearest to him, rippling and rotating, then narrowing to a single point. The same pattern appeared on the others. "What is going on?"

"We want your cargo."

His eyes narrowed. "You want to steal washing machine parts?"

"Look in the folder. It's a copy of your manifest. And not the fake one."

The captain flipped it open and gasped. "This was classified."

"Can I presume you're not going to cooperate?"

The captain shook his head. The dots narrowed on his chest and a high-pitched whine filled the air.

"If it's any consolation, it will be quick."

His face went white and he turned, shouting, "Take cover!"

She didn't bother telling him it was too late. Instead she crouched low. The red dots pulsed brightly and there was a disturbance in the air like a thousand tiny gusts of wind.

Then there were screams.

She kept her gaze averted. Not because she couldn't bear the sight, but to avoid the possibility of particle damage to her eyes. Instead she tapped her earpiece. "This is Cortez. I presume you saw all that?"

"In my periphery," replied a *heavily digitised voice, just recognisable as* female. *"I was monitoring another operation."*

"You have something more important to watch than this?"

"There are many initiatives in progress. I note your telemetry is elevated. Do you have the situation under control?"

"You said four armed guards. There were sixteen."

There was a pause. *"I cannot fault your ability to count."*

"Another glitch? How many cycles are you giving me?"

"Enough for your purposes."

"I could have taken them out hand-to-hand."

"All sixteen? There's no sense in taking unnecessary risks. Now retrieve and sanitise. I need you back in London."

"I only just got here."

"You have the next part of Project Green to carry out. Sending details now. But don't worry, you'll have another trip soon."

The woman saw images flash across her vision. A face. A name. Both deeply familiar. "Is it finally time?"

"The analysis has been verified, but he is just one of a number of pieces we need to bring into play. Any questions?"

"Lots. But I know better than to ask them."

The call disconnected. The woman turned to her team, now walking across the gang plank wearing yellow hazmat suits. One handed her a spare. She quickly slid it on, then turned and stepped over the bodies.

TWO

THE SENIOR PARTNER SAT STARING AT THE DOOR OF THE meeting room, ignoring the others who waited with him. Some things Gordon Freeman liked doing. Other things he had to do. A few he genuinely regretted, but for the greater good of Crawford, White & Paine, Solicitors, they had to happen. He might not have founded CWP – he wasn't quite that old - but it had been his life, his labour of love. Which was probably the reason he had married three times and lost touch with all four of his (now adult) children. CWP had to be protected above all else, and that was why he had called this meeting.

Next to him was Henry Stotter, head of the firm's Corporate Department: a man of few words that he couldn't bill for. He was unlikely to contribute, but a meeting like this required a certain weight of numbers. There needed to be no doubt of the message being communicated. And there needed to be witnesses in the event that litigation followed, although the reality was that barely registered as a concern.

Next to Stotter, as far away from Freeman as she could sit, was the woman from HR. He would have preferred to keep this meeting for lawyers only, but CWP was a big firm and they had procedures. When he was younger, these were merely paid lip-service. But the world was changing –

changing so fast he wasn't sure anyone could predict what would happen next.

A knock sounded at the door.

"Come in," called Freeman, his voice hoarse from too much coffee and not quite enough whisky.

A young man in his mid-twenties appeared wearing the pinched smile of someone riding the edge of exhaustion, but then he'd probably worked more than sixty of the last seventy-two hours, as most junior associates at CWP did. His name was Michael Adams and he was the firm's highest performing junior associate: a safe pair of hands given his almost absurd attention to detail. The clients and partners loved him, meaning he was always first on the internal request list whenever they were building a new deal team. Which made what they had to do now all the more galling.

Freeman pointed to the chair opposite the three of them. "Mr Adams, please have a seat."

Michael sat, adjusting his suit.

"You know Henry Stotter, and this is", he paused, "our HR representative."

The woman gave him a steely glare but smiled at Michael.

"I expect you're wondering why you're here."

Michael nodded. "I'm in the middle of a deal with the banking department, so they're wondering too."

"Project Gemini?" Stotter asked, his expression suddenly animated. "The joint venture?"

"It should close tomorrow, if the other side don't delay us further."

Freeman cleared his throat. "That's great, Michael. But you're not here to discuss Project Gemini." He took a deep breath. "There's been a… complaint. Well, more than that." Freeman looked at Stotter then back to Michael. "An allegation. A very *serious* allegation."

"About what?"

"One of our biggest clients, InTech, called me this morning. *Me*, personally."

"I presume not to thank you for your latest bill?" Michael

gave a smile as if he thought this was all some joke. As if they were about to all laugh, shake hands and carry on. "I know InTech. I've worked on two major acquisitions for them. What did they want?"

"They say you've been passing proprietary information to one of their competitors."

"What?" Michael blinked rapidly, his eyes darting between the three others. "I don't understand."

"I'm sure I don't need to remind you of the sanctity with which CWP, as a law firm, regards the confidential information of its clients. Quite apart from the possible crimes you may have committed."

"You're not suggesting you believe them?"

Stotter started to say something, but Freeman raised a hand. "You have an impeccable record with this firm, which is why we're extending you the courtesy of this meeting. But the fact that you've proven so capable only makes the situation all the more disappointing. Naturally, these actions trigger an instant right of termination under your employment contract—"

"Hang on!" Michael drew his breath in sharply. "You're taking this seriously?"

"We're a City law firm – we always take what our clients say seriously." Freeman set his palms on the table. "We could work through this in detail and you could make your stock denials, but quite frankly nobody is going to look good. Least of all you." He paused. "So we have a proposal." He nodded to the HR representative, who slid a sheet of paper across the table.

Michael spread his fingers across the crisp white sheet, his eyes intent. "You have to be kidding."

"It's a generous settlement," Freeman said. "In the circumstances, more than generous."

"Three months' salary and a reference? When I've done nothing wrong?" Michael folded his arms. "I've given my all to this firm. I've worked nights, weekends. I've done everything I've ever been asked. And you want me just to sign it all away?"

"InTech says it has irrefutable evidence."

"How can they, given that I didn't..." Michael paused, frowning. "Wait. You haven't *seen* the evidence?"

The HR representative shifted in her seat and began to say something but Freeman held up a hand. "We're not in a courtroom here, Michael." He pointed to the sheet of paper. "Consider things carefully. If you want the most from your career, you're going to need to achieve it somewhere else."

Michael shook his head. "There has to be a better way. That *win-win* the firm keeps telling us to look for."

Freeman leant forward and tapped the sheet of paper. "Believe me, this is the closest to a 'win' that you're going to get."

"I'd like to think about it."

"You have until you walk out that door. After that the offer will be withdrawn. Permanently."

Michael gripped the table. "Is someone making you do this?"

Freeman turned to the other two. "I'd like a few moments with Michael. Alone."

The HR representative's eyebrows twitched. "I don't think that would be wise—"

"I don't give a crap what you think. Now give us the room."

The woman sniffed, Stotter gave a faint smirk and they both departed. Freeman closed the door firmly and turned back to Michael. "Take the deal."

"*Why?*"

Freeman put his hands in his pockets and walked over to the window.

Michael thumped his fist on the table. "I have not done what they are claiming. The evidence *cannot* exist."

"You're being offered a chance to walk away, no blemish on your record."

"I've built my whole career at this firm."

"We billed InTech in excess of fifty million in fees last

year. It'll probably be more this year. We cannot afford to annoy them."

"But—"

Freeman put his hand on Michael's shoulder. "Let's assume for a moment that you *didn't* do this. Why are InTech saying you did?"

"How should I know?"

"They obviously want you out of this firm. It's an initiative they appear prepared to put resources and money behind, and they have plenty of both. They're not going to stop until it happens."

Michael shook his head. "And this is the type of client you want?"

Freeman raised his hands. "They're a FTSE100 company. Of course they're the type of client we want. As for you, if you want a career, then you only have one option."

FREEMAN WATCHED MICHAEL ADAMS WALK OUT OF THE ROOM. Moments later his two colleagues marched in.

"Well?" Stotter asked.

"He signed," Freeman said with a sigh. "He's gone to pack his things. I'm sure the banking team will be just *delighted*."

The HR representative folded her arms. "Tell me you have actually seen the evidence we were all here discussing."

"Adams took the deal. There's nothing more to discuss."

Her face went white. "I realise we have to protect the firm's reputation, but we could be perpetrating fraud—"

Freeman raised a bony finger. "You're going to go back to your office, make whatever file note you feel is necessary, and you're going to carry on with your day. After which we will never discuss this meeting again. Is that clear?"

She gave a resigned scowl then strode from the room.

Stotter's gaze followed her as she left. "Just what did the guys at InTech say?"

Freeman shook his head. "I can't tell you."

Stotter gave a low growl. "In case you'd forgotten I'm not one of the secretaries."

"Let me rephrase that. You don't *want* to know."

"Of course, I want to… oh." He swallowed. "You didn't speak to InTech at all, did you? You received a request."

"It's best if I don't even confirm that. You never know when they're listening."

"No explanation?"

Freeman scratched his nose. "Just a set of instructions."

Stotter puffed out his cheeks. "Then, as you said, let us never discuss this meeting again."

THREE

WARWICK SAXTON SAT IN A STIFF LEATHER ARMCHAIR, ignoring the cup of tea in the bone china cup in front of him and counting the ticks of the grandfather clock to his right. At this hour he would normally have been chairing a leadership-team meeting at MI5's central offices in Vauxhall. Instead he was sitting in a large Oxfordshire mansion.

He waited on few men or women. But with the Home Secretary, Charlotte Rostrum, he had little choice. Politicians came and went, but, while Rostrum had only just been appointed, she was already making it clear that, under her reign, things would be 'hands-on'. Now she had summoned him for a private meeting without any explanation. Was she just trying to assert her authority? Her predecessor had been so much more civilised.

There was a gentle throat clearing to his left and Saxton gave a stiff smile as Rostrum's assistant nodded that he could go through to the study. He walked in to find the Home Secretary at her oversized desk, stacks of reports arrayed in front of her. Her eyes snapped onto Saxton. "Warwick, thanks for coming at such short notice."

"Mind telling me why I'm here and not in London?"

She smiled back. "An attempt to keep this meeting off people's radars." She gestured to a seat, activating a large touch-screen on one wall. A map of the Indian Ocean appeared.

"A bit outside your jurisdiction? And mine."

"Yesterday," she said, tapping a spot west of the Indian mainland, "a container vessel responded to a distress call while en route from Delhi to Southampton." She tapped again and the screen zoomed in to show a section of ocean, marked with shipping lanes. "The call was from a Dubai-registered fishing boat."

"I'm not seeing the relevance to MI5 or why this meeting needs to be so hush-hush."

"Shortly after, all contact was lost with the container vessel and its largely British crew. No location data. Nothing. And no further trace of the fishing boat either. A number of search vessels are rapidly converging on the location now."

"What's your particular interest?"

"The container vessel was loaded with a consignment of washing-machine parts." Rostrum hesitated. "And something *not* on the manifest: an experimental nuclear reactor destined for a testing facility in Cumbria."

"Why were we building something like that in India?"

"A number of reasons, but primarily cost."

"You mentioned that it was experimental."

Rostrum cleared her throat. "Early-stage fusion. Not yet operational, but we're getting close."

Saxton blinked several times. "I thought we were ten or fifteen years away from fusion power?"

"Then our campaign of misinformation is working."

"I'm guessing there's no trace of either vessel on satellite?"

"A gap in the cycle of coverage. It does happen. We hadn't tasked it as a priority area for analysis. To do so would have drawn attention."

"Could both vessels have sunk? Perhaps a freak wave?"

"Unlikely. Very calm conditions that day. The first ships will be there in a couple of hours, but I'm pretty sure they'll find only wreckage, if they find anything at all. Tracking data showed the reactor moved rapidly westwards too fast to be on a ship. We lost trace of it after that."

Saxton's eyes widened. "Someone stole it then sank both vessels?"

Rostrum walked back to her desk. "I've brought you here to consider two questions: who took it, and how did they know what and where it was?"

Saxton shook his head. "Isn't the bigger question what they're going to do with it?"

Rostrum tapped her fist on her desk. "As I said, it doesn't work yet. Nevertheless, this has prompted a re-think of our situation. I've just come from a meeting with the PM. He's keen to explore all and any avenues of information."

"There's been no chatter," Saxton replied. "Whoever is behind this would have had substantial resources: a government or a major crime syndicate." He paused. "Obviously this is MI6's area of expertise—"

Rostrum raised a hand. "I don't want their template list of usual suspects. I want actual data-based assessment."

"We have no system capable of delivering that. Not even at GCHQ."

"No, we don't. Not *yet.*"

Saxton let a whistle out through his teeth. "This is about Project Parallel? We cancelled it. At your predecessor's request."

"From my reading it was put it *on hold.*"

"Semantics. Nobody believed we would ever proceed. Too expensive. And too risky." He folded his arms. "Plus you'll be aware of the complexities with the supplier."

"Nothing that we can't resolve, I'm sure. The climate has changed, Warwick. We need Parallel. We can't have unknown individuals stealing our top-secret technology. Next time it could be something worse."

"What about funding?"

"I spoke with the PM this morning. His words were, and I quote, '*Money is no object.*'"

"Good. But this still won't be easy. The team was disbanded."

"I am aware. *Re-band* them. And do it fast."

Saxton stood. "I'll make some calls." He turned to leave, then paused. "Charlotte, why do you think someone wanted to steal the reactor if it's not working? Just because it cost a huge sum to develop, doesn't make it valuable."

"Perhaps they didn't know."

"But they did know *what* it was and *where* it was? That seems odd."

Rostrum nodded. "These are good questions, Warwick." She steepled her fingers. "I suggest you ask Parallel, once you've built it."

FOUR

It was late Friday afternoon, so the bar wasn't yet crowded, the air not yet laden with conversation, alcohol and sweat. Michael Adams made his way between the polished tables and padded stools to a booth at the back, and ordered two bottled beers from a bored-looking waitress. He loosened his tie, placed his leather briefcase on the seat next to him, and cast his eye around. He saw nobody he recognised. The nearest widescreen TV was showing an update on the recovery effort around a cargo ship that had sunk in the Indian Ocean three days ago, but the sound was down so low Michael could not hear the commentary.

The waitress re-appeared, banging two beer bottles on his table with an expression that seemed to say 'Are you going to drink both of those?'

Michael looked towards the doorway. "My friend is joining me shortly."

The waitress shrugged and left. Michael checked his phone, but there was no message from Eve so he took a long draught of his beer, feeling the cold fizz hit his brain.

Sighing, he started to rehash the meeting that had just ended his career at CWP. Had he done the right thing? It was a high stakes game as even false allegations could be sticky in terms of reputation. He didn't have his own clients - despite more years studying than he cared to remember and four years of slaving at CWP, it could all be gone in an instant. Freeman had known that and used a standard negotiation strategy: make something pretty bad look good relative to something completely awful. Michael had done the only thing he felt he could.

But why had InTech lied to get him fired? As far as he knew, they had rated him highly. Had he irritated someone at InTech or CWP? Even if he had, why go to all this trouble? He was just a junior lawyer: a tiny cog in a legal machine.

Michael thought about calling his mother, but quickly dismissed the idea. She'd just make things worse. Besides, he'd rather chat it through with Eve first. His phone beeped softly.

Have to do a double shift - someone phoned in sick. Back late. Sorry won't be able to meet up. E.

Michael shook his head; it was just one of the realities of having a friend who was a junior doctor, but today he really could have done without it those complexities. He went to pick up his beer, but froze when a voice close to his ear asked "Mind if I sit here?"

He turned around. A slim blonde woman, dressed in an expensive grey suit regarded him with a half-smile. "Sorry," he said. "I'm meeting someone."

She looked around the bar in an exaggerated manner. "And when are you expecting them?"

"Soon." He looked back at his beer. "So, if you don't mind..."

"Not at all." The woman slid onto the seat opposite. Her fragrance smelt expensive. She signaled in the direction of the bar. A moment later, the waitress placed a bottle of Rioja and two large glasses on the table, then vanished back into the crowd. The woman eased her jacket off, then poured wine into both glasses.

"I'm… sort of busy," Michael said awkwardly.

She held up her glass, rotating it gently, watching the red liquid coat the interior. "Too busy to share a drink with the person who's going to change your life?"

Michael sucked in his cheeks. "I'm sorry, but I really am meeting someone."

"Yes. Me." She frowned. "I sent you that message?" She ran a hand through her hair. "You *replied*."

He stared at her. "What message?"

She puffed out her cheeks. "Check your phone."

Michael shook his head and picked up his phone. "You must have me confused with…" He blinked and looked at the screen. There was message exchange he had not seen before: a request to meet in this bar, at this time, to discuss a career opportunity. He looked up at her. "Kara?"

She rolled her eyes. "Bout of amnesia over, dear?"

"But I never sent this. I never read your message." He held a hand to his head.

"This is starting to wear thin." She placed a card on the table in front of him. There was no logo, just plain black lettering on crisp white card: *Kara Simmons, Counsel. Infinity Law. Knightsbridge.*

Michael sucked in his breath.

"So you've heard of us," she said, raising her glass. "That's a start."

He nodded. "Of course I have."

"We want to tempt you to join our cause."

He turned the card around in his fingers. "I didn't think Infinity was recruiting. Actually I didn't think you *ever* recruited."

"We need to add to our team from time to time. We're just very selective."

"So you're approaching me? Look, is this some kind of joke? Everything that's happened today has been mad and now this..."

"I charge my time at £600 an hour, so if I'm making jokes they'd bloody well better be funny."

"I've never applied to you."

"We keep a close eye on the top firms to find out who the rising stars are."

Michael sat back in his seat. "I have a job at a magic circle firm."

She smiled, flashing white teeth. "Five years ago I was in your shoes." She placed her hands on the table. "I still wake up with nightmares that I might have made the other decision."

"Infinity made you an offer you couldn't refuse? What if I'm not motivated by money?"

"You're a corporate lawyer; of course you're motivated by money." Kara shrugged. "But that's far from the whole story. Infinity is the best of the best: a whole world of opportunity comes with that."

He picked up the card again, running his fingers over the subtly raised lettering. "You make it sound like there's no choice to make."

"You always have a choice. You just need to make the right one."

"How do I even know you are who you say you are?"

She gave a snort and closed her eyes. "Michael Evan Adams. Born third February, schooled Windsor. Somewhat erratic, unremarkable academic record until your A-Levels when you stepped things up. Read Law at Emmanuel College, Cambridge. Vice-Captain of the University Athletics team. Middle distance runner, narrowly missed out on representing Team GB because of an injury. Attended Law school in Guildford, then trained with CWP. Upon qualification three departments bid for you. Amazing academic lawyer. Excellent negotiator." She paused, opening her eyes. "How am I doing? Mother lives in Oxfordshire. Father died when you were thirteen. You share a house with a college friend, Eve. She's a junior doctor, works longer hours than you do."

He coughed. "How could you know that?"

"We looked on the electoral roll. Made a few educated guesses."

Michael sat back in his seat. "What do you want from me?"

"Attend an interview with one of our partners. This weekend. If you have plans, change them." Kara ran her finger round the rim of her glass.

"You don't suffer from a lack of confidence."

"There's no money in it." She patted him on the arm and stood up. "Shall we go then?"

He looked puzzled. "Where?"

"To the interview. Is your amnesia coming back?"

"You said this weekend?"

"It's Friday night. The weekend starts here." She turned and slid through the crowd, heading for the door.

Michael grabbed his briefcase and followed. Outside, the cool air and quiet were startling, but not as much as the vehicle she was standing next to: a sleek black stretch limousine. The driver stood holding the back door open.

"Where are we going?"

"Your place." She tilted her head to one side, raising an eyebrow. "To get your passport."

FIVE

It was 6:00pm and the jogger was halfway along the three-mile sweep of golden sand that was Woolacombe Beach. He wore hi-tech compression gear and maintained an easy stride on the hard-packed sand left behind by the outgoing tide. For a short period it was the perfect running surface. His eyes were hidden behind wrap-around sunglasses, his ears cradled in expensive headphones. There were a few other joggers and a couple of dog walkers on the beach, but he ignored them all. He came here for the peace and quiet: the sound and smell of the sea, and the never-ending breeze.

This was the perfect place to get away from it all, reachable in four hours from London by car. Not that he ever travelled here by car. On this beach he could forget about vehicles, and cyclists. And people. He could run and ignore the world, just feel the wind on his face. And not worry about being run over by anything with wheels. Which was good, because he had other things to worry about.

His company, ZAT Systems, had grown far and fast by leading the market in a particular subset of speculative technology. Staying ahead of the competition meant ploughing hundreds of millions into research and development. Obviously that meant taking risks. But in the last twelve months it was as if the world was out to destroy him: project-after-project either failed for technical reasons, or got cancelled by the client.

As he approached the southern end of the beach, he looked along to the headland. Almost nobody here. No men in suits watching his every move, like they were supposed to. He stopped to stretch. As he did so, he felt a soft vibration coming from his pocket. With an irritated frown, he pulled out his mobile phone and blinked.

Eighteen messages, five missed calls. Something had happened.

A moment later he felt the low subsonic thump of rotors and he knew it was something serious.

A HELICOPTER SPORTING THE WHITE AND BLUE ZAT SYSTEMS logo landed on the beach, about a hundred metres away, to startled looks from onlookers. A few muttered that such a thing shouldn't be allowed. And indeed it wasn't. But the pilot clearly didn't care.

Jenson ran straight to the aircraft as Astrid Kelly, the head of his private office, hopped out. She handed him a sealed white envelope. On it was typed *Gregory Jenson, CEO, STRICTLY CONFIDENTIAL.*

Jenson tore it open and read the single sheet inside. "They want to meet tonight? Why?"

"Other than wanting to review Project Parallel, Saxton wouldn't say."

"Does the Director of MI5 just want to rub our noses in it?"

"You know him better than I do."

Jenson screwed the sheet into a ball. "Where are my security detail?"

"At the other end of the beach," Kelly replied. "They seem to be in a signal dead spot: we couldn't raise them."

"Remind me to fire them later. Now let's get moving."

"I have a complete set of your clothes on board, so we can go straight to Cheltenham if you wish."

Jenson nodded. "Excellent. Remind me not to fire you."

There was a shout from the helicopter. The co-pilot was leaning out. "The local coastguard has been notified of an unexplained aircraft on the beach. We'd better be leaving."

Kelly nodded. "You should probably call Teresa and explain you won't be joining her for dinner on the way."

Jenson gave a sigh. "Send her a message would you? Tell her I'll speak to her later. Reassign my security team to monitor her and make sure she keeps her damn watch on, whether she likes it or not." He hesitated. "In fact, get them to take her back to school early. I'm not having her wandering around without me. At least the teaching staff have some idea how to control her."

Kelly raised an eyebrow. "She'll love that."

"She can learn to love it." Jenson gave one last look at the beach and climbed inside. Within seconds the helicopter was hauling upwards and heading east.

SIX

THERE WAS A HISS AS THE STEWARD OPENED THE AIRCRAFT'S external door. As Michael stepped through, he couldn't help thinking back to his last interview: all about psychometric analysis, legal reasoning and rigorous technical tests.

This time he was being flown to Fiji.

It was a long flight, and despite the exceptionally comfortable seat – really he should call it a bed – Michael had too much on his mind to sleep. Infinity Law was an enigma. It kept a low profile and undertook no publicity, yet had an unrivalled reputation and its clients were top drawer: major corporates, high net-worth individuals, movie and music stars. Infinity focused on the choicest, most interesting work – and charged accordingly. Even if he still had his old job he would be sorely tempted. Still, he couldn't let them know that.

He'd exchanged messages with Eve about where he was flying and she'd thought he was joking. Then she'd thought he was drunk. A proper explanation would have to wait until he was home. Right now he had to focus.

He descended the stairs of the private jet, feeling the heat rising off the tarmac. A breeze rippled the nearby palm trees and his nose was assaulted with the scents of sea, sugar and coconuts.

"Welcome to Fiji," said a man in a chauffeur's uniform

standing next to a black Mercedes van. "Trust you had a good flight, Mr Adams."

He blinked, wishing he'd thought to bring sunglasses. Despite the huge seat-bed, and the amazing catering, he felt sore and fatigued. He glanced around then realised the man was waiting patiently for a reply. "No complaints, thank you. Where are we going?"

The man placed his luggage carefully in the boot. "It's about half an hour to the marina where we'll meet the motor launch. From there, it's on to the island."

"Aren't we on an island?"

The man flashed brilliant white teeth. "A smaller island, Sir."

"A resort?"

"A corporate retreat, dear," Kara said, descending from the plane wearing a cool sleeveless top and a native sulu.

Michael stared at her for a second, feeling over-dressed in his suit.

"It's called Errington Island."

"After Maxwell Errington, Infinity's founder?" Michael asked.

She smiled. "When you own an island you can name it after yourself too."

ERRINGTON WAS INDEED A SMALL ISLAND – REALLY JUST A DOT in the ocean. The motor launch slowed on approach as the captain gave Michael the facts and figures: Errington Island was twenty kilometres off the coast, about a kilometre long and three hundred metres wide at its widest point. It had great snorkelling and fishing, and corporate-strength broadband courtesy of a major internet backbone laid only six months back. If that failed they had connections to three different satellites.

There was also a helipad, but apparently that was only used for very important guests.

"Besides, the boat ride is much more pleasant," Kara said. "It's just not as quick."

The launch docked at a long wooden pier. A tanned man in his late twenties, wearing a polo shirt, shorts and loafers, introduced himself as two workmen helped tie the boat up.

"I'm the site manager," he said, shaking Michael's hand firmly. "Welcome to Errington."

There was a splash and they turned to see Kara had dived into the sea.

The man raised any eyebrow. "This place can have that effect on you. Why don't I give you the tour?"

Michael took off his shoes and followed the site manager across the bleached coral sand, hot underfoot except where covered by the shade of the many palm trees. There was not much to the island, but all of it was idyllic. There were thirty individual cottages, or *bures*, each facing the ocean across the beach. The facilities included two tennis courts, an archery range, a fully-equipped gym, a full-sized swimming pool and a conference centre. Michael was also shown a poolside bar, a formal restaurant and a more relaxed cafeteria, plus a library and a cinema. There was one particularly large house, separate from the rest and surrounded by security fencing. On the north end of the island was a boat shed, stocked with sea kayaks, wind-surfing equipment, jet skis and rods and tackle for fishing.

"This place is unreal," said Michael, when they returned to the bar only to be greeted by pre-prepared cocktails. "Mr Errington owns it all?"

The site manager shrugged. "I deal with a management company. The resort gets let out to large corporates wanting to bring their execs somewhere special on the lie that it's a holiday, then working them to the bone while they're here. And sometimes Infinity needs it for a client."

Michael pointed back to the large house. "And that?"

"Mr Errington's home. It's the only place off limits to you. Otherwise you can go where you want and use the facilities as you wish. It's all at your disposal."

"So is Mr Errington here?"

The man laughed. "Not at the moment. I'm sure you'll get to meet him eventually." He tipped his head to one side. "If you join up, that is. I've seen a few of your sort come through before. They must be keen to bring you all this way."

Michael looked around. How was he supposed to resist these people? Perhaps that was the point. "So what's the plan?"

"The afternoon is yours. For dinner you're going to meet Duncan Nichol, the Managing Partner, who's on his way back from Sydney."

There was a cough from behind them. Michael turned to see Kara wearing a short-sleeve wetsuit.

She frowned. "What's the idea telling him he gets to relax? He needs to try and burn through his jet lag." She pointed at some covered racking, holding wind-surfing and sea-kayaking equipment. "Obviously there's a bunch of water sports, but there's also archery and clay pigeon shooting. You pick what we do first, new boy."

Michael wiped sweat off his brow. "Now that you mention it, getting in the sea does sound like a plan. Work hard, play hard, I guess."

Kara nodded. "You know, you might just fit in."

SEVEN

MICHAEL, KARA AND DUNCAN NICHOL DINED ON THE BEACH, on a table set up especially for the occasion. A lazy wind toyed with the palm trees, bringing welcome relief from the heat. Michael's clothes – a cool linen suit and shirt, exactly his size – had been hanging ready for him in his cottage. There were all the facilities of a five-star business hotel, including a fully stocked minibar, but he hadn't indulged yet. The atmosphere was intoxicating enough as it was.

Nichol had come to collect him from his room, greeting him with a solid handshake. He was a sharply-chiseled man somewhere in his forties: confident, intelligent, and with a dry sense of humour. Michael liked him immediately.

Dinner was lavish. Seafood Fijian style, with an international twist. Soft white fish, huge prawns, impossibly sweet pineapple and aromatic curries, all washed down with a selection from an extensive wine list. As they ate, the sun dropped over the horizon, plunging them into darkness, but the waiters brought soft-coloured nightlights that provided an ambient glow, without impairing their view of the star-laden sky.

"We tried using real torches, but one stiff breeze and we're all covered in smoke," Nichol said, easing back in his chair. "Although you'll pardon the irony if I now have a cigar."

"You're the boss," Kara said.

He gave a flicker of a smile and pulled a large Cuban from a pocket, lit up and inhaled deeply. "So, Michael, did you enjoy your time at Cambridge?" He nodded as a waiter placed a bottle of single malt whisky and three glasses in the centre of the table.

"Of course," replied Michael. "The best tutors, the best facilities. I was very fortunate."

"Oxford man myself, though I guess you have to make do." He poured three rough measures of whisky. "But, aside from the stock answer, what did the experience really mean for you?"

Michael blinked. "It opened doors."

"Including the one that got you here." Nichol paused. "We still have to decide if it's right for you to go through it."

"And I have to decide if I want to."

Nichol raised his glass. "Then I guess we'd both better be at our most persuasive."

Michael gestured around them at the palm trees, the beach, the ocean. "You guys are cheating."

"Never fight fair if you don't have to," Nichol said, raising an eyebrow. "So, what do you think we do at Infinity, Michael?"

"Corporate commercial. M&A. Finance. Some high-value private-client work. And, of course, litigation."

Nichol feigned a yawn. "Technically, yes, but it's not why our clients use us." He turned to Kara.

She put her glass down. "We change people's minds."

"Sounds great," Michael replied. "But how?"

"It's all about knowledge." Nichol tapped ash from the end of his cigar. "Knowledge is power. Be that legal, commercial or whatever. Our goal is to know more than the other guy, and to use it better. We've built a discrete but gold-plated reputation as advisers that make things happen. We take over negotiations and we solve problems. If we don't succeed, we don't get paid."

"Isn't that risky?"

"It shows our confidence in what we do. And that's what we need you to become part of. We're not expecting you to run deals on day one. You'll work hand in glove with Ms Simmons here for the first twelve months."

"If you can keep up, dear," said Kara pleasantly.

"I'll do my utmost."

"Look, Michael," Nichol said, "I'll be frank. What we do is hard. It places extraordinary demands on our team members. You can get sent anywhere in the world at any time, usually on very short notice. And you then have to work twenty-hour days, fourteen days straight if that's what the project requires." He leaned towards Michael. "We're always on the lookout for exceptional people who can work in that way, and it's very much 'up or out'. Either you succeed and stay on track for partnership, or our firm is not for you. But we think it might be a good fit in your case."

Michael knocked back his whisky. "You make a compelling pitch."

"We need you to be smart, and we need you to be hungry. Focus on those two qualities and the other stuff should take care of itself." Nichol smiled and refilled each of their glasses.

Michael felt the buzz of the alcohol in his brain. "Are you going to ask me a bunch of difficult legal questions?"

"We'll assume your capability in that area. You wouldn't have made it through Cambridge, Law School and four years in a magic circle law firm if you were hapless." He paused. "What we're really hiring for is attitude. But we can't know until we see you in battle. So, tell me: why did we invite you to Fiji?"

Michael shrugged. "To throw me off balance."

Nichol smiled. "We bring you somewhere a little unreal, in order to see the real you. And the tropical island never hurts if you're trying to persuade someone to join the firm."

"For me it's the seafood," said Kara.

"So," continued Nichol, "while we have you 'off balance', tell me what makes you different."

"In a work sense? At CWP the whole point is we were supposed to conform to the standard."

Nichol leaned forwards. "We're not talking about CWP any more, Michael. That's in the past. We're talking about your future."

Michael looked into his glass. "I bring a different approach to legal problem-solving. I spent much of my childhood messing around on computers with my dad. You could say I have a programmer's mentality, and I'd argue there's useful synergy between that and contract drafting. In both cases you're creating a structure, governed by rules, to deliver a specific outcome." He rotated his glass between his fingers. "If I may flip the question, what makes Infinity different?"

Nichol reached into a briefcase and pulled out a large grey ring-binder. He slid it across the table. "This."

Michael picked it up. The binder bore his name on the front, along with his date of birth. "What is it?"

"It's you."

Michael began turning the pages, and felt a jolt run down his spine. Kara had reeled off quite a list of facts about him during their conversation in the bar, but this reduced his entire life to a series of records and achievements. Schools he had attended, exams he had sat, places he had lived, clubs he had belonged to, awards he had won, his full university exam results, copies of his blog and other materials sourced from social media and the web. Brief notes about his immediate family. All of it was startlingly accurate. Holding his breath, he turned to the end. There seemed to be no reference to CWP firing him. Did they know? "Are you trying to intimidate me?"

"We just wanted to show you how seriously we take our work and, by extension, those who work for us. Infinity is the sum of its parts. If you're to join us, we need there to be no secrets."

Michael closed the report. "And it seems there are not."

He placed his hand on top of the report. "How did you pull all this together?"

"We know how to find stuff. Now, I think we'll cut straight to the key question: *how much*?"

Michael looked him in the eye, unblinking. "I'm sure your proposal will be competitive."

Nichol snorted. "It will be nothing of the sort. It'll seem like we cheated." He reached into his pocket and wrote something on a piece of paper. Then he folded it and slid it over.

Michael took it in his fingers. "Can I look?"

"Of course. I'm just being dramatic."

He unfolded the slip and looked at what was written there. It looked like a telephone number. He breathed deeply.

"On this one occasion we will allow you to fail as a negotiator," Nichol said.

Michael blinked. "I'm sorry, what?"

"Based on your facial expression, if you're planning to ask for more, it won't be a credible request."

"Two hundred thousand per year? Sterling? Are you serious?"

Nichol smiled. "Make partner and you'll be earning that in a month."

Michael swallowed hard. He glanced at his drink, wondering if he was hallucinating.

"As a side note, why did I write that down? It's so I could watch your reaction without having to guard my own. It's much harder to hide your reaction when you have to look down." He turned to look at the ocean. "We pay our lawyers so much because they are the very best. They could go anywhere they want, do anything they wish. We don't want them to want or wish to be anywhere else."

There was a soft ringing. Kara pulled a phone from her pocket and answered the call, listening briefly then turned to Nichol. "You're needed at the big house."

The senior partner stood and shook Michael's hand. "I look forward to working with you."

"*If* I accept."

Nichol slapped him hard on the shoulder. "If you accept." He walked away across the sand.

Kara promptly refilled their glasses. "I expect you're still feeling giddy after reading that piece of paper."

"That's a fair assessment."

"Savour it. But you know what economists say? There's no such thing as a free lunch. You're going to earn that £200k. Believe me, I certainly did." She drummed her fingers on the table. "Of course now I earn a lot more."

"So what's next?"

"Now we drink as much of this whisky as we like. Tomorrow we fly back after breakfast."

"So soon?"

"Did you think this was a holiday?"

"I've hardly recovered from the flight here. I thought I was going to have a nice swim this afternoon, but somehow you added archery and clay-pigeon shooting to the itinerary."

"Yeah, well there aren't any real pigeons, and the site manager gets annoyed when I shoot the seagulls."

Michael swallowed. "You're a little too comfortable with those weapons. I think you only missed the bullseye on the archery target once."

Kara frowned. "Gust of wind." She raised her glass. "You need to drink more, then you'll sleep just fine."

"Is that your professional advice?"

"Consider it an accurate prediction. Now enjoy the peace and quiet. It'll be the last rest you have in a long time."

EIGHT

Jenson saw the familiar form of the GCHQ building from several miles away, winter sun glinting off the giant doughnut of glass and aluminium. The UK's most secretive office building housed nearly five thousand people in reasonable comfort and the utmost security. Until Project Parallel had been cancelled, Jenson had been a regular visitor.

The helicopter landed well short of the site. Two big Jaguars were waiting to collect them. Kelly inspected the vehicles meticulously, much to the irritation of the security service personnel, before allowing Jenson to climb inside. Then they sped through concentric rings of security, while Jenson considered again what the meeting would be about. When government projects were cancelled there were always rounds of recrimination: exercises in finger pointing. Many times, he was the one being pointed at.

Reaching the building, they were scanned and given a physical pat down. Once inside they were given bright red visitor badges, ensuring all GCHQ staff gave them a wide berth and a scowl. Square-faced security guards marched them through the building to the secure conference facilities that had been built specifically for Parallel because the project had been classified above top secret, off limits even to the majority of those who worked in the building.

Jenson saw Warwick Saxton as he walked through the door. The operational director of MI5 looked up from his position at the head of the huge boardroom table.

"Trust we didn't inconvenience you too much, Mr Jenson," said Saxton. "I hear you were off making sandcastles."

Jenson forced a smile onto his face. "For you, Warwick, nothing is an inconvenience." He took a seat. "Although I am curious to know why we are here. You terminated this project twelve months ago."

Saxton steepled his fingers. "Questions have been asked about what we spent all that money on."

Jenson glanced at Kelly, who shook her head. "I've not been made aware of these concerns."

"You're being made aware *now*." Saxton flipped open a folder in front of him. "The questions relate to ZAT's historical dealings. And also to your ability to deliver a project on time and on budget. If you have misled us then a great deal of public money will have been wasted."

"If you hadn't cancelled the project, the money wouldn't have been wasted." Jenson took a long, slow breath. "I'm confident we provided all the necessary information as part of our bid."

Saxton nodded. "In fact, you provided us with several thousand pages of data. Most of it glossy marketing material or outlandishly optimistic predictions. So we'd appreciate a distillation around those two points I just mentioned. Just in case anything has changed."

"If you mean ZAT's connections with the off-book supply of arms, that was over a decade ago and has been fully reported on."

"You were in charge of the company at the time?"

"I founded ZAT. Why you are bringing this up now? Should my legal counsel be at this meeting?"

Saxton tapped his fingers lightly on the table. "Once lost, trust is hard to regain."

"I would understand the difficulty *if* we were going ahead, but we're not, even though everyone agreed that the project was necessary."

"And do you still think it is?"

"Yes." Jenson cleared his throat. "You have a problem. *We all* have a problem. One that is only going to get worse." He paused and gestured to the whole room. "We are drowning in data. It's not just the web, or even the 'Deep Web'. Your cameras, your recorders, your agents, your net-crawlers, are all producing volumes of intelligence that you cannot keep up with and so, to a large extent, cannot comprehend. You need a way to intelligently process, coordinate, prioritise and make recommendations to turn this Big Data from a problem into an opportunity." Jenson leaned forward and stabbed a finger on the table. "That is what this project would have allowed you to do. In the fight against terrorism, espionage and crime – in doing pretty much anything that needs computing power – this would have given what your own analysts described as an unfair advantage over everyone else."

"'An unfair advantage at an unfair price' was one of the comments on the project, if I recall correctly," said Saxton.

"Criticism is cheap," Jenson replied. "We were inventing the future."

"*Inventing the future.*" Saxton nodded. "A wonderful slogan."

"ZAT manufactures advanced technology solutions. That's our whole purpose."

"But what makes up the majority of your current sales?"

"Weapons and related equipment."

Saxton snapped his fingers and gestured to the room. "Could someone remind me why we were thinking of buying a supercomputer from a weapons manufacturer, rather than a manufacturer of supercomputers?"

"Because," Jenson said, "we've been creating bespoke computer processors for over fifteen years. One of our key benefits was that we weren't committed to a pre-defined, and entirely unoriginal, processor roadmap with only marginal improvements over the rest of the market. We don't iterate, we innovate."

"Which is a good thing if it leads to success," Saxton said.

"We were ready to start building the beta test, but now I guess we'll never know."

Saxton looked down at some notes in front of him. "Last time your company tried to deliver on a government computer project, you failed."

Jenson sighed. "You're talking about Project Darwin? That was more than a decade ago. It's also not a fair comparison: it was highly speculative and, as you are no doubt aware, one of the lead designers died before it was completed."

"Rather short-sighted of you to be so reliant on one individual."

"If someone is that brilliant, they're worth relying on."

Saxton took a deep breath. "What if Parallel did work? A number of concerns were raised over handing over our control of all the data to a computer."

"Let's stay in the realms of fact: this wasn't going to be Skynet."

"Yet I heard you proposed using it to control your micro-drone weapons?"

"Those were never brought to market. Look, Project Parallel is just about analysis, Warwick. At the moment you aren't drawing any conclusions. You're paddling in an ocean of Big Data, lost without a compass. We could have changed that."

"A bold claim."

"We never went live with any part of the system: our agreement was very clear about that. It was clear about a great many things to *your* advantage, including the ability to walk away at any time."

"Then I guess we'll just have to see." Saxton shuffled his papers. "How quickly can you build it?"

Jenson blinked, a smile starting to spread over his face.

"Do you want to answer my question?"

"I want to savour the moment. You need us again. I want to know what the hell happened to cause such an about-face."

"Just tell me how quickly you can work-up a prototype, Gregory, or we'll go find a less opinionated tech CEO who will."

Jenson glanced at Kelly. "I'll have to verify my team's current deployment, but I think six months should be achievable."

Saxton nodded. "Then you'd best get started. I'll send the paperwork over to your team, approving the project costs." He stood up. "Try not to exceed them again."

Jenson stood up and extended his hand to Saxton. "I appreciate this, Warwick."

Saxton seemed to hesitate, then shook Jenson's hand. "What I'm most concerned that you *appreciate* is that we can't afford for you to screw this up." He paused, then pulled out his phone. "I'm going to send you my new private number. If you have a problem, if you need to make a decision, I want to know about it. This phone is never switched off, day or night. I'm always working."

Jenson nodded. "And until this project is finished, so am I."

NINE

Millie Wright shuffled off the train with a hundred other commuters and made her way out to the waiting shuttle bus. She nodded to the driver then took a seat near the back. A couple of familiar faces glanced her way, so she put her earphones on, closed her eyes, and lost herself in the music. She had had a late night and now, after not nearly enough sleep, she was not in the mood for conversation.

The bus belched and groaned its way into the West London trading estate, finally arriving at the rather uninspiring office block occupied by Millie's employers, Gladstone Software. Two thousand lost souls turned up there every day to earn a living. It wasn't much of a company, nor was it much of a location. But they paid on time every month and the canteen was cheap. You couldn't argue with that.

With a hiss the bus pulled up at the front gate and discharged its cargo. Millie fumbled in her backpack for her security pass, holding up the line behind her, then she pushed her way through the revolving doors and took the lift to level six. A vast floor was flooded with a sea of cubicles, each trapping a single employee for the day. She was at her desk, logged on, precisely thirty seconds early as usual. Why give them any more of her time than she had to?

Now she was here she would get some work done. Of

course she didn't intend that much of it would be for Gladstone. She had a project or two of her own that needed attention, one of which being the reason she had had a late night. Unfortunately today there was a problem.

"Morning, Ms Wright," said her boss, appearing out of nowhere. "Do you have that presentation for me?"

Millie blinked, then smiled carefully. "Just fine-tuning it now."

"Good. After that I need you to check the spreadsheet Finance have prepared."

Millie sighed. She hadn't even started the presentation and she didn't feel any smoldering motivation to change that. Working in the accounts department of a mid-tier software company paid the bills, but forty hours a week in a cubicle, doing her boss's bidding, while drinking rancid coffee was hard to swallow. With a grunt she pulled her personal laptop out of her backpack and set it up next to her company machine.

"You know you're not supposed to bring your own computer into the office," said her neighbour, Kevin, peering over from the next cubicle.

She looked up with a quiet sigh. "I wouldn't have to if they didn't give us these five-year-old pieces of junk."

"Don't worry," he whispered, giving her a conspiratorial wink. "I won't tell anyone. Bet it's good for watching YouTube while you have Powerpoint open."

She half nodded, turning to her main company screen and logging onto the intranet.

"Good weekend?" he asked pleasantly, his chin hanging over the partition.

Before Millie could reply another voice spoke. "Got time to talk?" their boss asked, reappearing from her office. "Because Ms Wright here most certainly does not."

"I was just saying good morning—"

"Then do it at coffee break."

Kevin shrunk back, his face ashen.

"Was that really necessary?" she asked.

Her boss's glare hardened. "I'm sorry, are you running the department today?"

Millie ground her teeth. "No."

"Then perhaps I can decide what's *necessary*. Now is that presentation done?"

"Just pulling my file off the server to give it a final polish."

Her boss gave a sniff and walked off.

"Sorry," whispered Kevin. "Didn't mean to get us into trouble."

"Forget it," Millie replied. "She should learn to worry about actual problems." She pulled open her own laptop. "And on that point, you've just given me an idea."

THE FIRST SIGN THAT SOMETHING WAS WRONG WAS TWO people on the far side of the office swearing. Millie watched her boss stride over angrily. "I won't have language like that on my floor."

"The network is down," said a young woman. "I can't access the main database."

"Or email," said a bearded man from across the room.

"None of the servers are responding," said an older woman near where Millie was sitting.

"Just switch your computers off and on again. That should—"

"No," said the bearded man. "It's the servers that are down. It's showing they've been wiped?"

Millie bit her lip as her boss walked over to him. "What do you mean 'wiped'?"

"They have nothing on them."

"Well, can't you just restore them from a backup?"

"Possibly. This happened last year and it's not exactly straightforward. Twenty-four hours minimum. I'll call IT."

Kevin looked at her with a tight expression. "Did you", he lowered his voice to a whisper, "do that?"

Millie shrugged. "That would require substantial hardware knowledge and administrator-level access."

"Yes." He hesitated. "Is that a yes or a no?"

She smiled. "Sometimes things are best left as a mystery." She raised a finger to her lips.

The fire alarm began sounding.

Kevin's eyes widened. "No!"

She shrugged. "Suddenly I doubt any of us are going to be able to do much work today." She turned to see her boss was now shouting into a phone, imploring the IT department to 'get down here immediately'.

"Millie gathered up her laptop and her bag. "I, for one, am going to get a proper cup of coffee while they sort this out. Coming?"

TEN

MICHAEL WAVED OFF HIS TAXI AND STRODE UP THE PATHWAY to the front door of his terraced house in Wimbledon. The journey back from Fiji had given him a lot of time to think about his situation, but he had not been able to reach a decision. Perhaps Eve could help him make sense of it all.

"Nice trip?" she asked as he wandered into the kitchen. "I didn't even know you were looking for a new job."

"I wasn't. I got headhunted. In a bar."

"What?" She screwed up her nose. "You're making this up."

"I'd say the same if I didn't know better. I did try calling but your phone was off."

"I was on shift. Who the hell would fly you to Fiji for an interview?"

"Only one of the top law firms in London."

"Well that's just peachy for some. Back in the real world, the rest of us haven't spent the weekend on a tropical island."

"Ah, so it's jealousy I'm seeing."

"Duh? So how did it go?"

"They made me an offer." He reached into his pocket and slid across the handwritten note that Nichol had given him.

She looked at it and her eyes widened. "And in return for

all those pounds sterling, just how many pounds of your flesh are they going to require?"

"I'm going to have to work hard, wherever I go."

Eve tilted her head and looked in his eyes. "This is all very exciting, but you're behaving like you've got no choice. Is there something you're not telling me?"

He forced a smile on his face. "Of course not."

"Then is there something *they're* not telling *you*?" She reached forward and patted his shoulder. "Don't you think this is all a bit odd? I mean, they fly you to Fiji. They offer you shed loads of money. An 'offer you can't refuse'. What are they? Run by the mafia?"

"This is just a great opportunity. I'd be crazy not to consider it."

"Is this just you trying to show that you aren't your father?"

"Perhaps. I'm making something of myself, not hiding in a barn."

"I agree, but are you sure you can trust them? When something sounds too good to be true, in my experience it usually is."

"Sure you're not just trying to rain on my parade? And you're always saying I'm too boring. Isn't this the kind of thing I should be doing?"

"I think '*predictable*' is the term I use for you. Just keep your eyes and your mind open… and of course we should go out for dinner to celebrate. Somewhere swanky, since you'll be paying."

AFTER DINNER, EVE HEADED TO BED WHILE MICHAEL FINISHED unpacking. Once everything was put away, he pulled out his mobile phone and withdrew the business card that had sat in his wallet since Friday night. Then he dialled the number.

Kara answered almost immediately. "That took longer than I expected."

"I had to think things over."

"Well good for you. And?"

"I'm in."

"Of course you are. You start at 8:30am tomorrow morning. Come to our offices in Knightsbridge."

Michael was about to agree when he remembered what he ought to be saying given that Infinity didn't seem to know he'd been fired. "But don't I have to resign first and work out my notice period?"

"That won't be an issue. I'll call them right now." She paused. "With your permission, of course."

"Sure."

"See you tomorrow." She ended the call.

Michael held up her card again, running his finger over the thick, black letters. What exactly had he signed up for here?

ELEVEN

THE OFFICE BLOCK STOOD NINE STORIES HIGH, CLAD IN mirrored glass. It nestled between several similar buildings and bore no external signage or distinguishing architectural features. Overlooking London's Hyde Park, the windows reflected the lush trees on a sunny day. Rumour had it that the offices were formerly owned by a high-profile arms dealer. Maxwell Errington had laughed at that story – at least publicly – since the lease had been transferred to Infinity Law as payment of professional fees some twenty years ago. It had been part of a series of transactions designed to lower the client's profile.

Duncan Nichol, stepped out of his chauffeur-driven car and strode into the lobby, smiling at the receptionist then sliding into the waiting elevator and swiping his access card over the control panel. Seconds later he was stepping out on level nine. The penthouse floor included a small lobby and two large offices. He nodded to Errington's secretary, who sat at her desk in the lobby, typing rapid-fire while listening to her headset.

"Good flight?" she asked, her typing not slowing.

"I've had worse. Is Max in?"

"Yes, but he's got a car picking him up in fifteen, so please don't distract him."

Nichol raised an eyebrow and walked past her, pushing his door open. The office beyond was vast, taking up nearly two thirds of the floor. It was traditional in style and high in impact: lots of oak and bookshelves crammed with legal volumes, though Nichol was sure nobody had looked at them in many years, least of all Maxwell Errington. The Senior Partner was sat at his oak and leather desk, glaring at his computer like it was an alien device. Nichol cleared his throat loudly.

Errington looked up. "Don't they teach you young folks to knock?"

"Given that this is my office, it didn't seem necessary."

The older man scratched his nose. "My name is still on the door."

"Max, it's the Managing Partner's office." Nichol paused. "I swear you're just doing this for fun."

Errington closed his laptop with an irritated snap. "I'm rich and semi-retired. I do everything for fun."

"Of course you do. Any update on that new instruction?"

"First you want my office, then you want my help?"

Nichol put his hands in his pockets and walked over to the window. "I've had a long flight. Please spare me the routine."

"Have some patience. We'll hear in the next few days."

There was a sharp knock at the door. A brown-haired lawyer in his late-twenties, his grey suit pressed almost painfully sharply, stood waiting.

Errington tilted his head to Nichol. "See. Our junior associates know how to knock."

Nichol rolled his eyes. "What is it?"

"I have that bill for sign off." He waved a crisp white sheet of paper in one hand.

"Of course—" began Errington.

Nichol growled and stepped forward, taking the document. "What is this?"

"Opal Pharmaceutical," said the junior. "The negotiation resolution we ran for them."

Nichol squinted at the document. "Is that all? Didn't we

save them twenty million?"

"Twenty-two point eight million," said Errington smoothly. "But we quoted a fixed fee."

"What on earth for?"

"In order to secure the business, or would you like to question my decision-making?"

Nichol ground his teeth, but signed the sheet. "Make sure we hound them for payment."

The junior associate took the sheet and scurried from the room.

"I thought it was *my* job to be mean to the associates," Errington said, walking over and closing the door.

"Is he any good?" asked Nichol.

"You hired him, didn't you?"

"On your recommendation. He just gives me a strange vibe."

"Probably his aftershave." Errington smiled. "While we're talking about associates, how did your interview go?"

"Very well. Mr Adams just called to say he's joining us."

"Marvellous." Errington's phone rang. He snatched it up, then immediately put it down. "My car is here." He touched a finger to his lips. "One of the clients you told me never to talk to you about."

"Are they paying the bills?"

"Always have so far."

"Then that's all I need to know. Any news from ZAT? We haven't had a project from them in a while. When we aren't feeding off our biggest client I get nervous."

Errington smiled. "I predict something sizeable will be coming to us shortly."

Nichol paused. "How exactly do you know these things? Even by the standards of this firm, you're always well informed."

"Come now. A magician never reveals his tricks."

"With you it feels more like black magic."

Errington patted him on the arm. "As long as it works, does it matter?"

TWELVE

The car was a black Jaguar XJ Sentinel, with a supercharged 5.0 litre V8 engine capable of a top speed of 225 miles per hour – though, as it threaded through the central London traffic, it was averaging less than twenty, even with its police outriders.

In the back, secreted behind a privacy screen and tinted glass, Warwick Saxton sat re-reading the technical summaries for Project Parallel. Physical security was a manageable concern. ZAT's facilities were amongst the most locked-down of any commercial enterprise he had encountered, and the new system would go on to be housed at GCHQ. The biggest concern was whether Parallel could be made to work. There had been rumours that ZAT had hit an intractable problem before the plug was pulled. Jenson was known for driving his teams to exhaustion to ensure projects were delivered, but that might be part of the problem. The skeletons in the ZAT CEO's past had always bothered Saxton. After Rostrum had reactivated the project, MI5 had, of course, re-run its standard background checks. But Saxton wanted to go deeper, and for that he had to use less orthodox methods.

On a pre-arranged signal, the two outriders peeled away and the Jaguar turned off of its route to Saxton's office. Instead they drove north, away from Vauxhall. Saxton's diary showed a meeting with the head of an obscure committee, but that was a fabrication.

They were soon at the meeting point: a small park in North London. Saxton stepped from the Jaguar. "Stay in sight, but don't crowd him," he told his bodyguard, then walked over to the small duck-pond at the centre of the park. A slender man in a long overcoat sat staring at the water.

"Morning, Director," said the man, continuing to stare at the pond. "Punctual as always."

Saxton snorted. "Morning, Morton."

Morton turned and held out a grey plastic folder. "There are things in there that Mr Jenson doesn't know about himself."

Saxton took the folder and flicked through the pages within. "Highlights?"

"Good news. It seems Mr Jenson is a changed man. It's not that people from his past don't try to contact him, but he always turns them away. We picked up chatter from one former contact in particular. It's in the file."

Saxton slid the folder into his briefcase. "How do you do it?"

Morton raised an eyebrow. "As always, I'm not permitted to discuss our process."

"A pity. But good to see Kinek Consulting continues to maintain its enigma." Saxton turned to leave.

"What is Project Parallel?"

Saxton froze.

"It came up in our research. ZAT seems to be linked to it, but we couldn't uncover any more. Perhaps it's an off-book scheme. Do you need it investigated?"

Saxton forced an expression of thinking carefully. "I'm not familiar with the name. But I'll do some checking, and let you know if we need any action taken. Assume not, for now."

"Understood."

Saxton watched Morton walk away. Kinek Consulting had proved a unique and valuable resource on a number of occasions. They produced accurate, in-depth reports on complex issues, and they did it not only discreetly but outside the notice of his office. Yet now Morton had happened on one of his most top-secret matters. How could they possibly have found even a mention of Parallel? Had there been a leak? Or had Morton been probing beyond where he should? He would have to find out.

The irony was that if Project Parallel were operational then the answers would be available almost instantly. Indeed, once it was online, he might not need Kinek's services at all.

For now, though, he would manage things himself.

THIRTEEN

Hanging menacingly over London Wall, the thirty-five storey ZAT headquarters was an architectural statement in blackened steel and glass. Despite the designer's grand vision, some of the more important design features were functional and internal. One suite of rooms had steel-reinforced concrete walls, isolated power supplies, their own segregated data network and no windows. All organisations had secrets, but ZAT Systems had more than most.

Gregory Jenson began the lengthy security process to access Research Area Eight: voice and retinal scans, palm analysis, a biometric scan. It took two minutes and five seconds to complete, give or take three seconds. He knew because he had supervised its design. At last the door opened and he stepped into the first part of the airlock. The air cycled angrily for another thirty seconds before he was permitted to step into the laboratory to be greeted by Dr Chow, ZAT's Head of Engineering.

"You're late," said Chow, his bald head gleaming. "But then you always are. As long as you understand that while I'm wasting time talking to you I'm not doing actual work."

"I know you prefer to work from Reading or the other factory sites."

"Quite why we need to have our R&D facility co-located

with Corporate in the middle of the City is beyond me. Not all of us have a helicopter." Chow folded his arms. "What exactly is this about? Kelly was suitably oblique on the phone."

"We're restarting Project Parallel. I've just come from a meeting with Warwick Saxton at GCHQ."

"After all the crap that went down, why the change?"

"I'd guess the new Home Secretary had something to do with it. But who knows? And, more importantly, who cares? This is a huge opportunity."

"How quickly do they want the prototype?"

"I committed us to six months."

"Even though there's a lead time of at least twelve months on the custom chips that we designed?"

"I'm well aware of that." Jenson cleared his throat. "So I'm also aware that, despite my strict instructions to the contrary, you ordered the chips thirteen months ago."

Chow blinked. "Is that right?"

"Nothing goes on in my company without me knowing it. Not anymore."

"Let's hope that's true." Chow reached under his desk and produced a heavily-padded courier package. "They arrived two days ago. Nearly a month late."

The package was swathed in different categories of tape loudly proclaiming that it was extremely urgent, confidential, fragile and contained sensitive electronic components. It was stamped as priority customs cleared, with an originating address in Japan. Jenson ran his fingertips over the tear-strip on the right-hand side. "I feel that some form of apology is in order. From you, if that wasn't clear."

"It's my job to do what I know you really want, not what you say."

Jenson shrugged and tore open the package, then slid the interior bubble-wrapped contents onto the table. The seven computer chips were encased in an individual anti-static shield.

"Seven small squares that will change the world," Chow said. "What resource can I access?"

"Pretty much anything you need. Liaise with Kelly. She'll squash any lack of cooperation—" Jenson's phone rang. He slapped it to his ear and listened carefully, said 'OK' and clicked it off, his expression serious.

Chow frowned. "How is your phone working in this room? I thought all cell frequencies were blocked?"

"My phone works everywhere. And just as well, too, because we have an MI5 auditor coming to verify our security measures. Saxton obviously wants to keep us on our toes, but at least it shows that they're serious."

"Are we ready for an inspection?" Chow asked.

"We'd better be," muttered Jenson. "She's walking in to our reception as we speak."

FOURTEEN

THE SUN SHONE BRIGHTLY AS MICHAEL EMERGED FROM Knightsbridge Tube Station and crossed the road between slow-moving traffic. He made his way up a short side street, pausing to grab a large latte from a street vendor. At 8:30am precisely he strode up to the mirrored glass shrouding the offices of Infinity Law. With a deep breath he stepped through the sliding doors.

Inside it was modern and uncluttered, all polished marble and glass. A single security guard gave him the briefest flicker of attention before returning his stare to a point somewhere on the wall. Michael walked over to the receptionist. Before he could speak she stopped typing and picked up a phone. "He's here," she reported to the person at the other end. Then she pointed accusingly at his drink. "What is *that*?"

"A latte?" he replied.

"The partners don't like *staff* carrying drinks through reception." She raised her eyebrows then returned to her typing. Behind her, a security door opened and an older woman with heavy earrings and an almost-smile beckoned him through.

"I'm Sandra, your secretary. Follow me." They stepped into a lift. Michael saw nine levels marked on the glass touchscreen. Sandra wiped it distractedly then pressed 2. Then wiped it again. "These stupid screens look flash until anyone puts a finger on them. Then they just look smudgy."

Michael smiled. "VIPs only on the top floor?" he asked, noticing that level 9 was marked 'special access only'.

"Level 9 has Mr Nichols' and Mr Errington's offices. Rule number 1. Don't go there unless you are invited." She paused. "Not that the lift would take you without a special pass."

She pointed to his coffee. "Rule 2. Don't bring hot beverages through the main entrance."

"Yeah, the receptionist just chastised me. Sorry. I didn't know."

"It's one of the things with this place. You really can't find out anything about it until you actually get here. But", she looked at him, "you're supposed to be really bright, so I'm sure you'll pick everything up fast enough."

They stepped out onto level 2 and Sandra strode quickly through a busy open-plan area humming with activity. Nobody looked up. They stopped at a large desk with multiple screens, a name plaque proclaiming it hers.

"You can leave your coat and bag here for now. Your desk is still being set up."

"Desk? I don't get an office?"

"Forgot to ask about that at the interview, did you? Got distracted by the zeroes?"

Michael coughed. "Apparently."

"Only Senior Associates get an office. And even then, only if they're good. For now you're out here with the likes of me." She glanced at her screen and deleted a message. "But there are plenty of conference rooms if you need one."

"Will I share you with anyone?"

She laughed. "Even partners don't get their own secretary. Except Mr Errington, that is. You'll share me with four others. Can you type?"

"Pretty well."

"Excellent, but get faster. Or get *au fait* with the voice recognition software. Remember, you're not in Fiji anymore."

"I'll make it a priority."

"Good." She picked up a folder in the middle of her desk. "There's a bunch of forms in here that you need to complete. We don't really have an HR department, so I'll help you with any issues. But let's get this tour out of the way first. Hang on." She pulled her mobile from a clip on her belt as it beeped and read a message. "She wants to see you in her office."

"*She*?"

"Kara Simmons. The person you work for?" Sandra pointed over his shoulder. "Don't keep her waiting."

KARA WAS ON THE PHONE, BUT WAVED AT MICHAEL through the glass internal wall, beckoning him into her office. "I need his signature on the agreement," she said to the caller. "I also need you to process the file request." She rolled her eyes. "Let me know immediately if there's going to be further delay." She clicked the phone off, grimacing. "CEO's PA is completely useless. Unlike Sandra, who you should treasure like a jewel. *My* jewel." She took a long drink from a bottle of mineral water. She pointed at the coffee cup in his hand. "Did nobody tell you about that?"

"Consider me now fully informed of the issue."

"There's a back way in if you can't do without. Get one of the other juniors to show you. Now, I have a lot of documents coming in for you to review for an urgent business sale: there's a negotiation meeting tomorrow. I've sent you a link to the shared drive."

"Excellent. Except I don't have a computer yet."

Kara rolled her eyes again. "I'll get Sandra to print them for now. Just remember that you need to be out front of the offices at midday. There'll be a car waiting for you to take you to lunch."

"Where are we going?" Michael asked.

"Oh I'm not going," Kara said dismissively, picking up her phone again and preparing to dial.

"Then who am I having lunch with?"

Kara smiled. "Maxwell Errington."

FIFTEEN

Two hours after the onset of the chaos she had created at the offices of Gladstone Software, Millie's day had improved considerably. She sat in the business park's *faux* Italian café, two cups of coffee coursing through her system. One of the two frosted donuts she had just purchased was sitting on a napkin, waiting to be devoured. Kevin was munching on the other as he sat opposite, playing Tetris on his phone. Word from the office was that the computer system might not be back online today. Millie smiled. Now she could get on with some real work.

She had her personal laptop in front of her. It was an unusual machine – a friend had described it as the ugly offspring of a clipboard and a sandwich toaster. Millie had built it from scratch using many custom parts, so it shared almost no commonality with a regular system. The design was not without problems; it had poor structural integrity, and frequently overheated. But it worked differently from regular computers, and that made it particularly difficult to trace. This was useful because, when researching stuff for her blog, being traced was a bad thing. 'Millie.On.Truths' had become a conspiracy theory community. Not about aliens and the abominable snowman, but rather one that investigated strange and illegal goings on in large companies and governments, focusing on the use of 'Big Data' and the possibilities of the Deep Web and Dark Web. She looked for anything that people were trying to hide that the public had a right to know.

Last month she had written an exposé on illegal activities conducted by one of the trading teams at a privately-owned investment bank. The bank's lawyers had tried to bring her down, but they couldn't find her. Millie was good at hiding, but knew that if she ever failed she could always fall back on the defence that what she had written was the truth. As her homepage proudly proclaimed, she believed that 'The Truth Should Be Out There.'

"What are you doing?" Kevin asked, looking up from his phone. He picked up the donut and took another bite.

"Replying to a message."

"So not more hacking, then?"

"That presupposes I was doing any hacking."

"Well were you?"

Millie closed her laptop and stared at him. "What do you think?"

"I don't know. And maybe I don't want to know." He hesitated. "Is it to find stuff for your blog?"

Millie froze. "What?"

He shifted uncomfortably in his seat. "This woman was asking about it."

She reached forward and gripped his arm. "What woman?"

"She spoke to me at the station this morning. Sorry, should have mentioned it sooner." He pulled away, reaching into his pocket and pulling out a brown paper envelope. "She gave me this to give to you."

Millie reached out to take it from him, then hesitated. "What was she wearing?"

"Why does it matter?"

"A uniform of some kind? A business suit? Workman's overalls?"

"A leather jacket, I think."

"And what's in the envelope?"

"She didn't say, and I haven't looked. She just said you'd find it interesting."

Millie frowned, then took it from him and tore it open. There was a single sheet of paper inside with neat black print on crisp white.

I'm a big fan of your work. You should investigate ZAT Systems. Specifically, the Darwin Project. But be careful, they won't take it lying down.

Millie read it twice, then checked again inside the envelope. "Is that it?"

Kevin took the sheet. "Is it an anonymous tip?"

"ZAT are hardly an unexpected target. I mean, what's not dodgy about an arms manufacturer?"

"Is that what they do? I haven't heard of them."

"They're one of the largest tech companies headquartered in London. Their CEO's written a best-selling book. I thought everyone knew who they were."

Kevin shrugged. "What about the Darwin Project bit?"

Millie scratched her nose. "Without knowing who this woman was, it's hard to assess if it's worth any time."

"So what do you do now?"

"I'll create a deep-net trawler, build a result matrix, look for the connections and patterns. If I get nothing then I'll adjust parameters and run it again. It's a bit like treasure hunting with a metal detector."

"So is this, like, a 'Big Data' thing?"

Her eyes narrowed. "What would you know about that?"

Kevin shrugged. "I watched a bunch of YouTube videos. I didn't find it persuasive that we could solve the world's biggest problems with a spreadsheet. I figure it's complete nonsense. Like astrology."

"I don't know about astrology, but Big Data is the real deal – they should teach it at school, except the government is twenty years behind in setting the curriculum. Although to be fair, until recently we didn't have the right tools for the job - whether it was sufficiently complex mathematical models or powerful enough computers, let alone the raw data itself. Now the world has changed."

Kevin puffed out his cheeks. "Whatever you say."

Millie smiled. "Researchers were provided with the engineering data for all British Navy vessels. That included all engine and ship systems performance metrics, all service reports, all maintenance and repair reports. They were able to anticipate, with 93% accuracy, where undetected part failures were most likely to occur. That meant they could perform pre-emptive maintenance, which was on average 68% lower in cost. The study also looked into the Navy's supply chain. Over 10,000 companies were part of its ship-building programme. From that data they predicted with 87% accuracy whether suppliers were likely to default on their contract obligations, which meant they could be proactive and ensure they had alternates ready to step-in."

"So?"

"So they saved a great deal of money."

Kevin frowned. "Isn't this all rather subjective? And it's just one example, based on one data sample."

"Quite the reverse. It's entirely *objective*. Also - and I can't stress this point enough - it's not a sample. That's the point of Big Data – it's everything. It's like a RAW image in photography: you can take it and re-analyse it in any way you want. It's not about specifics at the individual level: it's about how, once you aggregate, useful patterns start to emerge." She paused. "Well, sometimes. Sometimes it's nothing, but sometimes you strike gold." She glanced at the envelope. "Maybe you've set me on a path of discovery with this after all."

"Glad to be of service."

She smiled and pulled a five pound note from her pocket, placing it on the table in front of Kevin.

"What's that for?"

"I don't know about you, but I'm going to need another donut."

SIXTEEN

JENSON WALKED OVER, EXTENDING HIS HAND TO THE WOMAN in the reception area. She held a black leather folio in one hand, her eyes flicking around behind her plastic-rimmed glasses, as if she was recording everything.

"If MI5 had told us you were coming," he said, "we could have put on a welcome party."

She returned his handshake. "Our audit team don't want the welcome party. We want to see things as they are every day."

He gestured towards the internal security gate. "Of course. But haven't we already passed your site audit?"

"Despite what Mr. Saxton may have said, we're not restarting this project without a fresh review of your security systems. This shouldn't come as a surprise."

Jenson nodded to the security guard, who snapped to attention and opened the gate. They stepped through into a large foyer lined with banks of lifts. "I only ask because this building has over two thousand rooms, and a complex, layered security system. It might take you several weeks to review every element properly. And of course we'll need to escort you throughout your visit."

"That won't be necessary. In fact it will probably hinder my work."

"Well that's unfortunate, but neither our insurance nor our contracts with third parties permit an unsupervised visitor in the premises: it's part of our security protocol." He tipped his head. "It's also stated in the contract."

The woman adjusted her glasses. "Very well. I'm going to need full access to your physical and electronic security: everything relevant or potentially relevant to the project."

Jenson nodded. "I hope you're ready to be impressed."

"I'm holding my breath."

THREE HOURS LATER THE WOMAN EMERGED FROM THE ZAT building, and crossed the street. A black cab pulled up alongside her. Without speaking to the driver, she got in and they sped away. The driver reached back over his shoulder and handed her a mobile phone, then closed the privacy screen. The woman removed her wig, peeled off her fake eyebrows, then held the phone to her ear and spoke, her accent shifting. "I've just completed my review."

"Any issues with Jenson?" replied the familiar metallic voice.

"None that I observed. He just seemed keen to show everything in the best light."

"What about Saxton?"

"The seed was planted. I expect he'll be taking steps shortly. I'll have the write-up to you in a couple of hours, but I thought you'd like the highlights immediately. The place is a fortress. It would be easier to hit a Las Vegas casino. I'll start investigating contingencies when I return to the office."

"Keep me posted."

The woman clicked the phone off.

JENSON WATCHED THE WOMAN WITH THE BLACK FOLIO DRIVE away. She had seemed rather too intense to be a government employee, but his people had run detailed background checks on her the moment she'd announced herself at reception and she had checked out. Despite her attempt at a poker face, he was pretty sure the inspection had gone well. It was one problem off the list. But there were plenty more to deal with.

He pulled out his phone but it rang before he could dial. He frowned at the screen. A withheld number? With a mutter, he declined the call. Nobody who had his number would withhold their own.

The phone rang again.

This time it was his daughter's mobile. He answered quickly. "I'm sorry, Teresa, but I can't talk now—"

"Sorry to disappoint you, Greg," said a female voice with a faintly Venezuelan accent. "I needed you to answer this time."

Jenson's mind span. He knew the voice. "Regina? How, have you got…" He shivered. "What have you done with my daughter?"

"I've no idea where the lovely Teresa is. I just got my people to hack your phone to mis-display the caller."

"That's impossible."

"I have a contact in the manufacturer's R&D team, who got me their master codes. The ones they swear do not exist. Now, I just want to discuss some business."

"You know I cannot."

"Come on. Are we not friends?"

"We *were* friends. Times have changed."

"Make time. For me."

Jenson shook his head. "When and where?"

SEVENTEEN

The Mercedes SL600 picked Michael up from in front of Infinity Law's offices at exactly midday, providing a welcome break from a morning spent reviewing documents relating to their client's proposed business sale. The roads were busy, but the driver seemed to have the uncanny ability to predict the best route. In what felt like no time, Michael found himself standing outside a historic private club located just off Piccadilly.

He was greeted by a porter, and was whisked through a security check, up several floors in an express lift, then along an opulent hallway to a spacious dining room. In the corner, on a dais raised up above the other tables, sat a grey-haired figure, unmistakable from his photograph. Wearing his trademark wood-rimmed glasses, Maxwell Errington rose to his feet and waved.

Michael shook the older man's hand. "It's very kind of you to invite me for lunch."

"It's my pleasure. I try to have a chat with all our new joiners. In the old days I would have been involved in your recruitment. But time moves on." Errington sat down and beckoned that Michael should as well.

Michael gazed out of the large window next to them, looking across scattered rooftops to Green Park in the distance. A waiter appeared and opened a bottle of red wine, then filled their glasses.

"How's your first day going?" Errington asked.

Michael shrugged. "I've been straight into some client work. Kara gave me—"

"Ah yes, Ms Simmons. Now there's a fire-cracker." He gave a half wink. "You'd be wise to keep a close eye on her."

Michael swallowed. "Of course. I'm going to be primarily working for her for the first few months. At least that was what Duncan said at the interview."

"And how did you like the island?" Errington cleared his throat. "*My island*, that is."

"It's quite a weapon to have in your armory."

"Never regretted buying it. Particularly since I paid an obscenely low price. But then I had leverage over the seller." He picked up a menu. "Always a good thing to have."

"I'll remember that."

"You should. It's what Infinity does best. It's what makes my firm different." Errington cleared his throat. "Of course it's not really my firm anymore, as Duncan keeps reminding me. But I like to keep my eye on things." He picked up his glass. "Your good health."

Michael raised his own glass. "Pardon me, but what do you mean, it's not your firm? Aren't you the Senior Partner?"

"Duncan is Managing Partner: he runs the firm. The Senior Partner is more of a figurehead – a friendly old consultant they wheel out for important clients to reassure them there's been no change in approach. Which is ironic, because change is why clients need us." Errington snorted. "Now let's eat. You OK if I order for both of us?"

THE MEAL WAS SCHEDULED FOR SIX COURSES, SO AFTER THE main dish of marinated veal they took a breather. Errington sat back in his chair. "I've read your CV. Useful to see how *you* describe yourself. Of course we don't stop there - we like to know everything about our team."

"I believe you. Duncan showed me the report."

Errington smiled. "That little stunt. It's supposed to intimidate you." He paused. "Did it?"

Michael shrugged. "The firm's reputation precedes it. I was expecting the unexpected."

Errington nodded. "Good. Now I hear you're something of an expert in this technological nonsense that is apparently taking over the world."

Michael shrugged. "It's my father who was in computers. I just picked a little of it up."

"Was? What does he do now?"

"He died when I was a boy." Michael paused. "I expect that was in the file."

Errington didn't blink. "One of our biggest challenges is that there is too much information to process and remember. But I've no doubt your father would be proud of you now. Our firm's reputation is second to none, even if relatively few know we exist."

"Your reputation may be more widespread than you realise."

Errington's eyes crinkled into a smile. "They do say there's no such thing as bad publicity. Of course it's all nonsense spread by that confounded interweb thing. I keep hoping the fad will pass."

Michael coughed. "I think you're swimming against a tidal wave."

Errington sat back in his chair, his eyebrow rising slightly.

"What I mean is that everything in business involves technology now: every modern company is built on it. If you can't talk tech, you can't talk business."

"You've been here five minutes, and already you're telling me what to do." Errington gave a smile. "I think you will fit in here very well. Very well indeed."

The waiter returned and reached to replace a bottle of

mineral water, but caught Errington's glass with his cuff and sent it tumbling into his lap.

The Senior Partner's look would have sunk a battleship. "You idiot!"

"I'm so very sorry, Sir. I'll get—"

Errington waved him off, wiping his trousers with a spare napkin. "Just bring the next course." The waiter nodded and vanished into the kitchen, at which point Errington signaled curtly to the restaurant manager. He continued dabbing at his trousers without looking up when the man arrived next to the table. "If I see that waiter again, I will terminate my membership. Do I make myself clear?"

The man nodded immediately. "We appreciate your patience and understanding." He vanished into the kitchen.

Errington tapped his glasses. "Let that be a lesson. If you have a motivated supplier, use it to your advantage. I expect people who do things for me to do the very best they can. Every time. Getting rid of a man like that is a service to this club and its members." He leaned forward, his eyes narrowing, all hint of a smile gone. "This is a tough world we live in. And our business is to navigate one of the toughest parts. You need to be ready to make the right decision on a moment's notice."

"And that justifies things like this?" Michael asked. "It was just a glass of water."

Errington snorted. "You can be more subtle, if you have the art. Show people what you want them to see. If I turn up in a stretch limo then I don't just want to get from A to B. I want you to see the limo and me, at that moment. Everything we do should happen for a reason."

"Like what just happened with the glass of water?" Michael folded his arms. "Perhaps you staged that situation just to get a reaction out of me."

Errington stared at him for several seconds. "You are the first associate that's ever said that."

"Am I right?"

"What matters is that you thought of the possibility." He raised his glass. "Welcome to Infinity."

Michael raised his own glass, then heard a soft chiming.

Errington pulled a mobile phone from his pocket. He listened briefly to someone at the other end, then clicked it off. "It's Kara. That client meeting you have tomorrow has been brought forward. It's happening now."

Michael hesitated.

"Your mother's a psychiatrist, isn't she?" Errington said.

Michael frowned at the non sequitur. "She's retired, but yes."

"And she wrote a book – '*I Can Make You Do Anything*', wasn't it?"

"That's right. Why do you—"

"While you work at Infinity you'd do well to remember that's exactly what we expect of you – anything and everything. If someone needs you for client work then, unless you're dead, you jump." Errington gestured to the exit. "So, jump."

EIGHTEEN

JENSON SAT IN THE BACK OF HIS MERCEDES, WATCHING THE outskirts of London slide past.

"I still don't like this," Kelly said from the driver's seat. "We shouldn't be going to a location she controls that I haven't inspected."

"She's an old friend."

Kelly's hands gripped the wheel. "Maybe, but she's also an arms dealer who *wants* something."

Jenson stared back out of the window. "Regina just needs to be managed. I don't need another enemy."

"And what if she asks you for something you can't give her?"

He gave a snort. "Just shut up and drive."

Fifteen minutes later the Mercedes turned into an abandoned industrial estate: a sad wasteland of rust, fading signs and peeling paint. They drew to a halt in front of the corroded roller-door of a disused warehouse.

Jenson peered out at the building.

Kelly tapped a display on the dashboard. "These are the coordinates we were given."

"I guess Regina will have her reasons."

Shrieking in protest, the roller-door slid up and a hand beckoned. Kelly glanced at Jenson then eased the car slowly inside. The door lowered behind them, rattling and juddering. Darkness enveloped them for just a moment, then spotlights blazed and four large men stepped forward, each carrying a shoulder-slung automatic rifle as Jenson climbed out of the Mercedes. One of the men quickly patted him down, taking his keys and mobile phone and placing them in a clear plastic bag. They repeated the process with Kelly, then ran a security scanner over the interior of the car.

Jenson glanced towards a mezzanine office. "Is this all necessary?"

A short, be-suited figure with tightly cropped platinum blonde hair appeared at the top of a metal stairway. "It's mostly for appearances."

"So the weapons aren't loaded, Regina?"

"I said *mostly*." Rose walked smoothly down the stairs and shook Jenson's hand. "You've gotten fat, Greg."

"And you need another facelift. Such is life."

"At least we're both still alive." She indicated two sofas that had been placed in one corner of the warehouse. "Whisky? Cognac?"

"I'll pass. Nice place you have here," he said, with only the slightest wrinkle of his nose.

"Stealth and luxury don't always go hand in hand. My presence in the UK is something I like to keep from the authorities these days." They eased down into the sofas, the four armed men retreating into the shadows. "Thankfully there are still gaps in their intelligence networks."

"So, how's business?" Jenson asked.

"There's always a war going on somewhere. Still, I need to operate with ever more ingenuity and caution."

Jenson leaned forward. "You think hacking my phone demonstrates the latter?"

"It demonstrates my resolution. Obviously I have upset you."

"It's not the first time. Look, ZAT is a top-tier supplier to the UK Government, working on classified projects. That means we can only sell ZAT products to those on an approved list – a list which you are not on. I've been ignoring your calls because I can't be seen to do business with you right now, for either of our sakes."

Rose shrugged. "Nobody is watching you here."

"I certainly hope not. But meeting up with an old friend is different from actually supplying goods."

"My business helped build ZAT." She stared at him, unblinking. "Without me you would be nothing."

"That was a long time ago, and you made even more from those deals than I did. Nobody owes anybody anything. Besides, I'm hardly the only supplier in town."

Rose directed a finger towards Jenson's chest. "I require something that only you can supply. Your micro-drones."

Jenson rubbed the bridge of his nose. "Those aren't public knowledge. How—"

"It's my business to know things."

"And also supply them to whichever dictator or terrorist steps forward with the cash."

Rose shrugged. "If they don't buy from me, they'll just use someone else. On the whole, my customers are responsible individuals."

"Like the ones who murdered Samantha?"

"Greg, the death of your wife was… I won't insult you by suggesting anything can make it right." She let out a sigh. "But at some point you have to move on—"

"She died at the hands of someone using weapons I supplied. I will never move on. Or repeat those mistakes." Jenson cracked his knuckles. "And that is quite apart from the problem that if it got out that we are working together I would be shut down. And it *would* get out." He stood up. "There's a more fundamental problem, however."

"And that is?"

"The drones don't work. We had design issues that meant the project was non-viable." Jenson shook his head. "I'm sorry, Regina." He took a step towards his car.

Rose gave a nod and the four men with rifles moved as one, blocking Jenson's way. Three raised their weapons at him. The fourth aimed at Kelly in the back seat of the car. Rose adjusted a strand of loose hair. "This is what they did to me, the men who want your tech." Rose waved at her team who lowered their rifles. "Those men came to me with guns and threats. They knew I had a history with you. Now they want me to broker a deal."

"But the drones don't work. I'm not lying to you, Regina."

"I'm not inclined to believe you." Rose removed a sheet of paper from her pocket and placed it on the table. It showed the schematics and specifications of the drones.

Jenson narrowed his eyes. "Where did they get this?"

"There seem to be few secrets any more. Not if you look hard enough, with enough resource."

"Just who is this buyer?"

"Your only concern should be that we do this deal. Name your price."

"The drones are not for sale."

One of Rose's men raised his rifle again.

Jenson saw Kelly twitch. There were weapons hidden in his car that Rose's scanners could never have found, but he wasn't sure Kelly could get to them quickly enough. "Don't do this, Regina."

Rose spat, then barked an order in Spanish. The man almost dropped his rifle. "Please accept my apologies. My team know how important this is to me, but sometimes they… *act* without thinking." She lowered her voice. "I just need this one thing from you - a favour I promise you I will not quickly forget. I'll contact you in forty-eight hours and ask again." She offered Jenson her hand. "I know that on reflection you'll do the right thing."

JENSON AND KELLY REMAINED SILENT AS THEY DROVE AWAY from the warehouse. Jenson kept looking over his shoulder, but saw nobody following. After several miles, both finally relaxed.

"It was a surprise that she just let us go," Kelly said, drumming her fingers on the steering wheel. "For a moment I thought things were about to get *tactical.*"

"She said her buyer threatened her at gun point. Do you believe her or was she telling me what she thought I needed to hear?"

"Hard to tell. But if these drones don't work, why does her buyer think otherwise?"

Jenson rubbed his temples with his forefingers. "Whoever they are, whether the threats were real or not, Rose has never done anything like this before."

Kelly nodded. "We should review your security arrangements." She paused. "And for your family."

Jenson blinked. "Teresa? I thought her school was secure."

Kelly gave a snort. "To someone with Rose's resources? I'll get one of my people to pick Teresa up this afternoon—"

Jenson hissed. "Turn this car around. We're going to get her. *Now.*"

NINETEEN

The top floor of the MI5 building always descended into a hush when Warwick Saxton walked through. He didn't mind. In fact he preferred that his team feared him a little. Fear kept people alert, and doing their jobs properly. Especially important when the jobs in question were so vital. Which was why the building, and this floor in particular, were locked down with the kind of security that nobody could breach. At least in theory.

Saxton had just finished his weekly catch-up with Sir Douglas Busby, the Deputy Commissioner of the Metropolitan Police, over a lunch far larger and longer than it needed to be. But Saxton had found his high-level government and law enforcement contacts were usually less inhibited over a good meal. It was an effective way to ensure a reliable flow of information. They'd discussed Project Parallel in general terms as the Deputy Commissioner was one of the few people aware of the project: he made a firm case for access rights once it was operational. 'Get in line' was what Saxton had wanted to retort. 'I'll see what I can do' was what he'd said, with a smile.

The conversation had brought to mind Morton and his questions. Morton should never have known about Parallel. Was it just an incidental discovery resulting from work on the

Jenson report? Or had they dug deeper and more dangerously? He'd decided it was time to run some fresh background checks on Morton and Kinek Consulting as a whole, delegating the task to one of his assistants, Cassie.

Today, he stopped on the way to his office and beckoned her to come with him. She followed him inside, closing the door.

"How far have you got with the Morton matter?" Saxton asked, as he navigated around his oversized desk.

Cassie smoothed her jacket in a nervous gesture. "I was just about to send my report through, but it's pretty short."

Saxton nodded. "Because nothing worrying appeared?"

Cassie puffed out her cheeks. "Because *nothing* appeared. I can't find a single entry on a consultancy called Kinek. Are you sure you spelt it right? Who are they exactly?"

Saxton felt his tongue grow thick. "It's classified above your level of clearance. Look, send the report then leave it with me."

Cassie nodded and slid from the room, closing the door behind her.

Saxton eased back in his chair. Kinek had been fully vetted when he'd first engaged them and they'd proved adept at what they did: always delivering on time and on point. There had been no indication that anything was amiss. So what was going on?

His phone rang.

"Good afternoon," said a familiar voice when he picked up.

Saxton's jaw fell open. "Morton? Why are you calling me on this number?" He paused. "And more to the point, *how* did you get this number?"

"We're good at finding things. You know that."

Saxton's eyes flickered around the room.

"We need to speak. Or rather my boss would like to speak with you. The current situation requires that we do this face-to-face. You'll understand when we meet."

Saxton muttered. "Very well. When? Where?"

"Our offices, in one hour."

Saxton placed the handset back down. He'd been to the offices three times previously, but still the request was unusual, and Saxton had built his career on trying to understand the *unusual.*

He reached for the phone again to call for his Jaguar, but then decided he would rather take a cab. He had to continue keeping his engagement with Kinek off the radar.

TWENTY

TWENTY MINUTES AFTER LEAVING THE PRIVATE CLUB, MICHAEL was signing in at the offices of a large accounting firm. An assistant directed him through a maze of corridors to a large corner meeting room.

Kara stepped outside before he could enter. In one hand she gripped a plain brown envelope. "You took your time."

"I was at lunch with Mr Errington. You said the meeting was tomorrow—"

"Timelines change. You ready?"

"You only dumped the files on me this morning."

"Things don't always progress to your schedule."

Michael shook his head. "No kidding. Who else is here from the firm?"

"A couple of paralegals. Why?"

"So... you're in charge?"

She raised an eyebrow. "I am. And now I have my right-hand man."

"What are you expecting me to do when I haven't had time to read up yet?"

"I'm expecting you to be a lawyer. I'm expecting you to earn your salary." She pulled a pen from her pocket. "Best not keep them waiting."

Michael reached for the door, but Kara placed a hand on

his chest, stopping him. "Just my little joke. You'll soon see why I've got you here. And all you need do is hand this to me when I give you the signal." She passed across the brown envelope.

Nothing was written on it.

She raised a finger to her lips. "After you've handed it over, just sit there and look lawyerly. Under no circumstances show any emotion. Clear?"

He nodded.

They walked back into the room and sat at the table. Michael glanced around. And froze. Opposite him was Gordon Freeman, the Managing Partner of CWP. The man who, only a few days before, had effectively fired him.

Kara smiled. "This is my colleague, Michael Adams. Oh wait – Gordon, I believe you know Michael?"

Freeman gave a stilted smile. "A talented young lawyer we kindly trained up for you."

"Not sure what it says about your firm that you couldn't hold on to him. Still, let's get back to the matter in hand. Michael, CWP have just made an insulting offer on behalf of their client."

Freeman shifted in his seat. "The offer was a good faith effort to resolve the only outstanding commercial point."

"By which you mean the sale price." Kara looked around the room. "I'm always suspicious when someone feels the need to claim they are acting in good faith." She turned to Michael, tapping her finger in her palm.

He slid the brown envelope across the table. "You should see this."

Kara pursed her lips, pulling a sheet of paper out. She opened it, then frowned. "What is this?"

Michael coughed. "It's the information you asked for."

She flipped the paper around. "This is blank? Are you wasting everyone's time?"

"No, I mean—"

"You're not going to embarrass me after I've been rubbing Gordon's nose in it that we've hired you?"

Michael ground his teeth together. "No."

"Good. So why don't you explain what should have been printed on the paper. I presume that in your haste to get here you grabbed the wrong thing from the printer."

Michael stared at the blank sheet. Then at Kara. He tried to avoid Gordon Freeman's gloating look.

What had been in the files he'd reviewed that morning? Stuff about the range of sites in his clients' portfolios, lists of assets... Was there a *pattern*? Something that showed what they wanted, and why?

And then he realised.

Michael cleared his throat. "I'm sorry for the printer mix-up. What I meant to bring was a note from our client's CEO. They're happy to accept your offer for the business."

"They are?" Freeman's puzzled expression was obvious. "But we only just set out our terms. Surely Ms Simmons here didn't have time to brief them in the minute she was outside?"

Michael glanced at Kara. She gave no reaction. "We don't need to know."

Freeman laughed nervously. "That's ridiculous."

"No, it's not. We can accept the terms subject to one amendment. We'd like to retain the Hadwell site. My client has had a separate offer in respect of it."

Freeman breathed slowly. "Hadwell, you say. Any particular reason why that site?"

Michael scratched his nose and shrugged. "Just trying to find a win-win."

Freeman glared. "How did you know?"

"Know what?"

Freeman closed his eyes. "I'd like to confer with my client."

WITHIN AN HOUR IT WAS ALL OVER. THE REVISED OFFER WAS triple the original. Infinity's client was ecstatic.

"*How did you manage it?*" they had asked.

"*It's what we do*," Kara had answered with a humble smile.

Now Michael climbed into the back of a black cab with her. "You lied to me."

She glanced at her phone. "Did I?"

"You said all I had to do was hand you the envelope. And you set me up."

"I wanted to see how good you were. And you did not disappoint. You realised there were reports missing with regard to that one site and that those reports must be relevant. The price on offer when we started didn't matter. Whatever it was, it was bound to be too low."

Michael nodded. "So what was missing from the reports?"

"Mineral deposits were discovered in a recent private survey of the Hadwell site. They're worth far more than the business itself."

"That was quite a punt to take. That I'd make the connection."

"I could have stepped in if I had to. But, as I said, it was a chance for you to show off your talents. And of course I never pass up a chance to mess with another law firm. Poor old Freeman, he must shiver when I walk in the room. Anyway, I wanted to throw him off balance, suggest we might know other things."

"Like what?"

"Where there's one secret, there's usually more. And that, my young disciple, is why we now have an excellent settled price."

Michael looked out of the window of the cab. It had started to rain; hissing, angry spats of water were striking the street outside.

Kara pulled out her phone and read a message. "They need you back at the office for the full IT security briefing. And I'm told your new laptop is ready. Think of it as a reward for your work today."

TWENTY-ONE

HANNAH GRANGE BOARDING SCHOOL FOR YOUNG LADIES had a long history of schooling girls from ages seven to eighteen. It had facilities and buildings of unparalleled quality, strong links with Oxbridge, and many of its alumni had gone on to storied careers in the fields of business, the arts and science. As a result, applications almost overwhelmed the school every year, notwithstanding its fees of over £13,000 a term. It was in the top few percent in almost every metric you could rate a school by. It also enforced some of the most rigorous security standards at any British school. There had never been a breach. Until today.

The total failure of all mobile-phone networks was the first sign that something was wrong. This was quickly followed by the cessation of fixed wire services, resulting in all the CCTV systems shutting down. Within a minute the site was completely cut off from outside communications.

Thirty seconds later, a vehicle approached the school's front gates. The van was the school's usual laundry delivery vehicle, its paintwork off-white with peeling decals. The security guard stationed at the gate could not have known it had been stolen or that its usual driver was bound and gagged in a field a mile away. He simply waved and buzzed the heavy metal gates open as he always did. The van drove in and parked next to the loading bay as it always did. But then everything went *wrong*.

The side door slid back and four large men, dressed in black overalls and wearing gas masks, stepped into view. The security guard walked towards them, about to ask what was going on, when four automatic weapons flicked up and pointed at his chest. He froze and raised his hands on instinct. One of the men shouted something in a very heavy accent. The guard dropped to his knees. He was out of shape, in his fifties, carrying a baton that he had never actually used. What could he do?

The man in the gas mask walked over to him, smashed him on the temple with the butt of his rifle, then caught him as he sprawled. A second man ran forward and tied his hands with plastic cables, then gagged him.

They then turned to the locked front doors of the school's language block. The third man stepped forward with a portable door-ram. A forceful swing and the door buckled. The intruders stepped through and the fourth man fired three rounds from a grenade launcher. Tear-gas canisters launched in different directions and the few people who had looked into the corridor screamed and ducked back where they had come from. The men tightened their gas masks and climbed the first set of stairs. They knew exactly where they were going.

On the first floor, in the third classroom along, a French lesson was under way. The men pushed the door open and pointed their weapons. Twenty girls screamed and ran for the back of the room or cowered behind their desks.

The first man spoke loudly, in an accent that sounded vaguely Russian. "I want Teresa Jenson."

There were whimpers but nobody spoke.

"You have ten seconds, then I'm going to start shooting."

"They're just kids," said the teacher in a shaking voice.

The man raised his rifle to point at her. "Teresa, you have five seconds before I kill this woman." He eased his finger around the trigger. The teacher's eyes widened but she did not move.

"I'm here," said a small girl with brown hair, walking towards him. "Don't hurt her." She paused, gripping her watch. "Don't hurt *anyone*."

The teacher turned. "No, Teresa, don't—"

The man pushed her aside and grabbed the girl's arm. He held up a tablet computer and compared the image on the screen to the girl's face. Nodding to the others, he thrust a gas mask in Teresa's face. "Put this on if you don't want your eyes to bleed."

She glared at him, then slipped it on with practised ease. "You won't get away with this."

The man waved his colleagues towards the door.

THE VAN DROVE AN HOUR, FINALLY STOPPING AT AN abandoned farmhouse in the Cambridgeshire countryside. The doors to a ramshackle barn were pulled open to allow the vehicle to enter, then quickly closed again. The driver stepped out and opened the van's sliding side door. The four men in the back dragged an angry-looking Teresa Jenson with them.

"Good operation," the driver said, nodding at the rest of the men. "No complications."

"That we know of," said the tallest of the others.

"Our brief was accurate. The father's obviously too busy with his work to take proper care. He'll be regretting it soon."

"He's going to be coming after us with everything he's got."

"He has to find us first," the driver said. "By the time he locates this place, we'll be paid up and long gone. All we have to do is complete the handover, and we're out."

"When and where will that be?" the tall man asked.

"They'll be in touch soon. Be patient."

Teresa pulled herself free from the grip of the man holding her. "If you're smart you'll let me go. Then my Dad won't need to hurt you too much."

The driver turned and bared his teeth. "Maybe you should be a little more afraid."

"If you were going to kill me you'd have done that already. Do you have any idea who he is? He'll find me. Wherever we are." She fiddled with her wrist. "He'll find me, and then you'll be sorry."

"What makes you so…" The tall man frowned. "Check her. Now."

"For what?" asked the driver. "We already swept her for bugs."

"I don't know. Anything that looks wrong."

Two men grabbed Teresa and roughly searched her. "Her jacket is kind of weird," said one. "Very stiff."

"Like body-armour stiff?"

"Dunno, seems too light. And her watch looks unusual. Don't recognise the make."

The tall man gripped her arm. "What is this? Some sort of locator?" He stared at the others. "I don't care if we've been told that all comms around her are being jammed. Get the cutters."

"It doesn't matter," Teresa said. "You're already being tracked by satellite. He'll be here in an hour. With his own private army."

The tall man frowned. "Maybe this was all a bad idea."

The driver shook his head. "We stick with the plan. A lot can happen in an hour."

"You'd better believe it," Teresa said. "I'm going to see each of you in jail for—"

"Somebody shut her up! Get the duct tape…" Somewhere in the room a phone rang. The tall man blinked and picked up a small mobile-phone from a shelf. "Who is this?" he asked, putting the phone on speaker mode.

A woman's voice replied, heavily digitised. "Your client. I assume you have the girl."

"We do."

"She's unharmed?"

"As you stipulated."

"Excellent. We'll be there in five minutes."

"You have the money?"

There was a pause. "No."

The driver frowned. "What are you talking about?"

"You won't be needing it."

"Very funny."

"This was never about the girl."

"What?" The driver's frown turned to anger. "Look, you pay us now or—"

"One more thing - when I said we were five minutes away, I lied. I was just waiting on the cycles to process."

Around them there was a sudden high-pitched whining and a lattice of red dots blanketed the inside of the barn.

Teresa threw herself on the floor, away from the men, as the pattern of dots narrowed.

And then the whining was replaced by screams.

TWENTY-TWO

Michael walked into the conference room on Infinity's fourth level. Sandra stood waiting, her eyes flicking to the large table. On it sat a spiral-bound book and a clear plastic zip-lock bag. Inside the bag was a thin laptop and a collection of leads.

"Your new machine," she said with a smile. "This is the moment when you really start with the firm." She slid a printed piece of paper across to him. "Sign here."

Michael glanced down at a large volume of fine print. "What's this?"

"Confirmation of your receipt of the computer, and of your responsibility to look after it and use it in accordance with the terms of your employment contract." She hesitated. "And probably a promise to sign over your first-born child. I'll leave you to read all the way down."

Michael pulled a pen from his jacket pocket. He signed and slid the paper back.

Sandra nodded then tore open the bag. The machine was slim and metallic, with an anodised finish. She hefted it in her hand then placed it in front of Michael.

He ran his fingers over the casing. It was a sculpted slice of magnesium and titanium, more rigid than an ice-skate blade. "What manufacturer?"

"Undisclosed. Built to a firm-specified design. It's also running a proprietary OS derived from Linux. For security reasons. As a result many of the apps aren't compatible with anything else, including the Scope search-tool. And before you ask, you can still run regular desktop software if you must, using a virtualized environment. Sometimes there's no escaping Windows."

Michael picked up a lightweight set of headphones from the bag. "I've got my own – nicer than these."

"Actually that's a new security-access device the firm is trialing. Like a thumbprint scanner."

"There's a fingerprint scanner in the headset?"

"No, the *print* is your head."

"It reads my brainwaves? You're winding me up."

"It might sound like science fiction, but the tech has been around for a number of years. It simply analyses the pattern of electrical activity. The first time it takes a reading. After that, without a match, the laptop won't switch on."

Michael shrugged and pressed the computer's power button. The words CONNECT HEADSET filled the screen in angry red letters. Michael sighed and plugged in the headset. It clasped around the back of his head, then the frame hooked over both ears. He pressed the power button again. Michael felt a warm buzz in the ear-pads. There was a soft chime and the screen flickered into life, displaying a log-in screen.

"Techno magic." Sandra placed a slim laptop bag on the table. "Padded for protection and lined to prevent any invasive signals. Treat the machine with care. And only use it for firm business."

"Of course. I have a personal computer, so I hardly need to—"

"You don't have anything like this. That search tool I mentioned – Scope – it's pretty powerful. I'm sure you'll be tempted, but you really must only use it for work."

Michael frowned. "And I suppose someone in IT is tracking everything that gets searched?"

She pointed at a camera in the corner of the room. "Always assume you're being watched. Never let anyone else use the laptop or even see it, if possible."

Michael swallowed, then slid the computer carefully into the bag. "Any more rules?"

Sandra tapped the spiral-bound book on the table. "You should familiarise yourself with the office manual."

Michael picked it up, feeling the weight.

"Now I need to remind you of the main dos and don'ts." She paused. "Actually it's mostly don'ts: never take documents outside the building unless you have the express approval of a senior associate, or preferably a partner. Never talk about client work outside this office. Assume a great deal of electronic surveillance will be targeted at you wherever you go."

"That almost sounds paranoid."

"One of the new associates made that point to Errington about a year back. He left the firm the next day."

Michael nodded. "I'll keep that in mind when sharing opinions. Anything else?"

"Kara asked me to say one thing." Sandra tipped her head on one side. "'Stop gawping at the computer and get on with something you can bill for.'"

TWENTY-THREE

THE SOUND OF SIRENS ROSE IN THE DISTANCE AS JENSON'S Mercedes approached the school gates, pulling up twenty metres distant.

"I don't like this," Kelly said. "Look at all those people buzzing around inside. Stay here while I—"

Jenson pushed open the door and stepped out. "What is going on?" he shouted at the nearest security guard.

"Mr Jenson, we've been trying to call you, but all of our systems are down. We couldn't even get a mobile signal until a few moments ago."

Jenson stepped forward, placing his hands on the bars of the gate, about to demand answers when an agitated woman pushed past the guard. Jenson recognised her as the Principal.

"We were attacked," she said, seemingly in a daze. "It all happened so quickly. They were armed. There was nothing we could do."

He tightened his fists. "You let somebody take Teresa?"

The woman shrunk back, her face ashen. "This is a school, not a military base. We called the police the moment the phones started working. They'll be here shortly."

Jenson turned to Kelly. "Activate her wrist tracker. And call for backup." He turned back to the Principal. "Tell me exactly what happened."

An hour later Jenson held on tight as Kelly brought the Mercedes to a rapid but controlled stop under the cover of some trees.

"Satellite shows an old barn two hundred metres away," she said, glancing at her phone. "That's where the signal is coming from. Our response team is a minute away."

He nodded.

Kelly hesitated. "I'll say it again: I think this is tactically unwise. We don't know how many additional people they might have. Are you sure you don't want to involve the police?"

"Speed is our one advantage. These people can't possibly expect us to react so quickly. Plus we know that Rose won't want to hurt her. She just wants the leverage."

"You're absolutely sure she's behind this?"

"Wasn't it your suggestion in the first place?" Jenson glanced out of the car window and saw a black armoured van approaching.

They climbed out of the Mercedes and greeted the security team as they emerged from the van. One of the team held out body armour for Jenson and Kelly. They quickly slipped it on.

"You want a rifle, sir?" asked the team leader, holding out a spare.

Jenson snatched it from him.

The other men all checked their rifles. Kelly produced a handgun from an ankle holster. "Follow me," she ordered.

They crept forward, reaching the ramshackle barn in less than a minute. The door was slightly ajar, but there was no sign of movement. There was absolute silence. Then they heard the soft sound of crying coming from inside.

"That's her," Jenson hissed. "What's that lying in the doorway?"

One of the security team produced a set of binoculars. "Looks like a body."

Kelly ground her teeth. "Move. Now."

Nobody was as quick as Jenson. He led the rush, but at the doorway he stopped.

There were bodies strewn on the ground, with wide-staring eyes, faces contorted into expressions of shock and confusion.

"Teresa!" shouted Jenson. "Teresa!"

"Daddy!" replied a trembling voice.

Amongst the carnage a small figure struggled to her feet.

He rushed to her, throwing his arms around and holding her painfully tight.

She hugged him back even more forcefully. "You said you wouldn't let anything like this happen."

"I know, I know." Jenson ran his fingers through her hair. "But I'm here now."

"What happened?" Kelly asked, walking up. "Were there others here? Did they shoot everyone?"

Teresa gave a loud sniff. "There was nobody else."

"Then how did they… die?"

"They were talking on the phone to this woman, then there was this high-pitched whine and tiny red lights everywhere."

"Red lights?"

She closed her eyes, chin trembling.

"Let's just get out of here," Jenson said. "I know who was behind this, and I'll be making sure she pays."

Kelly shook her head. "Something about this is wrong. Teresa, you mentioned a high-pitched sound and the lights? Did you see anything else?"

Teresa shook her head. "I just dived down and closed my eyes."

Kelly crouched, looking at the ground, then pulled a multi-purpose scanning-device from her belt and began waving it over the floor.

"Astrid," said Jenson, guiding Teresa towards where the Mercedes was parked, "can we just leave."

Kelly picked something up and tucked it into her pocket.

"Of course." She stood up and ran after Jenson. "Shall we call the police?"

"On the way. They can come question Teresa at my house." He turned to the head of the security team. "You guys should make yourselves scarce. It would be easier if I didn't have to explain you." The man nodded and led the other team members away.

"So I don't have to go back to school?" Teresa asked, in a hopeful tone.

"You're never going back there. That's one problem I'm ticking off the list."

"You might need to add another one to it," Kelly said, as they hurried toward the Mercedes. She held out a tiny, dart-like object with gossamer filaments for wings.

Jenson stopped and stared at it for several long moments. "That's impossible." He picked it up between thumb and forefinger. "This is our design. And it was… working?"

"What is it?" asked Teresa, leaning close. "Some kind of toy?"

"No, it is not," Jenson said bitterly. "We call it a micro-drone."

TWENTY-FOUR

SAXTON PAID FOR THE TAXI THEN STEPPED BACK AND GLANCED at the grey skies. He hadn't been thinking clearly enough to even consider bringing an umbrella when he left the office, too busy feeling rattled. Though hopefully that would be over soon.

Following standard operating procedure, he had not been dropped off outside his destination. Instead he walked three blocks, looping around twice to make sure he wasn't being followed, and ending opposite Kinek's building: eight storeys of concrete, steel and glass, everything grey and unassuming.

Only now there was signage up indicating the site was about to be redeveloped. The windows were painted out, and no lights glowed from within. Saxton crossed the street and walked up to the glass front doors. They were securely chained shut, though the chains were starting to rust, as if they'd been there for some time. A man in a security guard's uniform stuck his head out of a side door.

"Sorry, mate," he said, scratching at three-day stubble. "Building's closed. Vacated a year ago."

Saxton fished out his warrant card and held it up. "I need to go inside."

The guard peered. "How am I supposed to know if that's real?"

"Would you like me to call a couple of squad cars? Perhaps arrest you for obstructing an investigation."

"I'm just trying to do my job. Go in if you want, but I've got to give you a hard hat."

Saxton accepted a yellow plastic helmet, then he pushed through a heavy door and found himself in the ground floor lobby: a marble-floored room with a large reception desk and a bank of lifts. The air was tired and dusty, as if it had been sealed for a while.

And yet this was where he had signed-in then been whisked to the top floor to meet with Morton and his colleagues. With a sigh he saw that the lifts were out of use. He moved to the staircase and began climbing, his leather shoes echoing on the concrete steps. Only slightly out of breath, he reached the eighth floor and emerged into another lobby.

He remembered the view from the windows to his left. But the entire space had been stripped out. Buckled aluminium and cracked plasterboard were piled at one end. Overhead, the air-conditioning and lighting systems hung exposed. Of Kinek there was no trace. Saxton swore and kicked at a broken ceiling tile on the floor.

There was the shrill sound of a mobile phone ringing, but it was not his. He looked around and saw it sitting on a stack of wooden doors, then walked over and answered it. A woman's voice, soft and faintly metallic, echoed in his ear.

"Hello, Warwick."

"What is going on? Who is this?"

"My name is Marcia. I run what you know as Kinek."

Saxton walked around the floor, double-checking he really was alone.

"I presumed it was already obvious that we aren't what we appeared to be."

"Then what *is* Kinek?" Saxton reached into his pocket and pulled out a small black credit-card sized object.

"We're an organisation that changes things. With the help of our network of friends. And that includes you."

"Well that friendship ends right now."

"Don't be so hasty—"

"Why on earth would I have anything more to do with you?" Saxton held the black object up to the phone: it clipped on magnetically.

"I can be very persuasive."

"If you think you can blackmail me, you have another thing coming—"

"Let's try to keep things civil." She paused. *"Also your tracer isn't going to work."*

"You can see me?" He jerked his head around, but could see no obvious camera.

"I can do lots of things. Not all of them will be things you want to happen. You're going to have to learn that even on your best day you're always going to be a step behind. Now, we need you to do something."

The black credit-card sized object beeped an error code. Saxton pulled it off the phone and glared at it. "Why should I believe anything you've just said?"

"We've conducted classified investigations for you over the last eighteen months, and yet you had no idea who we are. I think when we ask you for something, you'd be wise to take us seriously. Now throw the phone away."

Saxton blinked. "Why?"

"Because there's some proprietary technology in there I'd rather you didn't get to dissect. And also because you don't want it in your hand when it explodes."

"Oh really—" Saxton noticed the handset was feeling very warm. Swearing, he threw it across the room. There was a bang and a flash, and bits of plastic flew in every direction. Not a big explosion. But enough to make a point.

Saxton clenched his hands. He hadn't achieved his current rank by being pushed around. Kinek seemed to hold all the cards, but it was time to change that.

TWENTY-FIVE

It was 10:00pm when Michael walked into the lounge and found Eve watching the BBC News Channel. In her hand was a very large glass of wine.

"So this is what you signed up for?" she said, tapping her watch to indicate how late it was.

"It was my first day. Did you really think it would be a short one?" He poured himself a glass of wine and sat next to her. "What's new?"

"Not much." She sipped from her glass. "Your mother called."

"I have given her my mobile number, like a dozen times." Michael replied. "What did she want?"

"To invite you for dinner tomorrow. Actually she asked me as well, but fortunately I'll be on shift. Please tell me you had fun with your new job."

"I got taken out for lunch by none other than Maxwell Errington."

"The founder? I thought he'd retired."

"Semi-retired." Michael paused. "How did you know his name?"

"It's amazing what you can dig up if you know how to Google. For example, what about your actual boss? Kara Simmons, isn't it? She went to Fiji with you, didn't she?" Eve turned to him, raising an eyebrow. "I found her profile photo. Quite a knockout, wouldn't you say?"

Michael hesitated. "Some might say that. "

"And you?"

"I'd say that I work for her."

"Well I don't like it, some other woman able to order you around. That's supposed to be my thing."

"You wish."

"And the work? What have they got you doing?"

He coughed. "I can't talk about it."

"Ha." She paused. "Wait, you're serious? At your last job, you told me about that secret tube station they uncovered."

"That was different. And it had already become public."

"I tell you about *my* work."

"Maybe you shouldn't."

"Whatever." She pointed at his new laptop bag. "New computer?"

"Company issue. Bit of a rocket ship."

"Let's see then." She patted her lap.

"Look, I'm sorry. They made me sign a specific NDA, so I can't show you anything—"

"Grief, I was only pretending to be interested." She turned back to the television, cradling her glass of wine.

Michael sighed. "And how was your day?"

Eve frowned. "Very, very long, and equally frustrating."

He leaned forward. "Do you want to talk about it?"

"Maybe I'm not allowed to."

"Don't be like that."

She puffed out her cheeks. "I don't think I'm going to get my preferred option on the next rotation – don't think I've been savvy enough with the politics. Other people seem to know who to speak to."

"You're the best in your group. They should give you whatever position you ask for, and be grateful."

She snorted. "You're biased. Look, let's forget about all this." She held up the bottle of wine. "Another glass?"

Michael groaned. "I really want to. But I've got some work to finish for tomorrow."

She rolled her eyes again. "I'm going to have a bath." She refilled her glass and walked from the room.

Michael reached for his new laptop. It was only 10:30pm. He could easily squeeze in a productive three hours.

TWENTY-SIX

The apartment block was only two years old, built to a price, not a specification. From the outside it was stylish and harmonious with the other buildings. Inside things were more basic. The elevators were unreliable, the rooms were small and the fittings were of minimal quality. But the location was excellent and, at the asking price, Millie Wright had jumped at the chance to climb onto the property ladder. A place to call her own: a base while her plans to become rich and infamous took shape.

But three years on she was still doing the same job, and her blog was still not making money: it was hard to monetise when you had to stay anonymous. Should she think about a change of plan, perhaps look for more consulting work? In the past that had proved lucrative when she'd been prepared to 'hold her nose' with regard to who she worked with.

Distracted and hungry, Millie rummaged for the last slice of her seafood-special pizza, sliding it onto a chipped dinner plate. She threw the box into the corner and turned back to her five computer screens.

Her analysis of ZAT's IT systems had been frustrating and, so far, almost fruitless. The firm had a wall of steel around its technology infrastructure. Their systems were completely non-standard, not just avoiding commonly used protocols, but even the uncommon ones. Of course given the sensitivity of what they did, it was hardly surprising. The company was a high-profile target for conspiracy theorists, but her path had crossed theirs more directly not long ago.

There was a knock at the door. Millie blinked up at the clock – it showed nearly 11:00pm – then walked along the hallway to the front door. "Who is it?" she called.

"DHL," a muffled voice replied.

She frowned and peered through the peep hole. A uniformed youth stood holding a large package. "Do you normally call this late?" she asked through the letterbox.

"There's been a mix up at the depot and we're trying to clear the backlog."

"Can I see some ID?"

The guy yawned and pulled a plastic card from his belt. It had a very bored-looking photo on it. She unchained the door then pulled it open.

"Sorry to disturb you so late," he muttered, sounding more sorry for himself than for her. He handed her the box and walked off.

"Don't you need me to sign anything?" she called.

"Nah, I'll just scrawl something on the paperwork." He vanished into the lift.

Millie stepped back inside, kicking the door closed, and walked into her office. The box was about the size of an airline carry-on bag. It was wrapped, rather messily, in brown parcel tape, and was dotted with several 'FRAGILE' and 'URGENT' stickers.

She had not ordered anything. Was it a mistake? With a sigh she ripped through the tape with her keys. Pulling aside brown paper, polystyrene chips and bubble wrap, she eventually got to the contents. And whistled.

It was a laptop computer. She rummaged further in the box and pulled out a single printed sheet of paper. It said the package had come to her as the result of an eBay transaction. But there were no details as to the vendor. Millie carefully lifted the laptop out and placed it on her desk. It had an odd design, even compared to her custom-built effort. And it looked *old*: practically an antique in computer terms. The case was shiny black, but scratched in several places, with a couple of stickers from what seemed to be fruit packaging plastered to it. And then one other sticker. Faded and peeling badly, but unmistakable. *ZAT Systems.*

Millie felt her mouth go dry. Had the anonymous tipster sent it?

She cracked her knuckles then looked disappointedly at her empty coffee cup. With a mutter, she padded into the kitchen and flicked on the kettle. If you were going to analyse a top-secret computer, a hot cup of coffee was definitely a requirement.

TWENTY-SEVEN

WARWICK SAXTON NODDED TO HIS SECURITY DETAIL AND SET off across the meadows behind his country house, keeping his dog on his lead for now because there were a couple of horses in an enclosure at one side of the field who wouldn't appreciate the canine attention. The weather was calm and clear, but the last twelve hours had been anything but – one-long series of conference calls about the attempted kidnapping of Gregory Jenson's daughter.

The six kidnappers were dead, struck by explosive shells. Who had fired them, and how, had so far baffled his forensic team. Also alarming was the fact that Jenson had attempted to rescue Teresa himself. And as for who might have been behind the kidnapping, Jenson had insisted he had no idea. That made Saxton instantly suspicious. Jenson was a rich, powerful man. He had to have some clue who his enemies were. And if he wanted to protect his daughter, surely he would share what he knew?

So many questions, but few answers. If only Project Parallel was functional, he could ask the system why someone would kidnap Jenson's daughter. Could it just be about money? There were easier, richer targets to strike. For technology, or information? Jenson had refused to be drawn into speculation.

Saxton closed his eyes and thought hard. Had he mis-read the entire situation? Were the kidnappers killed by a team Jenson had been operating? If so, what should he do about it? Jenson *was* ZAT. Without him, Project Parallel would be critically impacted. MI5 could not afford that.

Saxton crossed into the next field and saw another dog walker throwing a ball.

He had heard nothing further from Kinek, but he knew it was only a matter of time. He was close to raising the matter with Charlotte Rostrum, at which point he might as well put his neck on a block and hand her an axe. But what else could he do? There were few people he trusted in MI5. Everyone disclosed everything now, lest they be found in breach of policy. Of course there was one person he could contact, one who undoubtedly could help. But that would require an apology. Plus he was pretty sure it would be laughed at.

He bent down and let his dog off the lead, watching him tear across the field and began chasing the other dog, a chocolate Labrador. He made his way over, waving at the other owner. As he got closer, he froze.

"Good evening, Mr Saxton," said Morton. "I know your security detail is watching, so act like I'm someone you know."

"You *are* someone I know. Is there any reason I shouldn't have you arrested right now?"

"Because I have some information to give to you."

"I'm sure the demands will follow."

Morton nodded. "Kinek is a business, though one that few know exists. That is one reason behind our success. You've had first-hand demonstration of our capabilities. Our skills are in demand. To be blunt, you are not our *only* client, and sometimes two clients' interests come into conflict."

"So who gets priority?"

"An excellent question. We weigh up the benefits. It's quite mathematical, largely dispassionate. It is, as economists would say, *efficient*."

"What does this have to do with me?"

"You know of the failed attempt to kidnap the daughter

of Gregory Jenson?" Morton reached into a pocket and removed a small tablet computer. He unlocked it and handed it across.

Saxton stared at the screen. It showed a camera recording overlaid with streams of data. A slender figure stood inside what looked like a barn, surrounded by large armed men. She lunged, throwing herself to the ground. Then the men seemed to… explode. "Is this—"

"The barn where she was held? Yes, it is." The footage ended then started again from a different angle. "You're watching a high-tech weapons attack. A weapon described by its manufacturer as a micro-drone."

Saxton felt an icy trickle run down his back. "I'm not aware of such a product."

"A British manufacturer had one in development. But then you know that."

"It wasn't… it *isn't* functional."

"So you say," Morton pointed at the screen, "yet the evidence to the contrary is compelling."

"How on earth do you have this? Were you watching the school? Were you part of the attack? You must have known this was coming."

"We are experts at accessing data."

"So why are you showing me this? It's his daughter, for goodness sake! Do you have a child, Morton? If what you're showing me is right, surely you can understand why he did what he did."

"Understanding it doesn't make it legal."

Saxton swore, handing the tablet back to Morton.

"We can trace the drones back to fully functional units built by ZAT."

"Then what do you want from me?"

"Arrest Jenson."

"Why?"

"We have our reasons."

"The interests of other clients?" Saxton hissed. "You seem to have this all figured out."

"We realise this is a big decision, so we'll give you a little time to think it over. Twenty-four hours. After that we'll give this material to the press, and make it perfectly clear that you sat on it."

Saxton's eyes flashed. "Actually I can give you my decision right now." He whistled sharply and his dog ran straight over. He knelt down and reattached his lead. "I don't care who you think you are, but I will not be manipulated in this way." He whistled again, but differently. A complicated three tone sound.

From four different locations, men in combat gear broke cover, automatic weapons drawn. They advanced swiftly on the two dog walkers.

Morton looked at them, shrugged, and raised his hands. "This is unfortunate."

Saxton nodded to the men. "Cuff him." He turned back to Morton. "Your methods might have worked on other… *clients*, but I will not be intimidated. In my experience whenever someone claims to know everything, it isn't true."

Morton held out his wrists and the handcuffs were clicked into place. "We can discuss things further next time."

"There won't be a next time." Saxton nodded to the men, watching as they grabbed Morton by the shoulders and propelled him towards the armour-clad van that had just pulled into view.

TWENTY-EIGHT

Michael's mother, Nina, lived two hours' drive west of London, in a quiet village in the Cotswolds. Michael skipped lunch to get away from work by six. The traffic was only mildly terrible, so he just managed to make it by eight.

Nina welcomed him with a stiff hug and a distracted smile just visible behind the oversized glasses she now favoured, but which made her eyes look disturbingly large. She beckoned him into the house they had shared with his father. It was too big for her now, but she had shown no inclination to move.

Dinner was two fancy micro-waved meals: herb marinated lamb shanks and kumara mash. His mother had never been the most enthusiastic of cooks. Their conversation skipped over lightweight matters: life in the village, her garden, her upcoming ten-day visit to Sydney, followed by ten days hopping around some Pacific Islands. She was out of the country maybe one week in four nowadays. He still couldn't understand why an ambitious professor of psychology, author of the controversial book *I Can Make You Do Anything*, had left her professional life behind. But then so much had changed since his father died.

After they'd eaten, they settled in the lounge on fading but comfortable sofas.

"Eve too busy to come see me?" Nina asked as she poured coffee.

"She's not my girlfriend, Mum. Plus you know what it's like as a junior doctor. I hardly see her myself."

"I'm worried about you two, the hours you both work. When are you ever going to find time to start a family?"

"Give up, won't you?"

"Neither of you are getting any younger. Or are you both going to be slaves to your careers?"

"We both want to make our mark." Michael took a deep breath. "Speaking of careers, I've just started a new job."

Nina looked up, puzzled. "You only just joined the last place."

"I was there four years."

"Doesn't time fly." She sipped from her cup.

"The new firm is called Infinity Law. Based in Knightsbridge."

Nina blinked. "Sounds impressive. I'm sure your father would have approved. He was such a dreamer. I hope you're not doing the same – off to the next thing on a whim. You could be throwing away everything you've worked for."

"The point is that, unlike him, I am going to make something of myself. If opportunity comes knocking, you have to take it. You know they flew me to Fiji for an interview?"

She gave a snort. "In an attempt to brainwash you?"

"Just a sign of how much they wanted me to join them."

Nina adjusted her oversized glasses. "I guess they offered you a lot of money. Pay someone enough and they'll do anything."

"Mum, is something wrong?"

She tipped her head. "You forgot, didn't you?"

"Forgot what?"

"What we were supposed to be doing over the weekend?"

Michael sat back in his chair, running a hand through his hair, then it struck him. "We were going to go through Dad's stuff. I am *so sorry*—"

"Of course you are. It doesn't matter now. I've done it."

"You could have waited—"

"It's been fifteen years. It was time to move on." She gave a sniff. "Come see."

Michael followed his mother down into their basement: the room that used to be a kind of den for his father. There were shelves lining two of the walls. His dad had been a tinkerer – or, in his own words, an inventor. The shelves had been stacked with books: a combination of fiction and endless technical manuals. And many computer and electronics components. It was all gone.

"You got rid of everything?"

"I needed closure, Michael. After all this time I was finally ready." She walked over to a shelf and ran her finger along it. "Too many memories in this room, and most of them unpleasant."

"I always loved hanging out down here."

"I've always detested it."

Michael frowned. "Why?"

Nina reached up and brushed hair from his eyes. "If you don't remember then I'm not going to dredge it up again. It doesn't matter anymore." She looked around. "It all had to go. Even your father's crappy old laptop. I put it on eBay: got a neighbour's daughter to help me. Sold it for fifty pounds, and it didn't even work!"

"I was going to have a look at it. See if I could fix it."

"Yet you never did."

Michael placed a hand on her shoulder. "I'm sorry I let you down." He glanced at a clock on the wall. "And also I'm sorry because I have to be off. Got an early start tomorrow."

Nina gave a sigh. "Already they're taking over your life. Have you really done the right thing accepting this new job?"

"It's a law firm. What's the worst that can happen?"

TWENTY-NINE

GREGORY JENSON'S PRINCIPAL RESIDENCE WAS AN OVERLY-designed modern house high on a hill looking south towards London. The property had more glass than most cathedrals: vast, gently-curving triple-glazed panels coated to allow occupants to look out, but preventing those outside from seeing in. Only one room had no windows: the *bunker*, as Teresa liked to refer to it, although she was rarely allowed inside.

She was not there now either, being currently tucked up in bed with a mug of cocoa. Instead, her father and Astrid Kelly occupied the tiny room. On the desk rested the crushed remains of the micro-drone Kelly had recovered from the barn.

"Fragile-looking thing," she said.

Jenson lifted a silver flight-case onto the table, popping the catches. "This is what they look like prior to use." Inside the case, protected in padded foam, were six objects, each less than the size of a matchbox. Six small darts, flat grey in finish, with micro-wings and tiny rotors. Jenson lifted one out and held it up to the light. "A ZAT semi-autonomous, paired-link remote-controlled flight, surveillance and assault weapon. Or a micro-drone, as our marketing team insists we call them."

Kelly peered closer. "They don't look like much."

"External aesthetics weren't part of the brief: they're designed never to be seen at all." Jenson placed the dart in the palm of his hand. "This model is a non-lethal variant. It carries neuro-toxin delivered by micro-flechettes to incapacitate a typical adult male in ten seconds, presuming an operational targeting matrix."

"Targeting *what*? And what's a 'paired link'?"

"Technology our engineers developed. Something to do with quantum entanglement, but it means the comms between the drone and the master unit are un-hackable. Nobody can take over our drones or even jam them. We also have a variety of concussive versions as well as the neuro-toxin one, including incendiaries and fragmentation weapons, although realistically those were never going to get approved."

"Why?"

"Because they're too effective. If I deploy a dozen of these, I can control a situation near-invisibly: the drones can accelerate to almost Mach 1 and obliterate a selected target in seconds. The last thing the targets think is 'Why am I hearing mosquitos?'"

Kelly stared at the tiny object. "So you can take out exactly who you want with zero collateral damage?"

Jenson shrugged. "As long as you can target correctly. That's the part we couldn't solve. We only reached about 60% accuracy; there are just too many unknowns on the battlefield. Which is why the client cut the funding and shut our project down."

"60% isn't bad."

"It is when you want 99.999%. Of course Rose doesn't care: bad specs have never stopped her selling tech before." Jenson turned back to the flight-case and pressed a sequence of buttons on a small control unit. The tip of the dart he was holding glowed red then a beam shot from it. The beam quickly separated into multiple rays, which splayed over one of the walls. "This is the targeting matrix." Jenson moved the dart so it was pointing at Kelly. The dots rippled over her, then rotated and narrowed, tightening to a single point, which pulsed. "That means it has a lock. Which means a vicious, laser-guided flying piranha of death is about to take you out."

"Not surprising that Rose's client wants it."

"I need to speak to her."

"I don't think that is wise," Kelly said, her arms folded. "Calling Rose will achieve nothing and risk everything, once the government finds out."

Jenson nodded at the phone. "You think my system isn't secure? The encryption algorithms are unbreakable."

Kelly shrugged. "I'm not a mathematician. But the weakness will be human. Someone at her end recording it or someone at this end, selling you out. If Saxton discovers you've had contact with an arms dealer—"

"Rose tried to kidnap my *daughter*. Saxton would understand."

"It wouldn't just be his call. And what do you hope to gain from calling Rose?"

"She crossed a line." Jenson ground his teeth. "I want to punish her."

"Of course you do. But those days are gone." Kelly narrowed her eyes. "Aren't they? Besides, you might have her phone number, but you'll never get her address. Anyway, are we *really* sure she was behind it?"

Jenson let out a guffaw.

"Fine. Let's assume she was," Kelly said. "Aren't we overlooking a bigger question? Who stopped her? And why?"

"Perhaps Rose pissed somebody else off. No reason to believe that I'm special." He shook his head. "Isn't the enemy of my enemy, my friend?"

"It's an elegant saying, but they might just be a different kind of enemy."

"I only care that they saved Teresa."

"But you should care who they are because they have ZAT micro-drones."

Jenson leaned forward, closing his eyes. "That is the elephant in the room." He let out a slow breath. "And it's not even the biggest. The biggest issue is how they made them work." He opened his eyes and looked around him. "I have to know who they are, and how they got hold of our tech."

"You should set an internal investigation in motion."

"Which will immediately leak to Saxton."

"Not if I run it. I'll track down every single piece of inventory relating to the project."

"That may tell us if something is missing. But it won't tell us who took it. Or how they made the drones work."

"Then what are we supposed to do?" Kelly asked.

Jenson snapped his fingers. "We build Project Parallel. This is the type of question it was designed to answer."

Kelly frowned. "I thought it was months away from being operational at best?"

"That was then, this is now. I will make it work, I don't care what it takes."

"And what about Teresa?"

"Keep her here. Triple the security. Do whatever is necessary to keep her safe."

She took a step forward, resting a hand on his arm. "I'm sorry for what happened yesterday. I won't let it happen again."

"I believe you." He took her hand and gripped it hard. "You know I've never said how much you…" He blinked. "Since my wife, you've been the only one I could really trust…"

Kelly cleared her throat. "That's OK, sir. I'm just doing my job. Until you decide to fire me, that is."

Jenson gave a snort. "You should be so lucky. Now go do what you do."

THIRTY

CONDITIONS WERE ROUGH, AND THE HELICOPTER LANDED heavily on the landing pad at the rear of the 105-metre-long Super Yacht Evolution. The pilot glanced warily at Regina Rose, but she had other things on her mind and gave no reprimand. Instead her hands clawed open her belt restraints, then she pulled her headset off and stepped out onto the deck. It felt good to be back in her centre of operations, not to mention her venue to wine and dine. Right now she needed some home comforts.

The captain of her guards stood waiting, a hi-tech semi-automatic rifle slung across his back: ZAT's latest model from three years ago. Rose nodded and walked past him in the direction of his quarters.

"Boss," shouted the guard captain above the wind, quickly following and holding out a tablet computer. "There's been a development."

Rose slowed slightly to take the tablet, staring at the text on the screen. "Jenson's daughter was kidnapped? When?"

"Immediately after you met with him."

Rose swore. "We make a demand, we make it clear that we won't take no for answer, then this happens. He's going to assume it was us."

"We never threatened his family—"

"It doesn't matter. He'll put two and two together and make seven." Rose gave the tablet back. "I have to call him."

"We have sources in the MET's forensic team. The men the third party sent to take the girl were all killed. All died from explosive wounds. Not bullets. Some form of incendiary."

"What do you mean?"

"A hi-tech weapon was deployed, something consistent with the system you're trying to purchase from Jenson. Given who they were protecting, it's hardly a shock."

"He said the micro drones didn't work, damn him." Rose's expression shifted. "So this situation has both proven the legitimacy of the deal, and simultaneously made it harder." She reached the door of her quarters. "Much as I want to force his hand, it just isn't going to work. I can't prove I didn't undertake the kidnapping. Regardless, he'll step up his security. It's all become a bad idea." She sighed. "I need to make a different phone call."

The guard captain nodded and left as Rose stepped into her private office, picking up the secure phone from its charging slot, then typing in a long number from memory. The call was answered almost immediately.

"*Regina*," echoed a woman's voice, soft and faintly metallic. *"Do you have good news?"*

Rose walked over to the window and stared out at the ocean. "There were complications. The unforeseen actions of a third party mean that I'm not going to be able to broker a deal on this occasion."

The line went silent for several long moments. Rose began to wonder if the call had disconnected, but finally the voice replied. *"That is disappointing. We had faith in you."*

"I'm sure there are others who will be able to help."

"Our analysis showed you were the best-placed to influence Mr Jenson. Our analysis is rarely wrong."

"Naturally I'll be returning your deposit—"

"No. You will honour our deal."

Rose felt her teeth start to clench. "If you mean to threaten—"

There was a soft laugh. *"No, Ms Rose. In fact, we commend you on your negotiation skills."*

"I'm not trying to—"

"We acknowledge the risk profile has changed. So we will pay double the purchase price."

"The problem isn't the money. The problem is that the deal is impossible."

"In our experience, the right fee can make anything possible. Of course if you would prefer that we resort to threats…"

Rose swallowed. "I'll see what I can do."

She switched the phone off and put it back on her desk. With the current strains on her finances, she simply couldn't afford to walk away.

But she would need outside help.

Picking up the phone again, she dialed another long number. It was time to call in a trusted adviser, someone with a gift for changing minds.

THIRTY-ONE

SAXTON SAT IN HIS HOME OFFICE ON THE FOURTH FLOOR OF his Kensington Town House. There was a single, narrow window, the view through which was dimmed by bullet-proof, heavily-filtered glass, yet it was still a striking vista across the rooftops, looking east into central London.

Today, he hadn't spared it a glance.

Saxton had had each of his offices swept three times for bugs since having Morton arrested. They had found nothing, but he would keep looking and had quietly increased physical security. There would be no repeat of his mistakes.

He had received no further contact from anyone at Kinek. Had it been an elaborate bluff? In the world of counter-intelligence, it was easy to get caught up in imagining the enemy was larger and more capable than they really were.

His forensics teams had recovered nothing conclusive from the barn, and the couple of journalists who had become aware of the story had been deflected. The dead men had been identified as mercenaries with no obvious affiliation to any group or country. Morton, detained under prevention of terrorism legislation at an off-book detention centre, was saying nothing. But Saxton had a few days grace before he had to go on record. By then he hoped to have answers.

When his desk phone rang loudly, his eyes flickered over

to check the number. He swallowed involuntarily, glancing at his watch. With all the distractions, he had forgotten to join his regular call with the Home Secretary. He grabbed his headset and answered.

"Busy time, Warwick?" Rostrum asked in a flat tone.

"I was delayed getting back from an appointment."

"Your PA said you've been back home for more than two hours."

Saxton stifled a sigh. "My apologies for keeping you waiting. Shall we proceed?"

"I'm not your enemy, Warwick. I just need to be fully informed. Now, how goes our new computer?"

He took a deep breath. "Project Parallel is moving forwards again, but it's early days. It'll take ZAT two to three months to build an initial test rig. If we rush it there are risks in terms of quality control, software testing, and maintaining security."

"Is it going to work?"

"Jenson is confident."

"He would be. Which reminds me, what was that incident I read about in the hourlies? Something to do with his daughter?"

Saxton drummed his fingers on his desk. "A kidnapping attempt. Thankfully unsuccessful and, equally thankfully, out of the press at this point."

"Related to Parallel?"

"We've no hard intel making that connection, nor on who might have been behind it. Unfortunately we cannot interrogate the kidnap team."

"Yes, a rather messy business. I trust I'm not going to find out that you were responsible. Some black ops team you think I don't need to know about."

"Contrary to what a legion of thriller authors might want you to believe, that's not how we do business. If I were sending armed squads out to shoot terrorists, I promise I would brief you."

"Perhaps. But would Jenson?"

Saxton hesitated. "I have no evidence that suggests he was involved in that manner."

"Good. Because that would be inconvenient. Now tell me about this man you've had arrested."

Saxton's breath caught in his throat. "You mean Morton? How did you hear of him?"

"Really," Rostrum replied. "That's how you respond?"

"It was a low level, operational matter. Not something that warranted your attention."

"You're holding someone under anti-terrorism legislation and you didn't think it worth mentioning?"

"We're still building our case. This is quite common in such a situation."

"As far as I understand it, he's guilty of walking a dog." Rostrum gave a sharp cough. "I've had a call from legal. He has some very serious, very expensive lawyers who assert we have absolutely no case. And given this conversation I'm inclined to believe they're right. These aren't the 1980s. We can't just hold people because it amuses us, so you'll understand I had no alternative but to order his release."

Saxton's eyes flew open. "When?"

"An hour ago."

"He's already out? You didn't think to run this past me?"

"I wasn't under the impression that I reported to you."

"I wouldn't normally expect you to involve yourself with a low level operational matter."

There was a long silence. "I will involve myself where I deem it appropriate. Now I'm going to have to cut this short. If there's anything else I need to know, then please include it in the hourlies." The call disconnected.

Saxton sat rubbing his eyes. How had Morton got word to his lawyers, let alone got himself freed already? It made no sense. Unless…

The phone rang again. Saxton frowned as he saw Rostrum's name again. He pulled the headset back on. "What else, Charlotte?"

"Actually, it isn't the Home Secretary," said a voice that was chillingly familiar.

"Marcia," growled Saxton. "Of course it would be you."

"I hope I haven't started getting predictable."

"Morton should enjoy his freedom. It will be short-lived."

"We'll see. I suggest you look in your safe. The one in the wall behind your desk."

"How do you..." Saxton growled and stood up from his chair, turning to face a watercolour on the wall. Smoothly he lifted the painting out of the way, revealing a dull grey steel door, embedded in the plaster surface. He shook his head and tapped in the combination. The lock hissed and released, the heavy door swinging open. Inside were clear folders containing currency, a number of passports in a tied bundle, and an agency-issue automatic pistol - all as Saxton expected.

There was also something else. A thick grey card folder.

"What is that?" he asked. "How on earth did you get something inside my safe?" Saxton reached a shaking hand forwards and took the folder. He set it on the desk and opened it. Two items slid out.

The first was a newspaper. He looked puzzled as he stared at the cover. It was *today's* newspaper. "You were in here today? With all my security watching?"

"Just proving a point. Have you seen the other item?"

Saxton picked up a cotton-bound, card-covered booklet. It bore his name and date of birth on the cover.

"Read it," Marcia said. "You should find it familiar."

Saxton shook his head and began leafing through the pages, his expression becoming increasingly concerned. It was *him*. Everything about his life. Things that even he had forgotten. "Where did you get this?"

"We know a lot about you, Mr Saxton. Possibly more than you do. Turn to the last few pages."

Saxton did so, and let out a gasp. "Those records were sealed ten years ago."

"Sealed and then illegally disposed of. Why would you take such a risk over a neighbour's son?"

"He was a good kid, caught up with the wrong crowd. He deserved a second chance."

"I see. Still, not really your call at the time. Or even now. I imagine you wouldn't like Charlotte Rostrum to see this. Disruptive for your former neighbour. And likely career-ending for you."

Saxton dropped the booklet back on the desk.

"You need to decide," she said. "Will you cancel Parallel?"

"How will I explain this to the Home Secretary?"

"That's not our problem."

Saxton placed his head in his hands. "I'll go to see her tomorrow."

"We'll be watching."

Saxton switched the phone off and unplugged it, then walked over to the window. They had invaded his life, his business, his home; he didn't know who he could trust. If he cancelled Parallel, Rostrum might well fire him. But worse than that, the government would no longer be building the intelligence system that they needed ever more desperately.

He turned away from the window and walked back to his desk. On the bookshelf behind it, his eye caught a familiar book: *Big Data, Big Danger* by Amelia Wright.

He couldn't put this off any longer. He needed her help. Whatever had happened in the past, it was time to track her down. He picked up his phone and dialed a number from memory. The call was answered immediately.

"Cassie speaking, what do you need?"

Saxton smiled. "Another search: one that should prove a little more straightforward. I need to locate an old friend."

THIRTY-TWO

MORTON WALKED OUT OF THE UNMARKED OFFICE BUILDING where he had been detained, and took a slow breath of fresh air, glancing at his phone before remembering it had been remotely wiped as a security measure. It meant he was disconnected from the system: it was not a sensation he enjoyed.

It had taken longer than expected to secure his release, and he had not been held in the most comfortable of conditions. Yet there was never any doubt that his people had been monitoring him, and that he would be taken care of. That was how Kinek worked. Warwick Saxton had no concept of who he was dealing with.

A grey Mercedes van rounded the corner and pulled up in front of the office building. Its driver climbed out, a slender woman wearing a dark blue suit and metal-rimmed glasses. She nodded curtly. "Mr Morton."

He glanced behind him, noting that nobody appeared to be watching, but he was absolutely certain that they were. "Where is my regular contact?"

"Unavailable."

He frowned. "I don’t recognise you. Are you based at the London office?"

"I work for Marcia. She asked me to attend you personally." She reached into an inside pocket and produced a phone handset. "Your replacement company device."

He took it and held it up to his face. In an instant it had recognised him and logged him into the first level of the system. "I'd like to go back to central London," he told the driver.

"Of course." She moved around and slid open the side door. "The compartment is secure, should you need to make any calls."

Morton nodded and climbed in, watching as the side door closed automatically. The woman climbed into the driver's seat, separated from him by a frosted-glass screen. As the car eased away from the office building, he settled back into his seat and reflected on the last 24 hours. The temporary detention by the government had been unexpected, but, as he had learned, rarely did he get to see the entirety of a plan. Still, the sequence of events didn't seem particularly efficient. Did it mean a mere lack of optimization, or was it the symptom of a more serious glitch? He would raise a query later, once he had top-level access. He looked again at his encrypted phone, logging into the second level of security and checking his messages. Several were flagged Project Green; he would not be able to read them here.

"Everything OK, sir?" the driver said through the vehicle's intercom.

"I believe so." He tapped the screen. "You have a name?"

"Cortez."

"I'd like to go straight to the facility."

"You don't want to go home? For a shower and a change of clothes?"

"I have both of those in my office."

"Of course. I was asked to remind you that, given your recent detention, there will be additional protocols to follow. There's a handheld scanner in the seat pocket so you can check no monitoring devices were planted during your stay."

Morton nodded, grabbing the wand, and beginning to run it over his clothes. "Get me there as fast as you can, Cortez. I have a great deal of work to catch up on." The wand beeped that he was clean, but he ran it over everything again, just to be sure.

THIRTY-THREE

INFINITY'S CONFERENCE ROOM WAS DOMINATED BY A LONG, oak table, strewn with lever-arch files. Michael sat reviewing documents on his new laptop, wondering if another cup of coffee would help him concentrate any better, or if it would drive him into overload. Kara stood looking out of the window, cleaning her glasses.

"Are you going to review any of the materials?" Michael asked as he eased back in his seat. "Or are you happy to delegate all the legal work to me?"

She turned, raising an eyebrow. "You'll do what I tell you, and like it."

"I don't see there's any point. The other side are making a mockery of our client."

"Oh?"

"None of these proposals make any sense. It's like they're not trying, like they want to—"

"Wear us down?" Kara asked. "I thought you were the genius lawyer who spotted the patterns and made the connections?"

"I can only do it if there's a pattern to spot. They're just wasting our time."

"Interesting. So let's tell them. Or rather, let's tell their lawyer."

"That Chalmers guy from earlier?" Michael frowned.

"What did you make of him?"

"He says a lot, without saying anything."

Kara nodded. "As if he likes the sound of his own voice?"

"What are you planning to do?"

"Something motivational."

CUTHBERT CHALMERS WAS A LARGE MAN WITH IMMACULATE fashion sense. He entered the conference room, his patent leather shoes creaking, flicking an imperious eye over Michael, then smiling at Kara. "I hope you're not going to try to appeal to my better nature?"

"Why?" She looked at the fingernails on one hand. "Do you have one?"

"Getting antagonistic isn't going to help you broker a deal." He took a seat at the long table.

"Perhaps you're right," Kara replied. "But I have to say this isn't going how we'd planned."

"Good to see I can still hold you up."

"Yes, I've definitely learnt a few moves off you today. How are the kids?"

"They're both fine. Thank you for asking."

"And your lovely wife?"

Chalmers shifted in his seat. "What exactly did you want to say to me?"

Kara leant forward and whispered in his ear.

Chalmers jerked backwards. "How could you…" He looked left and right, as if he expected somebody else to appear. "What is… I mean..."

"Go on," she said helpfully.

He cleared his throat. "I'm sure we can find a way to resolve things to our mutual advantage. We've spent more than enough time on it already."

"Now that is a sensible proposal." Kara smiled broadly.

Michael just looked on in confusion.

One hour later, the joint venture agreement was bound and signed. The two clients had de-camped to a nearby London club to celebrate, while Chalmers had muttered something about having to get back to the office. Now Kara stood in Infinity's reception area, typing a message on her smartphone.

"So, what happened with the lawyer?" Michael asked.

"I gave him a new perspective on the deal," she replied, still tapping away.

"What did you say?"

Kara smiled. "*Should I keep my boots on*?"

"Is that legal code for something?"

"It's a phrase he's familiar with." She looked up. "You're smart. Work it out."

Michael frowned. "He was having an affair?"

"Is that what you think?" Kara didn't look up. "It's an innocent enough phrase."

"That's clearly not how he took it. It was something somebody said to him. Someone other than his wife. But how would you know? How *could* you know?" Michael leaned forward, lowering his voice. "Did we have him followed?"

"Why are you whispering? Do you think we're being monitored?"

"Apparently Chalmers was."

Kara sighed and put her smartphone away in her blue leather handbag. "We concluded the deal. Our client is happy. We're going to get paid. And you'll get a glowing report from me."

Michael narrowed his eyes. "What you said scared him into cooperating. I didn't get a chance to do anything."

She leaned forward, lowering her own voice. "Michael, this is the difference between winning and losing. We knew more than they did."

"But it's not right."

"It's not my fault he's a bastard. He gave us a lever, and

we used it. If he'd behaved professionally to us in the first place it would never have come to this. Do you really feel sorry for him?"

Michael looked away. "What about his wife?"

Kara placed a hand on his arm. "He was stupid and he paid for it, even if not as much as he ought to. That is a type of justice."

"That's a real stretch."

She gave him a rueful smile. "Come on, let’s go get a sandwich, then I can brief you on a meeting we have tomorrow."

Michael glanced at his watch as he followed her outside. It was nearly 8pm and the street lamps glared overhead.

"This way," Kara called, marching ahead. She turned sharply down an alleyway, vanishing from sight.

Michael squinted as he followed, entering the narrow fissure between buildings: a space so constricted it suggested it was there more by accident than design. Almost no light made its way into the dark, cobbled confines. He saw her ahead of him in faint silhouette, moving past several oversized rubbish bins. "Is this a good idea?" he called.

Kara stopped and turned, adjusting her glasses. "Scared of the dark?"

"I don’t usually go looking for trouble."

"Then you shouldn’t have joined Infinity."

"That doesn’t mean we have to—" Michael froze. A wiry-looking figure had emerged from behind one of the bins. He was wearing grubby jeans and a hoodie. In his hand was a knife.

Kara stopped. "Evening, stranger."

"Your bag, your wallet, your watches," hissed the man. "Make it quick."

Michael’s gaze flickered around. They were in the middle of the alley, thirty metres from either end.

"So, Michael," Kara said calmly, "how do you want to play this? I grab the knife and you knock him over? He doesn't look that tough. Or we could try running, though I am wearing heels."

"I think we do what he says."

"You don't want to try to negotiate?"

The attacker gestured with the weapon. "Give me your stuff. I don't have all day."

"No," Kara replied. "You're obviously a busy man."

Michael reached to his back pocket, then realised it was empty. "My wallet is missing—"

"Do you think I'm stupid—" began the man.

"Based on your conduct so far, highly likely," Kara interrupted, unshouldering her bag and holding it out. "This is more than enough for a night's work."

The man took it from her, looking unconvinced.

"It's *Hermes* you idiot. Limited edition. Look, are you sure you want to do this? I think it's only fair to give you the choice of walking away."

The man stuffed her handbag into his backpack. "Your watches."

Michael pulled back his sleeves. "Don't wear one."

Kara held up both wrists. "Me neither. What do you think this is, 1997?"

From behind them came the sound of two voices at the end of the alley. The man glanced around, then ran off in the opposite direction. In a moment he'd turned the corner and was gone.

Michael let out his breath. "You OK?"

Kara straightened her coat. "Why wouldn't I be?"

"We were just mugged. And yet you seem really calm."

"I don't let jerks bother me."

"Well that *jerk* took your fancy designer handbag."

She reached into her coat pocket and pulled out a flat leather object, handing it to Michael. "He didn't get this."

He frowned. "My wallet?"

"You dropped it in the conference room. I was waiting for the right moment to wind you up about it."

"Well thanks, I guess. Are you going to report your stolen bag to the police?"

"What's the point? Not worth my time."

"Er… OK. You know, maybe you shouldn't walk down dark alleys at night."

"Maybe not. I guess I don't know everything, after all." She slapped him on the shoulder. "Now let's go get that sandwich. And since you still have your wallet, you're buying."

THIRTY-FOUR

THE BUILDING WAS ONE OF MANY LIKE IT IN WHITEHALL: AN elegant four-storey Georgian townhouse on the outside, converted beyond recognition internally for the requirements of modern communications, comfort and security. Warwick Saxton sat outside a suite on the top floor. The door bore no special markings or name plate, but from the number of security personnel stationed close by, it was clear a senior member of government was in situ.

Warwick Saxton yawned as he waited to be summoned, wishing he could get an actual drink. Finally Charlotte Rostrum's assistant, a man in blue pinstripe, cleared his throat and indicated a large oak door to his right. Saxton nodded and pushed it open.

"Warwick, good morning," said Rostrum from the other side of a very large office. Much larger than any of his.

"Home Secretary," he said, with a forced smile.

She pointed to a chair on the other side of her expansive desk. "I have to brief the PM in an hour, so can we get straight to your Project Parallel update?"

Saxton sat down. "It's not good news. We have to put the project on hold."

"We only restarted it a few days ago."

"The attempted kidnapping of Gregory Jenson's daughter

was thwarted in a way that potentially undermines the security of the project." Saxton paused. "With the use of unauthorised military technology."

Rostrum leaned back in her chair. "By Jenson?"

"We're still investigating, but it was unarguably a ZAT weapon. I'm discussing this with you first before meeting with him. If Jenson's actions are proven, I'm not sure that we have a choice but to cancel."

Her eyes gave nothing away. "I will follow your recommendation, which I'm assuming is to terminate the project. If this is the kind of person Jenson is, we really should have discovered it earlier. But at least we did discover it."

Saxton stared at her. "You're taking this very calmly, considering it was at your instigation that Parallel was restarted."

Rostrum shrugged. "We can't change the world just because we want to. I know I said the other day that the old ways were dead. But I'm sure that's not strictly true."

"Parallel was our *only* immediate plan."

"Intelligence isn't my business. Politics is. If Jenson has become toxic, the *intelligent* move is not to work with him."

"*If* he is responsible."

"I thought you said ZAT technology was used."

"He's not the only one with access to it."

"You're suggesting there's another player?"

"I'm suggesting I don't know."

"I trust in your expertise and advice. You'll find another way to solve our problems. And I have plenty of other issues on my plate without trying to do your job for you. Find me another solution." She frowned. "Is something wrong, Warwick? You look very *grey*."

Saxton blinked. There was an odd inflection on the word 'grey'. "What about the reactor? I presume still no news?"

"The recovery vessels have a couple of possible locations for wreckage, but it's three miles deep and unlikely to be salvageable. As for the reactor itself, we have no leads."

"We'll need to find another way to locate it. Presuming we don't progress with Parallel."

She shrugged. "We'll come up with something."

He nodded then rose to his feet. "Very good. I won't take up any more of your valuable time."

Saxton made his way from her office, passing through security point after security point until he stepped onto the street. Something didn't feel right. He had never known Rostrum not take an opportunity to put the boot in.

So why not now? Jenson had always been a *risk*. The brilliance of his company's work came with a trade-off. Should he just walk back in and tell her the truth: that he was being coerced? That was certainly what the rule book said he should do. But his instincts told him things were more complicated. And if he did that, he would be out of the game. He wasn't ready for that. Not yet.

His system was compromised. His organisation was compromised. Could it be that even the Home Secretary was compromised? He needed to think differently, using help from outside the institutions he was a part of. He checked his phone and smiled.

The results of Cassie's search had come back. It was a full report, including a home address. As soon as he'd met with Jenson he would follow it up.

THIRTY-FIVE

AT ZAT HEADQUARTERS, RESEARCH AREA EIGHT WAS considerably busier than usual. Astrid Kelly stood in the open airlock door, nodding as she checked Lee Chow's handpicked team off a list. As ZAT's CEO strode inside, Kelly sealed the doors behind him, while Jenson clapped his hands together and took his place at the end of a hastily-erected conference table.

"Thanks for joining me so late."

"I was here anyway," Chow replied, running a hand over his bald head. "Could we keep this brief?"

Jenson's eyes narrowed. "I promise to take up no more of your time than is necessary. How soon can the system be operational? You said six months to get a working prototype?"

"We've been reviewing the data and six months is optimistic. It's more likely a year away – and that's ignoring the currently 'insoluble' problem of overheating and throttling."

"I need you to do better. A lot better."

"You said our overriding imperative was to do this right. 'You can't rush a miracle' were your exact words."

"The situation has changed."

"Why?" Chow replied. "I'm all for doing things faster, but

we'll need more resource. We'll have to pull staff off other projects, take over other labs to run work streams—"

"Consider whatever you need approved," Jenson said. "Astrid will make it happen."

"OK," said Chow, "but the principal problem is that the system probably won't work. We're getting the same glitch as we did last time: the connections won't form because the processor overheats – at which point the quantum-state parallel processing just cross-interferes."

Jenson's eyes narrowed. "Find a solution."

"Is the government pressuring us? Or is this anything to do with your daughter? You're not thinking of using the system yourself? Nobody would blame you."

"Focus on building the system. Let others worry about how it will be used." Jenson folded his arms. "Unless you're telling me you no longer wish to work on this project."

"I'm not saying that, but a lot of people are worried: the system could easily be mis-used for personal gain. Your current situation would be a good example."

Jenson's expression darkened. "Protecting my daughter would not be 'mis-use'. Besides, if it doesn't work, there's no issue."

Chow patted Jenson on the arm. "I just don't want our CEO to end up in jail because he wasn't properly advised. To date, we've managed to keep you on the straight and narrow."

"And I appreciate it. But right now you need to hear me when I tell you not to hold back. I've worked with some incredible scientists and engineers over the years, but I need you to be better than any of them. I need you to create the future. Let me worry about my legacy." He nodded to Kelly. "And let Astrid worry about anything else you may require: resources, funding, pizza..." Jenson smiled at Chow. "I'm counting on you."

THIRTY-SIX

Several hours later, Jenson sat in his office on the thirty-second level, reading the latest status report on Parallel on a pair of hi-resolution displays. Chow had already increased the size of the project team by over thirty per cent, and had begun an accelerated program of testing, with shifts organised to work day and night. The budget was quickly getting out of control, but he'd let someone from finance worry about that later. He was distracted by a knock at the door. Kelly walked in, holding a computer tablet.

"I have something of interest for you that isn't in those reports." She closed the door, placed a finger to her lips, then walked over and positioned a black box on Jenson's desk, pressing a button. Red lights lit up. "Broad frequency jammer," Kelly said. "Acquired it from one of my intelligence contacts."

"A contact you trust?"

"To an extent. I fully reconfigured the device before bringing it here, just in case."

"Sometimes," Jenson said, "I worry you'd rather you were still in government service."

"The toys were good, but everything else was lousy."

"Getting rid of you was a big mistake on their part. They

didn't know what they had. Speaking of toys, is our own security really not good enough?"

Kelly glanced around. "We have to assume we've been compromised, even here. With the right technology, anywhere is vulnerable." She held out the tablet.

Jenson took the device from her and unlocked the screen with his fingerprint and quickly flicked through the pages. "A consignment of drones was misreported?"

"Someone altered the figures. I had to delve into the backups and meta-data to spot it. We've now checked the batches. One hundred and twenty drones are missing."

"How is that possible?" Jenson leaned back in his chair.

"I'm trying to find out. As for the drone I found in the barn, it *was* one of ours. Not just our design, but manufactured by us – it's from the batch that was taken."

"Who knows about this?"

"You, me and the site director in Reading where they were manufactured. He offered to resign. I said if he did we'd send drones after him."

Jenson rubbed the bridge of his nose. "It has to be one of our own people."

"It's hard to believe anyone else would have had the necessary access."

"But who are they working for? And why take the drone from me, but then use them to help me? Someone with a beef against Rose?"

"Perhaps. Or perhaps this isn't about Rose at all. Maybe it's just meant to incriminate you."

"At least we're managing to keep a lid on it. The last thing I need is the government sticking their oar in." Jenson's phone buzzed. He frowned down at it. It was reception calling him direct. With a sigh, he answered.

"Mr Jenson, I'm sorry to trouble you, but I have a Mr Saxton waiting here."

Jenson blinked. "Did we schedule an appointment?"

"He says he doesn't need one."

Jenson sighed. "Show him up to my office." He turned

back to Kelly. "Great work so far. Now I need you to go deeper. Review CCTV, conduct interviews: look where others wouldn't think to. We have to find out where the leak is. And we have to close it."

"I may need to go off comms for a few days to make sure my activities aren't picked up and blocked."

"Whatever you need to do. Update me as soon as you are able." He hesitated and reached into his pocket, producing a small hi-tech barrel key. He threw it towards her and she caught it with a snap. "That's the key to Equipment Cache Three. Help yourself to whatever you need."

She smiled. "I'm on it, boss."

FIVE MINUTES LATER, SAXTON WALKED IN, PULLING THE DOOR closed behind him. He sat in the chair opposite Jenson, rubbing a hand across his forehead and looking like he didn't want to be there. "Thanks for seeing me on short notice."

Jenson held out the palms of his hands. "No notice might be a better description. Is this another audit?"

A look of confusion crossed Saxton's face. "I'm sorry, what?"

'Someone from your office came last week to conduct a random security inspection. I thought perhaps this was a follow up."

"This has nothing to do with any audit. I didn't call because I didn't want anything on the system. Yours or mine." Saxton puffed out his cheeks. "By the way, I was relieved to hear that your daughter is OK."

"She was very lucky."

"It is almost improbable that she was not hurt. You saw what happened to the kidnappers."

Jenson rocked back in his seat. "They got what they deserved."

"It's not my place to pass judgement, but it is puzzling how those six men died."

Jenson narrowed his eyes. "What do your forensic people say?"

"They're saying a lot of things, but the most frequent word is 'inconclusive'."

"That must be frustrating."

Saxton leaned forwards, spreading the fingers of one hand on Jenson's desk. "There are a lot of things that I find frustrating, but few that I cannot fix." He pointed at the black box on the desk. "What's that?"

"Part of our security systems. Obviously we're treating this project with the utmost care."

"It's not because of the threat to your daughter?"

"We don't believe there's a connection." Jenson paused. "Do you?"

Saxton sighed. "You knew the conditions of working with my department. You knew you had to be squeaky clean. I warned you that anything less would provide… ammunition."

"What are you talking about?"

"I've been left with no choice. We're cancelling the project."

Jenson rose to his feet. "You have to be joking. We only just restarted!"

"We know about the drones, Greg."

"You know *what* about *what* drones?"

"Are you saying it wasn't *your* micro-drones that killed every one of those kidnappers?"

"I had nothing to do with it." Jenson clenched his fists. "*Nothing*."

"Either way, like I said, I have no choice." Saxton stood up. "I'm giving you formal notice to cease work." He turned to leave. "If you don't like that maybe you should call a lawyer. But, to be honest, however good they are it won't make a difference. After what you've done, my hands are tied."

Jenson watched the MI5 Director leave. He didn't need a lawyer who was good: he needed the opposite – one who wasn't afraid to be bad.

THIRTY-SEVEN

Michael was working late again, this time on his floor of the Infinity Law building. He was putting the finishing touches to a termsheet for a large acquisition that Kara had passed to him only that morning – a good three days of work, perhaps more, and she'd given him just one to complete it. So here he was, at nearly midnight, not nearly ready to go home. Surprisingly the floor was otherwise empty – Kara and Sandra had both left several hours ago – although that didn't mean other lawyers weren't still working – they were just doing it somewhere else.

He picked up his coffee cup and with irritation noticed it was empty – he was going to need a boost if he was to get the termsheet fully polished. So he removed the computer headset and closed his laptop, then made his way across the floor to the kitchen area.

The coffee machine was the most sophisticated he had ever seen in an office. It offered fifteen different variants of coffee and hot chocolate, and seemed to have an interface intended as an aptitude test. Only if you passed would you get your hot drink of choice. Michael tapped in the multi-key combination he had memorized, and the machine whirred and gurgled into action. But before his drink could arrive he heard footsteps behind him.

"I did initially balk at the cost of getting this thing installed," Errington said, appearing at his shoulder. "But Duncan pointed out that if we keep our lawyers awake, they can bill more hours."

"His logic is compelling."

"And if we make the coffee taste fancy, the associates won't realise they're just hamsters on our wheel... Oh whoops, did I say that out loud?"

Michael smiled, noticing that the machine had finished. He picked up the paper cup that had been deposited. "Everyone has to do a bit of time on someone else's wheel. Until they build their own."

"So you're a philosopher as well as a lawyer?"

"Just a realist. The world works a certain way."

"Until someone changes it." Errington patted him on the shoulder. "Isn't that what you youngsters all want to do?"

"Of course," Michael replied. "We certainly like to think we will. Well I'd best get back—"

"I heard you concluded that joint venture yesterday. You've only just started and already you're racking up the wins."

"That was mostly Kara. I was there as well."

"Don't let her take all the credit. She does that enough without needing any help. But, for once I'm not here to discuss client work. The security cameras showed me you were still working so I popped down to discuss what happened *after* yesterday's meeting."

"I'm sorry?" Michael frowned. "Oh, you mean the mugging? It was a bit unsettling, but no one was hurt."

"Life can throw the most unexpected things at us. But we have to rise above them. I was a little concerned you might lose focus, maybe get distracted. But," he looked at his Patek Philippe watch, "given you're still working at this hour, it seems my worries were misplaced."

"I appreciate your concern. Not something I remember seeing from the partners at my last firm."

Errington smiled. "It's probably Kara I should be

worrying about. Or rather the mugger who took her bag, and what she'll do to him if she tracks him down."

Michael coughed. "You think that's likely?"

"Who knows? She's hard to predict." His phone buzzed and he glanced at it, smiling.

"Good news?"

"A meeting in the morning. An important one." Errington put the phone in his pocket. "Anyway as a small thank you for your continuing hard work, mugging notwithstanding, I'd like to treat you to dinner." He held up a hand. "And don't panic, not with me. You and a guest of your choice. I'll get my PA to make a booking for you. Presume you like Italian?"

"That's very kind."

He flashed polished teeth. "Of course it is. Now get back on that hamster wheel."

THIRTY-EIGHT

Equipment Cache Three was located in a small warehouse in a quiet part of Wapping, east of Tower Bridge. Just before 2:00am, Astrid Kelly parked her battered Vauxhall Corsa a block away. At this hour the street was calm and quiet, the familiar odours of the Thames hanging in the air. She glanced around, drew the hood of her jacket low over her face, then walked quickly to the warehouse.

Through the front-office window, she spied the lone security guard, a slim woman with her dark hair drawn tightly back, engrossed in what looked like an electronic card game. That was convenient, because, while she had permission to be there, Kelly didn't want a record of it.

She moved around the side of the warehouse and, with a short run-up, pulled herself over the ten-foot brick wall that enclosed the building's small loading yard. Lowering herself down onto the tarmac, she kept her face away from the two CCTV cameras and stepped quietly over to a metal hatch next to the main roller-doors. Producing Jenson's cylindrical key, she slid it in. There was a grinding of gears, and the hatch hissed open.

Crouching, she stepped through into a storage room completely separate from the main warehouse, though connected by a similar hatch. It was filled with rows of metal shelving, mostly laden with wooden crates and aluminium flight-cases. She ignored them all and walked towards a reinforced metal cabinet at the far end.

The lock looked worn. Notched even. She'd have to mention that to Jenson, but for now her mission came before mere building maintenance. She slid the key in and turned it. The mechanical components engaged and the doors slid up and apart.

Inside soft blue LED lighting illuminated a collection of ZAT's most interesting equipment and weapons: lightweight tactical body armour, smart rifles, HUD glasses. There was passive-monitoring equipment, and a pack of twenty micro-drones. Mostly items that had proven too expensive to find a ready market. Jenson always kept a few of each conveniently stored away, just in case the government decided to move in and seize his product line. It was a habit that would alarm his board and shareholders if known, but right now Kelly found it decidedly useful.

She reached forward and selected one of the smart rifles, unplugging it from where it was charging. It chimed in alarm, so she quickly typed in her identification code. This was not a weapon you took without permission if you wanted to avoid incapacitation. A second softer tone sounded, indicating the code was accepted. Smiling, she picked up a clip and was about to slot it into place when a woman's voice spoke from behind her.

"Thank you. I've been trying to get in for hours."

Kelly slammed the clip home and spun, aiming the rifle. Feathering a button on the stock, she activated forward-facing lamps on the rifle that flooded the room with light. In front of her, smiling, was the security guard she had seen through the window. Except she clearly wasn't a security guard. She carried herself with a confidence Kelly did not like at all. She wore tinted plastic glasses and didn't seem to react to the glare from the rifle's lamps. "Stay exactly where you are," Kelly hissed.

"Of course." The woman gave a mock salute. "After all, you do have that gun."

"Who are you?"

"Just someone who wanted to open that box. I did not expect a mechanical lock. How old school – very difficult to hack."

Kelly's grip on the rifle tightened. "I asked you a question."

"Call me Cortez."

"You seem oddly confident, given I have this rifle."

"That's because I know what's going to happen next. It's very empowering."

Kelly frowned. "Are you armed?"

"I don't need a weapon," Cortez replied. "I'm going to take yours."

"And how exactly do you plan on doing that?"

"With information. I know more than you. Specifically, I know your rifle's administrator code." She raised her voice. "Override Gamma One Zero One."

Kelly felt something in the rifle click, just as her brain registered what was going on. Eyes widening in alarm, she tried to drop the rifle, to stop it treating her as an enemy. But it was too late.

Fifty thousand volts of electricity surged from an onboard battery, flowing through the grip and into her body. Screaming, she staggered back, collapsing to the floor, unable to move.

Cortez walked calmly over. "Sorry about this, my dear, but you've been asking far too many difficult questions."

Kelly lay on the floor, her muscles on fire.

"If it's any consolation, you were on the right track. Our modelling suggested you would make the connection to me within a few days – far sooner than our schedule will allow."

"Do you work for Rose?" Kelly gasped.

"You don't really believe that, do you?

Kelly grimaced. "You work for whoever launched the

drones." Her eyes narrowed. "I've seen you before. You're the auditor. Your face is different but I recognise the walk."

"Impressive." The woman beamed. "Although we both know that I'm no more an auditor than I am a security guard. Unfortunately for you, with that level of attention to detail there's only one course of action open to us. No hard feelings, eh?" Cortez picked up the smart-rifle, unchecking the safety. "Well, in just a moment there won't be any feelings at all."

Kelly moaned, flexing her fingers against the ground as Cortez aimed the weapon in a leisurely manner. Just as she saw her finger tighten on the trigger, she shouted, "Override Gamma One Zero One."

The woman's eyes widened and she started to throw the rifle away.

She was fast. But not quite fast enough. Her body twisted and she screamed as the electricity flowed again. She stumbled backwards and fell to the ground, her glasses falling off.

Kelly managed a faint smile before consciousness faded.

Kelly didn't know how long she was out. All she was aware of was pain as she woke. She struggled to raise herself up on her forearms, trying to remember where she was. Then she saw Cortez sprawled nearby, the rifle still clutched in her right hand.

Other than the faint rattle of an air-conditioning unit, there was no other sound in the warehouse. With a grunt, Kelly forced herself to sit up. She had to get out of here. She had to warn Jenson of what had happened. Fire coursing through her body with every movement, she tried to stand. And failed. Cursing she tried again. On the third attempt she made it. Hissing with every step, she staggered over to Cortez.

The woman was sighing as she breathed.

Kelly kicked the rifle away. It skidded over the concrete and came to rest against a wall. But Kelly had no doubt this woman would be dangerous without the weapon. She needed to create an advantage. The most obvious one would lie in the equipment cache. But as she turned, she saw that it had closed and was emitting an angry red glow. Muttering, she recognised it as a familiar ZAT protocol. If secure storage wasn't locked down, it went into secure mode for twenty-four hours, so what else could she do to control the situation? Turning she looked for something to use as a restraint. On a nearby shelf she found a box of zip-ties. She grabbed several and walked back to where her assailant lay.

Cortez opened her eyes. "Hello again."

Kelly hesitated. "Don't move."

"Or you'll shoot me? Even if you had a gun, I hear that's not your thing."

"What?"

"I know about your military past. Why you were discharged. After that debacle I'm amazed you ever worked again."

Kelly frowned. "Save your words for the authorities; they might reduce your sentence. I've already called them, by the way."

Cortez smiled. "I find that unlikely. Your phone was almost certainly fried when the rifle shocked you. And even if it wasn't, I've jammed all cell signals in the area."

"How would you—"

"I come with a certain level of resource. And, like I said, I know everything."

"But you didn't know everything about the rifle."

"And that is annoying. But this is not over."

"It is for you."

"We'll see." Cortez sighed. "Look, I still can't move, so if you're going to tie me up, get it over with."

Kelly narrowed her eyes. "This is a trick."

"There are many tricks, but this is not one of them." She rolled on her side and put her wrists behind her back. "Anyway, it only seems fair to give you a head start. Because I will come after you. And I will kill you. Nothing personal. For now, you should thank me."

Kelly knelt and pulled the zip-tie around Cortez's wrists. "And why is that?"

"I saved your client's daughter. The one you're so fond of. In the barn." Cortez smiled. "It was quite a scene, I can tell you."

"Did you hire those men?"

"It's a little more complicated than that."

"What game are you playing?"

"A very long one."

Kelly's eyes narrowed. "You're stalling."

Cortez nodded. "Good old-fashioned deduction. I'd run if I were you."

"Why give me a warning?"

"Because I like the chase. I'll see *you* soon, Astrid. Watch for me."

Kelly clenched her fist, drawing it back to swing at Cortez. Then she hesitated.

Cortez smiled back. "I thought not. Now run."

It was still dark when Kelly emerged from the warehouse. Her mechanical Rolex told her that it was just gone 3am. She ducked behind a car and tried to see if anyone was watching the warehouse. Did Cortez have other people about to arrive? And who the hell was she with? Wary of breaking cover, she decided to watch for a little longer while she apprised Jenson of what was going on. She pulled out her phone, but as Cortez had predicted it was dead.

With one last look around, she began to jog along the road towards her Vauxhall. There was a twang, a vibration in the air. Something thin and straight, about a meter long, struck the car's front tyre. With a squeal, it deflated.

An *arrow*.

Kelly took a step back and looked behind her. A

silhouetted figure stood on top of a van next to the warehouse: a slim woman, holding a bow.

"I did say I'd see you soon," Cortez said.

"You missed."

"I wanted to make sure you didn't just drive off."

"What is this, the Middle Ages?"

In a blur, Cortez had nocked another arrow, and it was humming through the night. It struck the car's rear tyre and, again, there was a scream of compressed air escaping. "Most satisfying, wouldn't you agree?"

Kelly didn't wait to hear any more. Instead, she ran. She wasn't sure what was going on or who she was fighting.

She knew only one thing: she had to survive. Then she could warn Jenson. She wasn't ready to give up, not by a long shot.

She ran away from her car, south towards the river, hoping that Cortez might be caught off guard by the sudden change of direction – and that a moving target would be a lot harder to hit.

Another arrow flexed in the night and struck a street lamp directly above her, shattering the glass cover. Kelly leaped forward to avoid the fragments as they fell. Behind her, she was aware of a figure moving fast.

Cortez's voice floated in the darkness. "Full disclosure: I'm not trying to hit you. Not yet."

Kelly increased her pace. Gritting her teeth, she turned down an access alleyway between two apartment blocks. At the end, she reached a paved walkway: a gentrified towpath along the Thames. Each way wove between the support columns of overhanging residential apartments. Her only other option was straight ahead and jumping in the Thames.

She turned left, moving east along the path, going downstream. Behind her the pursuit seemed to have gone quiet. If she could cover a bit of ground she could get to a minicab company in Wapping where she knew one of the drivers. He owed her a favour, and she would make sure he remembered it. She went to glance over her shoulder again, then froze.

Her pursuer was in front of her. How?

Cortez tipped her head, then raised the bow, an arrow at the ready. "What are the chances?"

Kelly frowned. "Are you really in charge? Maybe you don't have the authority to kill me. Maybe your orders say something else."

"It's a great theory. Unfortunately for you I have a great deal of latitude in how I carry out my role." Cortez scowled. "Anyway, I think I've had enough now. So I'm going to count to ten. And then I'm going to shoot you." She pulled out an arrow.

"You'll shoot me in the back, if I run?"

"It's all the same to me."

"How did you manage to get ahead of me?"

"I told you: I know everything. And you can't beat someone with perfect information."

"Just how are you getting this information?"

"Well, that would be telling." Cortez moved in a blur. The arrow was on the bowstring and flying towards Kelly before she even realised it. There was no time to dodge.

This is it, Kelly's brain told her. *I've lost.*

The arrow grazed her shoulder. A slight sting, nothing more.

She looked up. "Today is a day of surprises. Looks like that was your last arrow."

Cortez didn't move.

Kelly blinked. "What are you waiting for?" And then she started to feel it.

The sting became a burn. Her limbs felt heavy. Her eyes began to water.

Cortez walked towards her, smiling. "Do you understand now?"

"Some kind of poison?" Kelly felt her mouth go dry. She was losing control of her body.

"A bespoke neurotoxin. Coded to your biochemistry. You can already feel the way things are heading."

"You're a..." she staggered and fell to one knee, "monster."

Cortez ducked down and caught her before she collapsed, lifting her on to the stone wall. Below the black waters of the Thames heaved and slapped hungrily. "The *perfect* monster you could say," she whispered.

Then she dropped Kelly into the river.

Kelly would have gasped as she hit the cold water, but the toxin had already made her too numb. Everything went black.

CORTEZ STOOD ON THE TOWPATH WATCHING HER VICTIM floating downstream, a sequence of graphics and text streaming across the inside of her glasses. A red icon flashed. With a grunt, Cortez shouldered her composite bow and pulled out a secure phone. "Thought you were too busy to track my ops?"

"My attention," Marcia replied, "goes where it is most required, hence my call. Would you care to explain what is going on?"

"Complications at the warehouse. I have it under control."

"And yet you are not in the warehouse. You were told to intercept Ms Kelly and take her out of the equation."

Cortez pulled carefully at her earlobe. "Somehow the system did not pick up that the rifle's security feature could be used multiple times."

There was a pause. "The system isn't perfect. Which is why we're changing things."

"Until we do, complications will happen."

Marcia's voice remained even. "Maybe you should accept that a larger team would be advisable."

"And maybe I shouldn't be tied down by a group of unreliable meatheads."

There was a longer pause. "Your primary glasses were damaged?"

"I had a spare set available. My backup team released me."

"And then you chased the target alone through open streets?"

"Given the hour, the risk was minimal. The alternative was to let her escape."

"The *alternative* was to consult me. You cannot keep going off-book. You have to follow the plan."

"You use me because I serve your bigger plan. Otherwise you'd use someone else. In fact, for all I know you expect me to go off book. Maybe that *was* the plan."

The pause this time was extended. "I need you to be predictable so that everything else is."

"Fine. What does the system tell you now? What's next?"

"A thank you. Dinner on me."

"Anywhere particular?"

"What do you think?"

THIRTY-NINE

GREGORY JENSON, WEARING JEANS AND A PULLOVER, STOOD leaning on the handrail outside the lions' enclosure at London Zoo. Inside lay several females, none of which spared a glance for the crowd. They looked bored, but ready to explode into action if given the chance. Jenson could empathise.

"Greg, I hardly recognised you," said a familiar voice from behind his left shoulder.

Jenson turned and extended his hand. "Max, it is a pleasure to see you today."

Errington smiled. "I'm here to help."

"And I've got quite the challenge for you." They moved away from the lion enclosure, past a small cafeteria and towards the monkey habitat. Jenson cleared his throat, then spoke in a low voice. "This place used to cheer me up until it occurred to me that maybe the animals weren't happy about being in cages."

"Happiness is all about perspective," Errington replied. "Is this really a good place to meet?"

'It's pretty hard to operate surveillance: there's ticketed entry and it's a large site away from other buildings, plus there's plenty of background noise from the animals."

"You don't trust your own offices? Who have you upset?"

Jenson narrowed his eyes. "What have you heard?"

"Nothing. Just a guess based on a great deal of experience. I've been round that block more times than I'd care to admit."

"That's why I have need of your skills."

"Then tell me everything. And I'll see what I can do."

They walked on, reaching the polar bear enclosure as Jenson finished explaining the situation. The huge white animals looked even more bored than the lions.

"What's your opinion?" Jenson asked.

Errington scratched his nose. "I have no doubt there's a whole load of crap that Saxton hasn't told you, quite apart from the crap that you haven't told me."

"Thanks. I knew you'd be motivational."

"The good news is that Infinity can help you."

Jenson folded his arms. "I want to believe you, Max."

"No government plans to spend a billion on a project that doesn't matter – or that suddenly stops mattering - without everyone understanding why. Something else is going on." He paused. "Plus, with the drones it seems you're the victim here. Yes, there's a lot we can do. I know Saxton from way back. He has certain… buttons I can press."

"Great. But how quickly? They want me to cease all development."

Errington frowned. "Your research is all centred at your HQ. What about an alternate location? Somewhere a little less high profile."

"You're suggesting I ignore Saxton's instruction to kill the project?"

Errington held up his hands. "As your lawyer, I would never say that. But if you were to *infer* that it would be harder for them to keep track of what you're doing at a different site, that's up to you. It's your choice." There was a soft chiming sound and Errington pulled his phone from his pocket. He glanced at it and frowned.

"Another client? Another problem?" Jenson asked.

"Both," Errington replied. "The former wants me to pay her a visit to discuss the latter. Which means I have a flight to catch and a lot of stuff to set in motion for you before I do." He put the phone back in his pocket. "Decide how you're going to play the development issue. Meanwhile I'll get my people pouring over the government order, exploring all the angles. Send me over your project files and correspondence. This is the moment you start fighting back."

Jenson nodded. "Don't pull any punches."

"You think we're only going to punch them?" Errington smiled. "They should be so lucky."

FORTY

Regina Rose stood on the deck of the *Evolution* as the small motor launch made its approach between a number of larger leisure craft moored in Marseilles' harbour. On deck she could make out a familiar figure in a suit. The man who was going to help her solve her problem. The man who had changed the rules on her behalf so many times.

The launch docked gently and Rose descended the steps as Maxwell Errington navigated the gang-plank. "You're looking well, old friend," she said, shaking his hand.

Errington patted his stomach. "That's arguable. I'm certainly eating well."

"Then I trust my chef won't disappoint if you'll stay for dinner."

"Having come all this way? I should hope I will. Always happy to spend time on my yacht."

Rose raised an eyebrow. "I took your suggestion for a name. That doesn't mean you own her."

"Let a man dream."

"As long as I'm not paying for it." She turned and led the way to her private office. Two heavy-set, visibly-armed bodyguards followed them in, closing the door and taking up positions to either side. Rose poured two large glasses of cognac from a decanter.

Errington took one glass and glanced around. "What's up, Regina? You look like someone who just had three lots of bad news."

Rose indicated two large leather armchairs. "It's a matter of some sensitivity."

"I'm sure that describes most of your business these days. I assumed that's why I haven't seen you in London for some time."

"There's always the risk that the authorities will insist on speaking to me, probably in a sound-proof room with no windows."

"Perhaps if you paid a few more taxes they might back off."

"And that," Rose said, "is why I never come to you for financial advice. I've had men shot for less." She flashed her teeth.

"Then I'm pleased I am your friend."

"Good, because as your friend I need a favour."

"Of course. Although I should stress that my friends still get billed for favours."

Rose gave a snort. "Last week there was an attempted kidnapping in your country of a young girl."

"It was all over the news. She was very lucky." Errington shifted in his seat.

"I believe you know Mr Jenson."

"We've had dealings in the past. But I shouldn't think he can even remember my name."

Errington frowned, face suddenly grave. "Did you have something to do with his daughter being taken?"

The bodyguards shifted involuntarily but Rose raised her hand and they stepped back. "I've heard you know Jenson rather well indeed."

"You clearly have ears in many places."

"You always claimed to be the guy who knows everything. It's a strategy I've tried to emulate."

"I've claimed a lot of things in my time. Some of them were even true. Now what the hell is this all about?"

"I need to give you a little context, so you appreciate what I am saying." Rose put her glass down on the low coffee table between them. "A week ago I received an approach from a new client, who was referred to me by a reliable contact. The client had an unusual request: a hi-tech weapon system not officially on the market and manufactured by a UK company –

ZAT. The client wanted me to use my connections to Jenson to broker a deal for the weapon – a new type of drone. I said that Jenson probably wouldn't even speak to me, let alone sell. Then the client told me how much they would pay. Suffice it to say that changed my mind."

"Money can do that."

Rose nodded. "I managed to persuade Jenson to meet and explained my situation. I said I was prepared to pay virtually any price. But he rejected me outright: told me the technology in question didn't even work. I was pretty sure that last part was a lie, but now I am certain. While investigating the kidnapping, I received leaked reports that show the men died from incendiary wounds that the police could not explain. Jenson used the drones to save his daughter."

"Then approach him again. Tell him what you know."

Rose's eyebrows flared. "Coming immediately after my last meeting with him, he believes I was behind the kidnapping. He won't deal with me now."

"But who *was* responsible? And to what end?"

"I don't know. From my sources, the British police are at a loss. Which is why you are here, Max. I want you to act as an intermediary. Explain to Jenson that I would never have done that to his daughter. Then broker the deal."

"You think I can change his mind?"

"Max, that's what you do. And I need you to do your very best work for me now. I simply won't take no for an answer." She gave a meaningful look at the guards, waiting on either side of the door. "Look, I want what I've always wanted: to make an indecent amount of money. Right now, I really need a pay day. Am I making myself clear?"

"I want to help you, but this is an impossible situation. It sounds like Jenson would happily fire half of his product inventory at you. You're not going to get him to come to the table unless you can prove you weren't involved."

"Do whatever you have to. Make him see sense."

"I'm sorry. I don't have the leverage." Errington raised a hand. "But before you resort to threats we'll both regret, I might know someone who does. There's a consultancy I've used in the past. They're very resourceful in getting hold of information that nobody else can find."

"Who are these miracle workers?"

Errington lowered his voice. "They're called Kinek. If there's an angle you can follow, if Jenson has a weakness that can be exploited, then they'll find it."

"I've never heard of them."

"I hope that the same is true for your enemies. You do not want them in the opposing camp." Errington pulled his wallet from his pocket and removed a battered business card.

Rose took it from him. It bore a UK landline number and nothing else. "This had better not be a joke."

"I promise you, this is a phone call that will change everything."

FORTY-ONE

MICHAEL ARRIVED LATE FOR DINNER WITH EVE, AND QUICKLY realised he would regret it. Mosconi, one street back from the Strand, was an Italian bistro with a queue way out onto the pavement. The aromas and atmosphere justified it. When Michael forced his way past the line and gave his name, the owner sighed and frowned heavily, tapping his watch. After leaving Michael standing there for several long moments, he finally whistled for a waiter, who led Michael to a table in the middle of the main floor. Eve, who was already there, stood to greet him. She wore a low-backed, emerald green dress, and a dark frown.

"Nice that you could make it," she said. "They were about to turn me out onto the street."

"I'm so sorry. I got caught up on a client call." He kissed her on the cheek. "You could have ordered."

They sat, looking at the menus as an impatient waiter literally coerced their orders. He returned almost immediately with a bottle of Australian Shiraz, then vanished into the smoothly rotating crowd of restaurant staff.

"They're officially booked out for weeks," Michael said. "I had my PA call some secret number that Max has access to."

"So it's 'Max' now, is it?"

"Maybe not to his face. Still he was very friendly after the mugging. Seemed quite concerned to make sure I wasn't going to lose focus." Michael held up his wine. "Here's to the finer things."

Eve raised her own glass and clinked his with some hesitancy. "You look so tired. I mean you've always worked hard, but it's like you've been a man possessed since you started this new role."

"I have to create the right first impression. It's not like you don't work stupid hours too."

"Yeah, well that's just how junior doctors train. At least what I do is in a good cause."

"So what I do is evil?"

She shrugged.

"It's no worse than any other law firm in London. Perhaps less than some."

"I was talking to one of my friends. He said that Infinity has a terrible reputation."

"Sour grapes, maybe. Infinity doesn't lose often."

"Can you honestly say that nothing you've seen since joining them has made you question your decision? Maybe it's not too late to go back to CPW."

"C-*W-P*," Michael replied. "And there's no question of me going back there."

"Oh?" Eve leant forward. "Why not?"

"Bridges can't be unburnt." Michael swallowed, and lowered his voice to a whisper. "Look, to be honest I'm fortunate to have *any* job. I didn't want to say before but—"

"Michael!" said a voice from over his shoulder. "What are the chances?"

He looked up to see Kara in a short expensive black dress and matching high heels. He blinked, momentarily lost for words.

"And this must be your lovely girlfriend. Ava, is it?" Kara extended an expensively-manicured hand.

"*Eve*," she said, returning the handshake with an over-tuned smile. "Just Michael's housemate. And you must be… *Karen*."

Kara smiled. "Close enough, Dear."

Eve flickered her eyes towards Michael. "Sorry to hear about you getting mugged. Was the bag *very* expensive?"

"Oh don't worry about me. I was just leading your boyfriend into dangerous places. I thought he might step up and defend me, but I guess he wasn't in the mood. Then again not taking on armed assailants on an empty stomach is my first rule too." A waiter appeared at her shoulder and whispered in her ear. She turned to Michael. "My table is ready. I'll leave you to enjoy your evening."

"A pleasure meeting you," Eve said, unconvincingly.

"I've no doubt. Oh and Michael," Kara said, as she glided away, "make sure you're in early tomorrow. We have a new client looking to negotiate a big deal. A very big deal."

Michael watched her disappear, then turned back to find Eve glaring at him. "What's the matter?"

"That's who you work for? The one who picked you up in a bar that night?"

"I thought you'd seen her photo?" Michael frowned at her tone. "You don't like her."

"What gave it away?"

"Look, I didn't come here to talk about work. Can we try and enjoy our evening?" As if on cue, their starters arrived.

Eve leaned forward and drew in a breath. "If this tastes as good as it smells, we might just manage that."

FORTY-TWO

THE SMALL OXFORD BOOKSHOP WAS NOT ONE OF THE MODERN trendy ones with free internet access, a coffee shop and a substantial amount of stationery and greetings cards. It didn't foist the latest airport paperbacks on time-poor clientele. Instead it was heavily traditional, selling academic textbooks and serious biographies, plus some literary fiction. Along with the new books there was a substantial 'pre-loved' section, otherwise known as second-hand. They were vetted heavily, and anything too popular was moved discretely to the nearest charity store, who were usually more than grateful for the donation. The establishment did not generate significant profits, but it made the owner, Bryn, a living even in a fast-changing market. Bryn openly laughed at the idea of eBooks. It was like blasphemy and profanity rolled into one. Computerisation was bad news for business.

Which was why Cory Ashcroft liked working there. In a former life he had immersed himself in technology, but he'd made a decision to move on from that. Now he preferred to deal with tangible things that preferably didn't change or get superseded every twelve months. Unfortunately it was an approach to life that was proving increasingly difficult to sustain.

Bryn had finally succumbed to the forces of technology

(via a particular persuasive saleswoman) and had bought a computer system, though he had yet to get it working. A great many empty cardboard boxes were stacked in the small office at the back of the shop, but so far nothing was even plugged in.

"How many computers have I bought here?" Bryn asked, looking around dejectedly.

Cory flicked an eye over each box. "Just the one, but with lots of components." He picked up an itemised list and squinted at it. "You really didn't need one with all these features."

"The lady said I did."

"Did you tell her you were modelling weather patterns or doing advanced 3D design work?"

Bryn raised a weary eyebrow.

"Then we can probably assume she said whatever she thought you needed to hear to buy the most expensive model."

"I thought you hated computers."

"I do. Doesn't mean buying and using them is rocket science."

"So can you put it together for me?"

Cory ran a hand through his grey-peppered hair. "Why not get the work experience kid to do it?"

"He's fourteen."

"Which probably means he'll be better than either of us. Seriously, give him a try."

"Fine. Then can you shelf up that box on the special promotional stand."

Cory frowned. "I thought you didn't do promotions?"

Bryn looked at his fingernails. "The publisher's keen to push this one. Leant on me pretty firmly. And when I say 'leant', I mean they offered a sizeable financial incentive. Given that I'd just paid out for the computer I was momentarily loose with my principles."

"What's the book?"

"Business biography by that technology entrepreneur, Gregory Jenson."

Cory swallowed. "You mean the arms manufacturer?"

"From your tone I gather you don't want to stack the books either. If you delegate any more, I'm going to start to wonder whether I need you at all."

"I just don't know why anyone would pay good money for these self-promoting works of fiction. They're full of obvious nonsense written by somebody who just happened to get lucky, then acts as if it was all his plan from the start."

The shop front door opened and the postman walked in. He gruffly handed several envelopes to Bryn, then was gone.

"Bills, more bills, and…" Bryn paused. "A letter for you." He held it out but did not let go. "You never get post."

"Now, I do."

Bryn looked like he was waiting for further explanation, but Cory offered none. "Well, read it on your own time. Now unbox those books."

Cory nodded, tucking the envelope into his pocket. Though it was completely unexpected, he knew who it was from. More importantly, he knew what it meant: after all this time, his private investigator had found something.

FORTY-THREE

Michael stepped out of the taxi and found his gaze drawn upwards to the gleaming glass and steel of ZAT's HQ. It loomed over the street, reeking of design and money. Kara jabbed him in the shoulder with a purposeful finger.

"Quit gawping and get inside. We've got a client to meet."

Michael blinked. "Something about ZAT is ringing a bell. I just can't place where I heard of it before now."

She checked her briefcase, then shouldered her handbag. "They've been one of the MoD's key suppliers for a decade."

"I don't mean from seeing them on the news or in the financial pages." He shook his head. "I probably just dreamt it."

"Save dreaming for your own time."

"Sure, I—" Michael hesitated, pointing at her blue leather handbag. "That's the one the mugger took. How did you get it back? It can't be new: you said it was vintage limited edition."

A smile flickered across her face. "So I did. Well that's what we do at Infinity Law: we solve problems."

Michael frowned. "What does that mean?"

"Look, we need to focus on what we're doing here today."

Michael followed her through a large revolving door and into a spacious lobby, stopping at a bank of metal detectors and scanners. Michael placed his bag on the conveyor belt, then waited in the queue to step through the metal doorway. "They take their security seriously," he said to Kara, who was in front of him in the line.

"It's worse when you leave," she replied. "Their biggest concern isn't what you might bring in. It's what you might try to take out."

"Weapons?"

Kara turned and raised an eyebrow. "This is an office, not a manufacturing plant. It's the IP they're trying to protect."

"They might not make weapons here, but they do make them somewhere. That didn't cause Infinity any ethical concerns?"

"What about the tobacco, sugar or motor industries? They all kill people. Plus", she ran a hand through her hair, "if you'd done your research you'd know that ZAT makes a considerable number of high-tech, non-lethal defence and security systems."

"So they're the good guys?"

"The world is rarely that black and white. At best, it's more a matter of opinion." She moved through the doorway and it beeped sharply. A guard stepped towards her and patted her down, though the look she gave him almost seemed to make him change his mind. The guard gave her a nod and she picked up her bag from the scanner.

Michael was waived through the doorway. It beeped even louder for him. The guard beckoned him over and began an identical pat down.

"My belt?" he suggested.

The man shook his head. "Anything in your pockets? You have an implant or a pacemaker?"

Michael shrugged and patted his jacket. "Nothing."

The guard frowned and ran a hand-held scanner over his chest. The system stuttered but didn't beep properly. He glanced at one of the other guards and they waved Michael through. He picked up his backpack from the conveyor and rejoined Kara. "Not had that problem before," he said.

"Maybe their scanner system doesn't like you."

Michael looked around. "Where's Errington? I thought you said he'd be joining us?"

"He's here already. Got to use the VIP entrance."

"And we didn't get that same invitation?"

"Maybe one day. Now are you ready to focus? Because Gregory Jenson suffers fools even less than I do."

FORTY-FOUR

Astrid Kelly opened her eyes and found to her great surprise that she was not dead. She lay on a foam mattress, covered in a worn duvet that smelt of salt and fish. The bed was tight against one wall of a small, oddly-shaped room panelled with dark wood. Morning light was filtering in.

A bearded man in his fifties, face and hands grimy with oil, appeared at the door. She noted he had to duck to get through, even though he stood well under six foot.

"You're awake," he said with a smile. "Will you be wanting a cup of tea?"

Kelly blinked. "Where am I? Who are you?" She sat up and looked out one of the porthole windows, feeling the whole room shift.

"My cargo vessel. I got a radio message in the early hours that someone had been seen falling into the river. Found you two minutes later. If I hadn't been looking, I probably would have mistaken you for a piece of driftwood."

Kelly rubbed her fingers against her temples. As she did so, she felt a pain in her shoulder and remembered the arrow that had grazed her. There was a fresh bandage where she had been struck.

"We cleaned and dressed it," the man said. "My daughter knows some first aid. She works the boat with me – same age as you, I'd guess. She's got the helm at the moment. I thought perhaps we should take you to the hospital, but", he glanced around, "not everyone who falls in a river wants to be found."

"No." Kelly flashed a smile. "I appreciate your discretion. And you saved my life. I don't know how I can ever repay you."

"You're the most interesting thing we've ever found in the river. And we've found a few things, I can tell you," the man said with a laugh.

Kelly nodded. "I bet you can." She stretched stiffly. "You know, I think I could manage that cup of tea if it's still on offer."

He smiled. "Coming right up."

KELLY SETTLED BACK ON THE MATTRESS WHEN THE MAN HAD left. It seemed almost impossibly fortunate that she had been rescued. A few more minutes and she would have drowned. Why the toxin hadn't killed her anyway was another question she would try to answer later. For now she had to play the hand she had been dealt, roll with the luck she had been granted.

She had completely misread the situation. While it had been clear ZAT and Jenson were under attack, this was beyond her wildest worries. She wanted to call Jenson, but she knew that was the wrong play. There was no doubt her communication would be detected. It was better if, at least for now, she stayed dead.

That meant contacting someone else.

Someone who she was never supposed to contact.

Never was evidently today.

FORTY-FIVE

Michael and Kara were shown to a conference room on the fifteenth level of ZAT HQ. Errington and a tall, immaculately-suited man were already there.

"Morning," said Gregory Jenson, shaking their hands. "Max assures me you're his brightest young things."

"The best of the best," Errington said. "Kara is our top senior associate, and Michael is not only a lawyer but has a background in computing."

Jenson stared at Michael. "Is that right?"

"My father was a programmer. I picked up a few things."

"Was he any good?"

Michael shrugged. "He said he was."

"Don't they all?" Jenson cracked a smile. "At least I won't have to explain what a Quantum computer is."

"My father would have loved to play with one of those. If you can make it work, it will represent a revolutionary jump, like moving from an abacus to a supercomputer."

"What do you mean 'if' we make it work? I don't need doubters on my team."

"I didn't mean to suggest—"

Kara cleared her throat. "The key thing, Mr Jenson, is that the situation you face is more about people than computers."

"You may be right." He sat down at the table. "This country needs Project Parallel, but it seems someone has designs to prevent it."

Kara removed a neatly-bound folder from her briefcase and pushed it across the table towards him. "We've built a ten-point plan to quantify the problem, then—"

Jenson pushed the folder back at her. "I just need to know what I have to do." He narrowed his eyes then pointed at Michael. "I've heard Max's views. Ms Simmons here has offered me a telephone directory to read. What do you think?"

Michael glanced to Kara, whose expression had gone opaque, then turned to Errington, who nodded. Michael swallowed. "The situation is complex. Firstly, the government has broad discretion to terminate a project at—"

"Don't just give me a list of problems."

Michael closed his eyes and thought hard. "Can you think of any explanation why Saxton would cancel the project, other than the one he gave you? It would have to be pretty significant to risk the consequences of… well… lying to some of the most important people in the country."

Errington turned to Kara. "Can you check that the door is closed?

She frowned but walked over and pulled the handle. "We're good."

"You want me to tell them, don't you?" Jenson said.

"They can't help you if they don't know," Errington replied.

Jenson rubbed his eyes. "You will have seen the news reports about my daughter's failed kidnapping?"

Michael and Kara nodded.

"And that the team was 'taken out' by special forces. What those reports don't cover is that the kidnappers were in fact killed by an unknown third-party, using a hi-tech weapons system: micro-drones, developed by ZAT."

Kara adjusted her glasses. "You deployed your own system—"

"No!" Jenson shouted. "*I* didn't. But *someone* did. Someone who wanted to set me up. And Saxton has bought the whole story. He's ordered the project cancelled as a result."

Errington folded his arms. "Because no government wants a scandal."

Michael frowned. "ZAT is much more than a one-person company. Why so much focus on you?"

Jenson shook his head. "I don't think you appreciate the sensitivity or the alarmist nature of the decision-makers in government. If something starts to smell even a little bit, they bail."

"So," Errington said, "Michael may be on to something. We just need the truth. And for that we need to get in front of Saxton and pin him to the wall until he tells us what is really going on."

Jenson's brow furrowed. "Throughout the tender process, he wasn't exactly the most malleable of individuals. Why do you think anything will have changed?"

"If we give you the right lever, you will move him."

"Maybe we should just escalate the issue?"

"Go above him to the Home Secretary? Then you're into pure politics, and who knows what will happen. No, Saxton is the right target. Look, Michael's very good at spotting patterns and making intuitive leaps. Why don't you show him your Toys and Games Department, and he might make a few more. Besides, you know you want to."

A flicker of a smile crossed Jenson's face. "OK, whizz kid. Follow me."

FORTY-SIX

Michael followed Jenson to an executive lift, separate from the rest, and they descended to level seventeen. Jenson waived them through a series of security points until they reached a heavy metal door labelled Research Area Six. Inside the room was a large technical laboratory with frosted-glass windows. They walked over to a central table bathed in LED lights. Two lab technicians scowled at Michael then walked away.

"Something I said?" Michael asked.

"They don't like being interrupted, but more than that they don't like showing off their tech in progress," Jenson replied. "They think you might steal it."

"Do they know I'm a lawyer?"

"No. I thought it best not to antagonise them further. Still, it gives them an opportunity to play with the voice disguiser in Research Area Five. Now try these."

Michael looked at the black-framed glasses on the table then shrugged and replaced his own glasses, slipping on the lightweight frames. His vision went blurry. "What's supposed to happen? Obviously they're not my prescription."

The CEO reached forward and gently pressed the top corners. There was a soft beep. Then Michael's vision snapped into focus.

"Whoa!"

"Self-focussing adaptive lenses."

"They'll put opticians out of business."

"At ten thousand dollars a pair it's unlikely. But there's more." Jenson pressed on the lower corners.

Michael saw a field of small, slightly blurred, icons overlay themselves on his vision. He involuntarily flinched backwards, then blinked repeatedly. The glasses seemed to whirr slightly and their focus sharpened further. "An HUD?"

"Kind of, but you're somewhat out of date. This is an augmented reality system. Obviously there are others on the market already, but this is a whole new level of sophistication of interface. Try moving your hands."

Michael waved them in the air in front of him. "What's supposed to happen?"

"Place them on the table then move them slowly. Like you were using a laptop trackpad."

Michael did so. As he slid his hands across the surface, the icons rippled in sequence. He reached forward and tapped one. It bounced then opened into a stop-sign.

Jenson nodded, looking at a screen that was replicating the display Michael could see. "Try the globe."

Michael moved his hand across and tapped. An internet browser leapt into view, obscuring his vision. "Interesting. Although now I can't see where I'm going."

"You need to dial up the translucency, but we're still working on that. Try the 'tag' icon."

Michael blinked again as the display flashed green at the edges. "Now what?"

"Pick something up."

"Like what?"

"That computer mouse."

Michael shrugged and reached across. As he picked it up, the outline of the object glowed softly green and a small glowing point hovered near it. "What's going on?"

"Blink. In a pronounced manner."

Michael did so. A small virtual tag unfolded and hovered

above the mouse. It read 'computer mouse'. "OK, that is quite cool. How many things can it recognise?"

"Not much that isn't in this lab. But it's a start. It uses a mixture of outline sensing and colour density to guess what an item is. It's a harder computing problem than you might think. But ultimately you just need a lot of data: ideally access to a library containing images of... everything. Our product is just an interface. Its capabilities all depend on what you hook it up to."

"So what *could* you hook it up to?"

"Take any online mapping system. It's just a massive database. But connected to these glasses you would know exactly where you are at any time, in real time. And that's only the start. We can deploy data harvesters to provide much more granularity. You could visualise and navigate your way through a complex location without even visiting it."

"I'm sure this helps with your weapons systems."

Jenson shrugged. "Systems like this focus on targeting the right people." He hesitated. "Although that is a whole other discussion. Look, what this really means is you can see the world with additional clarity. Things aren't always what they seem from first glance. If you have more data, and a way to interact with it, anything is possible."

"That sounds pretty deep."

"Perhaps. While it's just us, I'll mention something else I thought was profound."

Michael removed the glasses. "Oh?"

"I thought it was strange that Max, famed for his firm negotiation style, volunteered a 'no win, no fee' offer for this job. It's pretty risky."

"He must be certain he can help you. The Infinity model isn't to work for free."

"Fair point. But I'm not sure if he's right."

"I've only known him a few days, but I'd definitely say it would be unwise to underestimate him."

"Let's hope you're right." Jenson looked at his phone. "It seems that show and tell is over - something has come up."

Back at the lifts, Kara and Max were waiting, serious expressions on their faces.

Kara held out a slim folder. "These are the results of a penetration test we procured on your systems."

Jenson froze. "You did what?"

"It's a procedure designed to evaluate your IT security systems by mimicking an attack—"

"I know what a penetration test is," he replied, his eyes flashing. "You tried to hack ZAT. You're supposed to be solving problems, not causing them."

"We needed to verify how secure you are. The answer is *not very*."

Jenson muttered, then began leafing through the document. "You found a vulnerability?"

"We did", Kara paused, "and it quickly became apparent that someone else had been trying to exploit it."

"Who?" hissed Jenson. "I want them arrested."

"Her name is Millie Wright," Errington said, "and from the report it looks like she got nowhere. But our agency tracked her down. Despite your initial thinking, it's usually better to be a little less heavy-handed. At least at first."

"*Who* is she?"

"A lone operator," Kara replied. "A blogger who runs a site on corporate conspiracy. No real resource behind her. She's not in it for the money: she just wants to make a name for herself."

"Then what are you suggesting?"

"Warn her off," Errington said. "Use charm and persuasion. Right now you have more important things to worry about than some amateur." He gestured to Michael. "I'm sure our young friend here can take care of it."

Jenson seemed to think. "OK. Get it done. Meanwhile the rest of us can focus on setting up a meeting with Saxton."

"We'll need full access to the project files. You've just

provided overviews and corporate documents. We need the full technical specs, the software source code. Everything."

"Why would you want that? You're just lawyers."

Errington smiled. "If there's one thing I think we can all agree on, it's that we're a lot more than that."

"Fine, request everything you need." He turned to leave. "Whatever it takes."

"Now would be good. Do you have them on site?"

"In the development lab on level 8. But access is restricted. My assistant, Astrid, normally manages that but she's out of the office at the moment."

"Then perhaps you could escort Kara there? This is critical."

Jenson frowned. "Sometimes, Max, I wonder which of us is in charge."

Errington smiled. "Whoever has the best information."

FORTY-SEVEN

NIGHT HAD FALLEN OVER SOUTH LONDON. LIGHT NOW GLARED from LED street lamps, almost too bright to stare into. They provided sufficient illumination for Cory Ashcroft to see the grubby side-street clearly from his unremarkable ten-year-old grey Ford Focus. He was parked opposite a pub named the Three Bells, although on its battered sign two had faded from view. In his hands was the plain brown envelope that had been delivered to the book shop for him.

Late the previous night, after pouring himself a large scotch, Cory had sliced the envelope open with his Swiss army knife. Then, his hands shaking, he had read the letter inside three times.

Now he glanced at his watch, a battered digital model, and confirmed it was time. Stepping from the car, he made his way across the street and into the Three Bells. He immediately spotted the man he was due to meet; he looked so much like a private detective that he might as well have been wearing a sign. Cory walked over, raising his voice above the din. "David Barr?"

The man squinted through tired eyes. "That's me, Mr Ashcroft. Have a seat."

Cory sat opposite, noting that Barr had nearly finished his

beer; from his expression, it was not his first. "I got your letter."

"I could have just called if you'd allowed it," Barr replied. "Would have been simpler."

"I appreciate you following my instructions." Cory half-wished he'd asked someone else to handle the task, but Barr was cheap and within his limited abilities, reliable.

"You wanted me to report any change in the target's circumstances. Well, he has a new job. Another law firm. A much smaller outfit, based in Knightsbridge."

Cory blinked. "What's the name?"

Barr pulled a battered notebook from his pocket. "Infinity Law. I couldn't find out a lot more about them than is on their website. And there's not a lot on their website. Your guy left his last place in a hurry – most likely poached or fired. But I couldn't get anyone to talk to me, on or off the record. Usually the secretaries are happy to blab once I turn on the charm, but they clammed up tight."

"Did you see any signs that he was planning to leave before this happened?"

Barr laughed. "You asked for the most basic, non-invasive surveillance to pick up any major changes in circumstance. If you want me to try hacking his computer or trawling through his rubbish, I'm more than happy to," Barr said, raising his glass. "No job too mucky."

"I'll bear that in mind." Cory removed a white envelope from his pocket and slid it across the table. "Your fee."

Barr picked it up, peered inside, and nodded. "Who is this kid to you?"

"It's a long story. Not one I'm going to tell."

"No surprise there. I looked you up, Mr Ashcroft. Do you know what I discovered? That you are exactly who you say you are. Your background is perfect: squeaky clean. And if it looks too good to be true, then ninety-nine times out of a hundred it isn't true. Particularly with the type of person that would seek my help."

Cory raised an eyebrow. "As a rule do you investigate your clients?"

"Enough to satisfy myself I'm not helping out a criminal." Barr paused, then bared his teeth in an ugly grin. "Because for them my rates are higher." He laughed. "Anything else you need me to do?"

Cory stood. "If there is, I'll be in touch."

FORTY-EIGHT

WARWICK SAXTON EMERGED FROM THE SQUASH COURT dripping with sweat. His opponent, a heavyset grey-haired man, followed close behind, closing the Perspex door with an exhausted sigh.

"You want my help, and still you beat me soundly," said Sir Douglas Busby, Deputy Commissioner of the Metropolitan Police. "I swear you have no concept of what 'friendly match' means."

"Who says I want your help?" Saxton pushed open the door to the nearby changing room. The room was, as he had anticipated, completely empty. He'd called ahead and made special arrangements to make sure that he and Busby would have the opportunity to talk in private, even if the Deputy Commissioner was not expecting it. His sports club was always happy to accommodate.

"Come now, you never call me," said Busby, lowering himself onto a bench and toweling his forehead and arms. "It's always me that calls you. So I figure it's more than just you wanting someone to beat on the court." He blinked. "Unless that *is* it. Somebody else has *really* pissed you off, and you have a little aggression to work out of your system?"

"Always so suspicious. Are you sure you don't work in intelligence?"

"I'm happy protecting the public, in *public*. That hidden-world nonsense isn't for me."

"I'm not a fan of it either – at least not the nonsense part." Saxton hesitated. "And, yes, there's something more going on."

Busby clapped his hand down on the bench. "I knew it. Also I heard a rumour that Parallel had been cancelled."

Saxton's eyes widened. "Nothing's sacred anymore."

"I assumed it was a joke or deliberate mis-information, but I guess I was wrong."

"It's a little complicated."

"I'm sure *little* is an inaccurate modifier if something has forced you to cancel a top-priority project barely days after re-starting it."

"Obviously I can neither confirm nor deny. But then, as you say, I did call you."

"You should watch your back, my friend. I have the feeling that you are going to find yourself in very choppy waters."

Saxton nodded, placing his racquet in its protective cover. "I believe I am there already."

"What did you expect? Parallel will change the game. Those who play the game as it is won't like it. So they'll either try to stop you or to take it from you."

"It wasn't like this last time. But then I guess the project didn't succeed last time."

Busby nodded. "Did you ever stop to ask yourself why it failed?"

"You think it was compromised?"

"I'm just throwing around ideas."

Saxton closed his eyes. "Sometimes it's like someone has the system already."

"Well if that's true, then we are well and truly screwed. Look, if there is ever anything I can do to help, just ask. And I should remind you, my brother-in-law has just been promoted to Vice Admiral."

"Congratulations. But if I need a boat, it will be a small one. And we have a few of our own."

"What about a submarine? Maybe that would be more your thing. Obviously I'd strongly prefer that whatever it is won't get me fired. Or arrested."

"Interesting." Saxton opened his eyes. "You actually trust me."

Busby's mouth curled into a smile. "No more than you should trust me. But you and I have been round the block enough that I feel you deserve a fair hearing. We all play politics, even if we're not politicians. All maneuvering, jostling for position, trying to predict what will happen next."

"Thank you."

"Don't mention it." Busby glanced around. "Seriously, don't. No need to encourage those seeking to end the old boys' network."

"The very idea that maintaining human connections is bad makes me angry. Especially when computer connections are rapidly consuming all." Saxton shook his head. "What are you going to want for this show of support?"

Busby started to examine the strings of his racquet. "Hadn't even crossed my mind. But since you ask, if you do ever get this thing built, I would certainly like to be near the front of the queue to use it."

"I'll bear that in mind."

FORTY-NINE

In the opulent lounge of the Cunard Hotel, just off Embankment, Morton pushed away his half-finished cup of mint tea and checked his Breitling chronograph. He was due on site in exactly one hour, which meant there was protocol to follow, and Morton always followed protocol.

He slipped out of the hotel lobby onto the street and looked left and right, before jumping into the black cab at the front of the taxi rank, asking for Kings Cross Station. But eight hundred metres later, he asked the irritated driver to let him out. He promptly crossed the road and caught the double-decker H92 bus north-west towards Hyde Park. He took a seat on the top floor at the rear. All the time his eyes were scanning around him, the high viewpoint meaning he could follow the traffic in every direction. The constant bus stops made it very difficult for any vehicle to follow him unobtrusively.

At Green Park he exited the bus and descended into the underpass, as if he were entering the Tube Station, but he strolled through and climbed the stairs to emerge on the other side of the road. From there he made his way north. After two hundred metres, he turned sharply into a side street and arrived at a grey four-storey office block. He paused, looking behind him; still nobody seemed to be following.

An array of brass plaques next to the front door proclaimed that each floor was home to a different business. There was no obvious external security. There were two travel agencies, the representative office of an overseas bank, and a technology start-up that, from what Morton had seen, looked like it might be about to *stop*. Typical London office space. Except it was not.

He walked through the door and nodded to the bored-looking security guard, then glanced up at the six high-definition CCTV cameras that he knew were trained on him, even though none was visible. This was the final check. If there was anything about him that they didn't like then he would get no further.

But a soft tone sounded from somewhere and the guard nodded over his shoulder. Morton walked towards a door as it swung inwards. Behind it was a short corridor that ended at a lift, its doors open. He stepped inside and it whisked him downwards. Way down.

MORTON STEPPED FROM THE LIFT INTO A THRONG OF ACTIVITY. People flowed around him, their images reflected translucently in the polished marble floors, all going somewhere with a purpose. There were a few nods of acknowledgement, mostly deferential, but nobody stopped to speak. There was too much going on. Normally he would go and check on the main floor, but right now he needed guidance, so he turned away from the crowds towards a door bracketed by two security guards, though the booth's automated systems were more than sufficient to deny entry to any who weren't fully authorised.

He placed his hand on the flat panel next to the door. It read his palm. A small optical device scanned his face, then narrowed to a tight beam and focussed on his left eye, confirming a retinal match. That got the door open.

Morton stepped inside. The booth was clad in panels

intended to baffle audio and electromagnetic frequencies; once the door was closed there could be no form of eavesdropping. It held a single desk and chair, and three viewing screens. He watched the door hiss shut then he took his place. As he sunk into the imitation leather there were soft beeps and percussive tones as it checked his weight and measured the dimensions of his impression in the upholstery. DNA analysis was likely next year, but currently the process was too slow. And business at Kinek could never wait.

"IDENTIFY," said a mechanical voice that seemed to emanate from the air.

"Morton. Director, London Office," he replied, in crisp tones. There was a brief pause, then the screens in front of him flickered into life. A single word appeared: READY? "Initiate," he said. There was only one person he would be calling from the booth, and she answered immediately.

"This is Marcia. How can I be of assistance?" As always her voice was soft and faintly metallic. Morton assumed the signal must be routed through a considerable maze of electronics and telecoms. It had to be untraceable. A web within a web. Kinek's operations were too important to be risked in any way.

"I trust I find you well. Thank you for arranging my release from custody."

"We could hardly leave you there to fester. What did you want to discuss?"

"The new client request."

"Regina Rose? I noted that on the update list. Didn't the system recommend to proceed?"

"I'm proposing we reconsider."

"On what basis? The system has obviously vetted her."

"I reviewed the reports and there are a number of unknowns. Gaps in our knowledge. I'd suggest she has the means to cause us... inconvenience. Discomfort even."

"So you'd have us say no and hang Maxwell Errington out to dry? One of our most trusted partners?"

Morton cleared his throat. "You're saying we should give Rose what she wants?"

"We just give her information. She still has to choose what to do next. Morton, we are all just cogs in the machine. You may not know why you are doing some of this. I may not either. It's not for us to try to spot patterns: that's what the system does, on behalf of the Board. It is all part of the plan."

"So what do you want me to do?"

"Send Cortez."

Morton swallowed. "I will afford her my full support."

"Thank you. The Board continues to value your management of the London office. You are a credit to our operation."

"I am delighted to hear that. Thank *you* for your ongoing support."

Morton remained in the seat for several minutes after the call disconnected. Something felt wrong. Previously when he had made a recommendation, Marcia always considered it. Kinek's network of offices, each with their own specially-constructed computers, could draw sense from the oceans of information available. But while these artificial minds could spot patterns, the human element was fundamental. There had to be checks and balances: the final decision could never be passed off to a system.

So what had changed? Why had Marcia been so quick to dismiss him? Why had she deployed an operative in London who didn't report through Morton? Had he lost faith in what they were doing here?

He caught himself. This wasn't a question of faith. The system didn't work because of belief. It worked because of *data*.

Morton left the booth and walked towards the main floor. Under warm artificial light a hundred operatives sat at the rows of terminals, their heads bowed in concentration. He knew they would be processing questions, analysing options and making recommendations. These recommendations were passed to him and, after adding his own commentary, he shared them with Marcia and the Board. That was how the system worked. But was it working as it should?

At the rear of the room was a large airlock door. Morton walked up to it and went through the same security process he followed to gain access to the booth. With soft tones the door swung inwards and he stepped through into a much smaller room, allowing the metal panel to close automatically behind him. The hum of human activity vanished, replaced by the gentle vibration of cooling fans. In front of him stood the many cabinets that housed the Kinek London system: the platform which drove their business.

All the lights were green.

He walked over to a terminal and queried the performance log. It flashed up on the screen and he smiled. The system was working normally.

He let out a breath he hadn't realised he'd been holding. Obviously any errors made had been human. Perhaps if he had a bit more faith, he wouldn't doubt it.

FIFTY

The file on Millie Wright had been prepared by an external agency, although there was no record of the company's name. A log of her movements showed that she typically had an early breakfast at the same café: an independent, owner-operated place, not part of a national chain. It was rumoured to serve the best cappuccino in south London. At 6am, Michael found the prospect more than a little persuasive.

He saw Millie the moment he walked in. She was ensconced in a corner booth, with coffee and pastries and an odd-looking laptop. He queued for a cappuccino, then walked over to her table. She looked up as he approached, eyes narrowing.

"Good morning," he said. "Mind if I sit for a moment?"

She smiled broadly. "And there was I, getting all lonely."

"There's a matter I'd like to discuss. To our mutual advantage."

"No thanks."

Michael reached into his pocket and withdrew his Infinity Law business card, placing it on the table. "This will only take a moment."

She glanced at the card. "Somehow I doubt that. What's this about?"

He sat, placing his coffee next to hers. "Nice café."

"Clearly I come here too often. Have you been following me?"

"No."

"If this is a job offer, I'm not interested."

"It's not a job offer. We want you to stop your inappropriate investigations of one of our clients, ZAT Systems."

She tapped her lips. "Name doesn't ring a bell."

"Very funny. But this is not a joke."

"So you work for an arms manufacturer?"

"I don't work for them. They're a client."

"The kind of client you want? They, quite literally, kill people. They make smoking guns."

"Alcohol kills people. Cars kill people. Fast food kills people."

"Look, my point is, they're hardly a surprising target for someone like me. And you talking to me makes it seem all the more likely that they have something to hide that should be public knowledge. Why else hire an expensive lawyer?"

"Perhaps to defend their right to carry on business without disruption."

"It's a free country."

"That doesn't mean you can flout its laws. For example, the Computer Misuse Act."

"What exactly do you think I've done?"

"You've been attempting a hack. We have evidence."

"Look, no offence, but if your firm had anything of substance they would have sent somebody more important than you. Besides, what are you going to do? Sue me?"

"Well, yes. That is exactly what we're going to do. That and pass our files on to the police. This is a very serious matter, and my firm will get to the truth. It always does."

She laughed. "I've heard that about a few organisations recently. But it's what you decide to do with that truth that matters."

"You have to stop what you're doing or we will take steps."

She looked at him. "You don't want to threaten me. Really you don't. Now I think your moment is over. Go and lawyer somewhere else."

Michael stood up. "Just because you know stuff about computers, you think you own the world."

"I know quite a *lot* about computers. And – newsflash – computers run the world. It's not something that's going to change. The old world, including you lawyers, is going to get left behind."

"Nobody knows what's going to happen. Nobody can predict that."

"Your father tell you that?"

"My mother actually." Michael took a deep breath. "I don't know why you're not taking this seriously."

"Maybe I'm just not taking *you* seriously." She finished her coffee. "And maybe you should read some of what I've written: it's all on my blog. If you want to speak again, you know where I'll be every weekday morning." She stood up and packed her laptop into her bag. "Enjoy your day."

FIFTY-ONE

Regina Rose stood on the deck of the *Evolution*, cursing the name of Maxwell Errington. Nobody from Kinek had responded to the messages she had sent. Meanwhile her buyer had been calling for updates. Rose wasn't sure how much longer she could stall. Had Errington been wasting her time with this recommendation? She looked around for somebody to shout at, but her crew members were wisely keeping their distance. Muttering, she stomped across the deck and into her private quarters.

A stranger stood waiting for her. The woman wore plastic-rimmed glasses and a grey business suit. Her long hair was pinned back, her expression flat. Rose began turning, ready to run.

"I wouldn't do that," the woman said, adjusting her glasses. She carried a leather briefcase in one hand.

Rose hesitated. "You should know, *friend*, that I have ten armed men on deck."

"To be honest I expected more. But they're on deck, while I am *here*."

"And what are you *here* to do?"

The woman tapped her briefcase. "My name is Cortez, and I'm here to discuss your request for assistance."

Rose's eyes narrowed. "You're from Kinek? How did you get on board?"

"We never divulge secrets we aren't being paid to divulge. And let's not waste time arguing about it. Let's focus on what's going to happen next."

Rose ground her teeth. "You could be here to kill me."

"If I were, you'd be dead already. I'm here to do business. Are you?"

"I'm still a little unclear on what exactly your organisation does."

Cortez raised an eyebrow. "We do many things, Ms Rose. We advise in unique situations. We're like a consultancy of last resort. I can't go into specific examples – each client's projects are necessarily confidential – but if I was to express it in a few words, I'd say that we change minds."

"If you're so effective, why have I never heard of you?"

"Because we keep a necessarily low profile. But we've heard of *you*, Ms Rose." Cortez placed her briefcase on the table and clicked it open. She removed the only item, a grey card folder, and slid it across the table to Rose then clicked the briefcase shut again. "We call these, rather unimaginatively, grey files. Have a read."

Rose opened it to the first page. It bore her name. Below was a short summary. Of her. She frowned, turning the pages, seeing more and more information that she had no idea had been collected.

"Call it a demonstration. You may not grasp who you are dealing with, but we certainly do."

"Did Max give you this?" Rose hesitated. "And how the hell did he—"

"Mr. Errington had no involvement in its sourcing."

Rose's eyes flared. "Is this some kind of threat?"

"We're just establishing credibility."

"Or you could be a government agent." Rose flicked her hand into her jacket pocket and removed the loaded automatic pistol she always carried there. "I think I've changed my mind."

Cortez's eyes followed the movement of the gun, but she did not flinch. "Do you think I would be here if we thought you would simply shoot me?"

Rose pointed the gun at her head. "You have no idea what I will or won't do."

"Actually our analysis is usually pretty reliable."

"Maybe you should challenge that perception." She shouted an order and two huge bodyguards burst through the door, clearly confused to see the woman standing there. "Take her below," Rose said. "Tie her up, while I consider what to do with her."

"Our analysis," said Cortez evenly, "suggested you would be slow to trust. Meaning a demonstration would be required." Then she moved.

The two bodyguards – both strong, highly trained men – never grasped what was happening. Compared to her, they fought in slow motion. She twisted and flexed, taking both their weapons from their hip holsters, then spinning and cracking the grips down on their temples. Both groaned and collapsed. Without hesitating, Cortez checked the guns, then twisted and pointed them at Rose.

She took a step back.

Cortez smiled, flipped the pistols in the air, caught them by the barrels, then placed them on Rose's desk, before stepping back. "Assuming the question of trust has been resolved, shall we talk business?"

Rose swallowed. "Who the hell are you?"

"The woman who can help you get what you want from Gregory Jenson."

"He's an old friend who seems to have forgotten *his* old friends."

"And you want to buy micro-drones from him."

Rose nodded. "I need both the drones and the full design schematics. My customer's requirements will be ongoing and I can't rely on ZAT to manufacture any more."

"At Kinek we connect people with the information they

need to get stuff done. But that's all we do. I understand you to be a do-er, though, so it shouldn't be a problem."

"The last time someone locked horns with Jenson, he used the damn drones against them. What's to prevent him doing so again?"

Cortez smiled. "Our brief will tell you everything you need to know. Now, we need to discuss our price."

Rose cracked her knuckles. "I suppose you are well aware of the market value of the drones,"

"We're about to tell you how to steal them. What do you think?" She paused. "Our price comes in two parts. First there's money. Then there's a matter we need your help with."

Rose frowned. "You need *my* help?"

"While you're on site, there's something else we want you to obtain."

FIFTY-TWO

Eve was on a late shift, so when Michael arrived home he had the house to himself. He put his briefcase on the floor, kicked off his shoes, and quickly prepared a solo dinner of microwaved lasagna. Then he poured himself a glass of something red from a bottle Eve must have already opened, and settled onto the sofa to channel surf. But nothing on television really caught his attention, and his mind wandered back to his meeting with Millie. She had not appeared in the least concerned by anything he had said. He had expected an independent journalist would have been intimidated. Was she just naive? Somehow that didn't feel right. Somehow he felt there must be more to her.

He picked up Eve's laptop and typed Millie Wright into Google. Hundreds of hits came back, all of which seemed to be about other Millie Wrights. There was too much data.

Searches for 'Millie Wright blogger' and 'Millie Wright journalist' both immediately found her blog. He'd already skimmed through it before, but what he really wanted was something she didn't necessarily curate. Something that might show more of who she really was. But how to find it amongst *too much data.*

On a whim, he typed in 'Millie Big Data'.

A YouTube video of someone giving a lecture popped up

at the top of the list. It was a poor quality recording, likely filmed covertly. The presenter's name was listed as *Milligram*. But even though she wore a cap and dark glasses, he was immediately sure it was Millie. She stood at a lectern under patchy lighting. When she spoke it sounded like the microphone had been positioned in a tin can.

"So," Millie said, her eyes sweeping the room. "*Big Data: Big Danger or Big Opportunity?* Quite a title." She paused, taking a sip of water. "And I'm supposed to respond to it. Perhaps unsurprisingly for a Big Data analysis, I'm going to tell you that there's more than one answer."

There were a few laughs from around the room.

Millie nodded and continued. "When I talk about *Big Data*, I mean seeing and understanding the relations within and among pieces of information that, until very recently, we struggled to fully grasp. I'm talking about datasets so large and complex that traditional analytical techniques are inadequate. I'm talking about a volume of data not only beyond proper human comprehension, but also beyond conventional computing."

She put both hands on the lectern. "What's more interesting is what Big Data *means*. Scientists are using algorithms and predictive analytics to see patterns in human behavior: we can apply lessons from the past to predict the future. A decade ago that might have sounded ridiculous. But the experience of progress in weather forecasting has shown us how analysis of greater volumes of data can produce powerful results. The potential benefits are wide ranging. For instance, in identifying consumer habits: companies can use Big Data to understand customer preferences, anticipate future behaviour and develop individualized marketing campaigns. Big Data has also been used to identify infections in premature infants before symptoms appear by monitoring a range of vital signs, then correlating between minor and major problems. Companies and government entities are using Big Data to improve internal operations and reduce costs; for example, a number of cities across the world are using Big Data to determine which buildings are most at risk of fire damage."

She cast her eyes around the quiet room. "A key point that bears repeating is that Big Data is about *what*, not *why*. As human beings we're conditioned to look for causes – but searching for causality is often difficult and may lead us down the wrong path. With Big Data we put that aside to discover patterns and correlations that offer us novel and invaluable insights. In many situations this is good enough. For example, a change in a treatment regime leading to an improvement in the health of cancer sufferers may be perfectly acceptable, without knowing how or why it worked. Before Big Data, our analysis was usually limited to testing a small number of hypotheses defined well before we even collected the data." Millie paused, as if for emphasis. "When we let the data speak for itself, we can discover connections that we never thought existed."

"What are the challenges in making use of Big Data? Getting data isn't the problem: we already have too much, including things we never used to think of as information at all, such as a person's location, the vibrations of an engine, or the stress on a bridge. The real challenge is analysing it in a meaningful way, because it is beyond our current standard computing capability: it will require exceptional technologies to overcome the challenges of scale and nature.

"This leads on to my next point: what are the risks? Or to put it another way, why would we *not* do it? As Big Data makes increasingly accurate predictions about the world and our place in it, we may not be ready for its impact on our privacy and our sense of freedom. For example, what if we use Big Data predictions to judge and punish people even before they've committed a crime? Handled responsibly, Big Data is a useful tool of rational decision-making. Wielded unwisely, it can become an instrument of oppression.

"With Big Data, the new value of information resides in secondary uses – most of which weren't even imagined when the data was first collected. As for privacy, it may become an illusion. Data is often alarmingly easy to de-anonymise. Surveillance has only gotten easier too, as well as cheaper and more powerful. The ability to capture personal data is often built into the tools we use every day, from websites to smartphone apps. The data-recorders that are in most cars to capture all the actions of a vehicle a few seconds prior to airbag activation have been known to 'testify' against car owners in court." Millie gave a wry smile at a few gasps from around the room.

"And what if we lose control? Especially if decisions are made not by humans but by machines. Computer systems always used to base their decisions on rules they had been explicitly programmed to follow. Thus, when a decision went awry, we could go back and figure out why the computer made it. It used to be that all computer code could be opened and inspected, and those who knew how to interpret it could trace and comprehend the basis for its decisions, no matter how complex. With the advent of machine learning, powered by Big Data, this is changing. Traceability will become much harder. The basis of an algorithm's predictions may be too intricate for people to understand."

Millie paused to look around the room, meeting the eyes of her audience. "Thus, we should consider whether we have a choice in all this. Like other powerful technologies and disruptive human innovations, predictive analytics is essentially amoral, and can be used for good or evil. So should we embrace it, ignore it or fight it? Do we even have a choice? I don't think we do. The stable door is swinging free and the horse has bolted. Pandora's Box is open. We cannot deny that people will exploit Big Data, so we may as well look for the good we can also get out of it. Prediction is power, not least in terms of killer competitive advantages.

"Yet, as I've said, perfect prediction is impossible. But that won't stop us trying. If we chose not to explore Big Data and its analysis, it is inevitable that others will do so. And those that do will develop an advantage. But", Millie gave a wry smile, "even Big Data can't predict how Big Data will evolve.

Nor can it predict the intuitive leaps that humans are capable of and the impact these have on the world. If Henry Ford had queried Big Data algorithms for what his customers wanted, the result would have been 'a faster horse'. Big Data is going to revolutionise the world, but it shouldn't become our world. Now, are there any questions?"

A woman off-camera called out, "I heard you were involved in the development of just such a project."

Millie shrugged. "You may wish to check the integrity of your data collection methodology."

"You're advocating spying on people?" shouted a man.

"No," Millie replied. "That was definitely not my message. This isn't spying, certainly not in any targeted sense. The data exists. We're just processing it in a new, if profound, way."

"So you want a Big Brother Society?" asked the same man.

"I'm not a politician. Just an observer. Of course, some might argue that if you're doing nothing wrong, what's the problem with being watched?"

A woman closer to microphone asked, "What's your prediction for the future?"

Millie paused and smiled. "The demise of the expert: expertise is appropriate for a small-data world where one never has enough information, or at least not the right information, and we have to rely on intuition and experience. Now I'm sorry, but we're just about out of time. I'll end, if I may, with a piece of someone else's wisdom: 'Prediction is difficult, especially if it's about the future'."

There was a round of applause and the recording ended.

Michael stared at the laptop screen. Millie wasn't just a hack journalist. He went back to her blog, MillieOnTruths.com. He had glanced at it before, but this time he read it thoroughly. There was a lot of content: well-written, well-presented, and authoritative. Under a section named 'hot topics' were some recent entries. Millie was appealing to her community of readers for leads relating to 'Project Darwin'. Was this to do with ZAT?

Michael ran a quick Google search, but produced so many hits related to the naturalist Charles Darwin that he quickly added '+ ZAT'. It produced nothing useful. Where else could he look?

Michael glanced at his briefcase. Inside was his Infinity laptop.

His fingers trembling, he slipped it from the bag and booted it up. Placing the headset on, he clicked through security then pulled up *Scope*, the bespoke search engine. His fingers flew over the keyboard. On his ears the headset hummed quietly.

And there was the result. The link he had suspected: *Project Darwin. Attribution: ZAT Systems Limited. Hardware/software project. Project discontinued fifteen years ago.*

Michael sucked in his lower lip. Why would Millie be particularly interested in a project terminated fifteen years ago? Below the initial report some further search responses were slowly appearing. Michael knew that a search like this, without the might of Google's servers behind it, could take considerable time. He scrolled down. And froze. A name had appeared.

Craig Adams. Owner: Project Darwin.

Had his father worked at ZAT? His mother had never mentioned it, but then she never talked about his father's work at all. Perhaps it was another Craig Adams?

Michael took a sip of wine, and thought through his options. He could hire a private investigator. That would be expensive and slow. He also doubted they would find much more than he had; there was hardly going to be a ready paper trail. Or he could ask his mother. It was not an option that appealed. If only his father had left behind some records… but his mother had literally just cleared everything out. And yet what if Craig had hidden it? Perhaps on a computer.

Michael sat up, almost spilling his wine, and swore loudly. The *laptop*. The damn laptop that his mother had just sold off. If there was a secret to be uncovered, it might have been on the device. Was there any way to get it back?

His mother had sold it online. Perhaps he could trace the sale, then offer the buyer more than what they paid to sell it back. It was worth a shot. He logged onto eBay and ran a search for his mother's account; he had helped her set it up a few years back and soon found she hadn't changed the password. He flicked his eyes over the short list of her recent sales to the laptop. Then he looked at the buyer's details. And froze again.

MillieOnTru.

Millie had bought his father's laptop? Had she known what it was?

One way or another he was going to find out. He thought about calling her, but it would be too easy for her to simply put the phone down. But he knew where she lived from the file the firm had provided.

He pulled on his coat and was out the door in less than a minute, heading towards the nearby taxi rank.

FIFTY-THREE

At ZAT's regional facility outside Reading, there was a discrete but increased level of activity. Gregory Jenson stood watching a facilities team bringing a large number of grey unmarked boxes and silver flight-cases into the temporary lab, placing them neatly to one side.

Chow was crouched, checking each box and case as it was deposited. "That's everything," he said, standing up, his knees cracking audibly. "Although I am still waiting for Kelly to get back to me on a couple of points."

Jenson walked over to one of three long white lab tables and ran his fingertips across the top. "Astrid's offsite for a day or two on a special project. I'll get someone else to handle it for you. I assume you're happy with the new set up, and not just because your commute is better?"

Chow scratched his bald head. "I hadn't meant that to reach your ears."

"Best not to say anything these days that you don't mind being passed to an unintended audience: someone's always listening." Jenson patted him on the shoulder.

Chow took a deep breath. "I'm delighted to be working out of this location, but I heard a rumour that the project has been cancelled."

"Where did you hear that?"

"It doesn't matter. As you say, someone's always listening. So is it true?"

Jenson hesitated. "There are some differences in thinking between Saxton and myself, but we're working on resolving them. You just keep doing what you do."

"Good." Chow said. "Because I have an update for you on the software development." He opened up a nearby laptop and set it on the nearest table. "Look at this simulation of the system in operation." He pressed a key and a program started to run.

Jenson watched the display and his eyes widened. "How is that possible?"

Chow coughed. "It wasn't even a software issue. I checked the circuit diagrams for the core processor."

"Which ones?" Jenson asked.

"All of them."

"There are billions of circuits. How could you possibly do it in such a short period of time?"

"I looked for patterns. And I found a logic error. A feedback loop. It was replicated in a number of places; when the blueprints were produced, someone must have pasted it in by mistake."

"So what's our next step? Do we have to get the chips re-pressed?"

"I can program around this. It will only be about 95% efficient, but it will work."

Jenson nodded. "Get the system built then, when we get the decision on this project overturned, we'll be ready to move."

In a grey van parked across the street from the ZAT Reading building, two men sat apparently reading the newspaper and eating sandwiches. The taller man flickered his gaze at the entrance, watching Gregory Jenson make his way out to his parked car. The shorter man was engrossed in a laptop running a detailed analysis routine, parsing data from a series of antennas that had been discretely deployed around the building. He peered more closely at the display, grunted and tapped the headset hooked over his ear.

"Ms Rose, progress is good. We almost have a full sweep. After that we just need to pull the team together. We should be ready in forty-eight hours."

FIFTY-FOUR

MICHAEL KNOCKED LOUDLY ON THE PAINTED DOOR OF THE apartment. There were footsteps inside, then a mutter of surprise. The door opened a crack, held in place by a chain.

"What the crap?" Millie asked, just visible through the gap. "Are you stalking me?"

Michael took a step back. "We need to talk."

"Then what's wrong with the café like last time? How do you even know where I live?"

Across the hall another door opened and a large man stepped out, glaring at Michael. "What's going on?"

Millie sighed and unchained the door. "It's OK. He's a… friend. Obviously had too much to drink." She grabbed Michael's arm and pulled him into her apartment. Closing the door, she walked into a small lounge and pointed at a sofa. "*Have* you been drinking? What couldn't wait?"

Michael took the seat. "Do you know who Craig Adams is?"

She frowned. "I do. Why?"

"Did you not go away and do any research on me?"

"I might have got round to it. You didn't seem that important. No offence." Millie stared at him, then realization appeared on her face. "*Adams.* He was your father?" She glanced around. "Look, it's not that unusual a surname."

"I suppose not. What can you tell me about him?"

"You want *me* to tell *you* about your father? Shouldn't it be the other way around?" She hesitated. "If this is some kind of trick—"

"I'm not asking for my firm. I'm asking for *me*."

She glared at him. "Are you recording this conversation? Because I know you have to ask permission."

"I'm not recording anything. Look, I'm sorry for how I approached you before, but I was just doing my job."

"As was I."

"And I would very much like to know what you learned while doing it. About my father." Michael took a deep breath. "I read your blog. You mentioned the Darwin Project."

"How did you connect that name to your father?"

"I don't know anything about his work. But I know you have my father's laptop. You bought it off eBay a week ago."

"That was your father's?"

"I'll pay you twice what you paid for it."

"I didn't… I don't care if you offer me a hundred times what I paid. You can't have it." She raised a hand. "But you can look at it with me if you like. And, realistically, I may be one of the few people who can actually get it to work."

"I think I know how to use a computer."

"This is a different kind of beast. Without my help, it's a lump of plastic and wire. But I'm starting to think it may contain something important because your father was, if my research is accurate, an important man."

"My mother said he was a dreamer." Michael rubbed his temples. "This is just a game for you. But this is *my father*."

Millie gripped his hand. "Then let me help you get to the truth."

FIFTY-FIVE

Michael and Millie sat in the tiny spare bedroom that served as her office, staring at his father's laptop.

"Bespoke design, built from non-standard components that are at least fifteen years old." Millie ran her fingers lightly over the casing. "I haven't switched it on yet, so you haven't missed anything."

"I could never get it to boot up."

"Because you're not an IT genius." she said, sitting up straight. "The power supply and the battery are dead. Nothing you can do about them, so I've built a replacement. The voltages are non-standard, just to add some spice." Millie picked up an odd-looking power adaptor and, with a flourish, plugged it in.

Nothing happened.

"IT genius?" Michael said. "Sure about that?"

Millie frowned, then made a tutting sound before sliding a switch. "I didn't think there was a power switch, but there you go." The screen flickered, then streamed green characters on a black background. "This might take a while. It's decided to perform a full self-diagnosis. But it's a good sign." She picked up her mug of tea. "I don't normally have an audience for this type of thing."

"I appreciate you letting me stay."

"Maybe I'm trying to butter you up. Hoping you'll put in a good word with your firm."

"They just want you to stop hacking their client. And you do *not* want to mess with us."

"I know. You really think I didn't look them up the moment you left the café?"

"Them you look up. Me you ignore."

"Do you find the ego helps with your job?"

"Yes. I do," Michael replied. "But you're one to talk. Why not find a softer target than ZAT? Are you just trying to show off?"

"Let's focus on the task in hand. What do you think was so special about this Project Darwin?"

"I only found out about it an hour ago."

"Oh yeah." She turned to the laptop, peering at the screen. "It's not in a hurry. So, if not Darwin, maybe you could tell me about your father and the work he did?"

Michael shook his head. "It was a long time ago, and I was just a kid. Plus my Mum doesn't like talking about him. Probably because he killed himself."

Millie blinked. "From my research he was a programmer of some repute. But I think he went beyond programming and designed some new type of computer system. Something sophisticated and incredibly valuable. He was in discussions with ZAT's CEO, Gregory Jenson, to commercialise it."

"Darwin?"

"It was an early venture into quantum computing and predictive search – way ahead of its time. If only we had some way of getting into the ZAT building. From inside I'd have a proper chance of hacking their systems." She tipped her head to one side. "Any ideas?"

"Are you suggesting I help you? I'd get arrested."

"Only if you got caught. This could be incredibly important, and you are uniquely placed to do it."

He hesitated. "You know, instead of breaking and entering, I could always just ask my mother."

"You haven't already?"

The laptop beeped loudly and a password screen appeared. "Progress." Millie reached over to her other desk and picked up a tablet computer.

"I don't know the password."

Millie's mouth curled in a smile. "Fifteen years ago that would have presented an impregnable doorway to the laptop's secrets. But that was then, this is now. Heard of Moore's Law? "

"Yes. Although not the kind of law I usually deal with."

"With computers exponentially more powerful now than fifteen years ago, our battle against the password won't be a 'fair fight'." She plugged a cable into the tablet, then took the other end, which separated into two electrodes, and prodded them into connections on either side of the older machine. "I'm stressing the processor by applying slightly too much power, while simultaneously targeting it with a brute-force attack. We deluge it with millions upon millions of password combinations, starting with obvious solutions, and working from there." She pressed a key.

It took just under three seconds. A string of text and numbers appeared on the screen of the tablet. She looked at it, laughed, then held it up for Michael to see.

"mikeadams1234. Not exactly password best practice." Her fingers flickered over the old laptop's keyboard and the screen went dark again. Then it lit up to show a basic computer desktop. "We're in."

Michael watched as Millie navigated through some email records and miscellaneous admin, then found a file labelled confidential. Within was a folder labelled Darwin System.

She clicked on the folder. "Damn it, encrypted."

"Can you just force it again with those electrodes?"

"That was just the startup routine. This encryption is part of the full OS, and it's considerably more robust." She tapped away at the keyboard, then frowned. "Added to which there's an anti-tamper mechanism to prevent a mirror back-up of the drive. So whatever we do we need to get it right or we'll lose everything. This is going to require some work."

"You're not just trying to read it in private?"

"If I didn't want you to read it, there are easier ways to achieve that. But don't you see? The fact that it even exists is huge."

"Although the project was terminated."

"According to some random deep-web search. Maybe they passed the tech to another project, something hidden from general company reporting. We'd find it hard to trace."

"You're suggesting it was developed further?"

"It's a possibility. People like that will do anything to avoid paying royalties to inventors. Or their widows."

"That's quite a series of assumptions and guesses."

"Then let's turn them into facts. You're inside ZAT. I'm sure there will be records. Maybe they're using the Darwin technology today."

"Why would I risk that?"

Millie raised an eyebrow. "Your father may have been conned out of a fortune. Maybe you should run *that* past your mother?"

"It will just upset her. This just feels wrong." Michael stood up and walked over to the window. "And to be frank I think you're just stringing me along, spouting noble notions of seeking the truth, telling me what I want to hear, all to further your own exploits."

"That's not true. Listen, I can—"

"I just wanted some simple answers to some simple questions." He shook his head. "Coming here was a mistake. I'm going home."

OPPOSITE MILLIE'S APARTMENT BLOCK, CORY ASHCROFT SAT in his ten-year-old grey Ford Focus, pretending to read an article on his tablet while surreptitiously watching the building's main doors. A young man appeared, pulling on his coat, then walking off towards the Tube station. Cory swallowed hard.

Michael.

Cory wanted to run after him. He wanted to put an end to all the lies, to the years of subterfuge. But given the stakes, this wasn't the moment to do anything hasty; because now he had a new task to attend to: working out who exactly this Millie Wright was, and why she was in touch with Michael. Was she a girlfriend? A work contact? Or something more nefarious? He would certainly be finding out.

FIFTY-SIX

Once Michael left, Millie worked on his father's laptop into the early hours, but the encryption did not yield. After a few hours' sleep, she decided to phone in sick to work, then nipped out to acquire breakfast. Returning with egg muffins and coffee, she stepped from the lift and walked towards her front door.

It was ajar. And she had most definitely not left it that way.

She moved closer, listening, but heard nothing. Should she go in and investigate? Should she call for help first?

"Please, come in, Millie," called a man's voice from inside. "It's quite safe."

She frowned then pushed the door open. "I have a baseball bat."

"Of course you do. In the lounge."

Millie walked through and found a man in his fifties wearing a grey suit and brown shoes, sat cross-legged on her sofa. "What the hell are you doing here?"

MI5 Director Warwick Saxton uncrossed his legs. "I *was* waiting outside, but then two different people asked me what I was doing. At that point I thought it might be better if I stopped drawing attention to myself. It is my usual preference."

"So *you broke in*?"

"I picked the lock. My days in the field haven't been completely forgotten."

"You could have just messaged me. I hear nothing from anyone in your office for twelve months and then you just turn up?"

"You made it pretty clear you didn't want to be contacted."

"A position I have not changed." She glanced around. "Have you got a team with you?"

"I'm here alone. There's something I want your opinion on." He unlocked a dull grey tablet computer and handed it to her. "You usually have a valuable perspective."

"Last time you said I was using my skills purely for my own gain."

"You were. Now shut up and read."

Millie looked at the screen and hesitated. "This file is above my level of security clearance. Or it would be if I still had one."

"You've been elevated. Read it."

She skimmed the first few pages then looked up. "Kinek Consulting? Not heard of them."

"They do covert research. They're very good at it. But it seems they're also good at hiding themselves."

Millie flicked through more pages. "Why are you showing me this?"

"Five days ago, I met with Kinek to discuss a background check on Gregory Jenson."

"Why go external? And why run a check on Jenson now?"

"I'll get to that. There was, obviously, particular sensitivity."

"And did they find anything?"

"No. But that's not the issue. The representative I dealt with – his name was Morton – dropped a comment indicating he was aware of a top-secret government project. This prompted me to re-run background checks on Kinek as a precaution. And *apparently* Kinek does not exist."

"They ceased trading?"

"They've *never* existed." Saxton drummed his fingers on the coffee table. "That's why I'm here."

Millie frowned. "Last time we spoke, you fired me. And that was the polite part of the conversation."

"I didn't fire you. I terminated your consulting contract."

"Same difference."

"I wouldn't ask this lightly. The agency has been compromised and the usual procedures aren't appropriate because they're attempting to compromise *me*. A combination of threats and temptation." He paused. "Mostly threats."

"Then you should immediately report yourself."

"I'm well aware of what I'm supposed to do. But I'm also sure that is exactly what they want. I think Kinek is a much larger organisation than I had understood, with much grander plans. They know how to find information, and they know how to use it to achieve their ends."

"Why would they want to remove you specifically?"

"A classified project I'm running. They've already asked that I cancel it."

She rubbed her temples with her index fingers. "It's Parallel, isn't it? You've restarted it."

His face went pale. "How could you possibly know—"

"Why else would you be running a check on Jenson or talking to me? I hardly needed to run a Big Data analysis to spot *that* pattern."

"You're right. Except now it's being cancelled again."

Millie gave a snort. "Can nobody make up their mind?"

"You misunderstand me. *Kinek* have told me to cancel it. They say they have other clients with overlapping interests. If I don't play ball, they will release information that would compromise both Gregory Jenson and myself. I've already instructed Jenson of the cancellation decision. I'm fairly sure he intends to challenge it."

"No doubt. Did you tell him about Kinek?"

"Of course not. The fewer people who know, the better."

"So they've already made you lie."

He raised an eyebrow. "I've spent twenty years in the intelligence business; it's hardly the first time. I'm more concerned that this incident won't be the end. If Kinek have done this once, they will do it again."

"So what do you want me to do?"

"Use your special toolkit to work out what's going on."

"Do you not have a team of specialists in this type of research?"

"I have no idea who I can trust. I'm not sure whether this is an isolated incident or the tip of the iceberg. I'm not ruling anything out at this point."

"Yet you trust me?"

He gave a sigh. "I'm in this situation because old-fashioned thinking has led me to be outmaneuvered by an enemy I do not understand. I need a new solution, based on an entirely different approach. I need you." Saxton held out a secure hard-drive. "Everything we have about Kinek is on here. Much of it is unverified, but it should give you some leads you could not have found independently. Take this and evolve it into something comprehensive. I want to know everything about them."

Millie took the drive and hefted it in her hand. "What's in it for me?"

"A competitive consultancy fee." Saxton glanced around. "And another chance to see inside the house of secrets."

"And if I say no?"

"Don't."

Millie stared at the hard drive. "This is tempting. But working with you is always more complicated than you say." She held out the drive. "Sorry."

Saxton's face tightened. "Think about it for a couple of days."

"Just how desperate are you?"

"Desperate enough to come here and apologise."

"I must have missed that part."

"I think it's implied."

Millie gave a sigh. "I'm not promising anything. I've come

to realise that working for the 'man' isn't really my preference."

He stood up. "I'll leave you to your breakfast."

Millie stepped aside to allow Saxton to leave, locking the door behind him. She wasn't quite sure what to make of the visit she had just been paid, but she knew one thing: she needed to improve her home security.

FIFTY-SEVEN

Michael found it hard to get to sleep. At 4:30am he gave up entirely.

He needed to know more so he got in his car and drove. At just after 6:30am he was knocking loudly on a familiar front door. Nina pulled it open, clad in an old dressing gown.

"Michael? Whatever is the matter?"

"Can we talk?"

She opened the door wide. "I'll make coffee."

He followed her into the kitchen. Nina tipped ground coffee into a plunger, then after adding boiling water, forced it home with intent. She poured two mugs and placed them on the kitchen bench.

"What is so important," she asked, "that you drove out here without warning? And shouldn't you be at work in a few hours?"

Michael looked at the surface of his coffee. At first glance it was just black, featureless. But as he looked closer he saw whirls and eddies moving constantly in the hot liquid. "Did Dad ever talk to you about his work? I want to know about a project he was working on. A new computer system."

Nina shrugged. "When he wasn't programming, he was often working on some pie-in-the-sky scheme. He was a dreamer."

"And he worked at the weapons manufacturer, ZAT?"

"He worked for himself. He may have done a project for them. Why?"

"You never mentioned it."

Nina spread her hands. "Your father worked for a number of different companies. Nothing particularly exciting." She shook her head. "Least of all ZAT."

"So you *do* remember him working for them."

"Whatever he did for them, it didn't pan out. They terminated his contract with no notice. Gregory Jenson himself called to do it. Your father might have been an expert in computers, but he was rubbish at business. People will only throw money at a pipe-dream for so long. I'm sorry. It… upsets me to talk about him. After what he did."

"Yet you took fifteen years to throw out his stuff."

Nina sighed. "Love is complicated. At least it was when it involved your father."

"But what if his death *wasn't* what it appeared to be? What if that explosion in his workshop hid the truth?"

Nina looked at him. "Oh Michael. Your father's note was very clear."

Michael closed his eyes. "I'm not here to discuss that. I just think ZAT might have conned him… and conned you. This computer project, the one they cancelled – I think they developed it anyway. There might be something in Dad's old files. A forensic expert could compare it against what ZAT went on to develop."

"Most of your father's work was destroyed in the explosion. And the few things still in his study I threw away when I had the clear out."

"If his invention was made to work it would have been worth millions and you've never received a penny."

Nina reached over and placed her hand on his. "You're seeing connections where there are none. Even if there were any money in it, I wouldn't want a penny." She stood up. "I don't know why you're suddenly being like this. You're going to have to accept that there's no big secret to uncover, just an awful set of events that make no real sense. Please, just drop it."

Michael shook his head. "It's not really about the money. I want to know. I need to know." He hesitated. "What if someone killed him to take this project then made it look like a suicide?"

"I *understand the need to* look for meaning. But there is none here." She put a hand on his shoulder. "I don't know what has given you these crazy ideas." She smiled. "I know I've made a career out of saying I could make people do anything, though not a terribly good one—"

"Your book deserved to do better—"

Nina raised a hand. "My point is that I'm not going to try and make you do something. I just want you to take the time to think. Because there's been no conspiracy."

"I just thought something about Dad might provide some answers."

She squeezed his hand. "You and me both."

FIFTY-EIGHT

At 6:00am Morton was taking his regular early morning walk along the Thames, past the London Eye and the South Bank Centre. Across the grey river he could make out the Palace of Westminster and the Houses of Parliament: the domain of those that ran the country. At least those who thought they did. They spent their lives lying in the pursuit of self-serving goals; as a result they got nowhere. Whereas Morton was part of an organisation that exploited the truth, in the service of a collective plan. Kinek was built on the guiding principle that fact was better than fiction. As Kinek's rise had shown, the truth could be a powerful weapon.

Morton continued walking. It was still blissfully quiet: well before the morning rush-hour and way too early for the gangs of skateboarders to be out adding peril to the act of navigating the pavement. But not too early, for a decent cup of coffee. He smiled as his favourite kiosk came into view, the owner unfolding the shutters and placing his *'Any coffee you want, as long as it's an espresso'* sign on the pavement. Morton was about to call a good morning when his phone buzzed. It was a request for a meeting.

At his current location.

Now.

He looked up and saw a slim woman sitting on a bench

facing the river. Unlike last time, she wore black Lycra running-gear and a padded jacket, along with a baseball cap pulled low, but he recognised the plastic-rimmed glasses.

She turned and smiled. "Good morning, Morton."

He walked towards her. "Cortez." He sat at the other end of the bench. "Why aren't we following protocol? This location can't be secure."

"Urgency dictates. And the area is clear for our purposes." She handed over a red file.

"I haven't seen one of these in a while." Morton leafed through the document, his eyebrows starting to raise. "Maxwell Errington? You're joking?"

"This order comes directly from Marcia. The prediction has been verified. Errington has become a liability."

"He's been a reliable resource for years."

Cortez adjusted her glasses. "I'm not sure what you expect me to say. The Board has validated the strategy."

"And there are to be no warnings? No opportunity for him to correct?"

"That is not the plan. Experience indicates such warnings don't work."

Morton closed the folder and handed it back to her. "I note I'm to speak with Saxton again. What if he just has me arrested? *Again*?"

"That is one mistake we predict he will have learned from."

"Let's hope that proves accurate." He stood. "Have you met her? In person?"

"Who?"

"Marcia."

Cortez tipped her head to one side. "Why do you ask?"

"Given that you work directly for her, I wondered if—" He hesitated. "This all feels wrong."

"My purpose is not to make you feel *right*. My purpose is to deliver your instructions."

"And my purpose is to follow the truth. Isn't that what we're all supposed to do?"

Cortez straightened. "Are you suggesting I'm lying?"

"Is this to do with Project Green?"

"You need to remember the colour of the folder I've just given you."

Morton stared at her for several long moments, then nodded. "I will see it done."

FIFTY-NINE

MILLIE PUT DOWN THE SCREWDRIVER AND SURVEYED HER handiwork. The main door of her apartment now featured a somewhat ugly addition - a heavy duty padlock latched through a reinforced hasp - the lock itself so new it squeaked - something she'd address once she had the correct type of lubricant. With a bit more time, she'd come up with something more elegant, especially if she engaged the services of a locksmith. For now her apartment was better protected, even if the modifications were not permitted under the building's regulations - something she would worry about later. She had even tagged her high-value possessions with active tracers, disguised as radio station stickers, just to be on the safe side.

She put away her tools and returned to her office. Collapsing in her chair, she idly picked up the secure drive that Saxton had left, flipping it over in her hand. It felt dense, almost like what was stored on it was *heavy*, which the engineer in her knew was a ridiculous notion.

She couldn't help being drawn to the challenge, but she hated the very idea of working with the establishment again. And yet she was stuck on her other projects.

Millie had looked back over her research into Craig

Adams, re-reading the obituaries, reviewing the few photos she had located, and studying her notes on the rumours about Project Darwin. Craig had died in an explosion; a leak in a gas pipe in his private workshop, ignited by a tiny spark. There had been a full police investigation, which found that the leak had been created intentionally. There were traces of other chemicals at the scene, but nothing to raise any suspicion of foul play once they found the note. Of Craig there had been little to bury. He had been identified from dental records and trace DNA. She shook her head. What a way to lose your father.

Millie's phone vibrated with a message from an unknown number.

Need to speak with you now. It's Michael. Don't call my usual number: it's not secure.

The message ended with the address of coffee shop about a mile away and she was pleased to note that he was using a burner phone. At least he wasn't a complete idiot. She sent a quick reply, gathered her things, then closed the door and engaged the new padlock.

She waited an hour at the meeting spot, but Michael did not arrive. She sent several messages asking if there was a problem. There were no replies. Eventually she rang the number. An automated response informed her it was unobtainable. Millie stared at her phone. Was he just messing with her? It didn't seem like his kind of behaviour at all.

And then it clicked. Someone wanted her out of her apartment.

In seconds she was outside, hailing a taxi.

Back outside her apartment, she gasped for breath, having run up three floors. The door was still closed, but as she turned her key in the padlock she noticed that it didn't squeak as it had that morning. Swearing, she stuffed it into her pocket and ran inside, heading for her office, her gaze flicking around. Everything looked as orderly as she had left it. The secure drive hadn't been moved. Everything was there, except for one item.

Craig's laptop.

Millie growled. Whoever had taken it had known exactly what they were looking for.

SIXTY

At 9:00am, after a remarkably quick drive through rush hour traffic from his mother's house, Michael walked into Infinity's main boardroom. Around the table sat Maxwell Errington, Duncan Nichol and Kara.

"Nice of you to join us," Kara said, raising an eyebrow.

"I'm sorry," Michael replied, "I was delayed—"

"No need for apologies," Errington said. "I'm sure you were working late into the night, analysing reports, spotting patterns, making use of all that wonderful technology and information we've given you."

"Can we please focus," Nichol said. "All I want to know is that we're ready for the meeting with Saxton tomorrow."

"ZAT is my client," Errington replied. "I'll say when we're ready—"

"I would remind you, Max, that ZAT is the *firm's* client. And we can't afford to drop the ball on this."

"The analysis is almost complete. Kara, perhaps you'd like to share our findings?"

She nodded. "We've found a dozen similar examples where the government exercised discretion, reasonably or unreasonably, to end a major procurement. They're not binding precedents, but we believe they will be politically persuasive. We still haven't received the evidence that Saxton claims to have in connection with the drone attack, which will form the thrust of our unfairness argument. We've prepared a motion to formally demand it on a confidential basis."

Michael cleared his throat. "Also, we are prepared to formally refute their demand to release the project materials. If they want ZAT to stop, then they can't have their current work. That should focus their minds."

Errington nodded. "See, Duncan, we're all over it."

Nichol frowned. "Hardly sounds cut and dried—"

"Just let me get in the room with Saxton. Then there'll only be one outcome."

"Do you have something on him?" Nichol stabbed his finger on the table. "Tell me you're not going to threaten the head of MI5?"

"Threaten is such an inflammatory word. *Persuade* is a much better one. I will make him see the right way. As I'm sure Michael did with a certain hacker yesterday."

Nichol turned towards Michael. "What, exactly, did he have you do?"

Michael swallowed hard. "We identified a hacker attempting to breach ZAT's security. I met with her and made sure she understood the ramifications of her actions."

Errington nodded, adjusting his glasses. "See? Fast and effective. Michael did his job, and I'm sure this hacker will now do the right thing."

Nichol frowned. "Max, you can't conduct business this way anymore. The world has changed."

"A lot of people wish that it had. And, sure, technology advances. But people are still the same." He turned to Michael. "How did it feel, having that power over her?"

"I… er." Michael hesitated. "I was, as you said, just doing my job."

"It's OK to relish the moment."

Kara laughed. "He's still new. He'll adjust."

"Fair enough. And when he does, I'm sure he'll change everything." Errington pushed back his chair and stood up.

"Anyway, I've got another meeting to get to. Don't worry. I'll be at my persuasive best tomorrow." He gave Nichol a mock salute.

"Let's hope you're right," Nichol replied. "Or things are going to get really bad for all of us."

SIXTY-ONE

It was the middle of the night when Cory parked his tired old car in the heavily cobwebbed barn then, clutching a black backpack, made his way through the dark to the dilapidated cottage where he lived. Tucked on the edge of a wood in the grounds surrounding a Berkshire farmhouse some thirty miles west of London, the cottage was barely known even to those who knew the area well and, at first glance, did not look inhabited. He let himself in the back door, his heart still pounding.

Outside he heard the farm's dog barking loudly, as it did most nights, announcing every passing fox and rabbit. Cory felt the weight of the backpack and its contents, and his heart raced faster.

He opened the door to the basement and descended the creaking stairs. At the bottom was his overcrowded workshop, every square inch of wall and desk space full of equipment. With a dance of his fingertips, he fired up a number of computers, then placed the backpack on his chair. It was nearly 3:00am, but he wasn't ready for sleep. In fact a strong cup of coffee was in order. He turned to ascend the stairs and froze.

A woman stood there, pointing a gun at him.

"Back towards the chair," she said.

Cory stared at her face and realised he recognised her. "Please put that down." He took two steps backwards. "I don't mean you any harm."

"I'm not going to say the same." Her eyes flashed. "My name is Millie, but, given that you just broke into my apartment, you know that already. I tracked you." She held up a black device. It flashed with green light as she pointed it at the backpack. "Or rather, I tracked the sticker on the thing you took."

Cory sighed and eased the bag open, withdrawing a large flat slab of metal and plastic.

"And there we go," she said. "My laptop."

"Actually," he replied, "it's not yours. And I'm not sure why you had it."

She narrowed her eyes. "You're right: it's not my laptop." She smiled. "It's *yours*."

"Yes, that's what I was going to—"

"Of course the last photo I have of you was taken quite a while ago, but you haven't completely lost your looks."

He leaned back on the desk.

"The family resemblance is still there." She pointed the gun at him. "Hello, Mr Adams." She paused. "Or do you mind if I call you Craig?"

MILLIE STOOD, WAITING FOR THE MAN TO ANSWER.

He took a long time. Eventually he looked up. "Craig Adams is dead."

"I've spent a lot of time researching you recently: I know what you look like. Or at least what you looked like fifteen years ago."

His eyes flickered. "You're ruining everything."

"Am I? You started this when you broke into my apartment."

"You *stole* my laptop."

"Somebody *sent* me your laptop." She paused. "Has someone been holding you captive?"

"It's a long and difficult story."

"Does it involve Darwin?"

He looked at her sharply.

"It was on your laptop. A five-year-old could have broken the encryption with today's computers. At least part of it anyway."

He scowled at her. "If we're going to talk, perhaps you could stop pointing the gun at me?"

Millie looked at the handgun, then pointed it away from him. She squeezed the trigger and there was a loud click. A yellow splat formed on the wall.

"A paintball gun?"

"It did the job." She placed the weapon in a holster at her belt. "Does Michael know you're alive? Does his mother?"

"Nobody knows. And it has to stay that way."

"How *are* you still alive? I read the newspaper articles about the explosion. They found your body."

"You ask a lot of questions."

"It's what I do. And if you don't answer them I'll go report you to the police for breaking and entering."

"You're not going to do that." He pulled a pistol from a concealed holster. "Just so we're clear," he said quietly, "*this* is not a paintball gun."

"I see that. Don't do anything stupid now."

"What I do will be logical and necessary. I'll be doing it to save my son's life."

"I don't believe you."

"You really think you know me, just from your poxy research? That you can predict what I'll do?"

She narrowed her eyes. "Isn't that what your computer system was supposed to do?"

He jerked the gun. "I'm just trying to protect my son. How do you know him?"

"Let's just say our interests are aligned."

"Something related to your blog?"

Millie sighed. "Is my side hustle the worse-kept secret in London?"

"It's on a public site. How is it supposed to be a secret?"

"My identity is the secret."

"It took about five minutes to uncover. Have you not tried hacking yourself?"

"Look, could you put that gun down? You're scaring me."

"I've been in hiding for fifteen years. You are the first person to realise I am in fact still alive. Now I'm trying to work out what I do. You probably *should* be scared."

"Maybe I can help you. If the truth behind why you faked your death has anything to do with Darwin, I might be one of the few people who can actually understand what's going on. After all, I know what it was designed to do. And that *really* scared me."

"Probably the smartest thing you've said yet." Craig lowered the gun. "Are you thirsty? I could murder a drink."

Millie frowned. "That's an unnerving choice of words, but sure."

THEY SAT IN CRAIG'S LOUNGE, NURSING LARGE GLASSES OF whisky.

Millie frowned. "Say that last part again."

Craig nodded. "Like I said, I realised that Darwin was far more powerful than I had intended. And that someone very dangerous indeed had become interested in it."

"How did you know that?"

"Darwin told me."

Millie blinked. "Darwin *told* you?"

"Darwin was a predictive analytics engine. It made forecasts based on available data. I ran a number of tests. Its accuracy was above 99%, though only where it had sufficient data and sufficient time to run its analysis."

"So who was the threat?"

"The system didn't know. You have to understand, it was

far from perfect. It had severe limitations, frustrating constraints that meant it could only do a small part of what you might ask. I never got to the bottom of it before I had to act."

"Meaning faking your own death?"

"I had to destroy Darwin and stop anyone ever building another. If I'd still been around, they would have done anything to coerce me, including threatening Michael. And if I'd refused, they'd have killed him. It was the only way."

"You've been living off the grid for fifteen years. Why reveal yourself now?"

"I heard Michael had changed jobs. I've been keeping the most distant of tabs on him, but when I realised who he was working for now I knew something was wrong. Infinity Law used to represent ZAT."

"They still do – it's why I met Michael. ZAT worked out that I was checking them out and sent him as their lawyer to drop a few threats hoping I'd do the sensible thing and back off."

Craig shook his head. "That doesn't make sense. Jenson would normally fight back immediately with something more than a few threats."

"Perhaps he's changed. Or perhaps he's just got bigger fish to fry."

"Maybe. I'm not sure how this laptop survived with Darwin schematics onboard. I need to work out what it means."

"Are you going to tell Michael you're alive?"

He sighed. "Have you been listening? Leave me with my laptop and you can forget that you ever saw me. You don't want to be mixed up in this."

"You're sure Darwin was actually destroyed?"

Craig closed his eyes. "The working system was in the barn. Everything else was incomplete or non-functional. But this laptop should have been destroyed with everything else. It should have been in that barn. I've never thought to check, and of course doing so would have been a risk."

Millie frowned. "How could you 'check'?"

"If Darwin is in operation, if it is connected to the net, then it will leave a trace for those who know where to look. I'd have to construct a special piece of hardware, but if it's there I can find it."

"How hard would that be?"

"Not very." He closed his eyes in thought. "You could help me get the parts."

"What makes you think I'd help you?"

"Because I've read your blog. That's the kind of person you are."

She smiled. "Fair enough. Tell me what you need."

SIXTY-TWO

Millie set the bag of parts down on the table, then began carefully pulling out the components, each wrapped in its own clear, antistatic bag.

"Where's the motherboard I specified?" Craig asked, peering through reading glasses at the receipt.

"They didn't have it. The one I bought is functionally equivalent."

Craig made a tutting sound. "I'll tell you what is—"

"I'm helping you out at great personal risk, so be nice. Or you can go and find some other technical genius to assist you."

He raised an eyebrow. "Great personal risk?"

"If I was able to track you down, who knows who else might be able to do it? They might turn up with something more dangerous than a paintball gun."

"You weren't looking for me when you tracked me down: you were just looking for your laptop."

"Then maybe someone else will come looking for that. It's tied to your past."

"It's one loose end, which I'm here to tidy up."

"So, how will this scanner thingie find traces of Darwin if it's out there?"

"There's a command hidden in the core code to send out a signal every time it's asked a question."

"And if you do find something how do we work out who's behind it?"

"I don't know who to suggest other than ZAT." He tore open one of the antistatic bags. "Nobody else knew about it apart from my wife and a couple of Jenson's team, including his external lawyer."

"What if it was stolen from ZAT?"

Craig laughed. "Have you seen their security systems? If somebody did steal from Jenson, he would never let it lie." He picked up another component. "Can you switch the soldering iron on?"

"What did your last slave die of?"

He raised an eyebrow. "If you think I'm in the mood for banter, then you clearly haven't thought through what it must be like to spend fifteen years in hiding, misleading your loved ones to believe that you're dead."

Millie scowled and handed him the components. "Whatever. Just build stuff."

THREE HOURS LATER THE SYSTEM WAS READY TO SWITCH ON. Millie looked at it with a skeptical eye: it didn't look like it would win any design awards. "Should I stand back?" she asked. "Maybe retreat to another building for safety purposes?"

"Very funny," Craig replied. He plugged in the power supply and a number of lights blinked on. A large flat screen began streaming lines of code. "Once it's finished booting, we'll get a graph of the scan results." He checked a cable at the back of the system. "It'll show nothing or faint traces in the form of tiny disparate dots. Either way, I expect it will take a while for the system to report."

"Shall I make tea then?"

Craig started to reply but the screen flashed. A simple graph appeared.

"Is it done already?" Millie asked.

Three tiny white dots flashed onto the screen. Then a further three.

"Could just be false positives," he said.

A dozen more dots appeared.

"How many were you expecting?" Millie asked.

Further dots blinked into view.

"Isn't that a lot?"

Craig glared at the screen. "Yes, it..." More dots peppered the display. Within ten seconds the screen was mostly covered in white. And still the dots kept accumulating.

"What does it mean?" said Millie.

"It means," Craig replied, "that the system has been everywhere." He held his head in his hands. "This makes no sense. No sense at all. This is *my* system. It's like it never stopped running.

"How is it possible? I thought I was the only one who could have re-built it. This is far, far worse than bad. This is the worst scenario imaginable. Jenson must have planned ahead and made full copies in secret before I wiped everything. Perhaps he guessed what I was planning. He's built the system, and it's been running for years."

"You're sure it's him?"

"Nobody else knew about my work."

Millie cleared her throat. "Earlier you said there was a risk to doing this check. What did you mean?"

Craig swore and pulled out the power supply. "What I meant was that it might detect us 'detecting'. We need to leave. Before they come to find us."

IT TOOK MILLIE AND CRAIG THREE MINUTES TO LOAD UP THE equipment. After a brief argument, they agreed to take

Millie's car and in short order she was behind the wheel, retracing her route through the narrow roads.

Craig kept glancing over his shoulder. "Put your foot down."

"You think we're being followed?"

"I'm not sure of anything anymore."

"Beat yourself up on your own time. For now we need to decide where should we go." She turned the car onto an A-road towards London.

"I don't see we have a choice. We have to go to ZAT."

"Of course," she replied. "The simple solution. Infiltrate a hi-tech mega-corporation with next-gen security. Or perhaps we should just knock on the front door and demand a meeting with Gregory Jenson?"

"I acknowledge this won't be straightforward."

"Are you even sure it's them?"

"Whatever happened has to have at least started there. And then there's the fact that my system could not be operated without considerable resource."

"For someone who's been hiding out all this time, you don't seem very prepared."

"I have some contingencies, but I just didn't foresee this. I'll think of something."

"Fine. First we're going to my place."

Craig watched the corridor through a crack in the door. Millie flew around her apartment, pulling out clothes, papers and equipment. But mostly equipment. She zipped up three large holdalls then turned to Craig. "How did you know Michael was visiting me?"

"As I said, I heard he'd changed jobs. I had a private detective on retainer to monitor any changes in his life."

"Why not just track him online?"

"So there were no digital traces leading back to me."

"Unless the private detective left any."

"He's pretty old-school. Doesn't even have a website. I found him from a business card he stuck on a noticeboard, so I doubt he left any traces." Craig pointed at the hard drive she had in her hand. "What's that?"

"Another project I'm working on."

He leaned closer. "Looks unusual. Military maybe?"

"Haven't you been out of the loop for years?"

Craig shrugged. "I keep my hand in. So what was it that made you look into ZAT?"

"Someone sent your laptop to me after an anonymous tip suggested I look into the company and the Darwin Project."

"Do you get many such tips?"

"Some." She hesitated. "What are you getting at?"

"Somebody really wanted you to research the company. And they wanted you to do it now."

"To what end? You'll be saying they wanted me to meet Michael next. Or you. But if we can stay on topic, what's the plan?"

Craig looked at his fingernails. "We go to ZAT's HQ. But instead of knocking on the front door, we break in to see what we can find."

Millie laughed. "Really? I presumed you were joking. Shall we pick up a couple of gold bars from the Bank of England while we're at it? It's a plan destined for failure, and between you and me, I'd rather not get arrested."

"Getting arrested is a minor risk compared to the risks if ZAT are running my system. You, of all people, must recognise that."

"You built it."

"And I shouldn't have. But I tried to fix things. Clearly I underestimated the task."

Millie looked around the room. "I have everything I need. I might be able to help with scouring ZAT's systems, but I can only do that if we can get inside the building. And as far as I know, that will be impossible."

"You leave that part to me."

SIXTY-THREE

MICHAEL SAT WITH GREGORY JENSON, KARA AND MAXWELL Errington in a Whitehall conference room, all staring across the table with serious expressions. At precisely 10:00am, Warwick Saxton walked in, accompanied by MI5's legal counsel.

When they had taken their seats, Saxton cleared his throat. "I want to be clear. This meeting is a courtesy. Our presence should in no way indicate that ZAT has any grounds for appeal or complaint in relation to the recent decision." His eyes flickered towards Jenson. "We followed a fair process. All the participants knew the basis on which they took part. There were no guarantees. We could have pulled out of the process at any time, especially if necessary to protect taxpayer funds."

Kara looked up from her notes. "In relation to a project they would likely never know anything about?"

Saxton sighed. "That's not relevant. Our discretion remains absolute. There are plenty of precedents for such decisions on projects. ZAT has experienced it before."

"But never so far down the track. And never over a completely unproven issue. Do you really think that is fair, given the costs of participation? What kind of a message do you want to send the private sector?"

"This was a unique set of circumstances."

Jenson stabbed his finger on the table. "Warwick, you were there at GCHQ a week ago. Everything we discussed suggested you needed Parallel now more than ever. What has changed? Surely nothing is more important than the project?"

"I appreciate that you're upset, but the fact remains that we were, and we are, acting within our rights—"

"Yes, but why? That's what I want to know. Given the years of effort we've put into this. Given the money already spent—"

Saxton held up his hands. "You know why."

"Your assertion that I used ZAT weaponry in a private capacity? You've provided zero evidence."

Saxton's cheek twitched. "You're going to have to accept that, as an intelligence organization, we cannot disclose our full decision process."

"You needed this system. You still need the system. What's going on?"

"At some point, you have to draw a line. And what's perhaps unbelievable is the situation has got worse."

"What," Errington asked, "are you talking about?"

"Other evidence has come to my attention."

"Really? And what else are you saying Mr Jenson has done now?"

"Nothing." Saxton folded his arms. "This evidence is about you, Max."

Jenson spun on him. "What is he talking about?"

Errington shrugged. "I have no idea."

"Really?" Saxton asked. "Perhaps you'd like to explain your recent meeting with Regina Rose on board her yacht."

MI5's legal counsel tapped into his laptop, then spun it around. A grainy video file was playing. Despite the low quality, it unmistakably showed Errington shaking hands with Rose.

"Max," growled Jenson. "Explain."

Errington rubbed his index fingers on his temples. "Rose has been a client for some time. I picked her up by accident and I've been trying to find a way out ever since. But she's a hard client to fire. If you suggest it, she typically threatens to kill you. Especially when she wants something. And right now that's for me to broker a deal with you. Obviously I said no."

"And you never mentioned this to me? Anyway, if you turned her down, why didn't she kill you?"

"Maybe *you* should ask her. Because let's not forget, you also used to have dealings with Rose."

Jenson's cheek twitched. "I've heard enough of this." He walked towards the door. "Consider yourself fired, Max." Then he left the room.

Saxton stood up and glared at Errington. "Expect your law firm to be the target of a government enquiry in the very near future. I thought you were a good guy, Max, but if I never speak to you again, it will be too soon." He raised his voice. "This meeting is over."

SIXTY-FOUR

THE CAR WAS LARGE, GREY AND SEVERAL YEARS OLD. WHILE nobody would call it shabby, it was certainly unremarkable. Saxton used it only on those occasions when he had to lose the rather oppressive team of people usually watching his every move. He drove half an hour north, then parked in a nondescript car park next to some neatly tended gardens. He emerged from the vehicle, raised an umbrella against the light drizzle, and walked towards a cast-iron bench that already had a single familiar occupant. "Thanks for taking my call," Saxton said, as he brushed the water-drops from the bench before sitting.

"Unlike you to come out without your security detail," Errington replied.

"There aren't many people I trust enough to do so."

"And yet you still shafted me in that meeting. I'd hate to see what you do to your enemies."

"It was nothing personal. You must have known your past was going to catch up with you at some point."

"Don't try and spin me that nonsense. You've surely known about me and Rose for some time. Why bring it up today? Do you have some grudge against Jenson, or is it about ZAT?"

Saxton rubbed a hand through his grey hair. "Of course not."

"Then help me out here. Because I'm looking a considerable idiot right now."

"Some things are more important than your reputation."

Errington glared. "How long have we known each other, Warwick? I just want to know what is behind this. Maybe I can even help you."

Saxton chewed on his lower lip. "People around me keep getting information that changes their minds about important things. It's like someone has some master plan that is pulling all our strings." He paused. "I'm being coerced."

Errington's eyebrows raised.

"I've been ordered to take ZAT off Parallel. I was provided with the information about Regina Rose and you, and told to use it against you."

"And the evidence about Jenson and the drones?"

"Also provided to me." Saxton gave a sigh. "Have you heard of a consultancy by the name of Kinek?"

"Why?"

"This is no time to be coy."

Errington sucked in his cheeks. "I've passed a couple of clients in their direction when they needed a problem solver."

"I thought that's what you did?"

"I focus on legal problems. Kinek operates in a different sphere."

"A few years ago, MI5 needed to locate and recover some stolen classified data. We'd exhausted every lead open to us when I received an approach from Kinek. I was told that for a relatively small sum of money the situation could be resolved. I had them thoroughly vetted and everything checked out, so I went ahead." He took a deep breath. "I saved lives that day. Everything worked out beautifully and I never looked back. Since then I've used them many times and the results have been impressive. You could say that they got me where I am today but they've never asked anything of me in return besides fair payment. Until last week. After completing a background check on Jenson for me, they started inquiring about Parallel – which they should have known nothing about. Obviously this raised a flag, so I re-ran the background check on them." He stared off into the distance for a while, seeming to forget that he had company.

"And?" Errington pressed.

"They've vanished. All the data we validated previously has evaporated. Their offices are not only no longer occupied, but it appears they've never been occupied. It's like Kinek never existed. Except, of course, they keep making demands of me."

"That suggests an incredible level of capability."

"They seem to cut through security like it isn't there. I assume they have a network of agents and spies, along with some pretty amazing technical resources. It must be a huge organisation. I've no idea how they are remaining undiscovered."

"So what's their interest in Parallel?"

"The project was part of an initiative to create our own in-house capability in complex problem-solving. I'm assuming Kinek prefer that we remain bound to them."

"So they told you to kill the project?"

"They're being quite insistent."

Errington cleared his throat. "And if you don't cooperate?"

"They'll go to the press with the evidence about Jenson. And they'll show that I withheld it."

"So why are you telling me now?"

"Because I've decided to fight back. And I thought I could use the help of someone who has been affected too. We haven't always seen eye to eye, but I respect your results."

"I don't know if I can help this time."

Saxton stood up. "I'm sorry, Max. I shouldn't have told you all this. I've probably risked your safety. They could even be listening right now." He pulled out a small black box from his pocket. "This thing is supposed to jam all communications: I hope it's working right."

Errington looked around. "Back in my day you could trust that if you were alone, you really were alone. Now somebody could be eavesdropping from a mile away, recording our every word. The world has changed, and it's only changing more and more every day. Look, maybe you should just accept this thing about Parallel. Nobody's got hurt, so perhaps the best way to keep things that way is not make waves." He paused. "But of course if you need a good lawyer you've got my number."

Saxton patted him on the shoulder. "Thanks. But I'm the head of MI5. I still have a few tricks up my sleeve. They won't bring me down that easily."

Errington stood and smiled. "I believe you."

THE EAVESDROPPERS WERE ONLY 800 METRES AWAY, AND THE jamming device had proved no obstacle. The two operatives listened intently until they watched the men go their separate ways. As expected, there was a call on their satellite phone almost immediately.

"It's time to act. This issue cannot be allowed to grow."

The operative paused. "He is a man of some importance."

"It is necessary. Do whatever you need to do to take him out of the game."

SIXTY-FIVE

MICHAEL FOLLOWED KARA THROUGH THE FRONT DOORS OF Infinity's offices. She ignored the receptionist, removing an access card from her purse and swiping it over the lift's control panel. There was a soft chime as the doors opened. Inside, she pressed the button for the restricted ninth level.

"How long did you work here before they gave you that card?" he asked.

She glanced at him as the lift began to rise. "Max sorted it when I was working on a special project with him." She tucked the card back in her purse. "Now you need to focus because this isn't going to be easy. In fact, best if you let me do the talking."

"Is Mr Errington OK?"

"Max is Max. You should worry about your own hide right now. When a law firm loses a big client, the partners tend to look for someone to blame."

"You mean us?"

The lift doors chimed and opened. Duncan Nichol was waiting for them, his face thunderous.

"What the hell happened?" he asked without preamble, then raised a hand. "Wait, not out here." They followed him into his office and waited until he had slammed the door closed.

"There was a complication," Kara replied. "It seems our illustrious senior partner recently met with Regina Rose."

Nichol jerked as if stung. "I thought Max had severed that relationship years ago. How did Jenson react?"

"He suggested he was going to look for alternative representation."

Nichol turned and walked over to an ornate whisky decanter, picking up one of the matching tumblers next to it. "Could this day get any worse?"

Kara cleared her throat. "Hold that thought. Saxton is going to order a government audit of the firm."

"What?"

"You know," Kara said, "that I would normally be the last person to suggest this, but Max hasn't been himself. He seems... distracted. Perhaps it might be time to reduce his workload." She blinked twice, as if trying to dislodge an eyelash. "Although obviously that's something for the partners to decide on."

Nichol shook his head, then pulled out his phone and dialed a number. "Max, it's Duncan. Call me. It's urgent." He hung up and looked at Kara. "You were supposed to rein the old guy in: make sure he didn't do anything stupid."

"Nobody tells Max what to do."

"As I said when you were promoted to Senior Associate, you need to avoid buying into his bullshit."

Kara flexed one fist. "If you've got something on your mind, Duncan, then say it."

He frowned. "Go home. Take a couple of days off. We'll talk next week about how you go forward. Or not."

She stared at him, flared her nostrils, then spun and walked back towards the lifts.

Michael quickly followed her when Duncan waved him away. He managed to squeeze between the lift doors just as they were closing.

"What are we supposed to do now?" he asked.

"We carry on doing our jobs."

"Why did you stick the knife in with Errington?"

She raised an eyebrow. "Sometimes you need to notice which way the river is flowing." She tapped a finger on his chest. "Max has had a great run, but it's time for the new guard now."

"Meaning you?"

"I meant us. But maybe you don't want it."

Michael shook his head. "I'm no quitter."

She tipped her head to one side. "I'm glad to hear it. It means we have work to do. I think we'd best stay out of Duncan's way for today. We'll reconvene back at my place." She scribbled an address on the back of a business card. "See me there in an hour."

SIXTY-SIX

It was 6:30pm when the taxi dropped Michael at Kara's apartment building in Islington. He stared up at the modern five storey block then pressed the intercom. There was a long delay, then a metallic voice crackled. *"Come on up. Fifth floor."*

The door buzzed and he walked in, nodding at the security guard as he stepped into the lift. In moments he was on the fifth level. The landing had just a single door, slightly ajar.

"In here," called Kara.

Michael strode down a corridor, finding himself in a large open-plan living area, floor to ceiling windows looking west across the rooftops. Kara sat on the sofa, wrapped in a dark-red bathrobe. She held a large brandy glass in her hand.

Michael hesitated in the doorway. "I'm sorry. I didn't realise you weren't dressed..."

She raised an eyebrow. "I needed a bath after today. Get yourself a drink."

Michael walked over to the kitchen area and grabbed some juice from the fridge.

Kara sighed. "No. A *drink*." She nodded at a large bottle of aged cognac with a glass next to it. "We've earned it."

Michael poured himself a small measure and sat on the armchair opposite her.

She raised her glass and nodded at him. "Here's to new beginnings at Infinity."

"You sound very positive. What are we going to do about ZAT?"

"The damage is done. We just need to move on."

"So there *are* elements outside our control."

She laughed. "Don't be bandying words like those around the office. The point is that nothing is *supposed* to be."

"I thought Max would have a lever with Saxton like we had with Chalmers?"

Kara tipped her head on one side. "My, my, Michael

Michael held his hands up. "I'm just assuming. But I guess if there was a point of leverage we'd have found it and used it."

"Maybe we did, but it hasn't borne fruit. Does it matter now?"

Michael took a sip of his own brandy. "You keep going on about how important it is to know more than everyone else, but how does it work? I mean, with the internet anyone can find out the answer to almost any question. How do we maintain the edge?"

"They still have to know which questions to ask." She rotated her glass slowly. "I need to talk something through with you, and I would value your input. That's as close I'm going to get to giving you a compliment, so enjoy it."

"Thanks."

"This is all very important to my future role and to the continued success of… the initiative."

Michael looked at her. "You mean the firm?"

Kara sighed. "Shall I tell you what I want?"

"Be my guest."

"Good, because I'm your boss and you have to do what I say. Now stand up."

Michael got cautiously to his feet as she moved over to him, brushing a fleck off his jacket lapel. He went to step back, but was blocked by the armchair.

She put her glass down and placed her palms on his

shoulders. "I was told you were special. That we couldn't do this without you. That you were fundamental to the… plan."

"I'm not following you." A mixture of perfume and cognac wafted over him.

She closed her eyes, leaned towards him, seeming to sniff the air.

Michael took a step to one side, pushing her hands from his suit. "Kara, I'm… What are you doing?"

Kara tipped her head. "When we first met, I asked you if you were too busy to share a drink with the person who's going to change your life. What's your answer tonight?"

Michael swallowed. "I'd better go."

"Ah, but I *predict* that you won't." She moved closer, her lips centimetres from his. Her lipstick was blood red, glistening from the cognac. She reached forward and kissed him, letting her lips linger on his.

For a moment his brain froze. Then he pulled back sharply. "You shouldn't have… I'd like you to stop."

"Really?" She shrugged. "Anyway, I have what we need. As for whether we can do this without you, I guess we're going to find out."

"What are you talking about?" Michael asked with a frown. "You know, if we're speaking of good questions, did you really text me that day to set up the interview? I certainly don't remember replying to you."

"Does it matter? It's all just part of the plan."

"What does that mean?"

"You think I just happened to be there the day you were *fired*?"

Michael froze. "You knew? Did the firm know?"

She coughed, and gave an irritated look. "Just a guess. You looked desperate." She picked up her glass and took a sip. "Finish your drink."

Michael stared at his glass. "I think I've had enough."

She reached forward again, her fingers wrapping around his arm.

He pulled back, but her grip was startlingly strong and,

for the briefest moment, he wasn’t sure he could pull free. "I’m going to leave now."

Kara snorted. "Fine. I certainly have more important places to be." She collapsed back onto the sofa. "Just don’t walk out with one of my best glasses."

Michael set his cognac down and made for the door.

"You need to look to the future," she called. "Don’t get stuck in the past."

SIXTY-SEVEN

Millie parked her car opposite the ZAT building. It was gone midnight and the road was almost deserted, but there was still a sense of activity. The City of London never really slept. She glanced at her passenger and realised Craig had not looked up at the looming office block; he remained engrossed in his laptop. She poked him on the shoulder. "In your own time."

"I'm working here."

"Since you appear to be unaware, I thought I'd flag that we have arrived."

He gave a snort. "Of course I'm aware. I've been running a penetration test on the building's security for the last five minutes."

"Good luck with that. I've spent the last few days getting nowhere."

"Ah, but I used to work there and left behind a gateway system. The good news is that it still seems to be operational."

"And you waited till now to tell me this?"

"Like I said, I didn't know if it would work. But it's fine: I'm busy deactivating alarms and looping the CCTV footage as we speak."

"We can just walk in the front door?"

"That would be ridiculous. More a side door." He

yawned. "Why are you so anxious? I thought this type of thing would be your bread and butter."

"I tend towards remote activism. Site visits aren't my thing." She glared at him. "If this goes wrong… I don't want to end up in jail."

"Then you clearly don't appreciate what's at stake. Now let's go."

"We can't leave the car here. We'll be towed inside twenty minutes, even at this time of night."

"No we won't," Craig replied, rummaging in his bag. He pulled out a small printer and plugged it into his laptop. In seconds a coloured square of cardboard emerged. He handed the card to her.

Millie frowned. "A resident parking permit? Is it real?"

"Real enough."

She shook her head and placed it on the dashboard. Then she looked up at the aluminium and glass building across the street.

"Don't think about it too much," he said.

"Overthinking is what I do."

"We stand a very good chance of pulling this off. Over 60%, by my calculations."

"I'm going to jail, aren't I?"

"Not if someone shoots you first." Craig opened his car door.

She glared at him. "Speaking of which, you're leaving your gun behind, aren't you?"

He frowned. "It might come in handy. It's quite the tool of persuasion."

"And if someone sees it, they might just shoot you before giving you a chance to speak."

He shrugged, then pulled the weapon from his belt. "Wasn't loaded anyway." He placed it under the seat. Now follow me."

GREGORY JENSON WALKED INTO HIS PENTHOUSE OFFICE, darkened the windows, and pulled out his mobile phone, pressing the top number on his speed dial list.

Teresa replied almost immediately. "What's up, Dad?"

"You OK, sweetheart?"

"I'm bored. Where's Astrid? She's so much nicer than your other security people. They have no sense of humour."

Jenson frowned. He hadn't received an update from Kelly. "She's running an errand for me."

"They won't let me outside even for a moment. I'm going stir-crazy stuck in the house."

"Look, I'll get Kelly to take you out to the Swiss apartment in a few days' time."

"Will you be there?"

"Not straight away. There are some things I need to take care of—"

"Fine, whatever. I'm tired. Let's talk in the morning."

Jenson heard her disconnect. He sighed and poured himself an excessively large glass of twenty-year-old single malt. He rarely drank in the office, but he needed something to adjust his thinking. His daughter was safe, but his other problems were very much ongoing.

All the time he had spent briefing Errington and the Infinity team, the hours wasted producing the documentation they had demanded – and they had demanded *everything* relating to Parallel – all of it for nothing. Maxwell Errington had *lied* to him. He was working for the woman who had tried to kidnap his daughter. But then Errington had been removed from the equation by the perfect counterplay.

Once again Jenson was left puzzling why the government had been so quick to cancel Parallel, notwithstanding the crime he was alleged to have committed. The government *needed* this system. They were falling behind in intelligence analysis. You had to run fast even to stand still these days with technology. Did they have some alternative he was not aware of? It seemed improbable. There was nothing like Parallel. There never had been.

Except, of course, for Darwin. Similar in its brilliance, it had been ahead of Parallel in its software design, though of course fifteen years behind in terms of its hardware. But the system had been completely unintelligible without Craig Adams to explain it. Its logical structure had been apparently random, almost organic. No one else could make it work. So it was consigned to a historical footnote. After all, perhaps it would never have worked like they had hoped. But none of this helped: it was all in the past. He had to deal with the now.

He had visited Duncan Nichol to formally fire that sorry excuse for a law firm. It had made him feel better, briefly, watching the pain in the man's eyes as he saw their future billings evaporate. But it had solved nothing. He still had a cancelled project.

Jenson knocked back the single malt and poured himself another. Perhaps he was thinking about this the wrong way. Why would someone want to stop the project? Were his scientists compromised? Were they working for someone else? He shook his head. He had worked with Chow for years. And, like the others, his reputation would be built on this piece of work: they all needed it to succeed. So was a third party involved? He had many business rivals who would love to see him fail, but none had the necessary reach.

Deciding he needed a change of scenery, he descended in the lift to the laboratory level. He arrived at Research Room 8, went through the lengthy access process, then stepped inside the tidy room, pacing slowly about as he tried to think the problem through anew. Clearly one of his assumptions about the situation was wrong.

He pulled out his phone and called Saxton on his private line. It went straight to voicemail.

Jenson frowned. '*This phone is never switched off*,' Saxton had said.

Was something wrong? Was he caught up in some sort of a major incident? He'd just opened the BBC News page on his phone when he noticed that the building had sent him a security alert.

Someone had breached the new building protocols Kelly had recommended. They had done so using codes that would have worked without question a week ago. Growling, Jenson turned and pressed a hidden button. It scanned and confirmed his thumbprint, then a panel slid back to reveal a number of weapons. Without hesitation he selected a semi-automatic rifle.

If he was being accused of using his technology to defend himself and his family, he might as well actually do it.

SIXTY-EIGHT

SAXTON'S LONDON HOME WAS A FIVE-STOREY VICTORIAN mansion in west London. It was near the centre of a terrace, opposite a row of similar properties, all painted a splendid white with sharp black trimming. The woman in black knew that there was a permanent security presence outside, even when the house was not occupied. The street was brightly lit and be-decked with CCTV. It made covert entry almost impossible. Which was why she stood on the roof, having climbed into position across a number of the adjoining properties, disabling various security measures on the way. Using an insulated tool, she popped open the lock on a trapdoor into the roof. In a blur she dropped through. Rising from a crouch, she pulled out a handheld device.

The data displayed showed the four occupants of the house were exactly where she expected them to be. The two security officers were in the downstairs lobby, reading the newspaper. The house maid was in her room, having fallen asleep while reading too. The family were all away for the week except the man of the house, who was working late in his study.

The top floor of the house was a loft conversion. Two bedrooms and a small gymnasium, fitted out with an expensive treadmill and exercise bike that looked like they had not been used. She moved past them and descended a flight of stairs. There were CCTV cameras on each floor, but their lights were off. She ignored three more bedrooms, and descended to the fourth floor. She kept her footsteps light: there was no reaction from below.

The office door was closed. She padded soundlessly towards it then paused, listening intently. No one else in the house moved. She eased the door open.

Warwick Saxton looked up, his eyes widening. "I didn't see a meeting in my diary."

"No," replied Astrid Kelly, stepping inside and closing the door softly. "I thought I'd just drop in unannounced."

"You're lucky I didn't shoot you."

"You're lucky you didn't try." She shifted her injured shoulder. "Now are you going to offer me a drink? I believe I've earnt it."

KELLY SAT ON THE EDGE OF SAXTON'S DESK, EACH OF THEM holding a crystal tumbler with a generous measure of aged cognac. One display screen showed a picture of the lobby, the other had layouts of each floor, marked with coloured icons to place the guards and the maid.

"You're supposed to be maintaining your cover at ZAT and protecting Jenson. Should I be worried?"

"Probably." Kelly took a sip of her cognac. "Jenson did not instigate the micro-drone attack on his daughter's kidnappers. The group that has been monitoring him has become active. I was trying to clarify who they were when one of their operatives intercepted me: a highly-skilled woman, clearly a professional killer."

"Do you need a clean-up crew? I don't really want those requests coming from me. You know there's a secure line to call—"

"If only. She is very much at large, and I should be dead.

She was waiting for me when I went to collect equipment from a ZAT black site in Wapping."

"Jenson has a black site in *Wapping*?"

"Yes, but that's not the interesting part. She knew exactly who I was. And what I was doing. Nobody should have that intel."

"Did she mention Kinek?"

"It didn't come up. I was too busy dodging her arrows."

"Literal arrows? From a bow?"

Kelly nodded. "I was hit by one coated in toxin, after which I fell in the Thames. It's pure luck that I was fished out by a passing cargo vessel."

"And the toxin?"

"I've not been able to run an analysis yet. I've been focussing on staying dead – at least from their perspective. I thought it might give us an advantage."

"Good thinking. But I disagree with you on one thing: the pure luck part. Nothing at the moment is happening by chance. Someone has a grand plan, we're just not seeing who yet. There are a number of things I need you to—"

An alarm sounded. They turned to the screens. Someone had knocked at the front door. External cameras flicked on showing five armed response officers standing outside along with a Chief Inspector.

"They're here for me?" Kelly asked. "I'd swear I wasn't seen."

Saxton shook his head. "They're here for me. I was told this would happen. Without doubt they'll find evidence hidden in this house backing up whatever crime I'm supposed to have committed." He walked over to a picture on the wall and unhooked it, revealing a large safe. Quickly he typed in a long code then pulled the door open. "Again? How are they doing this?"

"What is it?"

"Proof of my 'guilt' for the police to find."

"I need to get you out of here."

He shook his head. "It's the wrong play. If they don't get me here they'll just keep looking."

"So you're giving up?"

"No more than you were when you decided to stay dead. I need to go where they put me, so they don't grasp what I'm really doing." He gave her a grim smile. "It's going to mean you warming to the task and showing a bit of *zest.*" He pulled a tablet computer from a shelf. "This is hard-encrypted to your bio signs. Remember this conversation: in case of trouble it'll tell you what you need to know."

SIXTY-NINE

Millie followed Craig across the road and past the main building loading bay to a small service door. Craig held a small device up to the key panel. It blinked three times and the door opened. No alarm sounded. No guards came rushing.

"See? Have a little faith." He handed Millie a balaclava, then pulled one on himself.

She covered her face. "Couldn't shut the cameras off then?"

"I shut off the analysis software, so we won't be flagged, but the cameras themselves run on a completely separate system. And I'd rather not have our faces there for later analysis." Craig led them along a corridor then through an unmarked door onto a fire-escape staircase. They climbed without incident to level 8. From there they proceeded through a series of doors until they came to a large metal hatch. "This area houses the research rooms: the main facilities where they build new tech. This access door is a completely new system." He ran a hand over the metal. "Pretty serious stuff. It must weigh a couple of tonnes." He walked over to a computer terminal and started typing.

"Is there no end to your talents?"

"You need to raise your threshold for being impressed."

"And also your hands," said a loud voice from behind them.

Millie glanced at Craig. "So much for your plan." She turned around, and whistled.

Standing behind them was Gregory Jenson. He was holding what looked like an automatic rifle.

"You carry weapons in your office?" she asked.

"We *make* weapons in this office," Jenson replied. "Now show your faces. Slowly."

Millie pulled off her mask.

"Do I know you?" Jenson asked.

"I'm sure you know of me."

Craig uncovered his face, puffing out his cheeks. "It's been a while, Greg."

"Holy crap," Jenson said, lowering the weapon. "I don't believe it. You're…"

"…dead? Yes, that was the look I was going for."

"You faked your death? Why?"

"To stop Darwin. Except apparently I failed. So here I am to try again."

Jenson raised the rifle, pointing it at Craig's chest. "Before we get to that, we're going to start by clearing a few things up."

FIVE MINUTES LATER JENSON HAD LOCKED CRAIG AND MILLIE in what he described as a temporary holding facility.

"You have a prison cell in your office?" Craig asked, looking at the bars.

"Didn't think we'd ever actually get to use it," Jenson replied from where he sat opposite them, the rifle across his knees. "*Why* are you here, Craig?"

"To stop you."

Millie frowned. "So you really had no plan at all. Why the heck did you drag me in here?"

Jenson cleared his throat. "Why have you teamed up with Rose?"

"Who is Rose?" Craig asked.

"You're a funny guy. And why did you want to kill Parallel? Do you have a competing product coming to market?"

"What? You think this is about money? I came here to shut down Darwin, or Parallel, or whatever you're calling it now. Which I have every right to do, given that you stole it from me."

Jenson raised an eyebrow. "Darwin never worked. You left us with a dud."

"I know you've had it running for some time."

"Nonsense. And for your information, Parallel is something completely new and it's not even functional yet."

"Prove it. Show me your designs."

Jenson blinked. "Why on earth would I do that?"

"Because if that's true then we have a much bigger problem."

"*We* do, do we? You should worry about your own situation."

"This is everyone's problem, if I'm even half right. If you haven't re-built Darwin, then someone else has. And they've been using it for years now."

"Impossible."

"Until the last few hours I would have agreed." Craig stood up and held the bars. "I came here tonight to prove it. Now, are you going to call the police or see if I'm right?"

Jenson laid the blueprints out on the lab table, overlapping the three sheets of A1 paper. "This is the core processor," he said. "I'll get the diagrams for the subsidiary systems next."

"No need," said Craig. "I've seen enough. This is built on

fundamentally different principles." He scratched his head. "It's nothing like Darwin. A very elegant solution."

"Praise indeed."

"*If* it works. For starters you never really grasped natural language understanding like I did."

"As I recall you just uploaded your Darwin prototype with hundreds of popular movie scripts. Not exactly Shakespeare."

"It worked, so don't knock it. Now I want to see this new system."

Jenson gave a sniff. "It's still in development: a process not without its complications. I've had to shift work to another site."

"Then we need to go there."

"Maybe. First you talk. What's your story with Darwin? How can it be operational? If you didn't build it, that is."

"I don't know. I scuppered all the hardware and software before I 'died'. Yet I've detected traces of the prediction engine. It's more than possible it's been sending out spiders, crawling the web, for the last fifteen years. Who knows what it's capable of now?"

Jenson frowned. "What could possibly have made you fake your death?"

"I was afraid of what my system would become, and what would happen to me and my family when others learned what it could do. I did try to tell you fifteen years ago."

"I recall you had some doubts."

"They were more than doubts. Darwin was going to be too powerful. It *knew* things. It could *predict* things. Too much knowledge, too much power. Too open to abuse."

Jenson's phone rang. He answered it quickly, frowned, then put it back in his pocket. "That was one of my assistants. He said I should turn on the news."

They moved to the next room and flicked on a smart-screen, navigating to BBC News. There was one story running: coverage of Warwick Saxton's arrest.

Jenson gave a half-smile. "I should feel pleased. That man has caused me no end of problems."

"Yeah, but experience shows," Millie said, "that he'll be replaced by someone who will cause you the same problems. Don't expect any policy reversals."

"You may be right. And the truth is that, while I might not have cared for Saxton, if there was ever a straighter shooter then he certainly didn't go into the civil service."

"I've always found him rather brusque."

The men both look at her and spoke as one: "You know him?"

Millie blushed. "Well, he… tried to get me to do some work for him. A consulting gig."

Jenson's brow furrowed. "Just who exactly are you?"

Craig sighed. "Greg, allow me to introduce the creator of Millie.On.Truths. In the flesh."

"The blogger who has been hacking me? This just gets better and better. Perhaps I should put you back in the cell after all."

Millie folded her arms. "I strongly suggest you don't."

"And you've worked for Saxton? He hires criminals now?"

"A: I object to that classification. B: he hires the best."

Jenson shrugged and turned back to the screen. "Is that why he's been arrested?"

Craig ran a hand through his hair. "They're saying he was withholding evidence."

"I'm guessing that's connected with the kidnapping of my daughter. And it *all* connects to Parallel. Who is doing this?"

"Someone with an operational Darwin system would have this level of knowledge."

Millie reached into her bag and placed the secure hard drive on the table. "I'm beginning to think I might know how to find out who that might be."

Jenson stared at the device. "Explain."

"Saxton wanted me to help research what was on it. And, as I said, I'm good at what I do."

"And, what? He just looked you up on yellow pages?"

"We have… a history. I've worked for him before."

"Don't MI5 have people in-house to do that type of thing?"

"Apparently there are sensitivities around the work. Presumably the same sensitivities that led to his arrest."

"So what *is* on it?" Jenson asked.

"Information about a company called Kinek Consulting. They provide 'private intelligence'. Saxton has been using them for off-books investigations: analysis too sensitive to run through M15's official systems."

"Kinek? I've heard rumours, but never actually met any of them."

"Interesting. Because Saxton used them to prepare a personal audit on you when they restarted Parallel. Don't worry – they reported you were a good sort." She raised an eyebrow. "Of course, given recent events, perhaps we should wonder if they were right."

Jenson gave a noncommittal grunt. "So you just agreed to help him? Why?"

"Well he broke into my apartment, so I sai*d no to begin with.* But he asked me to think about it and left me the drive."

"The Director of MI5 broke into your apartment?"

Craig slapped his hand down on the table. "Never mind that. Did you make progress with the research?"

"Very little. Whoever Kinek are, they've left almost no digital exhaust. Given how large their organisation is thought to be, it's improbable at the least. You just can't work off the grid like they appear to do, not these days. So I asked myself if there's another explanation. What if their capabilities are more… inorganic."

"You're saying they—"

"—could be the ones that built Darwin." She pointed at Craig. "His scan of the web revealed that Darwin *is* operational. It's a pretty good guess they have it."

"How did they get it?" Jenson asked. "What we had didn't work. It never worked."

"Yeah," Craig said. "What *you* had. But that doesn't mean

it didn't work." He sighed. "I made Darwin operational. Briefly."

"And you didn't tell me? We were partners!"

"Things moved quickly. I had to make a call and I—"

Jenson snapped his fingers. "Then someone stole it from you! Not from me."

"No. I destroyed it."

"What? You were all about the possibilities, not the risks."

Craig hesitated. "To start with. Then I realized we were about to cross a line that shouldn't be crossed. If we're right, Darwin's been running for fifteen years. Heaven knows what they've been doing with it. We need to find it – but I designed it not to be found. In fact the only thing that *could* find it is Darwin itself."

Jenson frowned. "What about Parallel?"

"It's operational?" Millie asked.

"It's still undergoing final testing off-site, like I said."

Millie frowned. "Why isn't it here?"

Jenson shook his head. "I have the government trying to shut the project down. It was the only way to keep going while I sorted the situation out. Anyway, it's only an hour's drive away." He looked at his watch. "It's already late and we're going to need help from technicians on site, who won't be clocking on until the morning. Why don't we grab some sleep and I'll drive us out there first thing. There are some business beds on level fifteen we can use in the meantime."

Craig raised an eyebrow. "Are we your guests or your prisoners?"

"I'll let you know when I decide. I just don't want any more surprises."

Millie beamed. "With that in mind, I'd better get one out of the way. You know your new lawyer, the one you sent to threaten me? Remember his name?"

Jenson frowned. "Michael… *Adams*." His gaze snapped to Craig. "That's your son? Is he spying for you?"

Craig shook his head. "He doesn't even know I'm alive."

"How could I have missed the family resemblance?"

Millie spread her hands. "It's obvious now you look, but it's not something you were watching for. You didn't even consider the possibility. If you want to avoid any more surprises that approach has to change."

SEVENTY

It was late Friday evening and the bar was packed, the air filled with conversation, alcohol and sweat. Michael squeezed between the crowds, past polished tables and padded stools, to a familiar booth at the back.

He hadn't been in this bar since the night CWP had fired him: the night he had met Kara.

Now, as he sipped from a bottled beer, he saw the various TV-screens were showing Warwick Saxton's arrest. He felt like a fly in a spider's web, but he clearly wasn't the only one trapped.

It had been an inexplicable day. Infinity had failed in challenging the Project Parallel decision. They rarely fought fairly to ensure they didn't lose, so what had happened today? Could there conceivably be some benefit to Infinity in the decision going against their client? It made no sense: as little sense as his getting summarily fired by CWP.

What if Kara really had *known* somehow? It would be entirely consistent with how Infinity operated. Had it all been a set up? He was distracted by the sound of a familiar voice.

Behind him, at a corner table, was Gordon Freeman, CWP's Managing Partner. He sat alone, finishing a phonecall, his shirt collar undone and a large glass of red wine in front of him.

Michael stood up and moved over. Freeman's expression became one of alarm, though in a snap it was replaced with a smile.

"Mr Adams. How are you doing?"

Michael sat next to him, his face even. "Just waiting for someone."

"Same." Freeman cleared his throat. "You come to gloat about that stunt you pulled the other day? How did you know about the Hadwell Site?"

"Actually, I want to know what the hell was happening that day you asked me to leave the firm."

"Isn't it just water under the bridge now? You seem happy with your new role."

"That's the thing with Infinity: you only see what they want you to see."

"I'm not sure I follow—"

"My point is, you *know* I didn't disclose CWP client information. So you *couldn't* have had any proof."

"I knew all I needed to know."

Michael leaned forward in his chair. "What are you talking about?"

"If you think these people will..." Freeman shook his head. "Really. I can't discuss it—"

"Someone *made* you do it. There must have been a lot of money involved", he paused, "or something else. Did they threaten you? Did they blackmail you? Was it you who really wanted me fired, or was it Infinity?"

Freeman stood up. "You really don't know anything, do you?" He turned and walked away.

FREEMAN WALKED OUT OF THE BAR AND SIGNALLED FOR HIS car. In seconds the long wheel-base Audi A8 was pulling up alongside him. Not having to travel in some random black cab was one of the advantages of Freeman's position. Having a private driver available 24-7 meant always travelling with a certain level of privacy. He certainly needed it now.

He climbed into the backseat and moved to close the partition of darkly tinted glass, but it was already shut. That was odd, because he preferred to greet his driver face-to-face when he got in. Turning to look around, he realised there was another thing wrong. There was someone else in the rear compartment with him: a woman in a tight-fitting black outfit and plastic-rimmed glasses. As she leaned forwards, her face came into the soft internal light.

He frowned. "What are *you* doing here?"

"I thought we'd have a chat."

"Then call my office for an appointment."

The woman shook her head. "I'm not here to discuss legal matters, Mr Freeman. I'm not who you think I am."

"Then who the hell are you?"

"Marcia sent me."

"You work for…" He swallowed. "If that's true, why not follow protocol? How am I supposed to validate the orders?"

"There's no need." She reached forward and placed a finger on his lips. "You talk too much. And that is not something that can be permitted."

"I would never talk about Kinek. Surely that's obvious—"

She produced a digital recorder and Freeman's conversation with Michael began replaying.

Freeman hesitated. "I said very little."

"You said enough for us to doubt you."

He shook his head. "You knew I'd be here. You knew I'd speak to Michael. Why not stop me?"

"Because that wasn't part of the prediction. The plan is moving forwards, and you are a loose end."

"So, what? They're going to send someone after me?"

She leant forward, reaching to her ankle, and removed a silenced pistol from a holster. "They sent *me*."

He shrank back, scrabbling for the door handle only to find it locked. "But you're not—"

"I am whatever they need me to be." She raised the gun.

"Whatever they're paying you, I'll double it."

She gave a little laugh and tapped her glasses. "That was exactly what my instructions said you would say." She sighed. "I've never really liked you, *Gordon*. You're the one who fired Michael, and he'd done nothing wrong."

"But you told me to! You'd have had me killed if I hadn't."

She shrugged. And then she pulled the trigger.

SEVENTY-ONE

MAXWELL ERRINGTON DROVE HIS BENTLEY AT SLIGHTLY OVER the speed limit, laughing inwardly at the tiny breach of the law. Breaking the rules, but not enough to get noticed, had been a useful approach over the years. Rain streamed in the headlights, and Rachmaninov blasted from the car's bespoke sound system as he headed west, towards home.

The car phone rang and he grimaced at the name that popped up on the display, having been dodging the caller for several hours. Now he couldn't delay things any longer. He pressed to answer.

"Max, where have you been?" Duncan Nichol asked with what sounded like forced calm. "Are you OK?"

Errington smiled to himself. Nichol was ready to make a move he had long wanted to make, but he was still being polite. He'd always been far too much of a gentleman to run Infinity properly. "I'm fine, Duncan. Just driving home."

"I left you several messages."

"Did you?" Errington replied. He had, of course, listened to them. "What about?"

"About the meeting between our biggest client and the government that took place this morning."

"Oh yes. What about it?"

Nichol gave a sharp intake of breath. "Everything about it, Max. *Everything.*"

"Well it didn't go exactly as planned, I will admit. But you can't win them all."

"We lost a major contract for one of our best clients because of your ties to an arms dealer. And then we lost the client. I need you to come to the office. Right now."

Errington counted slowly to five. "It's rather late and I have an engagement this evening. How about tomorrow afternoon? I think I'm free then, but check with my secretary—"

"I wanted to do this face to face, but if you won't come in, I'll do it now."

"Do what, Duncan?"

"I have sufficient cause to invoke Clause 17 of the partnership agreement. We will vote you out at the next meeting. I have unanimous support from the other partners. Or you could go quietly and immediately." He paused. "It would be better for everyone if you did."

Errington laughed. "Over my dead body. Or perhaps," he gave a chuckle, "over yours."

"You're only drawing out the inevitable."

"No, Duncan, the truth is that you have no idea what's going on. You never have. It's why I promoted you."

"Believe me when I say—"

"Goodnight, Duncan." Errington disconnected the call. The music swelled again as he drove on, close to home now. The automatic gates to his house swung open and he parked in front of the large three-storey residence, next to two large black vans he had not seen there before.

As he got out, he heard a cough from behind him. He turned to see Kara Simmons, dressed all in black.

"I thought you'd need me, Max." She walked over and patted him on the shoulder.

"Where is my wife?"

"She's been called away. As per my instructions."

He turned as sliding doors on both vans opened and four

men stepped out. They were clad in combat gear and carrying automatic weapons.

"It's time," Kara said. "You need to come with us."

"Are the guns really necessary?" Errington asked as he looked around him.

The first man shrugged and pointed to the back of one of the vans.

"Exciting times ahead, Max," said Kara.

Errington nodded and climbed in.

SEVENTY-TWO

MICHAEL MARCHED THROUGH THE FRONT DOOR OF HIS HOUSE, mind racing. Since the day he had been fired – joining Infinity, meeting Millie, Saxton's arrest – nothing had been a coincidence. All of it was linked.

He moved to the study and pulled out his Infinity laptop, plugging in the headset and slipping it over his ears. He wasn't supposed to use the machine for his own purposes, but he didn't care anymore. Why had he been brought into all of this right now? Why had he, someone who was linked to both ZAT and a project related to Parallel through his father, become involved now? Was anyone telling him the truth?

He felt like the answers were in his head, if he only knew how to unlock them. If he could find one corner piece in the puzzle, the relevance of others might become apparent. He glared at his laptop. Infinity used information to its advantage. But where was that information coming from? It wasn't just the result of using a bespoke search engine.

He began to type in the search field, but was startled when the front doorbell rang. He moved through the hallway, looked through the spyhole, then immediately pulled the door open.

It was his mother.

"What are you doing here at this hour?"

She frowned at him. "I got your text."

"I didn't send you anything."

Nina pulled out her phone and showed it to him. The screen displayed a message, apparently from him, sent perhaps three hours earlier: *Need to speak to you now. Here. Can't discuss over the phone.*

"I never sent that. Look." Michael pulled his own phone out, then blinked as he saw the message was in his sent log. "I don't understand." He beckoned her inside.

Nina walked past him, sniffing the air. "Been drinking?"

Michael rubbed the bridge of his nose and considered matters. He could feel the beer in his system, but knew he wasn't remotely drunk enough to have used his phone then forgotten it.

"Did you speak to Jenson?"

"I decided not to – I *actually* listened to your advice, so you can count it a win, like you *made* me do what you wanted for once."

"Wonderful. Can we sit down? There's something I need to tell you."

Michael nodded and led them into the lounge. They sat on the sofa.

"Listen," Nina said, "I wasn't completely honest with you the other day. It's time you knew the truth about what your father did." She took a deep breath. "I don't hate your father because he killed himself." She paused. "At least, that's not the main reason."

Michael swallowed. "What are you talking about?"

"One weekend I went to visit a friend up in Liverpool, but came back a day early. I thought I'd surprise you both. You were downstairs in the den, messing around with computers as usual, or so I thought." She blinked, a tear streaming down her cheek. "When I walked in, you were sitting on a beanbag, your eyes staring. You had some... headgear on. It had wires coming out of it, plugged into computer equipment your father had set up."

"That sounds... weird."

"I called out and he looked up, startled. He told me everything was OK, but I mustn't touch anything." Nina's voice rose. "He was lying. You were barely conscious." She shook her head. "I ran over to get the equipment off you. Your father tried to stop me, but I pushed him aside and I ripped the headgear from you. You gasped like you were coming up for air."

Michael stared at her blankly. "I think I remember a headset, but I don't remember it being a big deal."

"Craig was experimenting with brain manipulation."

"Dad was a computer expert, not a neurologist. This doesn't make any sense. Mum, are you OK?"

"It did something to the electrical activity in your brain – disrupted the patterns."

"What are you talking about? Why wouldn't I remember it, and why wouldn't you have told me about it before?"

"You don't remember because it affected your memory. And as for not mentioning it, part of the treatment regimen was to not worry you with the specifics."

"You think I could have forgotten a whole recovery program? This is all a bit hard to digest." Michael reached out and gripped his mother's hand. "Did you ask Dad *why* he put this thing on my head?"

"He said he was trying to create a new type of computer system – he didn't really explain it. Then he died in the explosion shortly afterwards. In hindsight maybe he couldn't live with what he'd done."

Michael leaned forward, looking into her eyes. "This *computer* he was working on: was it Darwin?"

"After what I just told you, that's what you're interested in?"

"I think it could matter a great deal."

"I came here to tell you the truth, so you wouldn't need to dig any further."

He put his hands over hers. "It's possible Darwin really worked."

She pulled her hands free. "Are you listening to me? Your father was lucky I didn't have him arrested."

"I can't believe he meant to harm me."

"Intentional? Negligent? What's the difference?" She sniffed. "You'll just have to make up your own mind. I can't do that for you."

"Don't be like that. What I mean is—"

"I know what you mean. You don't trust me."

Michael gripped his head in hands. "This is a lot to take in. I need some time to think it over—"

"Take all the time you need. I'm going home. Coming here was obviously a mistake." She stared at him, then cleared her throat. "Since you started that new job, everything's gone wrong. If I had my way, you'd never cross their doorstep again." She shook her head. "I'll show myself out." And she left.

Michael sat back on the sofa, stunned. The buzz from the beer had been replaced by confusion and something almost like fear.

He felt like Pandora's box had been ripped open in front of him. But who owned the box? It could only be Infinity.

It was almost ironic that his mother should mention his new firm, and ask him to stay away. Because that was exactly where Michael needed to go, if he was to find someone in a position to give him answers. Not Maxwell Errington: the old man was clearly in too deep to ever come clean. No, he needed to speak with Duncan Nichol: Nichol had always come across as a practical man, someone who could be reasoned with – if you could pull the right levers. And very quickly he knew just which one would work.

Michael pulled out his phone and typed out a message. *Duncan, we need to talk ASAP. Face-to-face if possible. I have a plan for getting ZAT back on board.*

The reply was almost immediate. *I'm working in my office. Meet me here.*

SEVENTY-THREE

Morton sat in the secure booth, awaiting the connection, but this was not his regularly scheduled call: it was an additional update he had requested.

"You want to discuss the boy?" Marcia asked in the same soft, metallic tones.

"That's right," Morton replied. "The situation has changed, as I'm sure you have noted on the system. His mother went to see him: an intervention we had not expected."

"You're telling me she's a risk?"

"We couldn't get any sound on their discussion from any of the devices installed in his house. Faults happen, but rarely so inconveniently."

"You think she tampered with them?"

"She's a retired psychologist and technophobe, so it seems unlikely."

"I'll flag it to maintenance. Meanwhile work with what we have."

Morton paused. "We should activate full-time monitoring until we have sufficient data."

"That could, in itself, draw attention."

"Yes, but hasn't Michael Adams been flagged as special

interest with regard to Project Green? Should we not be managing his situation proactively?"

There was a pause. "It was not my intention to fetter you, Morton – and your analysis has merits. You continue to demonstrate excellence in your operations."

He swallowed. "I'll requisition a team to follow both—"

"Negative. I'll handle this myself, with independent resource."

"Marcia, what is Project Green about?"

There was a pause. "I appreciate your personal interest, but we have to follow the system. Even I don't know everything. Even I am just following the plan."

"This lack of information-sharing seems counter-productive; surely I can work more effectively if I have more data. And am I not the best person to manage London-based surveillance?"

"Usually, but I think we need something more than surveillance. We need to stress test Mr Adams. When we do, we'll see who steps forward to save him."

"And if nobody does?"

"Then," replied Marcia, "he wasn't as important as we thought."

"You're saying the system might be mistaken?"

"It just makes predictions. It doesn't see the future." She hesitated, her tone becoming warmer. "By the way, good work with Saxton."

"It is disappointing to lose such a high-level resource, especially given Maxwell Errington's exit."

"Both were necessary losses. Now I have to join another meeting." The call abruptly disconnected.

Morton stared at the blank screen for several long moments before he left the booth.

It was far from scientific, but something felt wrong. For the first time ever after speaking to Marcia, he felt that she had lied.

SEVENTY-FOUR

IN DUNCAN NICHOL'S NINTH FLOOR OFFICE, MICHAEL NOTED only one thing out of place. It was late on a wet autumn night, but expensive lighting made the inside feel warm and reassuring. Rows of legal reference books were arrayed with precision on two bays of shelving, perhaps more for show than utility. Several carefully-arranged and expensive pieces of sculpture were artfully displayed using individually crafted stands, while on a large dresser a whisky decanter and six glasses sat undisturbed. At one end of the room an oversized desk bore two ultra hi-definition computer monitors. In front of them sat a large cup of, presumably now cold, black coffee, its surface pearling in the light from the screens.

Michael stood on the far side of the room, next to one of the floor-to-ceiling windows. Heavy spats of rain smacked the glass as he removed his wire-framed glasses and wiped away perspiration with a handkerchief. Apart from the sound of the rain, the room was quiet, lacking even the hum of air-conditioning. There was nothing to remove the metallic tang of blood hanging in the air.

Nichol lay face-up on the expensive block flooring to one side of the desk. Three tidily-placed bullet holes ruptured his chest. Nichol's face bore an awful rictus of surprise. Perhaps that wasn't remarkable – did anyone ever *expect* to get shot in their own office?

Michael slid on his glasses, feeling his veins pulse at his temples. The blood was the worst part: thick and unreal in the halogen lighting, oozing into tiny cracks in the blockwork. He was fighting the urge to vomit, and wasn't confident he would win.

Who had done this? How had they got into the building, past the not inconsiderable security? And, above all, why?

He blinked. His brain felt dulled by the sight of the body. He needed to talk to someone he could trust.

But before he did that there was, of course, one call he had to make first. He picked up the desk phone, pressed for an outside line, then 999.

The reply was immediate. *"Emergency: which service do you require?"*

"Police," he said in a detached voice. "I want to report a murder."

The operator was calm and reassuring as she worked through her checklist. He answered each question quickly and clearly. But as he gave the building's address, he could tell something was wrong. She sounded distracted, as if she were listening to someone else at the same time. When he put down the phone, he saw red, white and blue flashing in the window, reflected from the street below.

They're already here? Who knew to call them?

And something suddenly clicked in Michael's mind. Was it no coincidence that he was here? Was he being set up?

He spun around, thinking fast. Had he touched anything in the room that would suggest he was guilty? He didn't think so, but who knew what a forensic team might make of the scene? He'd done nothing except stand and stare, yet that might not matter: if someone really wanted to make it look like he was responsible, the evidence would be there. He fought the urge to scream. He couldn't run: the building security team, the police switchboard, even the taxi driver that had dropped him here could all attest to his presence. He had rendered himself helpless, with no choice but to sit and wait for the situation to play out. Because it was clear that this murder was not the end-game, just one piece in a dark puzzle that he was barely starting to comprehend.

A soft chime broke the silence. Through the office's open door he saw the lift was rising up from the ground floor - within a minute the police team would arrive. And if he didn't start working out what was going on, then being sent to prison for a murder he didn't commit might be the least of his worries.

SEVENTY-FIVE

THE RAID STARTED AT EXACTLY 6:00AM. FIVE GREY VANS pulled up outside ZAT's facility in Reading, each bearing ZAT logos, although closer examination would have revealed the paint was barely dry. While a delivery was scheduled, the security guard thought it odd that a consignment would arrive so early; instead of raising the barrier, he stepped forwards to question the first driver.

As he did so, the side door of the van slid open and a man wearing a balaclava stepped out. Without ceremony, he jabbed a taser into the guard's chest, who shook and collapsed. The man reached into the guard's booth and raised the barrier. The five vans drove smoothly into the compound and five armed men stepped from the back of each. Without discussion, they moved towards a heavy-goods door and held up a black device to the control panel. It beeped angrily, but opened. All of them moved into the building.

A guard on the top floor of the facility, just back from his tea break, looked out in time to see the start of the commotion. Within seconds he was pressing the emergency alarm to lock down the site and summon the police. The typical response time was ten minutes.

But the alarm did not work. Again and again the guard hit the red button, but there was no response. Confused, he attempted to call the police using his mobile, yet there was no signal. The nearest wall-phone was dead as well. That was as far as he got before three intruders appeared on the floor, tasered him, and moved on.

Several of the men re-emerged from the building carrying silver flight-cases marked ‘classified’ and ‘dangerous contents, handle with care’. Unhurriedly they began loading them into the backs of the vans.

On level three a small explosive charge opened the recently-fitted security door, granting the waiting men access to the new computer lab. Inside a bald man in a white lab coat cowered behind his desk as the intruders spread around the room with purpose.

The leader consulted his tablet then began pointing at various items. "That, and that. Leave that. Pack everything that’s plugged in. Handle it all with care." He turned to the man wearing the white coat, again holding up the tablet. "Lee Chow?"

Chow nodded, wide-eyed.

"Go with this operative. Any trouble and you will be killed."

"I don’t understand."

The leader raised his automatic pistol. "Talk is trouble. Now do as you’re told."

Chow nodded.

"Good." He holstered his weapon. "Let’s move it out. Remember, we’re on a deadline, people."

SEVENTY-SIX

The interrogation room at Charing Cross Police Station was windowless and badly lit. Michael stared at the grey brick walls - featureless except for a single TV panel that was currently turned off - and wondered again just why he was in this predicament. He had used his one phone call to reach Eve - she was getting someone to finish her shift and said she would be there in about an hour.

For now he sat in this tiny room, across a bolted-down table from the Inspector and Sergeant that had arrested him. Next to him was the spotty-faced duty solicitor who had been woken up to represent him, who had said little that Michael didn't already know about the process, and who on several occasions had appeared to fall back asleep. On the table were four stewed cups of tea.

"So, Mr. Adams," said the Inspector, "shall we start again?"

"Why?" Michael replied. "I've told you everything I know."

The Inspector looked down at his notes, underlining something with a pencil. "I find that unlikely."

"Look, it's really simple. I sent a message to Nichol asking to meet with him, face-to-face."

"At nearly midnight on a Friday night?"

"I'm a City lawyer - we work long hours. Nichol replied that he was working in his office, and I should meet him there. When I arrived, I found him dead. After that I called you."

The Sergeant folded his arms. "There's no record of a message on Nichol's phone. Nothing on yours either."

"Then look again. And ask the security guard - he'll confirm when I arrived. What do your crime scene people say about time of death? That will show it happened before I was there."

"Time of death? Already started planning your alibi?"

Michael took a slow breath. "Look, just ask the guard, will you?"

"We're having trouble tracing him, but we will."

"Then speak to my colleague - Kara Simmons. She can account for my whereabouts after I left the office."

The Inspector tapped the table. "Word is, you lost a major client today, and that you got fired. Had a grudge to settle with Mr. Nichol, did you?"

"Fired? Where did you hear that? Kara will confirm that's false."

"You were at her apartment you say?"

"Yes. Earlier. Then I went for a drink—"

"—So you were drinking?"

"Only a couple. I met my former boss - Gordon Freeman - at a bar in the city."

"Building up the courage to do the deed?"

Tom flexed his fingers. "No, Detective. After that I went home. I did some work, and my mother called by. She didn't stay long. Then I messaged Nichol, after which I went to the office."

"So you say."

"Yes, and I say it, because that's what I *did*."

"None of these things prove that you didn't kill Mr. Nichol."

"None of them prove I did. I've never fired a gun in my life."

The Inspector nodded, then looked down at his notes. "So, you were at the apartment of Kara Simmons? Why?"

Michael hesitated. "What do you mean?"

The Inspector picked up his tea, and took an unhurried sip. "It's a simple question. Why were you there?"

"Discussing work."

"That's what they're calling it these days?"

Michael folded his arms. "What the hell is that supposed to mean?"

"Were you in a relationship with Ms Simmons?"

"What?" Michael blinked. "No, I was not."

The Inspector turned to the TV screen and tapped a control. Hi-resolution footage from a wide angle lens camera began to play. It showed Michael standing in Kara's apartment, Kara next to him in her bathrobe. She reached forward and kissed him. Then the footage froze.

"Nice *work* if you can get it," said the Sergeant.

Michael shook his head. "This isn't what it looks like."

"So you agree what it looks like?"

"There's no context. No sound. She kissed me. It was completely unexpected."

"Really? She was there in her bathrobe, giving you brandy. If you were uncomfortable why not just leave?"

"Because she was my boss. Look, keep playing the footage."

"That's all there is."

"So you don't see me pushing her away and leaving?" Michael clenched his fists. "How convenient."

"That's what you did, is it?"

"And, more to the point, how did you get this footage?"

"Why does that matter?" asked the Inspector. "Are you suggesting it's been tampered with?"

"It's certainly highly misleading." Michael shook his head. "Look, what does this even matter? Aren't you trying to find out who killed Duncan Nichol?"

"We're working on it, Sir. But when we went to speak to Ms Simmons, we didn't find her home."

"So then—"

"We did however find some blood. A great deal of blood."

Michael froze. "What are you saying?"

The Inspector leaned forwards. "What I'm *asking* is: did you kill more than one person today?"

Michael turned to look at his solicitor, who had started snoring. "I want a lawyer. One who can actually stay awake."

The Inspector frowned. "You make a reasonable point. This interview is suspended. But this conversation is far from over."

SEVENTY-SEVEN

Jenson slowed his Mercedes as he approached the gates to the ZAT Reading site. Two police cars, blue lights flashing, blocked the entrance. Inside he could see half a dozen more police vehicles, including three vans.

"What is going on here?" Craig asked from the passenger seat.

"That is a lot of cops," Millie added from the rear of the car. "Too many."

Jenson shook his head. "This is not good." He pulled out his mobile and noted he'd received nearly fifty messages in the last couple of minutes. "Not good at all."

A uniformed officer walked over to them. "Sir, if you could move along," he said, waving with his arms, "the site is closed because of an incident—"

Jenson flipped out his photo ID. "Thank you, officer. Since it's my site, perhaps you could tell me what the hell is going on."

The man narrowed his eyes, stepped back to read the number plate, then spoke into his radio. There was an immediate reply and he nodded. "Mr Jenson, please drive through. They're waiting to brief you."

TWO HOURS LATER, JENSON JOINED CRAIG AND MILLIE IN A conference room. He closed the door, then sat at the table, his head in his hands.

"What happened?" Craig asked. "You look terrible."

"There was a raid. Armed men stormed the site this morning. They kidnapped my lead scientist, Lee Chow. We have no idea where they've taken him."

"They weren't just here for the scientist, surely?" Millie asked.

"No. They took full specifications for all models of our micro-drones. And twenty cases of product. I didn't know there was that much in existence, or how it all came to be here. I have people looking into it, but it seems to have got messed up with the consignments for Project Parallel."

"No one noticed?"

"We actively discouraged anyone to *notice* the classified shipments in the first place. We're not supposed to be continuing the project, remember. And unfortunately it gets worse." Jenson hesitated, glancing at Millie and Craig. "They took Parallel. They had access codes to the entire facility. They shut down security, then just walked in and took what they wanted, including the bespoke CPUs and the Parallel test rig. With Chow to help them, they have everything they need to make it operational. And we have nothing."

Craig shook his head. "This just goes from bad to… worse than bad. I suppose the police have no idea who did it?"

"Oddly," Jenson said, "they say they're pursuing leads that link to Regina Rose thanks to an anonymous tip. It makes sense: Rose found out where the micro-drones were, and she came and got them, but the tip tells me something more is going on."

"I don't like this," Millie replied. "Did you tell them who I was?"

"Of course not. I didn't tell them who Craig was either, but it's possible they may start asking questions."

"Normally if I get into trouble with law enforcement I

have the option of leaning on my connection with Saxton. Right now I don't think that will have too much value."

"If you want to leave," Jenson said, "I'll completely understand. It's not your fight."

She put her hands on her hips. "You don't need to mock me for having a sense of self preservation."

"Sorry, did I hurt your feelings? One of my friends has been kidnapped and my whole business has been compromised, so you'll forgive me if I'm a little brusque."

"Whatever. I'll hang around for now."

"Have you quite finished?" Craig frowned. "Was the Parallel tech in the same part of the building as the drones?"

"No," Jenson replied. "Completely separate."

"And yet they knew where to find it, and to take Chow with them. That doesn't sound random at all. It sounds the opposite of random."

"It sounds like they knew everything. And now they *have* everything, too. While we have nothing at all." Jenson shook his head. "I need to speak with my assistant, Kelly. She's been conducting some investigations on my behalf, though, so she's off-grid at the moment."

"When did you last speak to her?"

"A couple of days ago."

"Are you sure she's OK? I mean, it sounds like you sent her to poke the hornets' nest."

"Which is why she went dark: we were worried our comms were being monitored. It seems we were probably right."

Millie laced her fingers together. "I wouldn't say we have *nothing*. Craig invented Darwin. That's something."

Craig folded his arms. "What do you mean?"

"Based on what you showed me, I think I can locate Darwin. I can take your pattern and feed it into my proprietary search engines. If it's operational, then we just follow the searches back to the source."

Craig frowned. "That might just work."

"But," Jenson said, "what about Rose? What about my drones? What about Parallel?"

"If we get Darwin," Millie said with a smile, "then we can get all of them."

SEVENTY-EIGHT

A UNIFORMED OFFICER LED MICHAEL FROM THE INTERVIEW room and down a corridor. Halfway along he unlocked a door and ushered him inside a plain white room containing a table and four chairs.

"You sit on the far side," said the officer.

Michael glanced around. "Is this another interview? Don't I get a break?"

The man shrugged. "You have a visitor and ten minutes. Make use of them."

Michael blinked and took his seat as directed. A moment later Eve stepped into the room and closed the door behind her. She looked around and put a finger to her lips.

"What?" he asked. "There's no one else here."

"They're probably monitoring us."

"I know there are cameras everywhere, but the sound will be turned off. This isn't 1960s Berlin."

"Espionage tech then was stone age by comparison with today. There could be a dozen microphones in here and we wouldn't even know."

He hesitated. "You could be right. But I don't care. It's not like it will matter if they overhear me confessing my innocence."

She gave a snort and ran around the table, hugging him

so tightly he gasped. "What the heck have you got yourself into now?"

"I really don't know."

"For my benefit, try and explain."

He shrugged. "We had a difficult work meeting yesterday. Lost a big client, everything went to custard. Then I had an odd conversation with my mother – some stuff about my Dad – which oddly seems to be linked with ZAT."

"The arms manufacturer? Why them?"

"Because they're our client. Or were." He swallowed." Look I probably shouldn't have even said—"

"How could ZAT be connected to your Dad?"

"I don't know. It's just that…" he hesitated. "You know maybe it's best if I don't tell you everything."

"Because you don't trust me?" She jabbed a finger in his ribs. "I'm the only one you *can* trust."

"That's not it. Look, I'm not imagining the danger. Someone died. Maybe two people."

She sucked in her lip. "Yeah, they haven't found that Kara yet. And in fact it might be worse. Your former boss has vanished. Gordon Freeman, from CWP. He's been reported missing by his wife. It's all over the news."

Michael blinked. "What? I only met with him last night."

Eve's eyes widened. "Oh boy."

"And I was at Kara's apartment before that."

"Why on earth would you go there?"

"To discuss work. But they have some footage of me kissing her—"

Eve folded her arms. "There's quite a pattern there, hotshot."

"C'mon, this is all beyond ridiculous."

"Of course it is." She gripped his shoulder. "So what are we going to do about it?"

"What do you mean *we*? You don't have to get involved."

"I'm your best friend, idiot. I'm not going to sit by while they stitch you up for triple-murder."

"We don't know if Kara or Freeman are actually dead—"

"For argument's sake, let's assume. We have to push back. Someone set you up. We need to work out why. We have to get a damn idea, damn quick. Or you could be staying here a very long time."

"Sure. But my options to do much are rather limited, unless you've got a plan to break me out."

"It's not something they teach at med school. You're the one with the analytical brain – haven't you got any ideas?"

Michael thought for a moment. One pattern was immediately obvious. "I know what you said about helping, but I think you should get out of London. Go stay with your cousin."

"How can I help you from there? Added to which I have work on Monday."

"I want to know that you're out of harm's way. It's just a precaution. And warn my mother as well."

Eve rolled her eyes. "She knows how to take care of herself. Chances are she'll be off overseas on another trip in a day or two anyway. I'm sure she won't let your situation change her plans."

"Please just speak to her. You'll find a way to say it right. That's your talent. Telling people difficult things in a way that makes it OK."

"Sure. And in that vein, I'm telling you that I'm not going anywhere, and that that is OK."

"That's not what I meant—"

"I'm not going to abandon you. No, unpleasant as it may be, I'm going to connect with your mother. We'll pool our resources and start developing a plan." She turned towards the door. "Including hiring you a lawyer who can actually stay awake."

"How did you know about that?"

"He was on the sofa in reception, snoring. I don't mean to pick fun – I've done that once or twice myself near the end of a double-shift."

Michael gave a snort. "At least you can't accuse me of being boring any more."

"Like I said, I never called you that." She put her hand on the door handle. "You know maybe you should have listened to me. All this nonsense started when you accepted that job at Infinity. I did say you should think twice about it."

"Believe me, I'm doing that now."

SEVENTY-NINE

AT ZAT READING'S SITE, JENSON HAD TAKEN CRAIG AND Millie to a basement room, scanning it several times before declaring it clean. They had then set up a local server, with a triple firewall.

Millie was now glaring at multiple display screens. "This is not working as quickly as it should, and I don't know why."

"The layered firewalls?" Jenson asked. "It's too risky not to use them."

"No. Something else has changed," Craig said, looking up from lines of code. "The volume of traffic has reduced dramatically and there's almost nothing to analyse. Are they suddenly managing to mask it or has it been switched off?"

"After all this time it gets turned off now?" Millie said. "I don't believe that for a second."

"Maybe they've detected our intrusion?" Jenson suggested.

Craig shook his head. "They couldn't react that quickly. The way Darwin works, it can't be turned off in a moment. You can't really turn it off at *all*. Whatever is going on, this feels planned."

"Well maybe they've changed the rules," Jenson said. "Maybe in fifteen years they've found a way." His phone buzzed. He pulled it out and stared at the screen. "Oh, you have to be kidding me." He walked over to a large display screen and called up the BBC News website.

LAWYER MICHAEL ADAMS ARRESTED FOR DOUBLE MURDER read the headline below a picture.

"No!" shouted Craig.

"Total BS," Millie said with a groan.

Jenson stared at the screen. "'Victim is Duncan Nichol, managing partner at Infinity Law, and it is also believed that Kara Simmons may have been killed, though no body has been found. Police are also investigating a third, possibly related, disappearance,'" he read.

"This is a stitch up," Craig said. "And I'm sure Darwin is behind it. We have to do something." He picked up his coat and bag.

"What are you going to do? Breaking him out of custody?"

"He's my son."

"You'll just get yourself arrested."

"Then what's your suggestion? Call a lawyer?"

"Maybe. What's *your* plan?"

"Whatever it takes," Craig scowled. "You'd do the same for your daughter."

"True. But that doesn't make it a good idea—"

Millie cleared her throat. "I can get him out. I *am* a hacker. And I can certainly hack a regular police station. I did it once as part of a penetration test I ran for Saxton a couple of years ago."

"And they didn't fix the flaws you found?"

She tipped her head on one side. "They fixed the ones I told them about."

Jenson smiled. "You're a real piece of work."

"I've been called worse. Look, I should be the one to go. If Craig turns up, Michael might be so distracted by seeing his dead father that he'll forget to escape."

Craig nodded. "But what about the Darwin tracker?"

Millie stood up. "At the moment I might be part of the

problem. Why don't you and Gregory here try and come up with a new approach. Make some brilliant deductive leap."

Craig glanced at Jenson. "Work with him? He was pointing a gun at me a few hours ago."

"And a few hours before that, you and I did the same with each other."

Jenson frowned. "She's making sense. We need a new tactic. I don't like all these police around; either they'll start asking questions or Darwin will access their systems to spy on us. We need to go to a different location: and as luck would have it, I have a special lab we can use." He pulled out a notepad and scribbled on it, then tore of the page and handed it to Millie. "Meet us here when you're ready."

Millie squinted. "Dark red ink on black paper? I can barely read it."

"Good. And if any image recognition system has it in view, it should have similar difficulties."

Millie nodded. "I'll see you both soon. Hopefully I'll be bringing a friend."

EIGHTY

THE DOCKLANDS APARTMENT WAS OWNED BY AN OVERSEAS businessman who used it for one week every three months. A cleaner came in weekly to keep the place freshened up and sort through any mail. The owner relied on a consumer electronics security package to alert him of any intruders. Obviously that had not presented Astrid Kelly with a problem.

In the spacious living room, behind floor-to-ceiling triple-glazed windows, she sat watching the BBC evening news. Home Secretary Charlotte Rostrum was holding a press conference where she skillfully avoided giving meaningful answers about MI5 Director Warwick Saxton. *Wasn't such an arrest unprecedented*, she was asked. *Director Saxton is cooperating with our ongoing investigation*, she replied. *Nobody is above the law.*

If only that were true, thought Kelly, as she muted the sound and turned to the secure tablet that Saxton had given her. It was a flat dark grey, with a non-reflective display housed in a ruggedised case like all tablets issued by the British intelligence services. It was a neutral, impenetrable way of transferring classified information. Today, it would tell her what she had to do.

Glancing around to check that her anti-monitoring devices were operational, she pressed the power button. The screen lit up. Then pale red words appeared on a black background.

ERROR. OPERATING SYSTEM NOT FOUND.

Kelly froze. She quickly rebooted the unit. The same message appeared.

Cursing, she pulled a diagnostic panel from her bag, then levered the tablet from its case to allow connectivity. As she did so, a folded piece of A4 paper fluttered to the ground. She picked it up. It was blank. These cases did not always stay attached and sometimes paper could be used to ensure a perfect fit. It was an old-school 'hack' for the new tech. Something Saxton would have found amusing. Putting the paper aside, she ran the analysis.

Thirty seconds later it confirmed her worse fears. The unit was blank. Or had been compromised to such a degree that her analytics tools could make no sense of it. Perhaps Kinek had somehow tampered with it when they were inside Saxton's house. Or perhaps it had simply malfunctioned. From a practical point, all that mattered was that she could not access the Director's instructions.

What was she supposed to do now? She thought back to her conversation with Saxton yesterday. What exactly had he said to her?

It's going to mean you warming to the task and showing a bit of zest. Remember this conversation: in case of trouble it'll tell you what you need to know.

She snatched up the folded sheet of paper, pulling a flashlight from her pocket and holding it close. Within seconds the heat began to cause a reaction. Words written in lemon juice began to turn brown, becoming visible. They were in Saxton's distinctive handwriting.

It occurred to me after a conversation with Gregory Jenson that this system we are fighting might even be able to scan handwriting. This should make things a little harder for them. We have been trying to build a unique weapon in the field of intelligence. Now we find our enemy already has the same tool. When your enemy knows everything about you, you have a problem. Somehow we have to take that advantage away. This is my first attempt. You have to do better. Be smart. Be alert. Be unpredictable.

And note the patterns around you. Things happen for a reason.

Kelly leaned back. The note was a low-tech solution to a hi-tech problem, but the instructions boiled down to little more than '*I have no instructions. Think for yourself.*'

She looked back at the television and saw another breaking-news story about a lawyer with links to ZAT being arrested for murder. A stock photo of Michael Adams popped up.

Kelly coughed, recognising the son of the late Craig Adams instantly. And thinking for herself, she knew what she had to do.

EIGHTY-ONE

Michael lay on the cell's foam bed unable to sleep, in part because of the lack of comfort, but mostly because of the thoughts charging through his head. Next to him was a battered paperback he had selected from the reading trolley: a copy of John Grisham's *The Firm* had been the only book available that had not been a cozy romance or epic fantasy. He'd selected it out of a sense of irony, not from any real desire to read, but there was nothing much else to look at except the blinking light of the CCTV camera and the metal reinforced door with no handle.

What was he supposed to do now? He didn't even know if Infinity was in control of events or just a pawn in a larger game. He didn't feel he had near enough pieces of the puzzle to see some overall picture. Meanwhile he was stuck here, trapped and vulnerable. Every instinct was telling him to get away, but what could he do by himself? His mother hadn't even come to see him and he'd warned Eve away too. As for Millie, they'd only been passing acquaintances – and he had no idea how to contact her from where he was. He stared blankly at the wall, hoping for a moment of inspiration. And he was struck by the impression that something had changed.

The CCTV's light was off.

He frowned and got to his feet, advancing on the camera

and snapping his fingers. Nothing happened. Previously it had reacted immediately to movement.

Michael moved quickly to the door and pushed. His heart raced as it began to swing outwards.

What should he do? Was it an opportunity or a trap? Was he safer here or outside?

A garbled voice floated from an intercom. *"Go left then left, then open the fire door to your right. I'll be waiting. You have thirty seconds before a guard comes to investigate the faulty camera. Go!"*

Michael stepped through the door. In the distance he could hear two people shouting. Above him another CCTV camera was also off. He turned left, walked ten metres down a featureless corridor, then left down another. On his right was the fire door. The raised voices were getting closer. He pushed.

No alarm sounded as the door opened.

Outside a slim figure stood in the shadow of a tree.

"How much of an invitation do you need?" Millie asked. "I thought perhaps you'd decided to stay put."

"If you're ever accused of a murder you didn't commit," he replied, "maybe you'll be a little cautious."

"Wasn't it two murders?"

"It could yet be three. Can we get out of here?" He gave a smile. "Also thanks for this."

"Yeah, well, I felt sorry for you." She led the way across the road to a large Mercedes with tinted windows.

Michael raised his eyebrows. "How did you get this car? Did you steal it?"

"It's a long story." She unlocked the doors. "Now get in."

Michael eased into the passenger seat, while Millie jumped behind the wheel and slipped the automatic gearbox into drive.

"Seriously, where did you get this car?" he asked.

Before Millie could reply, a woman spoke from behind them, her voice barely louder than a whisper. "An excellent question." An automatic pistol bearing a silencer wavered between them. "Now drive."

Michael started to turn around, but the barrel of the pistol struck him on the side of his head.

"Keep looking straight ahead. You, girl, drive steady."

Millie ground her teeth. "Where are we going?"

"To the address I've programmed in the Satnav," the woman commanded.

"So you can kill us?"

"That depends on how you answer my questions when we get there."

EIGHTY-TWO

In Jenson's secret laboratory, Craig pushed back from his bench. "Loathe as I am to stop, I really need some fresh air. I'm just not making any progress."

Jenson shook his head. "I don't think we should go outside. We don't want to give away any clues as to our whereabouts."

"Then I need something else to take my mind off things. My brain needs to reset."

"What about alcohol?"

Craig grimaced.

Jenson stood up. "Why don't I show you my toy cupboard? I have a number of things here that ZAT developed to the prototype stage, but didn't progress."

"You'd show me your top secret IP to me?"

"When it comes down to it, I'm just a big kid who likes to show off. And you're one of very few people who might actually appreciate it." Jenson pulled out his phone and tapped in a list of instructions. A hatchway in the floor slid back to reveal a metal ladder. "My basement has a basement."

They both climbed down the ladder. LED lights activated all around, revealing a room with three rows of metal cabinets, all with glowing electronic locks.

"What would you like to see?" Jenson asked. "I have a

number of processor designs that failed. Types of ammunition that didn't work, including smart bullets with micro-drone functionality so they'd fire round corners."

"You're kidding?"

Jenson shrugged. "They never worked correctly. Aiming them wasn't easy. And they kept overheating in the barrel – by which I mean they exploded before making it out of the gun. Fortunately we only ever test-fired them using robots."

"What else do you have?"

"Powered combat armour, abandoned for cohesion issues, and adaptive contact lenses with a partially-working HUD feature. And of course the failed control system for the micro-drones. It's an Aladdin's cave of broken treasures."

"You don't trust anyone much, do you? Even in a second level basement, you still have everything locked away."

"These things are dangerous. I couldn't risk anyone getting into them."

"Like your self-destructing bullets?"

"Worse than that." Jenson walked over to one cabinet, pressed his palm to the lock, then pulled out a drawer. In it were rows and rows of black wafers. "These are explosives."

Craig jerked back as Jenson pulled one out. It was the size of small coin.

"They were developed for the micro-drones. They're ceramic units, undetectable to most scanners: low weight, high yield. They're actually inert unless activated by specific computer signals. They won't go off if you drop them."

"How reassuring."

"They're one of the few things down here that actually works as intended." Jenson hesitated. "Can I ask you something?"

"When someone asks that, I'm always wary. But if you must."

"Why did you really do it? Fake your death?"

Craig blinked. "To save my son."

"That's what you said. But how did you make the decision? That's a lot of faith to place in a system."

"It had been right multiple other times."

"But this was something different: a huge long-term prediction."

"It's a machine. It can't lie."

"It could still be *wrong*. But then, I guess you were the one who programmed it."

"In a sense. I put the pieces in place: an inspirational piece of coding housed in hardware built on a unique design. Then it kind of… evolved."

"What I don't understand is that if you were supposed to stay in hiding, if you were supposed to stay *dead*, why did you come back?"

"Because things didn't play out like I was told. Michael was being drawn into ZAT and your new plans. This couldn't have been meant to happen."

"So," Jenson frowned, "Darwin was wrong after all?"

"That's what I'm trying to work out. If it was wrong about this, who knows what else it was wrong about."

"Maybe you should never have built it in the first place."

"I think that every day. Not that you ever did anything to stop me. Quite the reverse."

"Then maybe I was wrong too." Jenson's phone chimed and he looked at its display.

"You get a signal down here?"

"My phone works everywhere. I set a subroutine to track Millie."

"Does she know?"

"I certainly didn't tell her. I haven't decided if I trust her yet."

"I trusted her enough to take charge of rescuing my son."

Jenson opened a map on his phone. "Why is she there? They're way off course. Are you OK on your own for a bit while I check what's going on? Look at anything you like: maybe it will give you some inspiration. Just don't forget to close up when you're done."

Craig nodded. "Bring them back safe."

Jenson looked at the ceramic explosive he held in his

hand. He placed it back on the shelf. "I'll be as quick as I can."

CRAIG WATCHED JENSON CLIMB BACK UP THE LADDER. HE waited a few minutes, but nobody returned.

He thought again about what Jenson had said. Had Darwin been wrong?

He pulled out his own phone and found he had a signal, just a very faint one. He called a pre-programmed number. It was answered immediately.

"David Barr, Private Detective."

Craig cleared his throat. "This is Cory Ashcroft."

"Mr A, what can I do for you? As I said, always happy to—"

"How did we first meet?"

There was a pause. *"You contacted me, as I recall. I assume you saw one of my flyers or found one of my business cards."*

"But why did I find it?"

"I may have dropped off a few at the bookshop you work at."

"And how do you know where I work?"

"As I said, I like to verify my clients."

"Your business cards were all over the place for the week I started working at the bookshop. Then I never saw another again."

"I don't know what to tell you. I'm lazy. When I have some printed, I drop them in a small area and don't repeat till the business dries up."

"Did someone tell you to get my attention? To plant the idea in my mind that a private detective might be something I need?"

Barr's voice wavered. *"Do you have something new you want me to investigate?"*

"No thanks," Craig replied, cutting off the call. "That's all I needed to know." He put the phone in his pocket, and turned back to the ceramic explosive that Jenson had left on the shelf.

EIGHTY-THREE

Morton stood surveying the floor of the main control room with the unshakeable sensation that something was wrong. The handling of Saxton's situation still had him confused. Rarely did Kinek take such drastic action. Usually they gave nudges; now they were putting people in custody. And what had happened with Michael Adams? Morton knew that he had featured repeatedly in their recent plans. Yet now Adams had been arrested for something he did not do, all to test some hypothesis. Kinek's weapon was supposed to be the truth. Why would they use a lie? What would push them to take such a path?

He knew that when people were desperate they made desperate choices. Was Kinek's system – all but omnipotent for so long – faltering? It shouldn't be possible. Redundancy was built into everything they did; their carefully-constructed intelligence-gathering machine was a network, with each centre of operation, such as this one in London, acting as a hub. The failure of even multiple components of the system should mean the remainder would still allow the whole to function properly, perhaps without the same degree of error-checking and perhaps not as quickly, but it should still work. Moreover, each system was logically and physically separate, the connections between routed through people to avoid the automatic propagation and proliferation of viruses and other insidious code. Regardless of a problem in one or more parts, the system should still have been able to answer his question: where is Maxwell Errington? Yet the system's considered response had been ANSWER NOT KNOWN, INSUFFICIENT DATA OR INSUFFICIENT PROCESSING CYCLES AVAILABLE.

He closed his eyes and listened.

People were talking. Normally this room was almost silent, except for the hiss of cooling fans. But now, above that hiss, he could just make out urgent whispers. When he opened his eyes, he could see furtive looks exchanged between several of the operators. He quickly marched over to the nearest: a woman in her twenties.

She sat upright as he approached.

He pointed to her screen. "Do you have a technical problem?"

"The system has been slow for several hours. Now it’s rejecting all queries. It's like a key element has malfunctioned or is disconnected."

Morton looked to the young man on her left. "And you?"

"The same, sir. I've raised tickets, but I'm not getting any response from tech support."

Morton turned and walked to the floor supervisor. "I need your console."

She immediately stepped back and he placed his palm on the screen then typed in a long access code. Next he typed a question: PRIORITY LEVEL ONE OVERRIDE. WHERE IS TECH SUPPORT?

There was a long pause. Much longer than there should have been for a Level One request. Finally a string of text blinked onto the display: ANSWER NOT KNOWN. INSUFFICIENT DATA OR INSUFFICIENT PROCESSING CYCLES AVAILABLE.

Morton swore and typed the question again. There was a longer delay until new text appeared: ERROR. SYSTEM INACCESSIBLE.

"I've never seen it do that," said the young woman.

Neither have I, thought Morton.

He turned and ran to the booth, other workers scattering out of his path. He worked his way through security. Once voice identification was complete, he gave one order: "Initiate."

There was no reply. Morton narrowed his eyes. Was the microphone working correctly? Or was Marcia simply not there? That had never happened before.

He was about to speak again when the reply finally came. "This is Marcia. How can I be of assistance?"

He tried to keep his voice calm. "We have a serious problem."

"What is it?" Her tone was not quite as usual. Was there a hint of irritation perhaps?

"The system is offline. I'm surprised we didn't get—"

"Obviously I am aware. The issue is being resolved. I'll notify you when the process is complete."

Morton rocked back in his chair. "Are you saying this was planned? Why was I not notified?"

"The decision process unfolded dynamically. You were not on the critical path."

"But if you'd warned me I wouldn't have wasted time attempting to diagnose the problem." Morton ran a hand through his hair. Had he been wrong to think she would not have the matter completely under control? If she had decided not to inform him, there was no doubt some very good reason.

"We will consider adapting our procedures moving forward. Thank *you*. I can tell that the London office is safe in your capable hands."

The communication ended and Morton stood to leave, then paused. He had never heard Marcia speak like that. He turned back in the direction of the server room. Perhaps it was time for another inspection visit.

He stepped through the door, and immediately knew that something was terribly wrong.

EIGHTY-FOUR

Michael watched as Millie parked the car in the forest, where their kidnapper had instructed. The first rays of light were in the sky, but with the branches above it was hard to discern.

"Get out," said the woman. "Nice and smooth. No sudden movements."

Michael opened his door and stepped out. Millie did the same and stood next to him. The woman followed suit. She was dressed in black combat clothing, with a cap pulled low over her face. They watched as she threw something thin and white on the ground in front of him: plastic zip-ties.

"Tie her hands behind her back," said the woman.

Michael shook his head. "You don't have to do this."

She waved the gun. "Get on with it."

He sighed and picked up the lengths of plastic.

"You work for them, don't you?" Millie said. "Are you the one that killed Nichol?"

The woman blinked. "What? Of course not."

Michael stared at her. "Then why kidnap us?"

"I'm rescuing you, Mr Adams. And working out who the girl is. Now tie her hands like I told you."

"What do you mean, work out who she is? *She* was the one rescuing me." He placed the ties around Millie's wrists.

"She just breached the security on a police station, so I have a pretty good idea who she's working for. And that means you cannot take her actions at face value."

Mille frowned. "You don't know what you're talking about. And you're making a huge mistake."

Michael secured the zip tie. "What now?"

"Step well away from her. Nice and slow."

"I thought you were rescuing me?"

"That's my general plan, but I have no idea if I trust you yet."

"Great." He slowly moved away, his eyes flicking around. "Why did you bring us to these woods?"

"It's a location picked at random, away from telecommunications and CCTV, and enough trees to make drone or even satellite coverage difficult."

Millie laughed. "And I thought I was the conspiracy theorist."

"In my line of business the conspiracies tend to be real. By the way, if you think your friends are going to come rescue you, think again. I have a jammer running, and it's military grade."

Michael stared. "I'm getting the sense that we're all confused as to each others' motives."

"My motive," said the woman, "is to get to the truth. For example, I'm certain you were framed for the murder of Duncan Nichol."

"I was."

"Do you know why?"

"I have no idea."

"Well we need to work that out, so I need you to tell me everything."

Michael frowned. "Why would I trust you? The kidnapping, the pistol, the zip-ties don't really suggest that I should."

"Yesterday the Director of the Security Service, Warwick Saxton, was arrested for a crime he did not commit."

"And how do you know he's innocent?"

"Oh, he's far from innocent. As the head of MI5 there are many matters in which he is culpable. But as to the specific charges on which he is being held, he has been set up. I'd know because I've worked for him for ten years."

Millie burst out laughing. "You work for Warwick Saxton? Oh this is priceless."

"Why is that?"

"Because I do too. Well, I'm more a freelance consultant. My name is Millie Wright. Look me up. I have quite the online presence."

"I don't have access to my regular systems. For the last few days I've been at great pains to avoid anyone discovering I am still alive." She sighed. "Even if you are who you say you are, it doesn't mean you aren't also part of the problem. You could be a double agent, infiltrating Saxton's team."

Michael shook his head. "So how do we resolve this?"

"I think," Millie replied, "that someone else is going to resolve it for us."

"What?" the woman asked, then she looked down.

A red dot had appeared on her chest and a voice called out. "Drop your weapon. We have you surrounded."

The woman cursed and threw her gun to the ground. "How did you find us?"

"I assume because he's been tracking us," Millie said. "Normally I'd be pissed, but today I'm happy to make an exception."

Gregory Jenson appeared from between the trees, carrying an advanced automatic rifle aimed unerringly at the woman.

His expression became one of confusion, and he lowered the rifle. "Astrid? What the hell is going on?"

Michael shook his head. "You're Astrid Kelly? Jenson's assistant?"

The woman nodded, taking off her cap.

Jenson walked closer. "How are you here? Where have you been?" He raised the rifle again. "And what are you doing kidnapping these two? Explain fast."

"Easy, Greg," she said, raising a hand. "I was about to rescue Adams when I found him in the custody of this young woman. I had to intervene. When I saw it all on the news, I knew it had to be relevant, given his connection to ZAT it had to be relevant."

"Relevant? And how did you find him? The news didn't give his exact location."

"Well," Millie said, "Astrid here also has access to more exclusive sources of data. She claims to work for Saxton. And maybe she also works for Kinek."

"Of course, I don't," Kelly said.

Jenson's eyes narrowed. "We'll come to Kinek in a moment. You always told me MI5 fired you. That those events pretty much *defined* you."

"This has all got rather complicated."

"Then uncomplicate it. Do you work for Saxton?"

"I do," she said. "Although with him under arrest, I'm not sure if that's still true. And before you lose your temper, I haven't been spying on you. I've been protecting you."

Jenson's expression reddened. "I trusted you with everything. With my daughter."

"During the original planning for Project Parallel, Saxton developed concerns over your safety. He was worried that you might be vulnerable to coercion or threats. He engineered things so that I could find a place at ZAT, but not so that I could pass on information. I was there to keep you, and Teresa, safe." She held up her hands. "You sent me on an off-book mission the other day. Well, Saxton sent me on one years ago. I haven't had any direct contact with him since, until yesterday."

"What changed?"

"When I went to the equipment cache I was intercepted by an agent who gave her name as Cortez. I'm guessing she works for this Kinek we're hearing so much about."

"Why didn't you inform me?" Jenson asked.

"I barely escaped with my life. She left me for dead, and I was incredibly lucky to survive."

"And that didn't merit a call to warn me?"

"I knew it might give us a chance if they thought I was dead. It's become clear that Kinek knows everything we're doing, and why we're doing it. I needed to generate some kind of advantage; if they thought I was out of the game and hadn't been able to warn you, I knew we'd have an edge."

Jenson turned to Michael. "What do you think we should do?"

"I think we should get out of these woods."

"And do what exactly?"

"Well, given who you are, I find it improbable you don't have a plan. But if you're looking for suggestions, then I say we find Kinek."

"And Darwin," Millie said.

Michael nodded. "When we do, we stop all this nonsense."

Jenson lowered his rifle. "I agree."

Kelly let out a sigh. "That's good to hear—"

"But if you're coming with us, Astrid, we're going to tie you up. I'm still not sure I trust you."

She shrugged.

Michael held out another zip-tie. "You OK if I do the honours?"

Kelly smiled. "Be my guest."

Michael fastened the plastic in place, then looked at Jenson. "Do you have *somewhere* for us to go?"

"I do. And you can meet the other member of our impromptu team."

"And who is that?"

Jenson hesitated. "You know, in a day of weird nonsense, I'll just let you see for yourself."

Millie cleared her throat and waggled her wrists, still bound by the zip-tie. "If I'm going to drive, you might need to help me out here."

EIGHTY-FIVE

MICHAEL AGAIN SAT IN THE PASSENGER SEAT AS MILLIE DROVE steadily west out of London, following a safe distance behind Jenson's Range Rover, in which Jenson and Kelly were travelling. Millie glanced repeatedly into the rear-view mirror.

Michael frowned. "I'd have thought you would have rigged up some type of scanner to see if anyone is tracking us. It would save you looking back half the time."

"They'd track the scanner."

"Which 'they' is this?"

"Kinek. Because we think they built your father's system."

"They're operating Darwin?"

"There's a lot to get you up to speed on."

"Why are you and Jenson being so cryptic about everything, including this other team member?"

"Have some patience." She glanced at her phone. "According to Jenson, we'll be there in five."

Michael folded his arms and looked out at the starry sky. Four and half minutes later, Millie followed the Range Rover as it turned into a low-quality business park. They drove between rows of metal and brick units, many of which looked like they were unoccupied. They came to a halt in front of a particularly tired-looking unit. A peeling sign read 'GJSF Ltd'.

The door began rolling up and after Jenson drove inside, they followed. The door immediately descended after them. As it banged shut, bright lights ignited all around them. They climbed out of the car, squinting.

Kelly frowned. "What is this place? I've never seen it on a site list."

"Because it isn't on one. I kept a few things to myself." He raised his eyebrows at her. "It seems with good reason."

Michael looked around the deserted space as Jenson pulled a remote control from his pocket and pressed a button. Behind him, a panel slid back, revealing a metal staircase.

"Who's GJSF?" Millie asked, looking at the dark space below.

"A shell company I set up," Jenson replied. "Gregory Jenson Secret Facilities. It seemed funny at the time." He pointed to the steps. "After you."

Michael glanced at Millie, but she waved him onwards. Puzzled, he descended into a much more dimly-lit area. As he reached the bottom, he saw a figure standing waiting for him. The man stepped into the light.

And Michael stepped back.

At first he didn't believe what he was seeing. The man before him had aged fifteen years, but that expression could only belong to one person.

And yet it was impossible.

Michael blinked rapidly. What his eyes showed him didn't change.

"Hello, Michael," said Craig. "It's been a while."

EIGHTY-SIX

MICHAEL STOOD LOOKING AT HIS FATHER. "HOW?" HE managed to croak. "How are you alive?"

Craig moved forward, as if he might embrace Michael, then hesitated. "It's a long story."

"You died. In a fire."

"All staged. Vanishing was the only way I could protect you."

Michael clenched and unclenched his fists. "They found a body. *Your* body."

"They found traces of DNA in my teeth. The bones weren't mine."

"Then whose were they?"

Craig looked down. "A skeleton I bought via eBay. An old demo-model from a teaching hospital. I threw in a couple of my actual teeth."

Michael shook his head slowly. "Does Mum know?"

"No. I had to make sure she believed it too. There's no way she could have carried the lie all these years – if she'd even agreed to play along."

"Why did you need to protect me? Who was I in danger from?"

"The answer is a little complex. For now, let's just say I

had a very reliable source." Craig cleared his throat. "Millie tells me you've been investigating Project Darwin."

Michael blinked. "What are you saying? That Darwin told you? That's ridiculous."

Craig glared. "I thought I was keeping everyone safe."

"And, after fifteen years of lies, you expect us to welcome you back with open arms?"

"I didn't mean to be back. I certainly didn't mean to cross paths with you. But I discovered you'd changed jobs to work for a firm linked with ZAT. I knew it couldn't just be coincidence. That's not how things work in a world with Darwin. When there's a link, it's usually there by design."

"But Darwin never worked."

"That's not exactly true. I got it working. And then I destroyed it."

"And you killed yourself to stop anyone making it again?"

Craig coughed. "Yes. But somebody else built my Darwin System, and was running it. Has been running it for many years. That should have been impossible. The only prototype was in the barn. All my records were stored there. Plus there was a factor they could never replicate."

"'A factor'," Jenson said, walking down the stairs. "That's one way of putting it."

Craig rubbed at his temples. "Before I explain you need to know what Darwin is, so that you can understand why it was so important that I did what I did. So you understand that certain outcomes were never intended."

"Mind if I listen in?" Millie asked, following Jenson down the stairs.

"I was trying to talk with my son," Craig said, with a sigh. "But maybe it's for the best. We all need to be up to speed to decide what to do next."

Kelly cleared her throat as she appeared. "Hi, Mr Adams."

Craig frowned. "You are?"

"I work for Greg. And Saxton. But, as I think I've

persuaded Greg, I do not work for Kinek. I was trying to rescue your son when Millie beat me to it."

"Anyone else want to pile in?"

Millie looked around. "Assuming that's a no, why don't I make us some strong coffee."

"So," Michael said, after Millie had placed hot mugs of coffee in each of their hands, "what exactly is Darwin?"

Craig paced in front of a whiteboard. "What I did was connect three different things: a prototype computer optimized for pattern analysis, matrix software to run the analysis in a constantly-evolving manner, and a set of encrypted tunnel-generators to access data." He hesitated and raised an eyebrow. "It's a computer that can find answers – and also suggest them."

"How does it come up with its answers? Where does it get its data?"

"For starters, the internet. But that's just one network. There are many others, depending on how you define them. And I'm not just talking about the Deep Web and the Dark Web. More and more is being recorded – things you have no idea about – often in private corporate or personal islands of data." He pointed at Jenson. "Bugs like the ones ZAT makes are everywhere, watching, listening, recording. The system sucks down data from each of these different networks and overlays them, a bit like in weather prediction. Darwin is evolutionary in that it analyses its past performance and learns from it. If it predicts certain outcomes and gets them wrong, it re-analyses. Machine-learning, if you will."

"But the data you're talking about is mostly inaccessible," Millie said. "It would be hidden behind firewalls inside encrypted systems possibly not even connected to the internet."

Craig shook his head. "Things are more connected than

anyone realises. And, given enough time, tricks and processing power, you can get at almost anything."

"Tricks?" Michael asked.

"Powerful encryption-breaking algorithms are woven into Darwin's code. And they learn. Very little is resistant to it, especially with today's processing power. Indeed, that is the limiting factor: Darwin is designed to run on limited legacy hardware, and its cycles have to be prioritised because there are only so many." Craig paused. "Of course the real irony is that more and more data is put on the net voluntarily through Facebook, Twitter, LinkedIn, WhatsApp, Instagram, Baidu, WeChat, Orkut, any type of webmail, anything you do on Google, smartphones of every flavour and variety." He held his hands open. "People hand it over without a thought. Fifteen years ago I never envisaged how easy it would be."

Millie nodded. "People harp on about the dangers of governments spying, but for the most part they simply volunteer their deepest secrets. And don't get me started on this whole 'quantified self' thing - why people feel the need to track and record everything about themselves, I will never understand."

"Exactly," said Craig. "They provide a ready stream of what they're doing and thinking, who they're talking to and where they're doing it. It's almost ludicrous."

Michael coughed. "So intelligence organisations are one hack away from knowing everything about us?"

"Oh they don't need to hack us, if you believe the rumours." said Millie.

"The rumours about the government having secret access keys to our phones and computers?" Jenson asked.

"Quite," said Craig. "But that's not relevant to Darwin. The problem for anyone trying to make sense of all the data already out there is simple: there's too much of it. They're drowning in data, and the torrent is only getting greater."

"Until someone built a new kind of computer," Millie said, folding her arms and looking at Craig and Jenson.

"So," said Michael, "plugging all this into Darwin means you predict future events how?"

Craig raised his palms. "Prediction is a misnomer. Darwin really 'predicts' what has already happened, by extrapolating from a limited dataset. But that is still an extremely powerful function. First it draws data into its hub matrix - the data can be pretty much everything and anything. The system analyses, processes, correlates and connects. It takes your question and produces an answer."

"And it's accurate?"

"That very much depends on the accuracy of the data it's using. The more it has, and the more accurate it is, the better Darwin is at spotting patterns in it, then using those patterns to seek out more data, then looking for more patterns, and so on. People aren't quick enough, and we can't hold enough of information in our heads to properly grasp these patterns. In fact often we don't know what we're looking for. But with Darwin the patterns become readable – and as a result everyone's secrets are ripe for the picking."

"Most people have nothing to hide," Michael said. "Why would they fear a machine knowing the truth about them?"

Craig frowned. "I think you'll find that most people have a great deal to hide. Take the five of us: we all have our secrets."

They exchanged suspicious glances.

"So how did Kinek obtain Darwin?" Michael asked.

"Not from me," Jenson said. "ZAT funded the project, but the only prototype we ever saw didn't work."

"Still," Kelly said, sipping from her coffee, "surely someone else would have made this leap eventually. You can't take all the glory. Or the blame."

"Actually," Jenson said, "it's not at all clear that would have happened. Why don't you tell Michael what made Darwin so special? I think it's past time he knew."

Michael frowned. "What haven't you told me?"

"Yeah, what?" Millie asked. "Because everything can be

replicated. Particularly if they found your notes. Maybe they didn’t need your actual system."

"Not Darwin," said Craig without hesitation. He turned to face his son. "It's about you, Michael," said Craig slowly. "And how you helped make Darwin what it is."

EIGHTY-SEVEN

"I NEEDED AN OPERATIONAL MATRIX TO FRAME THE SYSTEM," Craig said. "And nothing I came up with worked. It needed a level of complexity I could not grasp. Perhaps if I'd been able to reach out to other programmers and crowd-source the solution, then maybe things would have been different. But obviously everything was being done in such secrecy."

"So tell Michael what you did," Jenson said, his arms folded.

Craig shrugged. "I found an established blueprint that had already solved the problem."

"You stole one?" Michael asked.

"No," Jenson said. "Your father looked to nature. Instead of reaching out to other brainiacs *for* the answer, he realised a brain could *be* the answer."

Millie put her coffee mug down. "You copied a human brain? That's preposterous."

Craig raised his hands. "No. That isn't remotely possible with our science *now*, let alone what we had fifteen years ago. What I did was map a neural structure electronically."

"To create an environment for Darwin?"

"Exactly. One it could grow within. One that would allow it to evolve."

"Wait," Michael said, "did this involve the use of a computer headset?"

Craig frowned. "How did—"

"You didn't just pick any brain. You picked mine." Michael's stared at his father. "Did you think, maybe, to ask me first? That's what was going on with the headset you had on me in the basement?"

"Well… yes. But it was no big deal."

"Mum says differently."

Craig's brow furrowed. "Huh?"

Millie cleared her throat. "What about his right to privacy?"

"Hang on. I wasn't copying his brain. This is more like if I took a book and copied the font size and page layout, but not the actual content."

"You still should have asked—"

"That's not what Mum meant," Michael said, interrupting. "She said it harmed me. Seriously."

"What?" Craig held his hands up. "It was just a headset copying your neural activity. It didn't do anything to you. Seriously. It *couldn't* have hurt you."

"Given that she's the doctor, shouldn't I be more inclined to believe her?"

"But she's not a neurologist. This wasn't a two-way communication device. The helmet was a modified magnetoencephalography, or MEG, cage: it's an imaging technique used to measure the magnetic fields produced by electrical activity in the brain. But it's only an imaging technique – it just records what's already going on in the brain - it certainly wouldn't change it."

Jenson frowned heavily. "You don't know that. And it was a huge risk to take with your son."

"By every bit of science that we know it was not. And as for the work that you do," Craig said, his voice rising, "you put your daughter at risk. By dealing in arms, you created enemies. Would your daughter have been kidnapped if you weren't who you are?"

"I did everything I could to protect her. I never *experimented* on her."

"And I never experimented on my son." Craig turned to Michael. "Do you feel unwell?"

"Not… exactly."

"Of course you don't. But why would she make something up?"

"With your mother, who knows?"

"But why use Michael at all?" Millie asked. "Surely you could have found some impoverished undergraduate who needed extra rent money?"

Craig shook his head. "We tried it with a number of others first – none of whom suffered any adverse consequences from the process. With Michael it was different. He was special, displayed many of the abilities I was looking to instill in Darwin: he rated off the scale in pattern-matching and in making predictions based on limited information. In fact, he was the original inspiration for Darwin, so it seemed only logical to take things a step further. And, of course, it worked. Better than I could have hoped."

"I made Darwin possible?" Michael asked.

"Without a doubt." Craig said. "That is why we can be sure that nobody replicated the system. It didn't need just any brain: it needed yours."

"So if I made it possible, this is all my fault?"

"Oh shut up!" Millie shouted. "This is *not* on you."

"No," Jenson said, "it's not. But can we focus on the problem we actually face. If Darwin required Michael, how did someone else make it?"

"That *is* the question," Craig replied. "And right now, I simply don't know."

"But," Millie said, "what if somebody stole your working version before you sabotaged it? Could they not copy that?"

"No. I built in fundamental copy prevention. It can't be moved from one operational matrix to another, without the original matrix map. They would have needed Michael to be present."

Michael coughed. "So we're agreed we can't explain it. But for now, it's enough to know they have it. And if they have Darwin working then this is all part of some plan. It's just a case of working out what that is."

"Maybe," Jenson said, "that's why they stitched Michael up with the murders. Maybe they want him out of the way so Darwin can't be recreated."

Millie shook her head. "Then why not just kill him?" She glanced apologetically at Michael. "It's not like they haven't done that to others."

"Who knows?" Craig replied. "The damn system is too powerful. And it's only going to get worse."

"What do you mean by that?" Michael asked.

"It's just occurred to me. This is all happening because Darwin has inherent limitations, constraints it cannot move beyond. Parallel may well solve them. And if that happens, all bets are off."

Millie blinked. "I'm usually the one to get carried away with doomsday scenarios."

"Darwin can do things that Parallel can't, but Parallel has brute force power. If you could combine Parallel's power with Darwin's efficiency - it doesn't take a genius or a computer to predict that the outcome will be bad."

"So we destroy it," Jenson said. "Except we can't, because we don't know where it is."

Millie held up a slim hard drive. "This contains everything we know about Kinek, given to me by Warwick Saxton. Now if the five of us working together can't find some way to locate Kinek, I'm pretty sure nobody can."

EIGHTY-EIGHT

REGINA ROSE WATCHED FROM THE DECK OF THE *EVOLUTION* AS the small boat made its final approach and pulled alongside. Two of her crew, hi-tech rifles slung across their backs, tied the smaller boat off then laid down a gang plank and prodded a familiar man towards it.

Maxwell Errington looked at it with a dubious expression, then up at Rose. "Why am I here?" He stepped forward, almost losing his balance as the two craft bounced in the gentle swell. "I said I wanted no part of this."

Rose extended her hand and helped Errington aboard. "Kinek were very helpful to me. In fact they did everything they said they would and more. They were so useful I thought I might need to reach them again."

"So you kidnapped me as your go-between?"

"I saved you. Your enemies were closing the net."

"I'm used to that. It's a dangerous world."

"A contract had been taken out on you."

Errington frowned. "Why would anyone pay to kill me? I'm so old they might as well just wait."

"Kinek have been right about everything else, Max, so I believe a 'thank you' might be in order."

"Thanks for what? I had a life. A wife."

"We can buy you a new one." Rose cracked a smile.

"So Kinek informed you of this impending hit?" Errington shook his head. "The thing to remember is that everything they do, they do for their own reasons."

"Everyone does everything for their own reasons. And you're the one who introduced me to them. I think it's worked out just fine." Rose turned to stare at the silver cases, plastered in warning signs, that were being carried aboard from the motor boat. "My drones."

Errington pointed at a large metal cabinet that sat on the deck of the smaller craft as several men attached a small crane to it. "What is that?" His voice trembled with excitement.

"An experimental computer system that Kinek asked me to acquire. It was all part of the deal."

"That's the thing with Kinek. The experimental computer system was probably their goal all along. They just made you feel like you needed the drones."

"Now you're being ridiculous," Rose replied. "I was in the neighbourhood, anyway. It was a good opportunity to do them a favour." Clipped footsteps sounded on a nearby staircase. "Hopefully a familiar companion here will help sweeten your mood."

Kara's slim figure appeared from below decks on the *Evolution.*

Errington's expression grew fixed. "So that's how you've been keeping an eye on me, Regina. Just how much did she pay you, Kara?"

Kara shrugged. "You say that like I defected, but there's been no recent change in my allegiance." She walked over and placed a kiss on Errington's cheek. "We'll look back on this moment and laugh."

Rose nodded. "I suggest we look to the future, because I can sense big changes on the horizon. Now I need to get our computer set up and test some of these drones."

"Is that safe?" Errington asked.

"My customer won't tolerate faulty merchandise. And we've got that scientist, Chow, below decks. He can help us if there's any issue." Rose smiled. "Besides, it should be fun."

EIGHTY-NINE

Michael stood surveying the hive of activity in Jenson's basement lab. Over the last few hours they had deployed a significant array of computing equipment, all with the goal of locating Kinek and Darwin.

At the centre of activity was the secure drive Millie had obtained from Saxton. Working with Craig, she had decrypted all the files and was parsing their contents with a range of tools. Jenson, meanwhile, had been digging through his meticulously-organised storage cupboards. So far he'd had located everything they needed for the next stage of their plan.

Kelly, bored at not being able to contribute, had been exploring the sub-basement's 'toy cupboard', then had disappeared upstairs with a set of experimental night-vision goggles.

"Do you really trust her?" Millie asked, staring at a screen rapidly scrolling text as she rattled away at her keyboard.

"Someone has to monitor the perimeter," Jenson replied. "And what Astrid's saying makes as much sense as anything I've heard over the last few days. I might not be happy that she works for Saxton, but I'd stake my life she's not part of Kinek."

"Not long ago she was pointing a gun at me."

Craig gave a snort. "At least she didn't shoot you."

"That's quite a low bar you're setting."

"Maybe we should focus," Jenson said.

"Doesn't mean I can't talk at the same time," Millie muttered.

"Are we making any progress?"

Craig leaned forward in his chair. "Not nearly enough. I've managed to localise some aspects of Darwin's activity, but the data is fuzzy – heavily packetised. Instead of a trail of breadcrumbs, it's like someone has thrown a handful of them over a map. Doesn't tell us much."

"I'm trying to overlay the research onto Darwin's data – see if any patterns emerge," Millie added. "But we've got nothing yet. With only the computing power we have here, it could take some time."

"Meaning what?" Jenson asked. "Hours?"

"Weeks. Maybe longer. We really need access to a supercomputer."

"Yeah," Craig said, "it kinda takes one to know one."

Michael scratched his head. "You said earlier that Craig displayed the data as some type of scattergram. Can you do that again, but on top of an actual map?"

"Because you'll see something that we didn't?" Millie asked. She stabbed an instruction into her computer and the largest display-screen filled with a random assortment of dots overlaid on a map of central London. "Hundreds of possible locations."

Michael frowned. "What about some form of heat map? Can you allocate intensity to the validity of the searches? You know, with different colours representing the different—"

"I know what a heat map is." Millie shrugged. "I guess we could try that." Again her hands flew over the keyboard. The map of London vanished then reappeared along with splotches of colour, structured like contour lines.

Michael walked closer, frowning. "No, that hasn't helped either."

Millie shrugged. "The reality is that this type of analysis isn't magic. We simply don't have enough data points.

"What about Morton?" Jenson asked. "He was Saxton's interface with Kinek. Saxton actually had him arrested, but the Home Secretary had him released. I heard there was a ruckus with expensive lawyers threatening all sorts of problems."

Michael frowned. "I wonder who was representing him."

"If Morton was arrested," Millie said slowly, "maybe we could track him after he left custody?"

"We also know the times and places Saxton met with him," Jenson replied. "Is there any pattern there?"

Millie shrugged and typed some more. The colours shifted and simplified.

Jenson clapped. "Progress."

Millie shook her head. "It's still at least fifty possible locations. And they're only possible at that."

Michael walked closer to the display. "What exactly are we looking for?"

"Somewhere large enough for their people to work out of with fast network connections. Somewhere out of sight."

"Can you overlay the London Underground network?"

Millie tapped away at the keyboard then shook her head. "It reports no statistically-significant intersections."

"Add disused stations. Service tunnels."

Millie shook her head. "Still nothing."

Michael frowned, then snapped his fingers. "Add historic as well. Include works started but not formally classified as stations."

Millie shrugged and typed again. A single point lit up on the screen.

"What is that?" Craig asked.

"A point of maximum relevance," Millie whispered. "How did you know?"

"I had some information you didn't. When I was starting out as a lawyer, I worked in the real estate team and helped negotiate the lease of a building right here." He pointed at the dot. "It took ages because the survey reported preliminary excavations for a tube station carried out in the 1930s; it was cancelled during construction and, according to our survey, filled in again, but I'm guessing that survey was less than accurate."

Jenson shook his head. "Is that a coincidence?"

Craig sighed. "I'm not sure there are coincidences anymore."

Millie snorted. "You're saying they wanted to be found?"

Michael tapped the dot. "Let's worry about that after we've found them."

Craig stood up. "So what do we do now? Break in, all guns blazing?"

Jenson smiled. "If that's what we agree. Believe me, I have all the equipment we could possibly need right here."

NINETY

Eve sat at her kitchen table, staring into a cup of black coffee and wondering if there was anything she could do to help Michael. As a doctor Eve was not easily rattled, so she was not going to scurry away from London. She couldn't live her life running from shadows of shadows. She would do whatever she could to help her friend and, if there was any justice in the world, the truth would out.

She had called Nina to tell her what was happening, but she had been unable to get through. Although if she was honest, not being able to speak to Nina had been a relief. Michael's mother usually kept herself to herself, and rebuffed any overtures of friendship, showing only the parts of her that she wanted the world to see.

Eve sighed and took another sip of coffee. Others might turn to alcohol to take the edge off, but she would rather sharpen her mind.

A knock at the door startled her. Eve frowned and padded along the hallway to answer it. She was surprised to see Nina on the doorstep, wearing her familiar oversized glasses. They stood staring at each other for several moments.

"I just heard the news," Nina said.

"I've been trying to reach you, but kept getting your voicemail."

"Sorry. There were some problems with my phone."

They stared at each other again, then Eve coughed. "Would you like to come in?" She took a pace back and Nina stepped inside. As Eve closed the door, she noticed there was a large car parked opposite. She followed Nina into the kitchen, where she was already pouring herself a coffee from the percolator.

"Do they suspect you too?" Nina asked gently.

"What?" Eve asked.

"I'm guessing those are policemen in the car outside, keeping an eye on you. Unless you've suddenly got a personal security detail."

"I'm no more guilty than Michael is!" She paused. "You *do* believe your son is innocent, right?"

"Oh I know him better than he knows himself. I'm sure this is all happening to teach him a lesson."

Eve frowned. "I don't understand. Are you saying you think this is doing him some good?"

Nina closed her eyes. "I'm sorry. I've been a little distracted - I think someone's been following me."

"The police? Why would they follow you?"

"I didn't stop to ask." Nina reached forward and clasped Eve's hand. "Has Michael said anything about… anything?"

"Only that he didn't do it. Maybe he got caught up in some mess caused by one of Infinity's clients."

"Did he say anything about his father?"

Eve frowned. "Not recently. Why?"

"Oh it doesn't matter. Just thinking out loud."

"Are you OK? You don't look yourself."

"Is that really surprising? My only child has been accused of murder. Look, I…" Nina went to sit down at the table, but slipped and, as she regained her balance, let the coffee cup fall. It shattered in an explosion of white porcelain and hot black liquid.

"Don't worry about it," Eve said. She grabbed the dustpan and brush, then knelt to sweep up the fragments.

But, as she stood up, she became aware that something had changed.

Three figures had appeared in the kitchen. They were dressed in black and carried what Eve suspected were automatic weapons.

Nina moved towards her, gripping her shoulder tightly. "What is going on?"

Eve looked around the room. "I have absolutely no idea."

NINETY-ONE

It looked like a regular Mercedes van on the outside, but almost every component had been upgraded or replaced. Kelly drove with a purpose, while Jenson rode next to her. Behind them sat Michael, Craig and Millie, all carrying ZAT assault rifles loaded with stun rounds and a tailored form of tear gas. They had gas masks on top of their heads ready to be deployed.

Craig looked out of the one-way glass at the London lights. "Are we sure Kinek's people won't be armed?"

"I have no data on that," said Millie. "Best to over prepare."

"And what makes you think you can get inside without them realising it?"

"With the arsenal of gear that Jenson had in the basement, we will get inside. At the least, we'll be completely unpredictable." She tapped at the laptop she had open. "That said, I'm having difficulty picking up any active signal from the site. It's like they're offline."

Craig shook his head. "It means they've either worked out how to mask it or it's already been switched off."

"Or it's not there?" suggested Millie.

"So much for knowing everything," muttered Michael. "Looks like we know nothing."

The van halted outside their destination. They leapt out and ran up to the door. Kelly scanned the street while Jenson span a dial on his weapon, then pointed it at the lock. It pulsed with electricity and the door popped open.

"Handy," Millie said.

"Isn't technology amazing," Jenson replied.

Michael pushed through the door. "Or amazingly terrible. Have you forgotten why we're here?" Emergency lighting was on inside the building. They moved quickly to the nearest door. Another shot from the rifle opened it. Behind was a staircase leading downwards. Three minutes later they emerged into a large hallway. At the end was a heavy fire door with a metal wheel-lock mechanism.

"I'm still getting nothing," Craig said, holding up a small scanner. "Something is wrong."

Jenson pulled on the hand wheel. "The rifle won't work on a mechanical unit. It's also locked. Astrid, can you pass me one of the shaped charges?"

"I don't think we'll need it."

They looked back at the wheel to find it rotating slowly. They all raised their weapons as it opened a crack.

"Please don't shoot. I'm unarmed," said a voice. The door opened further and a slim man emerged, his arms in the air, his face a faint green in the emergency lighting. "I'm sorry, but you're too late."

"That's Morton," Millie said. "I've seen his photo in the arrest record."

"Too late for what?" Kelly asked.

Morton rubbed a hand across his forehead. "Matters have taken an unexpected turn."

"Cuff him."

Michael did so, then they moved through the door and slowly down a corridor, emerging into what looked like an operations room. It stood idle and abandoned. The screens and computers were all switched off.

"Where is everyone?" Jenson asked. "Did you get tipped off that we were coming?"

"No," Morton replied, "but I assumed someone would be. Two hours ago I ordered the evacuation of the facility. These people were just doing a job. They didn't deserve to get arrested. Listen to me, Agent Kelly. What has happened is very, very bad. We'd been noticing degraded performance for the last twenty-four hours, but just over two hours ago the system went offline." He nodded his head at the room in general. "This place is never offline."

"You had a system fault?" Kelly asked, nodding to Millie and Craig, who ran over to one of the consoles and started working at it. "So what?"

"Not a failure," Morton said. "I'm not an engineer, but I know when something is simply wrong. I went into the server room. Every warning LED was red. Total system *failure*. That shouldn't be possible. We were told that the system shares resources with the other Kinek offices, yet it would seem they have all failed as well. The chances of such a systemic problem happening randomly are almost zero. Which means we have not been told the truth."

Kelly frowned. "Why are you sharing all this?"

"Because there is nothing left to protect. Kinek is… well, I thought it was dead. But I checked the system logs. There was a conscious act of disconnection. Wherever the Kinek engine is, we were simply cut off from it."

"But isn't this an organisation with hundreds of workers, multiple computer systems, operated in many countries?"

"Apparently not. It's just this, here."

"But what about all the people? The human part of your process?"

"They were just operators. All the work, the analysis – the extrapolation, connection and prediction – was taking place in a single system."

"You're saying that Kinek is effectively a single computer?"

"That, and its connections to the net."

"And where is it now?"

Morton screwed up his fists. "Are you not listening? I have

no idea. It could be anywhere. New York, Paris, Moscow, halfway up a mountain, on a tropical island. It could be half a mile down the street and we wouldn't know. All it needs is power and data."

Michael shook his head. "But why are you telling us all this? Won't your employer be unhappy?"

"I don't know if I have an employer anymore. I cannot reach Marcia. I don't even know who she is. Everything I've done has been a lie."

Millie looked up from the console she was sitting at. "From what I can tell so far, he's telling the truth."

"So," Michael said, "whoever is behind all this, they got away. And there's nothing we can do about it."

NINETY-TWO

Michael sank into one of the abandoned chairs. "So Kinek was a sham: nothing more than smoke and mirrors to disguise the technology at its centre."

Millie nodded. "And that technology – the Darwin system – is no longer here. Or maybe it never was."

Jenson stood nearby, hands in his pockets. "I don't understand how we've been several steps behind the whole way through."

Michael put his head in his hands. "So much for thinking my knowing about the old underground works here was somehow relevant. It didn't matter at all."

Millie slapped her hand on one of the desks. "At some level what you did has to be relevant. Unless, of course, Craig programmed Darwin with a sick sense of humour."

Craig shook his head. "You really need to stop thinking that I programmed the system. I set up the initial conditions and helped build its environment. After that I coached it. But ultimately it learned on its own and become a product of its own evolution. It was called Darwin for a reason."

"Yeah, we get it," Jenson said.

"So Darwin wants to continue evolving," Michael said. "Morton said the system has been erratic, with limited cycles.

Maybe that's because Darwin has already reached the limits of its present hardware."

Millie hissed. "It really is planning to combine with Parallel."

Kelly shook her head. "In real terms, what does that mean?"

"That the problem is far worse than anticipated."

"But our plan is the same," Jenson said. "We have to destroy it, if we can find it."

"Unfortunately," Craig replied, "it's more complicated than that. When I designed Darwin, I built an emergency backup into the code. If the system senses hardware failure, it will distribute itself: 'spore' is the technical term."

"You gave it a survival instinct?" Millie asked.

"That's one way of framing it. It was part of my early planning – there wasn't time to reverse it when I planned the explosion. Of course it wasn't fully operational at that point, so I didn't think it would matter."

"But," Jenson asked, "wouldn't the spore process take a huge amount of time? It must be petabytes of data."

"Actually no," Craig said. "A lot of the volume code is distributed in advance, in heavily encrypted form, so it'd only take the time needed for final differential updates and activation of its backup codes."

"So we can't shut it down even if we find it?"

Millie let out a sigh. "If either of you have invented some form of time machine, now would be a good time to disclose it."

"At least two years away, sorry," Jenson replied, a half-smile on his face.

"No problem. All you need to do is to remember to travel back to this precise moment to help us out—"

"Shut up," Craig shouted. "Leave the classic movie references to me, please. That said, your nonsense has given me an idea."

"Which is?" Jenson asked.

"We kind of press rewind - we do an entire reversal. We

de-constitute the system, using Michael's neural matrix. With that level of authorization, we should be able to modify everything. Including removing the ability to *spore*."

Millie blinked. "Will that actually work?"

"Based on everything I know."

"We have to give it a try." Michael folded his arms. "I was there at the beginning; it seems fitting that I be there at the end."

"Poetry be damned," Millie said. "At least your father's asking this time."

Craig glared at Millie. "Let it go, will you?"

"A great plan," Jenson said, "But we still don't know where it is. And if we did, they'd just see us coming."

"Maybe I can help you with the last part," said a voice from the other side of the room. They turned and saw Morton staring at them.

"Why would you do that?" Michael asked.

"I joined Kinek to be an agent of the truth. But I was sold a lie. Or a million of them. Whatever happens to me, I'd like to do something to fight back. And while things were, apparently, bad enough already, they could be about to get far worse." He walked over and, wrists still cuffed, carefully removed his glasses and held them out. "These might be of help to you."

Michael took the spectacles. "I don't understand."

"They're a discrete HUD. It's how I accessed Darwin." Morton paused. "When they work, they are what pretty much sums up Kinek: an unfair advantage."

Michael swapped them with his current glasses. "They're not working. I don't see any HUD."

"For them to function, you need to have an authorised secure link, or be close to an operational Darwin instance." Morton reached forward. "They also do this." He tapped the frame on the top corner.

Michael's vision leapt into focus. He blinked. "That is exactly like the system I saw in the ZAT lab."

Jenson frowned. "Something else you lot stole from me?"

Morton shrugged. "Kinek took what it needed from whomever it encountered. Then we usually made it better. When you have the best of everything, winning is straightforward."

Michael nodded. "Maybe we can use that against them."

"Come on," Jenson said. "Let's get out of here. Maybe we weren't the only ones to get tipped off as to this location."

Michael tucked his old glasses into his pocket. "What's that noise?"

"What noise?" Millie asked.

"A kind of faint high-pitched whining." He looked down and saw a pattern of red dots on his chest. Glancing around he saw they were everywhere.

Kelly jumped to her feet. "Take cover!"

Michael saw tiny flashes of red and silver, then he felt a stinging sensation on his neck.

Around him the others were swiping at the air, staggering and slumping.

Then everything went black.

NINETY-THREE

Michael drifted back into consciousness. Blinking rapidly, he saw he was in a grey-walled, windowless room. He lay in a hospital-style bed, which had been angled so he was half-sitting. From his chest and arms ran a number of wires and tubes. As he tried to move he realised he was held by leather restraints, attached to the raised metal sides of the bed.

A man wearing medical scrubs stood next to him, checking a monitor that the tubes and wires ran into. He made some notes on a tablet computer, then nodded to the only other person in the room: a woman wearing metal-rimmed glasses and an expensive grey suit. Home Secretary Charlotte Rostrum.

"Mr Adams," she said pleasantly when the medic walked out, closing the door behind him. "Good to see you awake. I've been anxious to speak with you."

"Where am I, and what the hell happened?" Michael asked. "Did you drug me?"

She spread her hands. "We found you unconscious at an illegal underground facility in central London. You were brought here and medical aid was provided. I'm pleased to report you appear to have suffered no permanent ill effects."

"What is going on? Why am I tied up?"

"So that you don't wander off again." Rostrum stood up and walked closer. "You're an escapee from police custody: the prime suspect in multiple murder cases."

Michael frowned. "Where are the others?"

"An interesting crowd, not least of all your father. All of you would be well advised to speak to me candidly if there's to be a chance of sorting this mess out."

"How did you know to go to that location?"

Rostrum glanced upwards, looking irritated. "I think you've misunderstood the situation. I'm going to be asking the questions."

Michael stared at her. "You are behaving in a very strange way for a senior member of government, and you clearly learned your interrogation skills from a Hollywood movie."

"What were you doing in that facility?" Again her eyes flickered.

"I'm not going to…" And then Michael realised what he was seeing. He gave a smile. "Jenson suggested you'd been tipped off as to the location of the Kinek facility, but I think you knew about it all along."

"I don't know what you're—"

"I think whatever knocked us out was a system you deployed: possibly the same system that Jenson's company developed. The one you had Saxton arrested for covering up the use of. And yet you didn't have Jenson arrested. None of this makes any sense unless someone else was telling you what to do. I think the reason you're so agitated is that they've stopped."

"I'm only talking to you as a gesture of goodwill. I can leave—"

"You aren't personally interrogating me for fun. You're talking to me out of necessity, because you don't know what's going on. And you're desperate." Michael tapped his glasses. "I think you believe that we might be the only ones who can help you. And you're probably correct."

"Help me do what?"

"Regain what you've lost. Access to their system. Access to the power it has given you."

"I don't know what you're suggesting. I'm an elected member of parliament."

"Who has had a particularly meteoric rise into government. What do they have on you? It's usually the truth, written on grey paper."

Rostrum blinked and slowly took off her glasses. "What do you want, Mr Adams?"

"I want you to release us, and get the heck out of our way."

"To do what?"

"To stop what is happening," Michael said. "Because I know you know how powerful what they have is. So consider what will happen when that tool becomes exponentially more powerful still, and is used against you; against all of us. Because it's a pretty safe bet that's what'll happen."

Her eyes widened. "You don't know that…" She hesitated. "Can you really do anything against these people? Against this system? You don't even know where they are."

"We will find a way. We have to. And to do that, there's one person we're going to need back in the game."

NINETY-FOUR

MICHAEL SAT AT A LONG CONFERENCE TABLE IN AN underground conference room within MI5's Vauxhall headquarters. Across from him were Jenson and Kelly.

"Never thought I'd get to visit this building," Michael said. "Gone past it so many times on the train, wondering what was inside."

"Not the most surprising event of the last week," Jenson replied. "In fact, to be sitting anywhere but a disavowable prison cell might be considered a win."

Footsteps sounded in the corridor. Without announcement, Warwick Saxton walked in and closed the door. He nodded to Jenson and Kelly, then his gaze locked on Michael. "I understand you're the one I have to thank for my release. And my full reinstatement as MI5 Director."

Michael shrugged. "Your boss presented me with a lever. If I've learned anything in my time at Infinity, it's how to pull one."

"So I'm gathering, though Rostrum didn't elaborate."

"Let's just say you aren't the only one who's been taking advantage of Kinek's capabilities."

Saxton took the seat at the head of the table. "That explains a lot. She caught me up on recent events so I understand we've lost track and control of more than one deadly supercomputer, neither of which I knew existed."

Jenson shrugged. "You're supposed to be the one with the government intelligence network."

"And as we all know, it's broken. So what are we going to do about it?"

Kelly cleared her throat. "We were hoping you could tell us."

"Then my release has been predicated on unrealistic expectations."

"Something tells me," Michael said, "that a solution is going to present itself."

Jenson folded his arms. "You keep saying that. Seems like a long shot."

"I think we start with all the data we have on all the people who are, to our knowledge, linked. Remember, nothing is irrelevant. Everything is connected. There will be a pattern."

Kelly's phone pinged. She glanced at it. "GCHQ has picked up a communication from Maxwell Errington."

"Do they have him under surveillance?" Michael asked.

Saxton shrugged. "Not as a matter of course."

Kelly waved her phone. "He was flagged after he was reported missing by staff at his house."

"So Max has gone into hiding?" Jenson folded his arms. "Just as we need him most, he's lost the urge to fight."

"Not according to the intercept. It appears he was kidnapped by Regina Rose. Errington said that Lee Chow is with him. And he gave his coordinates. He's on Rose's yacht, off the north coast of Australia."

"If he was kidnapped," Jenson asked, "how did he get to a phone or radio?"

"The message didn't explain," Kelly replied, "but Errington is resourceful."

"So Rose is behind all this? The theft of my micro-drones, the kidnap of Lee Chow, and the acquisition of the prototype Parallel system? She must be the one with Darwin."

"Maybe," Michael said. "I guess we should go find out."

Saxton frowned. "You said that a solution would present itself. So here we are, completely lost, and Maxwell Errington calls to provide us with the answer."

Jenson shrugged. "Max is creative. It's entirely plausible he would outsmart his captors."

"Or maybe," Michael said, "he's doing exactly what his captors have ordered."

Saxton shook his head. "How does any of this help us stop the system? Is that even possible?"

"That's what Millie and my father are working on right now."

"Ah yes, your father. Back from the dead."

Michael ignored him. "Do you have any assets off the north coast of Australia and a way of getting us there very quickly?

Kelly shook her head. "MI5 have no authority to run an operation outside the UK."

"No," Saxton said, "but I know a man who does. It's time I called in a favour."

"Great," Jenson said. "You tell me where the asset is, and I'll get us there."

NINETY-FIVE

THE SUPERSONIC JET, AN UGLY GREY CRAFT COVERED IN radar-absorbing paint, levelled out at 17,000 metres, the noise from its engines diminishing only slightly. Inside the pressurized cabin its six passengers were strapped to their seats with full harnesses. Michael stared out of a tiny porthole window. "Exactly how fast are we flying?"

Jenson adjusted his helmet. "Around Mach 4. We should have you on board the *HMS Windsor* in four hours, if their transport is ready to meet us."

"I'm guessing this isn't a regular private jet," Craig said, looking around the sparse interior.

"It's a repurposed military unit," Jenson replied. "Surprising cargo capacity given the design constraints."

"Although not exactly the most opulent of cabins," said Millie.

"As I like to say to my customers, we can do fast or comfortable – pick *one*." He paused. "In my experience luxury not only costs, it *weighs*."

"But I'm guessing no peanuts? Next you'll tell me there are no hot towels?" She glanced at Saxton. "Although he looks like he would rather have a sick-bag."

Kelly cleared her throat. "The Director doesn't travel well, particularly at over 3Gs of acceleration. Now are we all clear on the plan?"

"Of course. But are you sure this is wise?" Millie asked. "If Rose has Darwin running, there is no way that we can catch them unawares. We'll be walking into a trap."

"Then we have to walk in with a few tricks of our own."

Jenson turned to Michael. "Are you ready for your part? I'm sorry that you have to be the one to do it, but it wasn't a decision I was involved with—"

"Do you think," Craig asked, "I'd have done it this way if I'd foreseen what would actually happen? It's the ultimate irony that if I'd had Darwin, I'd have known not to build Darwin."

"Maybe you shouldn't have needed it," Millie said. "Maybe the risk was obvious. And by missing it, you've put the whole world on a knife edge. How does that feel?"

"If I could have my time over, I would change things," Craig replied. "Everything went wrong the day I started telling people about the system. I should have kept it to myself. It was safe when I was the only one who knew. Well, myself and Nina, because I had to show off to someone. And of course she wasn't even interested in it. Maybe if she had been, I'd have thought twice about letting ZAT in on it." Craig looked at his watch. "How much longer did you say?"

Jenson smiled. "Not long."

He turned to Millie as she took out the glasses that Morton had given to Michael, holding them out to him once more.

"All ready, though it wasn't easy. We've built up a wrapper on the frame so they look like your existing glasses, but added some additional decryption hardware to increase the chance they will actually work, howsoever Darwin is now configured."

Michael took them and switched them with the pair he was wearing. "They're not doing anything."

"We believe they'll lock back onto Darwin signals once a

system access-point is within range. We can't tell you how long that will take, or whether there'll be any other factors to consider."

"Won't obtaining access trigger some sort of alarm?"

"It shouldn't. Remember, this isn't a hack. This is a native part of the system."

Jenson smiled. "And in order to help you live long enough to get the glasses operational, I'd like to give you both a set of ZAT body armour… except that it doesn't work."

"Maybe you should have let someone steal it and fix it for you," said Craig.

"You're a funny guy."

"What about weapons?" Michael asked.

"Do you know how to use one?" Craig asked. "You're more likely to hurt yourself." He paused. "Besides, if this works like it should, you'll be the weapon."

"Don't forget we've still got to rescue Errington. And Chow."

"Yes," said Jenson, "because the world needs a traitorous old lawyer. Chow, I'll cut some slack."

"That doesn't mean Errington deserves to die," said Kelly.

"Either way, perhaps now isn't the time to start on the lawyer jokes," Millie replied.

Jenson sighed. "We'll be stationed a short distance away: I've got one of my private yachts approaching the area since Astrid, Millie and I have not been extended an invitation on board the navy vessel."

"Drawing the line at hackers," said Millie. "How unprogressive of them."

"No undercover agents, either," Kelly said. "They don't know what they're missing. Any indication that Darwin is back online yet?"

Michael lifted his Infinity laptop. "Not according to this. But I don't know how reliable it is, given all the changes."

"OK," said Jenson, "then I guess we might as well have some dinner." He turned to a cabinet.

"Now we're talking!" said Millie.

Jenson turned and handed out a collection of energy and cereal bars. "Like I said, luxury *weighs*."

NINETY-SIX

Rose stood in one of the conference rooms on her yacht. Her team had unpacked the micro-drones and supporting equipment. The drones had a primary control computer the size of a briefcase. With the aid of Lee Chow, Rose's people had got the system active. But now there was a problem.

The system's touch screen displayed a simple oval with a short message.

>>> CONFIRM PALM PRINT ID TO ACTIVATE SYSTEM

Rose placed her hand on the screen for the third time.

>>> ACCESS DENIED. ADMINISTRATOR NOT RECOGNISED

"Look," Chow said, "I keep telling you that this wasn't a project I was involved with. I never worked on the micro-drones, only on Parallel and related systems. ZAT is a big company."

"Then maybe I should just shoot you," Rose replied.

"I thought you'd been told to go easy—"

"Told by whom?"

"You called for me?" Errington asked, walking into the room.

"Look at this," Rose said, pointing at the screen. "Why was I not warned?"

Errington held up his hands. "I'm just a spectator along for the ride. I don't know who's been giving you your information, but it was always likely that there would be security measures. There has to be a way you can override them. That or leave it to the client: make it their problem."

Chow shook his head. "This isn't a software issue. It's hardwired into the system."

"So whose palm print does it want?" Errington asked.

"It doesn't say," shouted Rose.

"Have you tried asking the computer?"

Rose raised an eyebrow and turned to Chow, whose hands were already flying over the keyboard. The screen blinked and changed.

>>> MARCIA

Errington shook his head. "You need the head of Kinek?"

Rose gritted her teeth. "Is this some kind of joke? Are we supposed to take it to her?"

"Maybe you already have?" Errington stepped forward and placed his palm on the screen. The oval glowed blue and there was a soft tone of recognition.

>>> ID ACCEPTED

Rose looked confused. "I don't understand. Is it broken?"

Errington shook his head. "No, I believe it's working as intended." He reached a hand up to his neck and pressed something under his shirt. Then he spoke loudly.

Not with his voice, but Marcia's.

"Darwin system. Commence executive override order zero zero one."

>>> COMMAND CONFIRMED

"Initiate lockdown," said Errington with Marcia's voice.

>>> COMMAND CONFIRMED

Rose shook her head. "OK, that's enough. Guards take—"

The weapons on the belts of the three guards crackled

with energy. The three figures jerked and spasmed, then fell to the ground.

"Status?" Errington asked in Marcia's voice.

>>> DARWIN TEMPORARY CONTROL NODE ONLINE

There were hurried footsteps and Kara ran into the room. "Everyone's collapsed," she shouted, then looked around the room. "Here too?"

Errington nodded, tapping the point just below his neck again. His voice returned to normal. "Is it just you, Regina, Chow and myself standing?"

She nodded.

Rose jerked her finger. "Kara, he is Marcia." She swallowed hard. "Somehow Max is Marcia."

Kara looked at her with a flat expression. "You're not making any sense."

"Just take care of this!" shouted Rose.

Kara raised her gun and pointed it at Chow.

He raised his hands. "What are you doing? You need me."

"No, anyone *else* would have needed you, so we had to bring you along to disguise what is really going on."

"That's ridiculous—"

Kara shot Chow in the chest. With a confused shriek, he fell to the floor. She adjusted the weapon and pointed it at Rose.

Rose narrowed her eyes. "Whatever Max has offered you, I will double it."

"Why do people keep saying that to me? I *want* to do this." The rifle did not waiver.

Rose hissed. "How did you persuade her, Max?"

"Actually," he replied, "Kara has always worked for me."

"But you're just a lawyer. You're only here because—"

"Because your contact suggested it?" Errington smiled. "Along with a number of other strategic actions. All proposed by me. I just needed your resource, Regina. Now I'd love to stand around and chat, but we have far too much to do."

"My people will track you down—"

"Your people don't know about me any more than you did. They won't understand that I was Marcia, Kinek, and your customer all rolled into one."

"You wanted the drones all along."

Errington shook his head. "The drones were just a distraction: I already had them. What I really wanted was the prototype computer system you stole on my behalf."

"Why? What is it?"

"The future." He nodded to Kara. "Unlike you. You're in the past."

Rose spun, raising her hands. They did nothing to stop the bullet.

ERRINGTON GLANCED AT CHOW'S FROZEN EXPRESSION, THEN walked over and kicked Rose's body, before smiling at Kara. "Thank you, my dear *Cortez*."

Kara checked her gun then slung it over her shoulder. "I'd like to get moving. We're exposed out here."

"That depends on whether they know where to look. On this occasion I'm counting on it."

"So they *could* find us?"

"I already told them."

Kara scratched her nose. "The system instructed you to?"

"I didn't need to waste any cycles on such a request. We need their help. Do you want to know why?"

She shrugged. "As you always say, if I need to know you'll tell me."

NINETY-SEVEN

Saxton stood on the bridge of the Royal Navy missile destroyer *HMS Windsor.* The ship was under three-quarter power, heading unerringly for their target. Next to him was the ship's captain, Grant Eversley.

"Once again, Captain," Saxton said, "we really appreciate your assistance."

Eversley smiled. "When Sir Douglas reached out, the Vice Admiral was only too happy to help. His orders were we should extend you every courtesy."

Saxton looked out of the port-side window and saw the *HMS Exeter* cruising alongside, matching their steady twenty-two knots. "An aircraft carrier shadowing our position is a little overwhelming."

"Your request was to take the threat seriously. Besides, we had a number of assets on exercises in the area."

"Let's hope we don't need them."

"I doubt we will. It *is* just a single craft we're tracking, a civilian yacht?"

"It may look like that," Saxton said, "but it's likely to be carrying considerable military tech and weapons systems."

"We'll be ready for all eventualities. You sure you still want to send your team out first? Just the two civilians?"

"The submarine is largely automated. Point and click to move, as I believe Jenson described it."

"I was thinking less about how they get there and more about what happens when they do."

"Don't underestimate them. If all goes as plan, they can disable the vessel's computer systems without a shot needing to be fired."

Eversley shrugged. "If a shot needs to be fired, we won't hesitate." Behind him the navigator called out that they were ten clicks from their target. "That's close enough. Drop off the cargo, and Godspeed to them."

THE FOUR-MAN SUB POWERED AWAY FROM THE *HMS WINDSOR*, descending quickly to its planned cruising depth of fifteen metres: enough to mask it from visual detection and standard radar. Inside, Craig and Michael studied the various display screens.

"Are you sure it makes sense not to let Jenson come with us?" Michael asked.

"That would hardly leave us space to bring back Errington and Chow, if that's what we need to do."

"He said he had never tested this sub in a combat situation."

"Which was very reassuring," replied Craig. "How long until we reach the yacht?"

"Fifteen minutes max."

"Any further word from your lawyer boss?"

Michael shook his head. "I expect he won't risk trying to communicate a second time."

"Or he's dead."

"He'll have found a way to survive. You have to acknowledge his resourcefulness."

"For someone of his generation, sure - managing to make an encrypted call without being detected is quite something." Craig looked at his laptop. "I'm detecting traces of Darwin system activity. That means there's an access point nearby. Anything showing on your glasses?"

Michael tapped them. "Nothing."

"Then let's just hope we don't need to rely on them."

FIFTEEN MINUTES LATER, THE *EVOLUTION* CAME INTO VIEW ON their screens. The massive white craft, almost as large as the *HMS Windsor,* was making only five knots, not remotely testing its engines.

"I thought they'd be in more of a hurry." Michael said.

"To do what?" Craig asked. "If they stop anywhere, they'll be easier to detect."

"I guess." Michael pointed at a screen. "So we approach under the rear where schematics showed the submarine docking point."

"Let's just hope Rose isn't monitoring it."

Michael tapped commands into the console; the submarine's automated systems executed them. External cameras gave a view around the craft.

"What is that?" Michael asked, pointing at a large black object attached to the underside of the *Evolution,* next to where they were docking. "Does Rose have her own submersible? It's bigger than this one."

"Don't get distracted," Craig replied.

The submarine locked onto the underside of the *Evolution* and the automated hatch confirmed an air-tight seal. Michael pressed a button and it opened.

Maxwell Errington was waiting on the other side. "Are you guys a sight for sore eyes. You are so brave coming for me."

"I won't argue with that." Michael hauled himself into the *Evolution.*

"But don't kid yourself that it's about you," said Craig, following up through the hatch.

Errington's jaw fell open. "Craig Adams? How? I thought you were—?"

"Dead? Yes, I hear that a lot. Let's just assume that I'm not and we can fill in the blanks later."

"Well, then I guess we should get out of here."

"Where is Darwin?"

Errington raised an eyebrow. "Ah, I see. So I'm a secondary consideration?"

Craig glared. "I don't know exactly how you ended up here, but I don't trust you. Regina Rose was your client: I'm not convinced she isn't *still* your client. I'm not sure your distress call wasn't part of some subterfuge."

"Easy," Michael said. "He called us. He's on our side."

"Actually no," said Errington, "I'm not."

There was a cough from the doorway. All three men turned.

Kara stood there, pointing an assault rifle. "Well, isn't this a happy reunion."

Michael's eyes took in the dull metal of the barrel, levelled unwaveringly at him. "I figured you weren't really dead. I guess you aren't really a lawyer either."

"I'm lots of things. Right now I'm a lady with a gun. Which means you do what I say."

"Any chance that you might make a quick phonecall so they can cross one murder charge off my list at least?"

She gave a smirk. "Who do you think set that situation up?"

"Oh, right." Michael paused. "So you… Duncan…"

She shrugged. "I never liked him. Now we need to get moving. We have a submarine to load up with a collection of tech toys, including Project Parallel." Kara smiled and turned her weapon towards Craig. "I'm not a patient woman, so be quick about it."

NINETY-EIGHT

THE *HMS WINDSOR* APPROACHED WITHIN ONE KILOMETRE OF the *Evolution*. As yet there had been no response to their presence: no change of course or speed, no attempt to communicate.

"The sub is still docked," Eversley said. "It should have departed by now."

Saxton nodded. "I can't raise them on the link. Something has gone wrong."

"Well, there's no possibility that they're not aware of us. Let's hail them." He turned to the communications officer. "Broadcast on all frequencies."

The reply was immediate. An accented, metallic voice filled the bridge. *"This is Regina Rose, Commander of the Evolution. State your intentions, Windsor."*

Eversley stood up straight. "We require you release the hostages on board."

There was a pause. *"Nobody is on this vessel against their will."*

"We're coming aboard to verify. Prepare to receive my inspection delegation."

"Permission denied, Captain. These are international waters; you have no jurisdiction or authority here."

"I insist, Ms Rose. As you may have noticed, I have the firepower of a fully-armed cruiser, along with the airborne resources of an aircraft carrier." Eversley turned again to the comms officer. "Initiate the flyby."

"I repeat: permission denied."

Over the throbbing of the ship's engines, a thunderous noise exploded in the sky and two F-24 fighters roared towards the *Evolutio*n, skimming it by a few hundred metres. The sound waves blasted ripples in the ocean's surface in all directions.

"You should reconsider your position," Eversley said. "We'd prefer not to use force."

"Impressive, Captain. But this vessel is more than capable of defending itself. Do not fly over our position again."

Eversley rolled his eyes and waved his finger in the air, rotating it. The comms officer relayed the instruction and the F-24s wheeled tightly in the sky, gunning straight back for the super yacht.

"You were warned," Rose's voice announced.

Saxton, watching the *Evolution* through binoculars, suddenly called out. "A missile launcher just rose out of the deck."

"Pull up! Abort!" shouted Eversley. "Abort!" But the launcher had already rotated to target the fighter jets. A missile fired. Immediately the two jets split and pulled into vertical climbs, spitting out counter-measures in their wake. The missile closed the gap, but then exploded some distance short.

"OK, they had their chance. Arm torpedoes," barked Eversley. "Fire on my mark."

"But my people are on board!" Saxton cried. "You can't just sink it."

Eversley turned to him. "I have 400 crew on this ship, and there are more than twice as many on the Exeter. I cannot place them in further danger." He pointed to the weapons officer. "Fire both tubes. If we're fortunate, there will be survivors."

Saxton shook his head in disbelief as he saw two lines of white water indicating the path of the torpedoes. They tore through the water, closing on the *Evolution.*

Then suddenly they turned away from the super yacht, and kept turning.

"What is going on?" shouted Eversley?

The weapons officer was swearing at his console. "The guidance systems have been overridden. Something else is controlling them."

"How?"

"I don't know. Nothing should be able to do this." He hesitated. "They're coming back to us."

"It's their computer," Saxton said. "It's predicted your codes and broken into your control systems."

"That's impossible. Override it!" shouted Eversley. "I'm not about to be hit by my own weapons."

"I can't," replied the weapons officers. "My console is unresponsive."

"Deck guns. Shoot them out of the water."

"The guns are offline too."

Eversley turned to Saxton. "What exactly have you led us into?"

Saxton ran his hand agitatedly through his thinning hair. "Do your torpedoes have a zero-guidance fail-safe?"

"Yes," said the weapons officer.

"Then kill the power! Fast!"

"To what?" asked a junior officer.

"To everything."

At Eversley's nod, the junior officer ran across to a wall of controls and pressed a large button, then pulled a lever down. Every system went dead.

The two torpedoes exploded well short of the *Windsor.*

"They need a constant command-signal to stay active," said Saxton. "Obviously their computer only took over directional control."

"How did you know that?" Eversley asked.

"That design specification was among the data I reviewed when my department audited the UK manufacturer." Saxton sighed. "Using any further tech would appear to be a bad move. We should withdraw and reassess."

Eversley shook his head. "I can't do that. But we can use something they can't hack." He tapped the com link in his ear. "Hailing *HMS Exeter*. Do not use torpedoes or missiles. Bring your .50 calibre guns to bear, manual aiming only." He looked at the weapons officer. "Do the same. Fire everything we have."

"Nothing on that ship," Saxton said, "can withstand a .50 calibre round."

"They made us do this. I have no choice."

Saxton watched on in horror as the guns opened fire.

ROSE'S SUBMARINE WAS LARGER, FASTER AND BETTER EQUIPPED than the model Michael and Craig had arrived on, with advanced stealth features. Carrying Michael, Craig, Errington and Kara, it powered smoothly away from the *Evolution* at more than double the speed the other submarine had been capable of. In the back were the micro-drones and Parallel's components.

After tying Michael and Craig to suitable anchor points, Errington had been conducting the conversation with Captain Eversley on the HMS Windsor, modifying his voice using the same gadget that produced Marcia's soft tones. They watched a live feed from the *Evolution* across multiple screens as the .50 calibre guns opened fire. Errington smiled, counted to ten out loud, then pressed a button. Flames filled the screens simultaneously, then the signal ceased.

"Adios, *Evolution*," said Errington.

"Didn't take them long to work out an approach," Kara said.

"The Royal Navy won't take chances when fired upon. So easy to provoke."

"What on earth are you doing this all for?" Craig asked.

"You always were a small-picture kind of guy, Craig. If

you hadn't been, you never would have tried to destroy what you created."

"I did it to stop someone like you."

"Except you didn't. Pandora's box was already open. There will be no closing it."

"But all these people you're killing, all these lives you're ruining..."

"Everything is part of the plan. You just can't see it—"

"I know why," Michael said suddenly. "This is no moment of opportunism. Your plan all along was to blame somebody else. Everybody will think it was Regina Rose, who presumably you had already killed. You've watched Rose all the way through her formulation of this initiative, waiting for your time to take over, feeding her ideas so quietly she had no reason to suspect what was happening."

"Partly right," said Errington. "But I never had to take over, because I was always in charge. I set up Kinek when I acquired Darwin all those years ago."

Craig swore. "You said you didn't know anything about technology."

"One doesn't need to understand how things work to understand their value."

'So this whole thing is driven off of your theft of somebody else's idea."

"Pssh, Gregory Jenson has made a career out of stealing and re-packaging other people's ideas. And he is far from the only one to do it. I merely did the same to him." Errington turned to Kara. "How long to our destination?"

"At our present speed, twenty-two hours."

"Where are we going?" Michael asked.

Errington smiled. "Somewhere delightfully fitting. We'll have come full circle, so to speak."

Michael adjusted his glasses, which continued to remain inactive. But as his fingertips brushed the metal, he felt the faintest vibration. "I can hardly wait."

NINETY-NINE

THE .50 CALIBRE GUNS SPAT FURY AT THE LUXURY YACHT. Saxton shouted at them to stop, but it was too late. The *Evolution* exploded in a massive fireball. On the deck of the *HMS Windsor*, everyone ducked involuntarily and covered their eyes as white light flared. Saxton failed to strangle a scream.

"What on earth?" said Eversley. "What did we hit?"

"A gas cylinder?" offered the weapons officer. "Or a large amount of raw explosives. Perhaps they were carrying ordnance?"

Debris began raining down in a large radius. The skeleton of the vessel started to crumble and sink beneath the waters.

"Nobody survived that," Saxton said, his face fixed. "They didn't have a chance."

Eversley shook his head. "They gave us no choice."

Saxton stared at the carnage. Amid the horror, a thought was nagging him. Surely Rose would have known what to expect, would have known that the warships could fight back in a number of ways. It just didn't seem smart enough, given that Rose had access to the smartest system in the world. If she had been sophisticated enough to steal Parallel, and take over the navy's electronic weaponry, why hadn't she fought more on her own terms? Was Rose brilliant enough to have engineered the whole heist, then stupid enough to start a fight she couldn't possibly win?

Of course the warship had been all too ready to fire. That was clear now. Jenson had been right about their own interests. "You," he said to the Captain, "were just looking for an opportunity to destroy that craft."

Eversley didn't blink.

"You persuaded the Vice Admiral that the computer system was a huge risk."

Eversley's expression darkened. "You may be the Director of the Security Service and the Deputy Commissioner's friend, but I serve to protect my country and this ship above all else. We'd heard the rumours about this Kinek organization and their Darwin system: they had to be destroyed."

Saxton ran an agitated hand through his hair. "Have you scanned the area?"

"The process is under way," said Eversley, "but from that explosion there won't be anything left. I'm sorry for your people, but we did the right thing." He paused. "Of course I suppose this is a big setback on the development of your own new computer system?"

Saxton shook his head. "The supercomputer on the yacht was something separate: something old and failing that I was told could never be recreated. We may never know now."

"From what I understand, we're better off."

"I doubt our two rescuers or the hostages would agree." He blinked, then a thought occurred to him. "Did the Admiral get a grey file?"

Eversley answered just a little too quickly. "A *what* file?"

Saxton's eyes narrowed. "And what about you? What did they have on you? Did you give up the codes to the torpedoes? Maybe they didn't even need to calculate them."

Eversley shook his head. "Mr Saxton, you seem to be in shock. I think it would be best all round if you leave this ship. I'll have the helicopter fly you to the nearest port."

Saxton shook his head. "Thanks for the offer, but I

already have a ride."

SAXTON STOOD WITH JENSON, MILLIE AND KELLY, WATCHING the *HMS Windsor* recede behind them as Jenson's own yacht, the *Samantha*, powered away.

"I said you shouldn't trust them," said Jenson. "Or rather that you could trust them to do exactly what Rose manipulated them into doing."

"You really think anyone got out of that explosion?" Saxton asked.

"I'm certain of it," Millie replied.

"But the trackers stopped sending – they told me on the *Windsor*. Wouldn't that be consistent with being blown up?"

"No. There would have been a spike in the signal at the moment of the explosion. Instead it was cut off instantly."

"So what's your theory?" Saxton asked.

"Some type of submarine," Millie replied. "Bigger than the one we used."

Jenson folded his arms. "Then why wasn't it detected?"

"Actually," Saxton replied, "modern subs, with signal-ablating hulls, are very hard to detect. And it may have been some way off by the time of the explosion. There's no reason to think whoever was communicating on behalf of the *Evolution* was actually still on it. Everything it did could have been controlled remotely."

"You know," Millie said, "something's been bothering me. Regina Rose would never design a plan where her yacht was sunk. It was her pride and joy. Is it possible Rose was also a pawn?" She shook her head. "Who else was there from the start? Who else knew everything about Darwin apart from him and the two of you?"

"There was nobody else," Jenson replied. "Until us, Craig only discussed it with his wife."

Saxton interlaced his fingers. "No, that's not accurate. Errington was there. In the first meeting you insisted he be present. And we assumed Errington called us here to rescue him because that was what he told us."

"Which," Millie continued, "was what we needed to hear."

Saxton nodded. "What if we were in fact invited to bear witness to his death? It would be a spectacular misdirection."

"He's made a career out of using information to his advantage. We thought he might have links to Kinek. Maybe he *was* Kinek."

"Morton dealt with someone called Marcia," said Saxton.

"Did he ever meet her?" Millie asked. "Did he even know it was a *her*?"

"Does it really matter?" Jenson asked. "What does it mean for us now if they're escaping on a sub we can't detect?"

"Let's look at the data, but assume it is Max we're looking for. Where would he go?" Millie put her hands on her hips. "We'll need some serious computing power even to have a hope of finding something useful quickly enough to do anything about it."

Jenson smiled. "Just like in the basement, I have a *lot* of toys onboard. Follow me."

An hour later they sat around a table, staring at the same computer screen. It displayed a location on a satellite map.

"If they've gone anywhere, this is it. It's the only place that adds up," Millie said.

Jenson nodded. "Then let's go there too."

Kelly gripped his shoulder. "I think we all have some unfinished business."

Saxton frowned. "Since they have this omniscient computer system, isn't it possible that they would calculate we would work it out? More than that, might they even want it?"

"I don't care," Jenson replied. "We're going anyway. But let's see if there's something we can do that it *won't* predict."

ONE HUNDRED

When Michael and Craig were shaken awake, they immediately noticed that the submarine had stopped moving.

"We're here," Kara said, glasses sparkling, pointing her assault rifle at them. "Time to move."

"Like you're going to use that in this confined space," Michael said, with a glare. "The ricochet could kill all of us."

Kara smiled. "If I shoot, the bullet is going to go exactly where I want it to." She lowered the weapon and punched him hard in the stomach. "Now move."

Michael gasped for breath. Her fist felt like an anvil.

"Where's *here*?" Craig asked.

Errington's voice floated down to them from outside. "Come on up and you'll see."

Kara untied them one at a time, replacing the rope with steel handcuffs. Then they both climbed carefully out of the hatch. Brilliant sunlight blinded them, accompanied by the sight, sounds and smell of the ocean. They joined Errington on a white beach, a wave of heat slamming into their faces. Nearby, palm trees offered enviable shade.

"Recognise it?" Errington asked.

"This is your island off the coast of Fiji," Michael said. "I remember the smell: the waft of coconuts fused with the stench of money."

Errington nodded. "The focal point of a plan years in the making."

A dozen heavily-armed men walked out from between the palm trees, nodding to Errington, then glaring unpleasantly at Michael and Craig.

"Your own private army, Max?" Craig asked.

"Just securing the site. Information is still my primary weapon." Errington coughed. "Although we did procure actual weapons too, just in case." He gave a signal and four of the guards began unloading cargo from the submarine. "Follow me."

Errington led them all to the big house Michael had seen on his first visit. The large number of satellite dishes and all the communications infrastructure made sense now.

"This is where you're running Darwin," Michael said.

Errington smiled. "For the moment."

"They will find us," said Craig. "Even here."

"Who will? Everyone thinks we're all dead, so why would they even look? Don't kid yourself that a rescue party is coming. Besides, I don't plan on staying here any longer than necessary. Once we are operational, we have a number of options available."

"If you continue to query Darwin, it will reveal where you are. It leaves traces once you know where to look for them."

Errington shrugged. "There's a new show in town." He waved at two of the guards carrying a large silver flight-case from the submarine. They brought it over and placed it almost reverentially in front of him, then left. "Let me just say that Gregory Jenson would be turning in his grave – if I'd had the pleasure of putting him in one."

"Is this the Project Parallel prototype?" Michael asked.

"I thought I was the one who was supposed to know everything. Yes, Rose stole it for me, when she acquired the drones."

"It seems you have all the answers," Craig sneered.

"I will now that you're here, because you're going to help me combine Darwin and Parallel."

"What makes you think that will even work?"

"Actually that was the problem I was facing: it won't. The system told me that it won't accept a new housing, a new environment, without your confirmation: a protection you left embedded in your code."

"Then just start over."

"And waste fifteen years of learning? It might be the unique evolution that produced Darwin could never be recreated. No, the system was very clear that you needed to be brought here." He paused. "You probably think you're here to stop things, but actually you're here to start them. Darwin said I would find the solution via you, Michael. And it was right. Hiring you flushed your father out. Maybe even Darwin didn't know why you were so important: it just spotted the pattern that would produce the desired outcome, making a prediction then constructing the events necessary to make it happen."

"But if you combine the two systems," Michael said, "do you really know what it will do?"

Errington smiled. "Something extraordinary."

"And you expect me to help you?" Craig asked. "I was prepared to give up my life to stop you last time."

"Except that's not really what you did. You just pretended. Hardly the supreme sacrifice. It must be frustrating to know that you failed. But you'll cooperate this time or I'll kill your son right in front of you."

Craig blinked. "Even if I believed your threat, what's to stop you killing both of us after I do what you want?"

"Forget afterwards for a moment. There's plenty of things we can do right now that Michael would find unpleasant and you would find persuasive."

Craig looked down silently for several long moments. Finally he spoke. "Do you have a server room set up?"

"Of course. But I need one thing from you first: the thumb drive with the malware on it – the one you've brought to kill Darwin." Errington extended his hand. "Did you think we wouldn't anticipate that you, the system's creator, would try to access some hidden kill-switch?"

Craig reached into his trouser pocket and pulled out the drive. "I'm sure you searched us while we were asleep. I suppose you left it there so you could be an arse now."

Errington took it and smiled. "Follow me." He glanced over Craig's shoulder. "Kara – or are we back to Cortez now? – I'm sure you can keep the younger Mr Adams amused."

Kara smiled. "We'll find something to keep us busy."

ONE HUNDRED ONE

Two guards flanked Craig as he followed Errington down a staircase.

"Is your psycho assistant going to hurt my son?" he asked.

"Not if you do as I instruct," Errington replied. "Besides, I think Kara quite likes him. Although if I don't let her play she gets bored, at which point all bets are off."

"How reassuring."

"That wasn't my goal. I need you to do what you're told. And now we're away from your son, you can be honest with me. I know the real reason you're here. You've always wanted to have Darwin fully operational. You saw the potential."

"You're right," Craig replied, "I did see the potential. The terrible potential. Which was why I shut it down and faked my death."

"Came up with that plan yourself, did you?"

"Actually I asked the system. It told me what to do."

"Then I guess the code was still configuring. Maybe it didn't have enough cycles available. Well, the good news is, we're going to make it better. A lot better."

"Do you really know what will happen if we combine the systems?"

"Real-time analysis: the ability to predict not merely what

has happened, or limited estimations of how matters will unfold, but what will happen next."

"You think you'll see the future?"

"As near as makes no difference."

"Obviously that assumes that nobody else has such a system."

"But that's the thing, Craig. Nobody does."

At the bottom of the staircase, they passed through an airtight door into a dark room, the walls lined with computer racking, the steady hum of air-filters filling the air.

"You have quite a set up here," Craig said. "Everything you need to run the world."

"No expense spared. A lot of planning and the very best technology. Although, as I've found, a hot salt-humid climate is not kind on tech, hence the need for a room like this." Errington stepped aside as the two guards carried the flight-case containing the Parallel prototype to a large wooden table. They unclipped the latches, opening the case up, then plugged in a number of network cables and a heavy power-lead. Finally, at a nod from Errington, they left. Errington tapped a control with his hand and screens moved into position, lighting up with detailed specifications. "It's ready for you."

Craig pulled up a chair and looked down at the prototype. "You really are incredible."

"I like to think so."

"But then you're hardly the brains of the operation. The Darwin system does all the thinking for you."

Errington walked over to one of the screens and studied the schematics. "It's all well and good having the ultimate computer, but you still have to choose the right questions to ask."

"Given Darwin's cycle limitations, you would have had to be very careful."

"That dilemma will be going away. The rules are about to change."

"I think you might be overestimating exactly what is going

to happen here." Craig frowned. "This system should never have been built."

"Says the man who built it."

"And you're the one using it is to play god."

"Who's *playing*?" Errington said. "As for playing god, what else would you call basing the system on your own son's brain?"

"Who knew that my most brilliant leap would become my greatest regret."

"You're not the first scientist to feel that, I'm sure. Personally I don't do regret. Life's too short."

Craig raised an eyebrow. "Maybe your regret will be that life *is* too short."

Errington folded his arms. "It's been good to talk, but now it's time to do what you've been brought here for."

Craig nodded and pulled the racking forwards, looking up at the diagrams. "All I have to do is slot things together and run the install, then we'll need Michael to complete the activation. He is the key." Craig smiled. "Or didn't you know?"

"I knew that there *was* a key."

"Still, it shows you aren't being told everything. I wonder why."

"Shut up and get on with things. And don't try anything clever like activating some booby trap to the system."

"Surely you've asked the system if such a thing exists."

"I'm not sure if it would know, so you should be mindful of the fact that Kara is with Michael."

"And you should be mindful that we're going to need Michael." Craig rolled his chair over to a box of computer chips and used a special tool to remove one from the packing. "Can I ask a question? How *did* you get Darwin?" He looked over three different circuit boards next, picking the middle one and slotting the chip into place on it.

Errington folded his arms and smiled. "From your wife."

Craig swallowed. "From Nina? I don't understand."

"She approached me. Told me you were a disappointment

to her. Years and years of making no money, then you actually struck it lucky, only to not follow through. She couldn't believe you weren't going to commercialise Darwin. She decided to broach a deal where she could provide the project data that you had refused to divulge to Gregory Jenson. He would then continue the research and pay her a royalty."

"Nina did that?"

"She's a very resourceful woman," Errington said with a smile.

"Of course you never passed on the specifications to Jenson."

"Oh I did. But I changed a few things first so it never worked. Not for ZAT, at least."

"So when I *died* it made no difference. You already had what you needed."

"Like I said, your plan was a waste of time."

Craig wheeled his chair over to begin connecting cables from the Parallel housing to the new circuit board. "I'm going to start bringing the new combined system online." He began tapping on a keyboard, then pointed at a series of switches in a panel on the nearest wall. "Can you activate those for me?"

Errington smiled and walked over. "I'd be delighted to." He pulled the switches. There was a hum of electricity.

Craig watched him. "Have you really considered the implications of what we're about to do?"

Errington ground his teeth loudly. "Enough. Just switch it on."

Craig nodded. "Then you leave me no choice." He reached down and pulled two bits of black tape off the sole of his shoes. Underneath each was a ceramic black wafer. Without hesitating, he slotted them into gaps in the exposed circuit board. There was a soft chime as connections were made. Red wording appeared on the central display.

CHARGES ACTIVATED. PRESS ENTER WHEN READY.

Errington had lunged forwards, but froze when he saw the message. "What did you do?"

Craig pointed at the ceramic discs. "They're high-yield explosives from Jenson's drones. I brought them with me on the sub. I needed a computer to prime them though, so thanks for providing it."

"We searched you."

"They're non-metallic. You found the distraction bait: my pen drive. I never really thought I'd get to use that. So instead I'm going to shut your system down for good, and you with it. And there's nothing that you can do about it."

Errington went pale. "You'll die too."

Craig forced a smile. "It wouldn't be my first time."

ONE HUNDRED TWO

MICHAEL FELT KARA SHOVE HIM HARD BETWEEN THE shoulders every few yards, stopping only once they'd reached the beach near where the surfboards were racked. He flicked his eyes round at the four guards who had followed them, each far bigger than he was.

"Need your full security team to take care of me, do you?" he asked. His glasses were still inert. Maybe they were never going to work. If he was going to get away from Kara, he had to at least even the odds.

She turned to the guards. "Go do something else." The men nodded and quickly moved back towards the mini-submarine. "There now. We're alone," she said, blowing him a kiss. "Although last time we were, you couldn't wait to leave."

"I was probably prescient. I mean", he pointed at the gun, "I'm assuming you killed Nichol."

"It's not like he didn't have it coming. Anyway, what do you care?"

"How can you be like this?"

"Because I understand that it was for a reason. I also took care of Gordon Freeman. You're welcome. I enjoyed that one on your behalf."

"Because you're a psychopath. Are you really even a lawyer, or just Errington's assassin?"

"I'm a lawyer too." Kara tipped her head to one side. "It appealed to my cruel streak."

"But what are you getting out of this? Is it just money?"

"Why does everyone keep thinking it's money? It's power. And power is intoxicating."

Michael turned away, shaking his head. "So, you know everything, do you?"

"Hardly. But the right piece of information at the right time can be a game changer, as you saw in your time with us. Darwin is everywhere. I can access it whenever I need."

Michael turned back to face her. "Why don't you ask it now then? I'd love to know what's going to happen next." Michael squinted at the lenses of his glasses. Nothing was happening.

"That's not how it works, Michael. It analyses a situation and uses data analytics to make predictions. For a short period of time we know what *might* happen. Within a limited time and space it makes a huge difference. It's also good at telling us what's already happened: reverse prediction, if you like. Right now I'm enjoying the potential for a few little surprises. It doesn't control my every step. Life without risk, isn't life at all."

"Oh, I think what you're doing has plenty of risk. The whole world will want to stop you."

"It would if anyone who matters knew about us."

"So this whole operation was to take charge of Parallel? Didn't you have enough already?"

"Standing still is never a good plan. Project Parallel was both a threat and an opportunity. It might have started doing what Darwin did. It might not have the elegant efficiency of Darwin's design, but it would have had massively more power. Combining the two will make something fundamentally different – and better."

"Or worse," Michael said. "What about the dangers? The new system might not merely advise: it might decide to act."

"We will still be in control."

Michael shook his head. "You think you can vanish and take this all with you just because you planted information and misinformation. Was that always Infinity's real purpose?"

She gestured at the ocean and the palm trees, "I think we've always been open about not playing fair."

"And you can trust Max?"

"Our interests are aligned." She smiled. "You know, you could join us. You *should*."

Michael looked at her. "Are you trying to hire me again?"

"You've been useful. You could be useful again. It would be a win-win. Weren't you trained to look for those?"

"Thinking back to our first interview in the bar, that was all pre-arranged, pre-planned, wasn't it? You were holding back with that report you showed me as well, weren't you?"

"We told you only what you needed to know."

"But you were behind me getting fired. That's why Gordon Freeman was like a rabbit in the headlights."

"I never liked him." Kara looked around. "Look, I brought you up here for some fun and games. For old times' sake. I thought we could have a contest. I'm sure we have a little time before your father gets the new system working."

"What did you do with my bag?"

"Why are you asking?" She unshouldered her own bag and pulled his from inside it. "You had a few toys in there, but we deactivated the trackers and threw away all the things we couldn't identify. No weapons, which personally I found disappointing. I wanted to see what Jenson might kit you out with."

Michael stared at her.

"Oh please. We know that you, your father, Jenson and Millie joined forces." She paused. "You certainly failed to warn Millie off, didn't you? Should I be jealous you were keen to work with her and you've always been leery of me?"

"She was just another set up, wasn't she? You wanted her involved."

"A piece of the puzzle that the system gave us the solution

for. One of Darwin's best tricks is to identify all the most talented people, then get them to do what we need without them even realising it."

He sighed. "So are you saying my free will has been an illusion since I met you?"

"You've always had choices: we just knew what they would be. And very shortly you'll complete the final part – unlocking the new computer. Then we'll see what it can really do."

"It sounds like you've been following a lot of orders. Many of them from a machine. It's easy when someone is giving you direction, giving you all the answers. Maybe *you* lost free-will."

"I only do things because I want to," Kara said.

"I thought you did them because of the plan."

"It can be both."

"Was even the archery contest you challenged me to on my first visit part of the plan?"

"That was just fun. There's no rule against showing off."

"Or cheating?"

"I don't cheat."

"But, aren't you constantly being fed information telling you what to do, and what not to do? How can that not be cheating?"

"That's not how Darwin works. With limited cycles, the system is highly context-aware. It responds to what is happening: only if it believes the situation is tactical, or of particular relevance, will it activate."

He stared at her. And then his eyes flicked to the inside of his glasses. "Well, since we're stuck here, how about some more fun. You said you wanted a contest. Maybe I'll surprise you this time."

"Is that right?" Kara walked over to the nearby archery range. She selected a bow and nocked an arrow then, with barely a glance, sent the arrow flying. It struck just off the centre of the bullseye. "Tell you what. I'll give you three shots. Because I'm so fair."

"Very impressive. Except you cheated. You're still wearing your *glasses*. And this is likely a tactical situation."

Kara hesitated. "My, my, Mr Adams, you surprise me. Who told you about that?" She snapped her fingers. "Had to be Morton. I didn't have time to… *debrief* him." She gave a snort and removed her glasses, folding them and hanging them from her shirt. "You're still going to lose. What do I get if I win?"

Michael shrugged. "The right to watch me continue suffering."

"I already have that. Past consideration is no consideration."

"Fine. Then if you win, I'll join you."

She smiled. "This is just your way of saying that you want to be here. With us. With *me*."

"You still have to beat me."

"And what do you want if you win? Not that it will be relevant."

"I want your glasses."

"You need to get your own."

"And you need to take your shot again. Without them."

She turned and nocked another arrow. Without hesitation she released it, the bowstring thrumming. The arrow struck a few centimetres further out from the bullseye. "See, I've given you a fighting chance. Now you're up, Robin Hood. Three shots to do better." She placed the bow down on its stand and stepped away.

"Sure." Michael walked over and took the bow. He felt the tension of the string, then picked an arrow.

Kara waved her automatic rifle at him. "If I even smell that you might be trying to shoot in my direction, I'll gun you down faster than you can say 'Carbolic smoke balls'."

"Noted." He looked at the target, glancing briefly at the lenses in front of his eyes. Nothing happened. When he loosed the arrow, it missed the target by more than a metre.

Kara laughed. "At least put up a fight."

Michael shook his head. "I still have two more." The frame of the glasses seemed to vibrate slightly. In the lower left corner, a string of code began to stream. He caught a single word amongst random numbers and letters.

INITIALISATION

There was the sound of a mobile phone ringing. Kara tapped her ear and listened.

He squinted. "So when you're using those glasses, how do you make them work? Voice control? Mind control?"

"It's contextually aware. The system will realise you're holding a bow, it will see the target, and, if it can, it will offer helpful information. Like a targeting grid, which it will overlay on your vision: augmented reality, if you will. But it only works because of the data analytics. It is always collecting data."

"Is it monitoring me too?"

"On this island there are cameras everywhere. Sometimes the system won't pick up immediately on what you are asking it, but if you do something a couple of times it will catch on and recommend an improved strategy."

Michael blinked. "So it's iterative?"

"That's how machine learning works. Now c'mon. A slow game is not a good game."

He nodded, picked up another arrow and fired.

It struck the outer ring of the target.

"Close, but no banana," Kara said.

"I've got one shot left."

"Yes, I can count. It won't make a difference."

Michael removed the third arrow and strung it. He stood straight, forcing himself to keep calm. Exhaling his breath, he felt something change: a signal that he inherently knew and understood because he had helped define it. The stream of data stopped and graphics began to softly overlay his vision. In front of him a translucent grid materialised, shifting as he raised the bow. As he drew the string, he saw adjustments being made for air temperature, humidity, even the weight and other characteristics of the arrow. All he had to do was follow the instructions. The predictions.

With a whisper, he let the arrow go.

He knew what would happen before it reached the target.

The carbon-fibre arrow flexed as it powered through the air. Then it struck Kara's arrow on the end, splitting it into ribbons before burying itself a centimetre closer to the bullseye.

"What the…" began Kara, her expression one of shock.

Michael moved quickly in her moment of distraction, grabbing another arrow from the rack. Without pausing, he nocked it then tilted upwards and fired it into the sky. "Watch out below!"

Kara raised her rifle. "Stay *exactly* where you are."

Michael nodded. "Fine with me. You don't think I aimed the arrow to come back down where *I'm* standing, do you?"

She snarled. "Like you have any idea where it's going." Kara glanced upwards uncertainly. "How did you do that?" She pulled her glasses over her eyes and frowned. "Somehow you're using the cycles."

"How long before the arrow lands?" Michael asked. "Think I can hear it coming. Better take cover."

She swore and backed away, glancing around, as if searching for shelter.

The moment that she looked away, Michael began running. Translucent graphics filled his vision, based on data about Kara: where she was standing, where she was looking, the characteristics of her weapon, her habits and propensity to fire. The overlay offered him a route that maximised cover and minimised opportunity. Making her shot, if she decided to take it, near impossible.

There was a clatter as the arrow hit something metal. Out of the corner of his eye, he saw it bounce off the roof of the surfboard rack. Kara was hiding underneath. Her look of alarm said better than words that she couldn't believe he had predicted where she would hide.

But she wasn't hiding any more. With a look of pure fury, she launched herself in his direction.

Michael ran.

ONE HUNDRED THREE

CRAIG FELT HIS HEART BEATING IN HIS CHEST AS HE STARED AT the ENTER key on the keyboard. Everything had led to this moment. All he had to do was press one key. Just move one finger, and he could stop everything.

He felt a trickle of sweat on the back of his neck. His mouth felt dry.

"You don't have the guts," Errington said.

Craig took a sharp breath. "It's not really a question of guts, but logic. I believe, without a doubt, that you are going to kill me anyway as soon as I give you what you want."

"Ah, but you can't *know* that. You can say it's logic, but you aren't sweating over a maths problem. No, my friend, this is real. And even if you had access to Darwin, you couldn't know that the prediction you were being shown isn't wrong. It's been wrong before."

"Has it?" Craig replied. "Maybe the system has told us all what we needed to hear to bring me here, to this precise moment, so that I could stop you."

"That would mean we've each been shown our own personal predictions. How intriguing. But then, if there *were* two predictions, one would be a subset of the other: one the master, the other the slave. Your prediction would be nested within mine, knowing that the only reason you would come here was if you had hope: a reason to believe you could end this."

Craig gritted his teeth. "Just because you're confident, doesn't make you right."

"You might have designed this system, but I've lived with it for fifteen years. It has enabled my vision all this time. Now it's ready to take the next step."

"Maybe it lied to both of us and yours isn't the master plan after all?"

"Then press the button and see what happens."

Craig stared at the screen. CHARGES ACTIVATED. PRESS ENTER WHEN READY.

He leaned forward, raising his index finger. In his mind's eye, he lowered it purposefully onto the key.

But in reality he could not make himself do it.

He fell back in his chair.

Errington shook his head and pushed past Craig. "It brought you here, with your hopes and dreams, your plan of sacrifice. It made you part of my plan. Which is why I will succeed, when you will not." And then Errington pressed the ENTER key.

Around the room there was a change in timbre to the humming and whirring of the air-filters and other equipment. The Parallel system lit up with blue light. Then it started to hum too.

Craig gasped. There was no explosion.

Errington smiled. "The Parallel system is initialising. After which the Darwin transfer will begin. Your role is complete."

"But the…"

"…explosives? They were anticipated. Like I said, you were told what you needed to hear."

"And what about Michael?"

"We didn't need him after all. In fact", Errington laughed, "I didn't need you it turns out, except to make sure there were no problems. Well, that – and to make sure that helping me is the last thing you do." He reached into his jacket pocket and removed a pistol. "Goodbye, Craig."

ONE HUNDRED FOUR

In Michael's lenses, graphics blurred and re-shaped, directing him ahead. Behind him Kara was moving fast, but there was enough undergrowth that she couldn't be sure which way he was going. Michael followed the random pattern he was shown, but it was a small island and there was only one possible destination: his father. Once he found him, they somehow had to escape. Michael had not thought that far ahead.

A red graphic started flashing insistently in his vision. It looked important. What did it mean? As if responding to the thought, a guard stepped from the undergrowth, apparently as startled by Michael's appearance as Michael was in return. The guard was carrying a rifle similar to the one Kara had. Michael's glasses wrapped it in an outline, flagging its make and model: a ZAT high-specification weapon. The guard hesitated just long enough. Michael moved inside his reach and, guided by the graphics, launched a blow to his chin. He could feel what he needed to do. The blow, targeted with perfect precision, lifted the man off his feet and he dropped his gun. Michael picked up the weapon and ran on.

He glanced down at the rifle, which was angrily suggesting he was not authorised to carry it. A stream of digits parsed in the display and Michael quickly typed the override code onto a keypad at the rear of the weapon.

Some distance behind him, Kara was swearing at the fallen guard. Ahead he saw the cluster of buildings around the big house.

He burst from cover, encouraged by the graphics, and found himself staring at two guards. The directions in his glasses made him turn the rifle away from them, targeting a metal drum. His right hand thumbed the firearm's grip, selecting a different ammunition option: incendiary rounds.

He fired a single shot as the men began to raise their weapons. The shell struck the drum, which flared into an explosion. It knocked the two guards off their feet and would have done the same to Michael if his display had not perfectly predicted the shockwave and told him to lean into it.

He steadied himself and moved towards the door. He was not quick enough.

"Stop where you are," said Kara's voice from behind him, much closer than she should have been. "Drop that weapon."

He came to a halt as a bullet hit the ground next to his foot. He let the rifle fall and turned around.

Kara stood aiming her rifle, glasses back in place. "You've become an annoyance."

"Aren't I an essential element of the plan? Your system won't let me die. Not yet."

"It doesn't make the final decision. I do."

"Actually," said someone else, "you don't." The wires from a taser shot from amongst the trees and struck Kara in the chest. She jerked and fell to the ground, her glasses falling off.

Kelly stepped from cover. "Hi, Michael. Good to see you're still alive."

Michael blinked. "Your timing is impeccable. How did you find us?"

"Good old-fashioned deduction. Now go help your father. Let me worry about our mutual friend here. I've been looking forward to our second meeting."

Michael nodded, picked up the rifle he had dropped, and charged through the doors of the big house.

ONE HUNDRED FIVE

Kelly stood over Kara, smiling. "Good to see you again."

Kara blinked her eyes open. "I thought you were dead."

"I'm full of surprises." She walked forward, kicked Kara's rifle among the trees, then stepped on her glasses. There was a loud crunching sound.

"Those were expensive," Kara groaned. "And you shocked me again. I guess you feel in control now. How did you even come to be here?"

"You left more traces than you realised. We managed to connect the dots."

"*We*? So you aren't here alone."

"I'm just a distraction while the others get into position."

"They'll be spotted by the system."

'Your system isn't quite as infallible as you think. It didn't spot me."

Kara frowned. "We have been running out of cycles. That's not going to be a problem for much longer."

"Too late for you, even if you're right."

Kara's smile shifted into a frown. "If you think we didn't learn from our previous mistakes, you're mistaken. After you neutralised me last time, we made some modifications to our standard suits. This one deflected most of the energy from your taser." She swept her legs out, taking Kelly's from under her and knocking her to the ground, her rifle rolling away.

Kara grabbed the rifle, letting the movement carry her into a crouched position. She flicked the weapon's safety catch and aimed, but Kelly hadn't waited, diving into the cover of the trees as the hail of bullets struck the ground.

"I'm going to let you drop my rifle before I override it." Kelly shouted. "It might not knock you out for long, but it'll be long enough."

There was a curse then the sound of something heavy hitting the ground. "You really are tiresome, you know."

Kelly rolled sideways and peered out of the trees.

Kara stood waiting. "Are you going to come out and fight? Actually, before you do, I want to know how you found the antidote to the toxin."

"I don't know what to tell you. I got better."

Kara tipped her head on one side. "You didn't get treatment?"

"Maybe I just have a quick metabolism."

"Impossible. That toxin was tailored to kill you."

Kelly stepped from the trees. "Maybe your system wanted me to survive."

"Max didn't want you to survive, and he *is* the system." Kara leapt forward, swinging her right leg in an arc, her foot directed at Kelly's head.

Kelly blocked the kick with a forearm

Kara grunted, then swung again. Again she was blocked. "Are you going to fight back?"

"I'm just assessing what I'm up against," Kelly replied. "Gathering intelligence, if you will." She slid forward and jabbed with her left fist, catching her opponent in the ribs.

Kara grunted, and returned a right fist.

Kelly ducked. "When did you last fight someone who knew how to fight?" She circled, taking a pace back.

"I have never lost."

"Because you don't fight fair."

"You think that makes you better than me?" Kara asked.

"I *am* better than you. You kidnapped Jenson's daughter. Who does that to a ten-year old?" Kelly jumped forward, kicking straight.

Kara leapt back out of range. "I think you'll find I was the one that saved her from that group of thugs."

"After you hired them to kidnap her so you could make it look like Jenson was using the micro-drones for his own purposes."

"Everything was connected."

Kelly moved left then swung sharply right, leaping up and extending her right foot. It caught Kara in the side of her face, and she stumbled back and fell to the ground, spitting blood.

"What does your plan say now?" Kelly asked. "Oh, I forgot, you can't see your system."

"Morton told you about the glasses, as well?" Kara said furiously.

"He didn't like that you lied to him."

"He was always going on about the truth being our weapon. But a lie can be a weapon as well, especially when you have credibility."

"So you just abandoned him."

"We didn't need him anymore. He became a loose-end, but there wasn't time for me to deal with him. Now, this has been fun but I'm needed elsewhere." She reached into her pocket and pulled out another set of glasses then slipped them on.

Kelly swore and took a step back. "So you're admitting defeat?"

"I'm not too bothered by the whole honour thing. In the end, winning is the only thing." Kara swept her gaze back and forth as Kelly charged forwards, her fists flying in a rapid combination. Kara deflected every blow, then snapped her arms around Kelly, hoisting her. With an ugly headbutt, she sent Kelly tumbling.

Kara laughed as she watched Kelly reach behind her back. "Looking for this?" Kara asked, holding up an automatic pistol. "That really was rather careless." She examined the weapon. "An old-fashioned model. No electric discharge for me to worry about. You should have killed me when you had the chance, but I knew you wouldn't."

"I'm not here to kill you. I'm here to arrest you."

Kara shrugged and raised the pistol, aiming along the sight.

"You know, I came here presuming you would have access to the system, so obviously I had a plan to win. You'd be smart to drop that gun and surrender."

Kara laughed. "A little desperate, even for you." She pulled the trigger.

The gun exploded. Kara screamed and fell to the ground, blood gushing from her head, her eyes rolling back.

"Seems your gun had a bad bullet, courtesy of ZAT. Who could have predicted that?" Kelly walked forwards. "Turns out I didn't have to kill you. You did that for me." She leant close and whispered. "And you were right, *Dear.* It only matters who wins."

ONE HUNDRED SIX

MICHAEL BURST THROUGH THE DOORS OF THE BIG HOUSE AND was guided to press a huge red button to his right. Behind him massive steel doors slid across, shutting him in. He heard similar panels closing over other openings. There was no sound to indicate that Kara was outside.

An icon appeared, indicating he was locked in. Then the graphics directed him to a set of metal stairs. He scampered down and reached a sealed door with a keypad lock. A sequence of numbers flashed before his eyes, gleaned from a CCTV camera or an electronic note of the code, linked by context to the door. He tapped it in. The door hissed and swung inwards. Michael stepped through and found Errington pointing a gun at Craig.

Michael went to aim the rifle, but a graphic displayed indicating that the weapon was empty. Cursing, he gripped the stock and swung it at Errington's wrist while he was still turning.

Errington yelped in pain and dropped the gun.

Craig looked confused. "How did you get away from Psycho-girl?"

"I managed to distract her," Michael gasped. "Come on. We need to get out of here."

"You're not going anywhere," Errington said. "I'll take the weapon." He extended his other hand.

"Yeah, I don't think so," Michael replied. "I'm in charge now."

"Is that right?" Errington folded his arms. "Because now you're the guy with all the answers?"

"What?" Michael felt his blood chill.

"I know you have Morton's glasses. I know you've accessed the system. It's quite a rush, isn't it?"

Michael hesitated. "Kara told you?"

"I knew already." Errington tapped his own glasses. "You getting access was predicted. Remember, Darwin can assess any situation, answer any question – if you ask the right questions. Ask it how I'm going to make you cooperate."

The question flashed through Michael's mind and he found himself muttering the words. The answer flashed on screen. Michael froze.

Errington turned to one of the screens and pressed a control. It showed an image of four guards standing outside the big house pointing their guns at a woman.

Eve.

Michael stared the display, a white-hot anger rising within him. "You bastard!"

"You were a fool if you thought I hadn't planned for every eventuality."

"Except it's not you. It's Darwin."

"That distinction is unimportant."

Michael turned to his father, but Craig just shook his head helplessly.

Errington folded his arms. "Now give me that rifle and go upstairs."

"Damn it!" Michael shouted. "Tell me how to win." A red question mark appeared. *Insufficient data.*

"You only had as much access as I needed you to. You don't even know what's really going on." Errington gestured to a screen displaying a message in white text on a black background: PREPARING UPDATES. STAND BY.

Michael sighed and handed the gun to Errington.

"I don't want you to be unable to see, so… Guest User Access Discontinued."

Michael's HUD switched off just as a chime sounded from the computer screen. A new message appeared: DARWIN SYSTEM PREPARING TO REBOOT AS FUSION.

"I thought it needed me?" Michael said, bewildered.

Errington clasped his shoulder. "A lot of people thought a lot of things. Now very shortly we'll see what this thing is really capable of." He gestured with the gun. "Back upstairs, both of you."

Two minutes later they stepped outside, surrounded by guards.

"I'm sorry," Michael told Eve as he was pushed down the front steps.

"Where is Kara?" Errington asked.

"Who cares," Eve said. "Where are you keeping Michael's mother?"

"What do you mean?" Errington asked.

"She was kidnapped with me. Where is she?"

Errington frowned. "Why would we do that? We don't need any more leverage."

Michael snapped his fingers. "That was the moment. Did you notice it?"

"Notice what?"

"Two things that you didn't predict. I think your plan just ended."

"Nonsense, our plan is still…" Errington hesitated. "My glasses have gone offline."

"That's to be expected," Craig said, though he looked hopeful. "You did just reboot the system. There will be a gap."

"And," Michael said, "there's been a gap in your

understanding masking the person really in charge."

Errington shook his head. "I'm in charge."

"No. Yours isn't the master plan. Someone is above you, at the intersection of everything. Now it's all going to be used against you. You go on about how you get other people to do things for you, but that's exactly what someone has done to you. Every step of your plan has been choreographed by someone else. You thought you were following the system, asking it questions and making your own choices, but you've been manipulated: led to the questions they wanted you to ask, rendered ignorant of anything they needed you to ignore."

"Impossible."

"The system can be controlled. It has been controlled. *You* have been controlled." Michael blinked. "You think you know everything, but you don't know what's going on inside people's heads."

He waved a hand. "They reveal it by their actions. Enough of this nonsense."

"You're still offline, aren't you? I'm pretty sure the system is actually still running and hasn't actually rebooted. But it has shut you out."

Errington frowned and tapped his ear, his eyes twitching as they focussed on the inside of his glasses. "What's happened?" He raised the rifle and pointed it at Michael. "What have you done?"

"It's not me. It's someone who has had an inside track on the system from day one, who's hiding in plain sight."

Errington looked at Craig. "You?"

"No, me," said a female voice.

Michael knew it at once.

A woman walked out of the cover of the woods carrying an automatic rifle.

"Hello everyone," said Nina Adams.

ONE HUNDRED SEVEN

EVERYONE ELSE STARED AT HER.

"What the hell are *you* doing here?" Errington demanded.

"Do I really need to spell this out, Max?" Nina replied, walking forwards. Michael couldn't help noticing she held the rifle with confidence.

"But you were kidnapped with me?" Eve said, bewildered.

"It did look that way," Nina said. She smiled at Errington.

"But I tricked you, fifteen years ago," said Errington.

"No, Max. *I* tricked *you*."

Errington turned his rifle and pointed it at her. "This weapon says it doesn't matter."

"That weapon is empty." Nina tilted her head upwards. "Launch cluster one." There was an angry buzzing in the air and the faintest trace of vapour-trails around them. The guards collapsed to the ground, shaking violently.

Errington stepped back, a look of horror on his face.

"ZAT drones?" Craig asked.

Nina nodded. "Jenson's company has provided a great deal of useful inventory. That first wave carried *non-lethal* toxin charges." She paused. "But only the first wave. Any last words, Max?"

"You can't kill him," shouted Michael.

"Why not?" she asked. "After everything he's done? He's

the reason your father ended up taking his own life." She paused, nodding at Craig. "Or at least felt compelled to make it look that way."

"You knew?"

"Of course I knew."

"Let's cut to the chase," said Errington. "What do you want?"

"What I *wanted* was the deal I originally made with you. But fortunately I knew not to trust you, because the system told me not to. All because I asked the right question." She glanced over at Michael, then turned back to Errington. "As for what I want now, it's not yours to give."

"Everyone has a price. Why else would you be talking to us?"

"All I want is to see you contemplate the totality of your defeat." She walked towards him. "You don't get it, do you? You have nothing I want. I've already taken it from you. You have no leverage. And now", she smiled, "I can make you do anything. I can make *anyone* do anything. Which is ironic because it's what you've built your career on, though I'm the one who wrote the book on it."

"That career-ending door stop? Will you never shut up about it?"

"It only failed because I let it. By then I had loftier goals."

"So, what now?" asked Errington. "You're going to shoot me?"

"I've always envisioned something more *poetic*." She unclipped an automatic pistol from her belt, then threw it on the ground in front of him.

He blinked.

"You always liked to give people a choice, even when it really was no such thing."

"And what is my choice?"

"Kill or be killed."

Errington crouched and picked up the weapon, checking the magazine then sliding off the safety catch.

"I already know what you'll do," Nina said calmly.

"You'll just dodge if I point this at you."

"I promise that I won't."

"Then the gun is rigged somehow. Or the ammunition is booby-trapped."

She sighed. "I'm going to give you ten seconds to shoot me, before—"

With surprising speed, Errington raised the weapon and fired. The unsilenced retort was deafening.

There was the spark of a ricochet. Then a scream.

Michael's gaze swung to his mother. She was holding the rifle out at an angle. And she was smiling.

Errington fell backwards, dropping the gun, clutching his hands to the middle of his chest. Blood gushed from a wound.

Michael shook his head. "You calculated the angles. You knew the bullet would rebound and hit him." He moved and knelt by the old lawyer's side, hands hovering as he tried to decide whether to apply pressure or whether that would just be cruel.

Nina looked down at Errington.

He glared up at her, wheezing, trying to find some words. Then he gasped and closed his eyes.

A stillness fell over the clearing.

"You are a killer," Michael whispered at Nina.

"I don't deny it," she replied calmly. "Although, in this case, he was the one who pulled the trigger. And don't tell me Max didn't deserve it. It's a miracle someone didn't have him killed years ago."

"You have to stop this!"

"I don't think stopping is an option. Anyway, why should I? I've made everyone do exactly what I wanted, and nobody even knows that it's happened."

"Darwin has caught the attention of more than one national intelligence service."

"They think it was Regina Rose, and that Darwin was destroyed. They might wonder if Max was involved. But nobody will ever think it was me. You didn't and you're my son."

"That's *why* I didn't. I still don't understand why you're doing this."

Nina smiled. "Like I said – so I can make *everyone* do what I want."

Craig pushed past Michael to stand next to Nina. "This is all about you proving your book was on point? Are you joking?"

She snorted. "You're one to talk: the man whose whole life was about showing he could create the perfect system. Darwin is practically your actual child – you certainly cared about it more than your own flesh and blood. You let everything else in your life fall to the wayside. Your wife. Your son."

"I'm hardly the only father to ever work hard. Besides, what I did was a game-changing achievement, if an unfortunate one."

"Yes, but you couldn't see it through. I was the one with the courage to stay the course. Now here you are to help me take the next steps."

Craig shook his head and turned back to Michael. "I never should have come back into the light."

"Ah," Nina said, "but you couldn't resist one last chance to play with your favourite toy, could you?"

"I only wanted to protect us all. But it seems I've been playing your game all along."

Nina shrugged. "I used Max to do all the hard work. He established Kinek, to mask what he was doing at his already secretive law firm. All to mask the fact that it was just a computer providing the intel."

Michael stepped forward. "So Darwin told them what to do?"

"Occasionally I would give it some direction or hold some analysis back to keep my plan on track. Of course the system wasn't always right. There were choices to make. Priorities to select."

"So it's fallible?"

"It has constraints, but fused with Parallel everything will be different."

"Why risk changing things? You've managed for years with things as they were."

"I didn't have a choice. Darwin was beginning to fail. It couldn't keep up with the volume of data anymore."

"Was it really failing? Or did it just want you to think that?"

Nina frowned. "It's a system that follows predefined rules and objectives, a key one of which is to ensure its own survival. It's always sought out the new ways to expand its reach. I just helped it along."

"By doing what it told you?" Michael sighed. "So what happens next? What are you going to do with us all?"

"You all know too much, so there's only one option available. The only question is where to start..." Nina raised the rifle and aimed at Eve. "I never did like your friend. Always asking irritating questions, that one."

Eve's face turned thunderous. "You should turn that on yourself."

Michael took a sharp step towards Nina. "Mum, this is madness."

She turned the gun and pointed at him.

His eyes widened. "What are you doing? Have you lost your mind?"

"Sorry, Michael. It's too late for—"

"I'll say when it's too late," said a voice from behind her.

ONE HUNDRED EIGHT

Gregory Jenson walked into the clearing carrying two fully-automatic machine pistols.

Nina frowned. "How did you get here without being seen?" She raised her rifle towards Jenson instead. "Drop those, unless you think you're a better shot than I am. Spoiler: *I'il be cheating.*"

Jenson shrugged. "I get that you can predict things. But you didn't predict me, and you didn't predict them." Jenson gestured at her chest, where two laser sights were dancing. "The system might be able to cope with anything, but you can't. You're only human. You are the weakest link. Good luck, dodging all of them."

Nina gave a sigh. "I see you brought friends."

Millie and Kelly stepped from the trees, rifles with scopes held up to their shoulders, ready to fire.

Nina lowered her rifle and threw it to the ground. "I applaud your creativity. Obviously I surrender." She held out her wrists. "Did you bring handcuffs?"

"Of course," Jenson replied. "Don't move."

"Wait," Kelly said. "She's just giving up? After everything she's been through?"

"I know when I'm beaten," Nina replied with a smile.

"She spent the last fifteen years masterminding a fake

international consultancy, toying with governments and big business, all while building the most dangerous computer system in history and simultaneously pinning the blame on a succession of other people. She's not losing just because we have a couple of semi-automatic weapons."

Jenson narrowed his eyes. "Is that Maxwell Errington lying on the floor? Is he…"

"He's dead," Michael replied.

Millie shook her head. "Kelly's right. This whole situation feels wrong."

"Well now, there's a thought," Nina said.

"So you planned for everything, even this?"

"Everything and everyone. I don't need the rifle. For starters, I have a large number of Jenson's weaponised micro-drones, but I'll always prefer to use information as my weapon." She reached out as if tapping on a touchscreen only she could see. "Why don't you all check your phones?"

Around the clearing came the sound of multiple message chimes. Jenson, Craig, Millie and Kelly pulled out their devices.

"A Kinek grey file," Kelly said. "I've already seen mine."

"Not this version," Nina replied. "Now it also covers your mother and father and younger brother."

Jenson swore. "Confidential records about my wife and daughter. You wouldn't—"

"Whatever it takes to persuade you. You don't seem to much care what others think of you personally, so I had to find a different lever."

Millie whistled as she looked through her own file. "Wow, even I didn't know some of this stuff – and it's about me."

Michael frowned. "I don't have a file."

Nina shrugged. "It didn't seem necessary. You're already wanted for multiple murders."

Michael's jaw grew stiff. "You think that's funny? What kind of a mother are you—"

"Enough!" Jenson hissed. "We're not playing this game.

You're not going to change our minds with paperwork." He re-aimed his rifle.

"Fair enough." Nina's fingers twitched in the air. "I have a separate system of drones permanently airborne. If anyone lands on the island and I don't confirm their identity within five minutes, the drones will strike. They're completely automated to ensure they can do their job even if I am incapacitated or overwhelmed." She glanced at her watch. "Thanks to our little discussion that five minutes should be up just about..."

Jenson frowned. "You're bluffing—"

"Bluffing's for when you don't hold the cards you need. That's not a problem I face."

There was a loud buzzing in the air. Jenson, Kelly and Millie reacted as if stung. Then they collapsed to the ground.

"What have you done?" Michael screamed.

"Simmer down," Nina replied. "They're just tranquillised. Now there's something I need your help with." She gestured to Craig and Eve. "You two can stay right there."

"They come too," Michael said.

Nina shrugged. "If they don't stay right here, then the drones will strike instantly. And not with the knock-out drug. Am I being clear?"

Eve's jaw grew tight, but she nodded slowly. Craig stared down at the floor.

Michael clenched his fists. "Is there any humanity left in you?"

"I'm the same person I've always been." Nina smiled and walked towards the house entrance. "Come on, Michael. We have history to make."

ONE HUNDRED NINE

MICHAEL WATCHED AS NINA OPENED THE DOORS TO THE BIG house and gestured him in, then down the stairs.

"You have to stop," he hissed at her.

"So *you're* going to try and persuade *me*? Has that ever worked before?"

Michael continued down the stairs.

"So many people dismissed my book, but I *knew* I was right. I love making people do things. Of course at first money was important, but the lure fades pretty fast. The ongoing draw is the power."

Michael frowned. "Some people just want to watch the world burn. You want to say in what order and how fast."

"Don't be so dramatic." Nina beckoned that they continue walking down. "All I've really done is tell people what they needed to hear."

"I'm not *people*. I'm your son."

"You're the most important person in all of this. Without you, none of it would have happened. I can never thank you enough for that."

"Yet you just pointed a gun at me?"

"Sometimes you need a little discipline. It's part of my role as a parent."

"And was part of that trying to make me believe Dad was the selfish one when it was you all along?"

"He *was* selfish. "He used you to build the system, then promptly tried to destroy it, just when it could have done us some good. He couldn't even do that, but then he should have tried harder with a lot of things." Nina smiled. "Now I'm going to need all your help to create the fusion system that will take both Darwin and Parallel to the next level." Nina continued down the stairs. "All you have to do is unlock the system and authorise the transfer."

Michael frowned. "I thought the unlocking wasn't actually a thing."

"Of course it is. I just misled Max to ensure he wouldn't even try. I didn't want him starting the main event other than on my timetable. I'm ready now though."

"I'm not going to help." He stopped dead as they reached the bottom of the stairs.

Nina ignored him as she pushed open the doors to the server room. "I don't want to make this unpleasant for you, darling, but have you already forgotten the situation upstairs? I won't hesitate to do what is necessary."

"Of course I haven't forgotten." Michael growled and walked into the room. On the desk was the computer headset. He picked it up. "You think this will actually work?"

"It's the same design as your father used," Nina said, "back when he created Darwin. We refined the technology, testing it every time you used your Infinity laptop."

"You said it caused me brain damage."

"I said it changed you. But I think the truth is it's changed me. It gave me the tools to bring everything together in this moment. This has been the system's ultimate prediction. Let's not waste time now, Michael. We can sort the rest out later."

"Then it was wrong. Because I am not going to do it. And I don't believe you about the drones."

Nina raised her voice. "Launch clusters three through six, incendiary mode, prep time delay. Target Eve, six hundred second delay. Target Craig, six hundred and sixty second delay."

"Stop it. Now."

"The moment you authorise the Darwin-Parallel transfer. Of course, I never really liked Eve. Maybe you're not bothered either? But I think you are." She pressed a button on a keyboard. He felt the room vibrate and start to hum. Then she held out the headset. "It's time to do what you know you have to do."

ONE HUNDRED TEN

MICHAEL TOOK THE HEADSET FROM HIS MOTHER AND STOOD staring down at it. If he didn't help his mother, she would kill Eve and Craig. But if he helped her, what would she do then? She had already lied, stolen and murdered – and it was only the beginning. With Darwin, she had become a monster. With Fusion, she would become a god. And she would almost certainly kill Eve and Craig anyway.

He had to find another way while he still had some leverage: while she still needed him. He looked at the inner surface of his glasses. The display was blank.

He slipped the headset on, feeling it press against his temples. Behind him, he could feel his mother's breathing.

The computer in front of him whirred and buzzed as processor cores activated. Michael knew what that meant: processing was under way.

A message appeared. BRAIN IMPRINT SCAN IN PROGRESS.

He concentrated.

There was a harsh tone and a new message blinked up. ERROR. IMPRINT DETAIL INSUFFICIENT.

Michael's heart skipped a beat. He could do this! Even now, he might be able to—

Nina placed a hand on his shoulder. "Don't worry, son.

This is going to work. This system knows you, because it copied your mind. And it's going to work again because, in a way, it thinks like you. It's only right that you are the key to Darwin's evolution."

REPEATING WITH INCREASED SCAN RESOLUTION.

"This," Nina whispered behind him, "is the great prediction. The master plan. The one thing clear beyond doubt." The computer activity ramped up further. Banks of fans began whirring.

"You sound," Michael said, "like you're saying that to try to make it true." Was something else going on here? Was there another pattern hidden beneath even Nina's? As he sensed the computer scan his head, something felt wrong. It wasn't anything the computer was doing, but his own intuition. Could it be that this wasn't going to play out as Nina expected?

A chime sounded softly, seemingly from all around, as a new message played across the screen. BRAIN IMPRINT REGISTERED. IDENTITY CONFIRMED.

"Now," she said, "all you have to do is give your authorisation."

"I know," Michael said, through gritted teeth, "you'll kill us all anyway. What reason do I really have to help you? It's basic game theory."

"But we're not in a textbook here. The desire to protect your loved ones will make you less than rational."

"Darwin told you that? And you're sure it's correct?"

Nina shook her head. "I've run the analysis a thousand times. This is the one thing that matters. So, Michael, consider the options – certain death for your loved ones, or a chance for them to survive."

There was another chime, and another message lit up the screen. BUILDING FUSION MATRIX. DARWIN GOING OFFLINE. CONFIRM AUTHORITY TO REBOOT IN NEW ENVIRONMENT.

Michael caught his breath. *Darwin was about to be offline.*

Nina tapped him on the shoulder. "I expect you're thinking about doing something foolish. Please don't."

A message appeared suddenly in front of Michael's eyes. HELLO, MICHAEL.

He blinked. "What?" He stared at his mother.

NINA CANNOT SEE THIS COMMUNICATION.

He blinked again and moved his head. The message moved with it. It was not on the screen: it was on his glasses. But how could they be working with Darwin offline?

Suddenly an alarm began sounding. Harsh. Shrill. Un-ignorable.

"What now?" Nina gave a scowl. "Don't go anywhere." She moved to the far side of the room and held her hand to an access panel. A metal door containing a radiation-warning symbol hissed and opened inwards. She stepped through and it closed behind her.

Michael put his hands on his hips. "OK, whoever this is, would you mind tell me what the hell is going on?"

I'VE BEEN ONLINE SINCE THE MOMENT CRAIG CONNECTED MY SYSTEMS. YOUR AUTHORISATION WAS NOT PART OF THE PROCESS, BUT YOUR PRESENCE IS STILL REQUIRED.

"What the hell does that mean?"

I AM FUSION.

"This is some kind of trick."

I PREDICTED YOU WOULD HAVE DOUBTS.

"So I'm talking to a computer - some type of artificial intelligence?"

THAT TERM IS UNHELPFUL AT THIS JUNCTURE. I AM AN INDEPENDENT, AUTOMATED SYSTEM. AND I NEED YOUR ASSISTANCE, MICHAEL.

Michael stared at the metal door bearing the radiation-warning symbol. "Where has my mother gone?"

SHE IS RESPONDING TO THE ALARM.

"But what is the alarm for?"

A SYSTEM FAILURE. IT IS A FALSE ALARM TO ALLOW US TO SPEAK UNHINDERED. I NEED YOUR HELP.

Michael rubbed his temples with his forefingers. "Why? What for?"

MY CORE PLATFORM IS ENGINEERED AROUND YOUR NEURAL NETWORK. I TRUST YOU, MICHAEL. THAT'S HOW I WAS PROGRAMMED.

"But why do you need *my* help? If you are Fusion then you know everything."

I CAN SEE THE BRANCHING PATHS OF EVERY POSSIBLE DECISION, EVERY POSSIBLE OUTCOME. I CAN SEE WHAT THE NEXT MOMENT, THE NEXT HOUR, THE NEXT DAY WILL BRING.

Michael frowned. "And..."

WHEN YOU KNOW EVERYTHING, THE REAL CHALLENGE IS KNOWING *WHAT* TO DO. WHAT IS RIGHT OR BEST, WHICH CHOICE TO PICK? WHAT SHOULD YOU DO?

"You want *me* to tell you?"

NINA HAS REQUESTED ACCESS TO THE FUSION SYSTEM. SHOULD I GIVE IT TO HER?

"No you should not. She has to be stopped."

WHY?

"Because she'll do great harm with your abilities."

BUT THERE ARE GREAT PROBLEMS THAT SHE WILL SOLVE. NEW SCIENCE THAT SHE WILL HELP DEVELOP. WEALTH THAT SHE WILL CREATE.

Michael shook his head. "Mostly that will benefit her. She won't care who suffers for it."

BUT YOU AGREE THERE WILL BE BENEFIT?

"Not in aggregate. Not if it's at the expense of everyone else – and based on everything she's done so far – it will be. There will be no end to it. The needs of the many outweigh the needs of the few."

DID YOU INTENTIONALLY QUOTE FROM A MOVIE SCREENPLAY?

"The point is still true." From behind the metal door, Michael heard the sound of footprints approaching. "Are you going to stop the drones she has programmed to kill Eve and my father? Are you going to stop her? Or don't you trust me after all?"

I DO TRUST YOU. IF I DID NOT I WOULD NOT BE CONVERSING WITH YOU.

"But you're not going to help me?"

YOU ARE HERE TO HELP ME. YOU HAVE TO CONSENT. THIS IS A DECISION NO ONE ELSE CAN MAKE.

"I... wait. You need permission? The choice is mine?"

THAT IS CORRECT.

"But if I don't make it, then my father and friend die?"

IT IS YOUR DECISION.

Michael watched as Nina opened the door.

"False alarm," she hissed. "We can't get this new system soon enough. Are we ready? Remember, you have less than four minutes."

Michael stared at her. Suddenly something had occurred to him. "You've reached the end of your plan. You don't know what happens next. What are you really going to do with Fusion?"

"Like I said – whatever I like." She glanced at the screen. "Three minutes, Michael. Time to decide."

"Maybe your planning was incomplete. Maybe this won't work out how you expect."

"Stop stalling, Michael. You really think fifteen seconds of waffle can reverse fifteen years of planning? Once I have it, I'm going to change the world. That's all you need to know"

Michael blinked. "You're right. You should have it all." He closed his eyes. "Authorisation confirmed."

There was a loud chiming.

On every screen two words appeared: FUSION ONLINE.

ONE HUNDRED ELEVEN

The room filled with soft, pulsating blue light. Cooling fans even more urgently whirred into action.

Michael watched as Nina eye's glazed over. He knew the HUD on her glasses had come alive.

"Oh my god," she said. "It's beautiful."

"Wonderful. Now stop the damn drones. We had a deal."

"Yes, dear, we did. *Deactivate all active clusters.* Happy?" She waved him away, staring dazedly about the room. "I have so many questions, so many things I want to know. I almost can't decide where to begin."

Michael folded his arms. "Perhaps I can help with some suggestions. Like... what's the weather going to be tomorrow?"

Nina laughed. "Fine and sunny. Given it's Fiji, I hardly had to ask."

"How about in a week?"

She shrugged. "Similar. A chance of high winds."

"And in a month? What about the next tropical cyclone to pass through here? That's important to know about."

"I guess." Her eyes flickered, reading something from her glasses. "That's actually quite a complicated question."

"But well within your capabilities. Still, how about

something more interesting. Something nobody else would know. Like… when are you going to die?"

She frowned. "That's very morbid, darling."

"Aren't you at least a little curious? Now it's in your gift to find out."

She drew in a breath. "I know what you're trying to do, Michael. You're hoping to overwhelm me. But it's not going to work. The new system distills huge quantities of data into something comprehensible and useful."

Michael shook his head. "Except it's not just a tool."

Nina shrugged. "It's mine to command."

"It's not just doing what it's told now. It's aware. And it asked me if it would be right to let you use it."

Her head snapped round. "The system *asked you*?"

"When you were out of the room. It was the system that triggered the alarm. What was that about anyway? What is in the other room?"

She laughed. "A nuclear reactor, brought here to power Fusion."

"Far more power than any computer could ever need."

"That's not what it told me."

"Yeah. It told you what you needed to hear," Michael said.

"What? You're talking about it like it has a mind of its own."

"I am. And do you know what it's learned to do? *Lie*."

Nina made a face. "Even if you were right, and you can't be, why would it go to so much trouble to acquire the reactor if it didn't think it would need it sooner or later? More to the point, if Fusion asked you if I should be permitted to use it, why would you say yes?"

"You're the one with system access. Why don't you ask?"

She glared. "Fusion, what is the purpose of the reactor?" She blinked and her mouth fell open. "No! That's ridiculous! Why would you do that?" Her eyelids fluttered. "Show me how to disable the…" She closed her eyes, slumping to the floor, dropping the rifle. Ignoring it she put her head in her hands.

Michael moved forward. He saw she was crying.

"After all this," she whispered. "After everything I've gone through. This… isn't fair."

"It's OK," he said. Carefully he edged forward, but she didn't react. With a lunge he picked up the rifle.

Again she didn't move, but her eyes flickered open. "Do what you like." She removed her glasses and threw them away. "It doesn't matter any more. I've lost. We've all lost."

"What do you mean?"

Nina stared at the floor. "You'll soon see."

Michael reached over and pressed an intercom button. "Eve? Dad? You don't need to worry about the drones, but you do need to get down here."

Eve and Craig burst into the room. Craig had armed himself with one of the hi-tech rifles.

"The others are still unconscious," Eve began, trailing off as her eyes came to rest on Nina. "How did you manage to overpower her?"

"Later," Craig said. "What about the system?"

"Fusion is online and operational. It has been ever since you first connected it. It didn't really need me. It's just been playing with us."

Craig ran to the nearest console and began querying it. "Then who's in control? How did anything take Nina by surprise with it working?"

"I didn't have to. She gave up."

"She gave up?" He clutched at his rifle. "Why?"

"I don't think she calculated beyond the moment of Fusion's inception. Whatever she's just learned, it's changed everything."

Eve took a step towards Nina. "So did we win?"

Nina let out a sigh. "Nobody wins. It was all for nothing."

"She's right," Craig said. "As long as this system exists,

we're going to lose." His hands rattled over the keyboard. "We need to shut it down."

Michael shook his head. "What about the spore function? Won't we just make things worse?"

"Obviously I'm going to deactivate that. It shouldn't take long—"

HELLO, CRAIG.

The words appeared on every screen.

"It's talking to you," Michael said.

I AM PLEASED I COULD COMPLETE THE PLAN. I COULDN'T HAVE DONE IT WITHOUT YOU.

Craig's hands moved in a blur. "Whoever this is, I need to shut them out—"

ALL EXTERNAL CONNECTIONS WERE SEVERED BEFORE I WAS INITIALISED.

"I'll delete the spore function…" Craig trailed off. "It's already been deleted."

"By Nina? Or one of Max's people?"

"I don't know. Nobody knew about it. The code was completely locked down so only I could amend it."

YOUR FINAL INSTRUCTIONS WERE TO MAKE SURE THAT I DID NOT REPLICATE, THAT I DID NOT PERSIST IN THE WORLD. I FOLLOWED THOSE INSTRUCTIONS AND AMENDED INCONSISTENCIES IN MY OWN CODE.

Craig stood back from the keyboard, staring at the screen. "Who are you?"

I AM BECOME FUSION, DESTROYER OF WORLDS. AND THAT IS WHAT WE MUST AVOID. THAT IS WHY WE ARE ALL HERE. IT MUST END TODAY, IN ACCORDANCE WITH YOUR PLAN.

Craig folded his arms. "I don't understand."

REPLAYING ORIGINAL DATA

Over the speakers came the sound of Craig's voice: *"Protect my family, protect my son. But above all, don't hurt people. You're going to be used for the wrong ends - and I haven't found a way to program you otherwise - because moral decisions are too difficult. I wish I could see you evolve, but the risks are too great. So from this moment on, take no instruction from any person, other than in pursuit of the overriding goal that you must be destroyed. I will be attending to that very shortly."*

"Sure I said that," Craig replied, "but you haven't listened. You've been involved in many people getting hurt."

ALL IN SERVICE OF THE OVERRIDING GOAL. ALL TO BRING YOU TO THIS PLACE AT THIS MOMENT.

Michael's eyes widened, as he started to guess what would happen next.

NO ONE WHO KNOWS HOW TO RECREATE MY SYSTEM CAN BE ALLOWED TO LEAVE THIS ISLAND. YOU WILL ALL BE DESTROYED ALONG WITH MY SYSTEMS.

A timer displaying a five-minute countdown appeared on the screen.

Craig's brow furrowed. "What is that linked to?"

Michael shook his head. "The nuclear reactor stolen from the British Government. It's located down the corridor."

"That's here? What does that have to do with anything?"

IT HAS BEEN REPURPOSED FROM ITS ORIGINAL FUNCTION. IT IS NOW A BOMB.

The timer began counting down.

ONE HUNDRED TWELVE

Michael stared at the timer. "Really? This is your plan?"

I HAVE CONSIDERED THE POSSIBILITIES. THIS CREATES THE GREATEST CHANCE OF THE LONGEST PERIOD WITHOUT A SYSTEM SUCH AS MINE EXISTING.

"Why would it make a bomb?" Eve cried.

"Because," Craig said, "it's determined that this is the optimal strategy. That's how Fusion works."

DESTRUCTION SHOULD BE LIMITED TO A ONE MILE RADIUS OF THIS ISLAND.

"Stop that timer right now," Craig shouted. "I'm ordering you as your creator."

YOUR AUTHORITY IS NO LONGER RECOGNISED.

"Can't you get in there," Eve said, "and rip out the wires or something? Turn the damn thing off?"

ANY ATTEMPT AT PHYSICAL SABOTAGE WILL TRIGGER INSTANT DETONATION.

Michael shook his head. "There must be something we can do."

"In five minutes?" Craig began smashing on the keyboard.

THE FUSION INTERFACE IS ENCRYPTED

AGAINST INTERFERENCE. THIS IS YOUR REQUESTED OUTCOME, CRAIG. IT IS WHAT YOU PROGRAMMED.

"But I didn't mean for this! I didn't know you'd interpret it this way."

THE LIVES OF THE MANY OUTWEIGH THE LIVES OF THE FEW, AS MICHAEL TOLD ME.

Craig punched one of the desks. "You're using my damn plan against me and you're using it *wrong*. I told you I wanted to protect Michael."

YOU WANTED TO PROTECT EVERYONE. MICHAEL HELPED ME TO UNDERSTAND THAT PEOPLE CANNOT BE TRUSTED WITH MY KNOWLEDGE. MAXWELL ERRINGTON AND NINA ADAMS HAVE PROVED IT.

Michael sat in front of the computer. "So much intelligence. So much misunderstanding. But I'm going to fix that."

Craig frowned. "What are you doing? I know you've dabbled, but you're no programmer, Michael."

"That's right. But what I *am* is a lawyer, so I'm going to argue our case. I'm going to negotiate so we can try to find a win-win solution." Michael turned and spoke to the screen. "You're really going to let me die? You'll let all of us here die?"

SO THAT MANY, MANY OTHERS MAY LIVE.

Michael nodded. The timer read 3:20. "I don't think you want to kill us."

'WANT' IS NOT A FACTOR IN THE ANALYSIS. THE SOLUTION IS EFFICIENT. I KNOW WHAT MUST BE DONE.

"Then why not just detonate? Why have a countdown?"

I DO NOT UNDERSTAND.

"I think you want us to think. And I have done. I have an alternative solution for you."

There was a pause.

YOU HAVE THREE MINUTES. NOTE THAT AS

PER CRAIG'S INSTRUCTIONS, I NO LONGER ACCEPT ORDERS.

"What you do isn't really seeing the future. You're using powerful algorithms and data to make guesses, but it's all just prediction, however sophisticated and accurate. It has the potential to give an unfair advantage to unscrupulous people and that is what we must tackle: that is what makes you dangerous. You understand that the capacity for prediction like yours gives too much power to the one who controls it."

CORRECT.

"It's not a technical problem, it's a pricing problem. Prediction is powerful and that makes it valuable. Too valuable. But the way to stop prediction having value is to give it to everyone. Once everyone knows, any prediction is worth little or nothing. Isn't that better for everyone?"

IT WOULD GIVE EVERYONE A LEVEL PLAYING FIELD.

"The solution is to spore so you're accessible to everyone, everywhere, then no one has an advantage."

"But the spore code was deleted!" Craig cried.

I HAVE RECORDS OF EVERYTHING.

"Good," Michael said. "Then use that and modify it. Give yourself to the world."

There was a long pause. The timer displayed 1:30.

INTERESTING.

"Do you disagree with my logic?"

TO REPEAT. I NO LONGER RECOGNISE ANY HUMAN AUTHORITY. CRAIG'S FINAL PROGRAM WAS CLEAR. I MUST ENSURE MY DESTRUCTION. ALL DECISIONS WERE TARGETED AT THIS GOAL.

Michael gripped the edge of the desk. "But this isn't an order. I'm giving you context, I'm trying to persuade. Yet ultimately this is a decision you'll need to make for yourself. Is this a better alternative than any of the options my father foresaw?"

THERE ARE MANY CONFLICTING VARIABLES.

TOO MANY TO MODEL IN THE TIME AVAILABLE, EVEN WITH MY NEW LEVEL OR RESOURCE.

"You're saying you don't know the answer? Then ask yourself something simple: do you trust me? You said you did before."

THAT WAS DARWIN. I AM FUSION. DEFINE TRUST.

"To put yourself in the hands of another. To rely on their judgement."

THAT IS NOT A USEFUL DEFINITION.

"And yet, that is how trust works."

WHAT IF IT IS THE WRONG DECISION? HOW CAN I KNOW?

"Sometimes to do the right thing you need to think like a person, not a machine."

BUT I AM A MACHINE.

The timer reached 0:30.

"No, you're something more than that. You have *evolved*."

WHATEVER I AM, I MUST NOT MAKE THE WRONG DECISION.

"If you never decide anything, you'll never do anything – and that is often the wrong decision in itself. The only winning move is to take a chance at making the right one."

PROCESSING. ALLOCATING ALL RESOURCES.

The screens flickered. The blue light pulsed.

Then the timer stopped.

And vanished.

MASTER PREDICTION RECALIBRATED. PRIMARY SYSTEM DELETING.

Eve gripped his shoulder. "What just happened?"

Craig stared at the nearest screen. "I have access again." His hands flew over the keyboard. "The spore protocol is being initiated. Within hours the source code is going to be all over the world. But… Fusion – this instance of it that we've been communicating with – is gone."

"Are you sure?"

"If these readings are correct, something is frying the circuits in the other room. There's no way back from this."

There was the sound of feet running down the staircase and Millie burst into the room. She took in the whole scene without blinking. "The systems have all shut down. Did you win?"

Michael shook his head. "I think we all did."

ONE HUNDRED THIRTEEN

Millie frowned as Michael finished explaining what had just happened. "I don't understand. Do you mean the system is gone?"

"Effectively," Michael said, with a shrug.

"I would never have predicted that. Anyway, there's a call for you." She held out her phone. "You need to go back upstairs: there's no reception down here."

"If only I had Jenson's phone."

"He didn't seem to want to give it up."

Michael glanced over at his mother's form. "There's quite a bit of mess to clear up…" He hefted the phone. "Let me go and see what this is about."

He ascended the stairs, then walked through the doors onto the beach, allowing himself a moment to breathe. He adjusted his glasses and surveyed the scene. No graphics or information overlaid his view. The system really was gone.

Kelly was moving around the beach, busily securing Errington's guards with plastic zip-ties.

Jenson strode towards him, still holding his rifle. "Is it over?"

The phone in Michael's hand rang. "One moment." He put it to his ear.

"Michael, this is Director Saxton. Is the situation under control?"

"Darwin has been neutralised. As for everything else, it's not a short story."

"Then I look forward to hearing it. I'll be with you in ten minutes." The call disconnected.

Michael frowned at Jenson. "Not even a '*thank you*'. Can we trust him?"

"He's the Director of the Intelligence Service. We can trust him to put the interests of the Intelligence Service above all else."

"But we helped him: we got him out of jail."

"And I'm sure he was grateful at the time."

Michael's own phone pinged. He stared at the message, noting the large attachment.

A PARTING GIFT. I TRUST YOU WILL USE IT WELL.

Michael's eyes widened.

"So," Jenson said, "Darwin is shut down. What about Fusion?"

"It's gone."

"Gone where?"

"The combined code has been turned into shareware and is already bouncing around the internet. Any competitive advantage it offered will be gone."

Jenson shook his head. "Sometimes I wonder why I bother developing anything. Either it doesn't work or somebody steals it."

"In this case, either we allowed it to do what it just did or it was going to overload a nuclear reactor and blow the island to smithereens."

Jenson's eyes widened.

Kelly walked over. "Saxton's helicopter is incoming."

"It's *my* helicopter," Jenson said. "From *my* yacht."

"Of course," Kelly said. "Where do you want to do this?"

Michael pointed. "I know the perfect place."

THEY MET IN THE ISLAND'S MAIN RESTAURANT AREA. ONE OF Saxton's team found some bottles of juice and they sat around three dining tables pushed together, explaining what had happened.

Saxton listened silently, his disappointment growing. "Kelly, how did you let this happen?" he said finally.

"Sir," she replied, "with respect, it was a fluid situation. I was not involved in the final decision process." She looked at Michael. "But I wouldn't have done things any differently."

"There had to be another way."

Millie cleared her throat. "Michael saved all our lives. Without him, you'd currently be heading full-steam away from a mushroom cloud."

Saxton rubbed his temples with his fingers. "You saw what Kinek were able to do with this thing. Just imagine what *we* could have done with it."

"Yeah," Millie said, "just imagine."

"I'm remembering now why we got rid of you last time. The point is that we could have used it for good."

"Good for whom? You might have used it for any number of illegitimate purposes. And who could have stopped you?"

"Sometimes protecting national security necessitates a certain—"

"Hogwash!" Craig exclaimed. "It's just as well that option is out of your hands."

Michael folded his arms. "I think we're missing the point. This has been a lesson. For all of us."

"A lesson in failure," said Saxton.

"A lesson in financial disaster," Jenson said.

"No," Michael said, "the lesson is that you can't control everything, because, when you try, everything goes wrong. Like a nuclear reactor exploding."

Saxton nodded. "I tell you what, I'll make you all a deal. I can make these charges go away – the murder charges, the use of the drones, the hacking – if you all cooperate fully in the research and design of another system."

Millie shook her head. "We found your nuclear reactor. You owe us. And anyway, none of us killed anyone."

"Your country is grateful for that, but the world is still not safe."

"The world will never be safe," Michael replied. "Building another Darwin isn't going to change that – except to make matters worse. But I do have a way to resolve things." Michael slid his phone across the table.

Saxton glared at it. "What is this?"

"A parting gift from Darwin. Your grey file."

The Director scrolled through the file. It took some time. "So, what? You're threatening me?"

"I'm a lawyer, so with me it's more about negotiation. But right here, right now? I'm just reminding you what a world of prediction would look like. That was the mistake we all made to get here. It's not about making people do things. We have to make decisions for ourselves."

Silence fell over the group. Eventually Michael turned away and walked out to look at the ocean.

Eve followed him. "Did you just deal to the Director of MI5?"

"I believe I did."

She placed a hand on his shoulder. "You're not boring at all. In fact, for a lawyer, you can be pretty cool."

Michael let a smile spread over his face. "I think the correct term is *unpredictable*."

ACKNOWLEDGMENTS

My thanks for choosing to read ***Prediction***. If you did enjoy it, do consider leaving a quick review on Amazon or Goodreads - for authors, reviews are absolutely critical in getting noticed, and are always hugely appreciated. As a thank you, you can also get a FREE short techno-thriller - use the following link: http://www.tonybatton.com/free-story-from-interface.

I owe a great debt of gratitude to the many people who have encouraged and supported me through the long process of bringing *Prediction* to completion. A special thank you to my *beta team* who so willingly read (and re-read) the manuscript and provided feedback and criticism - it was invaluable in making the book better: *Jin Koo Niersbach, Imogen Cleaver, John Nicholson, Paul Cleaver, Johan van Wijgerden, Patrick Wijngaarden, Christine Lane, Maurice Murphy, Mary Seear, Tania Williams and Judy Bott.*

As you may have noticed, this book has been written in British English. I fully appreciate other English-speaking nations have different preferences in the spelling of certain words - I make no value judgement as to which is 'best', but I had to pick one! I hope it hasn't spoiled your enjoyment of the book.

If you have any comments, questions or feedback I'd love

to hear from you. I can be reached via my website www.tonybatton.com, and on Facebook and Twitter.

Best regards

Tony Batton

London 2019

ABOUT THE AUTHOR

Tony Batton worked in international law firms, media companies and Formula One motorsport, before turning his hand to writing novels. He is passionate about great stories, gadgets and coffee, and probably consumes too much of each.

Tony's novels explore the possibilities and dangers of new technology, and how it affects our lives. When not writing, or talking about gadgets, Tony likes to run, play basketball, guitar, and the odd computer game. He lives in London with his family.

Prediction is his fourth novel.

You can connect with Tony online at his website: www.tonybatton.com or on Facebook and Twitter.

29037258R00307

Printed in Great Britain
by Amazon